THE QUINNY HITE
MYSTERIES

THE QUINNY HITE
MYSTERIES

THE FOURTH STAR

SINISTER
STREET

RICHARD BURKE

COACHWHIP PUBLICATIONS

Greenville, Ohio

The Quinny Hite Mysteries, by Richard Burke
© 2014 Coachwhip Publications
Front cover: Texture © Sascha Duensing; Spider ©
    Tribalium
No claims made on public domain material.

Richard Burke (1886-1962)
The Fourth Star published 1946
Sinister Street published 1948

ISBN 1-61646-248-5
ISBN-13 978-1-61646-248-2

CoachwhipBooks.com

"The Corpse in Grampa's Bed" first published in *Murder Cavalcade*, 1946. The anthology was copyright renewed by the MWA, but they disclaim (pers. comm.) renewals of individual stories. No individual story copyright renewal by the author or estate.

CONTENTS

THE FOURTH STAR

Chapter One	9
Chapter Two	25
Chapter Three	50
Chapter Four	73
Chapter Five	94
Chapter Six	114
Chapter Seven	132

SINISTER STREET

1 · Lola Had Twin Daggers	155
2 · The Living Room	169
3 · The Stripper	182
4 · Beyond the Screen	192
5 · Sanctuary	202
6 · The Ruby on the Floor	210
7 · The Spider	222
8 · Mr. Silburn Intervenes	236
9 · Key	244
10 · The Glove Box	257
11 · Confession	270

12 · A Visit from Mrs. Page   280

13 · Maestring's Errand   290

14 · Sinister Street   302

15 · Tote Sheet   312

The Corpse in Grampa's Bed   323

THE FOURTH STAR

CHAPTER ONE

QUINNY HITE MOROSELY eyed the nickel and dime on the imitation mahogany bar, change for a half-buck he'd just handed over in payment for a slug of rye. Not so long ago, in a joint like Terry's Golden Turtle, a helping of whiskey added up to a quarter. Same whiskey, same thirst—nothing different except the bartender's increased take.

Money might be the root of all evil, like Father Moynihan used to say, but getting any of it came close to being the root of all work—which was worse. This job Quinny was presently engaged with was certainly no dish for a smart homicide detective, but material suitable to his talents had been deplorably lacking. Murders lately had been the work of dumb clucks whose clumsy technique left them soft touches for the Homicide Squad, not crimes offering a private operator chances of profit. During these low tides of mortuary prosperity, a man had to do what he could to keep meat on the frame, so Quinny Hite had taken on this job for Sixtus Nudel. It wasn't an enterprise likely to add much to his protein intake, either.

Sixtus Nudel, who boasted of being the only Jew in Manhattan to be named for a Pope, was a Center Street lawyer. He'd hired Quinny to locate a skull named Frankel, needed as a witness to an accident the detective assumed had probably not yet happened. Finding the man meant the collection of the balance of the fee, but so far Quinny had slapped his feet on East Side sidewalks for three days without getting so much as a scent of his quarry. This was Monday morning and he might just as well have spent his time in the restful atmosphere of the Hotel du Nord bar, where he lived. That is, he kept a room in the hotel, too, as bars closed at 4 a.m.

The Turtle Bay region of Manhattan, east of First Avenue and north of Forty-second Street, was clear across town from Quinny's normal feeding, drinking and sleeping territory. The chances of running into an acquaintance flush with new dough and likely to buy a drink were slim indeed this far from Times Square. Reflecting thereon, Quinny sighed and downed the rest of his rye, which, in his delicate financial condition, would be the last until sundown.

"I beg pardon, sir, but aren't you Quinny Hite?" a voice behind his elbow inquired.

Quinny shot a precautionary glance into the mirror back of the bar before answering. It revealed the image of a slight, sandy-haired man with sea-green eyes, whom the detective had noticed a few minutes earlier shutting himself into a phone booth at the rear of the cafe. Now that he'd had the chance of a good look, Quinny felt that he had encountered the fellow elsewhere at some time in the past—most likely in the playgrounds in or near Times Square. Under average height, he seemed to have the not unusual idea among short men that oversized garments would give an illusion of greater height. His clothes were tweedily Hollywood, but could be Park Avenue.

"Sure, I'll take a drink," responded Quinny, enthusiastically. He pushed his empty glass across the bar toward the bartender, who had shifted closer and was watching expectantly. "Rye, again."

The man in tweeds, slightly taken back, grinned affably and glanced at the bartender.

"Oh—fine! I'll have one, too." His odd eyes swept back to the detective as he fished a wallet from his pocket and took out a bill, thus reassuring Quinny that he hadn't rashly maneuvered himself into buying. The stranger smiled. "But, you are Quin Hite, aren't you?"

"That's right," nodded the detective. "I oughta know you, but it seems like—"

"I'm Morgan Sands. I used to see you around the Club Flamingo a few years ago. You had a girl in the floor show—"

"Yeah, yeah. I used to hang around the Flamingo—and I had a girl working there." A bit of nostalgia colored the detective's thoughts. When he had frequented Club Flamingo he'd had night-club money—most of the time. "The way things are set up now," he continued, "I don't have any girl and the dough is short."

"Not doing too well, eh?" There was speculation in Sands' sea-green eyes.

"No kidding, I ain't." Quinny sampled his drink. "How about you?"

Sands laughed and finished his drink, then plastered the five-spot on the wet bar.

"I've never had money trouble," he said lightly. "But, I've had most of the troubles money can buy, one time or another. I've been on the West Coast for the last two or three years, and too busy on a war job to get into mischief."

"What kind of war job?" queried the detective indifferently.

"Shipyard. You see, I'm a naval architect by profession, although I'd never worked at it before. Didn't need to—the Sands family have always been pretty well fixed, you know."

Quinny didn't know, but found the information of interest. It confirmed his first impression of the man's background and did a lot toward jolting his memory into recalling some items of Morgan Sands' past activities. Reports of some of Morgan Sands' more spectacular didoes had reached Quinny by way of the Club Flamingo songstress, Joan Fairley. The detective's thoughts dwelt momentarily on her. After three futile attempts at marriage, she'd walked out on him. Aw, well—

Mr. Sands was still speaking.

"Whatever became of Chinese Red?"

Quinny smiled reminiscently. He hadn't thought of the half-caste Chinese girl with the flame-colored hair for a long time—and she was *nice* to think about.

"I don't know, but wherever she is, my money says she's plenty lengths in front of the field. Did you know her? She used to move into uptown saloon society once in a while."

"No—not personally. I was just remembering the job you did in picking up the murderer of Tony Austen. Like another drink?"

"Sounds like a good idea. Anyhow, I never say no."

Morgan Sands nodded to the waiting bartender, but seemed to have something aside from conviviality on his mind.

"See here, Hite, I've just run into a screwy situation. Perhaps you could help me out, if you aren't too busy."

If there was to be anything in it, the detective was quite prepared to shelve the Frankel search. "Right now, I'm a drug on the market, and can be had cheap," he said feelingly. Then he hedged, "That is, cheap for me."

"It isn't much of a job," Sands replied. "Just a few minutes, probably. You see, when I left for San Francisco three years ago, I closed my house—it's right around the corner from here. In California, I found the right girl, a good, wholesome, sweet and lovely person who means everything in the world to me. But there's no use boring you with all that."

"Nope," assented Quinny. "I know already."

Morgan Sands' green eyes showed surprise. "You've heard about Anita?"

Quinny shook his head. "Only when her name was Rose, or Helen, or Shirley, or Minnie, or something else. When a guy which is in love sets out to tell about the dame he's overboard about, she adds up kinda familiar. Go on."

"Anita and I are to be married here next week. She's coming by train with her mother, while I came on ahead by plane to have the Sands house reopened and put in order—"

"Yeah—I know maids and butlers and stuff are hard to get nowadays, mister, but I don't do housework, if that's what you're working up to."

"Of course not. That isn't what's on my mind at all. I arrived last Saturday, so today I've come over to see what condition the house was in. What d'you think?"

"After three years? Probably lousy. What on earth do you want to move a bride into this crumby street for?"

"It's disintegrating, all right," Sands agreed ruefully. "It was a fine street when the house was built, and I'm planning to make it

so again. Buy up the rookeries on the street and build smart apartments, when materials are available. Well, I let myself into the
house a little while ago—and found the hall light on."

Quinny chuckled. "Boy, what a light bill you'll have, goin' away
and leavin' the lights on. Three years, you said?"

"I didn't leave 'em on," insisted Sands petulantly. "Lights, gas
and telephone were all shut off when I closed the house. I went on
in. The dust covers were all in place downstairs, so I went up to
the second floor. There are two large bedrooms there—one in front
and another at the back. The door to the back bedroom was partly
open, and the light over the bed was burning. Worse than that,
there was a woman sleeping in the bed. And a radio playing."

"Yeah?" Quinny laughed again. "Better wire the West Coast gal
that the situation has been filled. Did you wake this dame up?"

"Certainly not! I came away, thinking that the real estate firm
which manages my New York property had let the house without
informing me. That's how I happened in here to telephone and ask
what the dickens they meant by renting my house. They claimed
to know nothing about it."

"You think somebody just moved in, anyhow?" Quinny pursed
his lips. "Could be. Tough to get a place to live in lately in New
York."

"I suppose it is, but, just the same, whoever is occupying my
house has no right there, and I propose to get them out right now."

Quinny nodded. "You also propose that I do the job. That it?"

"Well, I—I don't feel up to tackling it alone. I'll make it worth
your while to go along with me while I order these intruders out.
You see, there's none too much time to get the place ready, and I
can't depend on my real estate firm to attend to it. They'll insist
on due process of law, and all that sort of business. I'm in a hurry."

Quinny felt keenly disappointed. There couldn't be much moola
involved in giving unauthorized tenants the heave, unless perhaps
he could convince Sands that the operation fell outside the law.

"It's not my line, of course," he said, "and I could get into
trouble about it, if these mugs don't heave easy. I know something

about this evictin' stuff, on account of when I was a rookie cop I got sent out regular to head off a neighborhod riot when somebody was getting the toss. I wouldn't want to risk my license for coffee money."

"That's not what I'm offering, unless coffee has gone up to fifty dollars a cup," denied Sands. "There won't be any trouble. I just want to have someone with me, in case these people get ugly."

Quinny drained his glass and turned away. "Leave us go, then," he said. Fifty smackers was almost enough to pay off on a dash of mayhem, if it came to that.

Leaving the Golden Turtle, they rounded the corner into the crosstown street, which dead-ended at the East River. What Quinny had said about the neighborhood was amply borne out. A row of boarded up and condemned houses, a small furniture factory and a couple of dingy warehouses were strung along the northern side, ending at a dead-storage garage nearer the river. The side Quinny and his new employer were on was no improvement. About halfway down the block, nestled between a five-story tenement and an apparently abandoned ironwork factory, was a three-story red brick house of more pretentious aspect. The windows, however, were fitted with well-made wooden covers, each with a crescent-shaped hole cut in the center, with similar construction covering the entrance as well. The literary section of the neighborhood gamins had made full use of the boarding. Florid letters in chalk declared that someone named Pete loved Elsie, with whom, later annotations indicated, Pete had been making excellent if reprehensible progress.

The house had a small stoop at the top of three worn steps. Sands nervously fitted a key to the door in the boarding, while Quinny surveyed the dismal street and sniffed at the faintly fetid atmosphere. A fine place to bring a bride, fresh out of California flowers and sunshine and stuff that Joan had freely mentioned in her occasional letters. Opening the temporary door, Sands applied another key to the front door of the house. Somewhat to the detective's surprise, the lock yielded without the stubbornness locks are apt to display after long disuse. Chances are, he thought, these tenants for free have been here for some time.

Morgan Sands opened the door and Quinny followed him in. The hall light, enclosed in a lantern of amber glass, shed a diffused, yellow glow that failed to give much illumination. The reception hall was narrow, with a flight of stairs leading to the upper floors, while an archway at the right opened into a drawing room. Cracks in the wooden window covers admitted thin beams of dust-ridden daylight, the cloth shrouded furniture looking like misshapen ghosts.

Their business was upstairs. Quinny could hear the metallic sound of a cheap radio coming from the upper regions. Sands glanced at him uneasily, and started up the carpet-covered stairs. The detective came along behind, with a curious glance at a pair of crossed battle-axes which decorated the wall about halfway up. At the top Sands paused and Quinny took the lead.

The door to the back bedroom was open a foot or so, and as the detective stopped to peer in he saw the head of an ornate bed where it stood against the wall. A bedlamp spread bright light down on the figure of a woman in yellow pajamas and a bed jacket, the quilt pulled up over most of her body. She was lying half on her side, her back toward Quinny. An open paper-backed book lay face down on the quilt, and a newspaper had been dropped onto the rug at the side of the bed. A portable radio on a fragile table at the bed-side droned on with one of those conversational programs meant for housewives.

Quinny glanced back at Sands, who had paused at the top of the stairs and was watching the detective with an uneasy expression in his queer eyes. Doubling his fist, Quinny smacked it sharply against the door panel. The sound crashed through the surrounding silence of the house, but the woman did not stir. Somehow, the detective hadn't thought she would. Thrusting open the door, he stalked into the musty room. After eyeing the still figure on the bed for a prolonged moment, he snapped around to see what Sands was doing. The man had come on as far as the door, and now he definitely looked frightened.

"What is it?" Sands asked, shakily.

Quinny pursed his lips, then moved his hand deprecatingly.

"Dead, I think."

He turned back toward the bed, leaning over for a view of the woman's face, then straightened up. A medical education wasn't required to determine that his first impression had been correct.

Only the dead stare without seeing.

Sands, his sea-green eyes increasingly vivid against his growing pallor, moved hesitantly into the room and tiptoed part of the way toward the bed. As the woman's face became partially visible he gasped and halted abruptly.

"Good God!" he exclaimed.

"Yeah?" returned Quinny caustically. "Friend of yours, eh?"

"It's Paula!"

Quinny grunted. "What was your idea bringing me here, Sands?"

The house owner's expression blazed into anxiety and for a moment he struggled with his vocal cords.

"Do—do you mean that you think *I* killed her?" he blurted. "That's ridiculous. I—"

"Murder ain't funny, mister." Quinny's hazel eyes stared harshly. "Go on. Who is this dame? What did she mean to you?"

"This—this is too horrible!" Sands glanced at the dead woman, shuddered, and closed his eyes tightly.

"Yeah—ain't it?" The detective's lips curled. "Pull yourself together, Sands. You cracked a while ago about the trouble you'd bought with your dough. So far, you ain't bought nothin'. Maybe you can spend your way out of this. Maybe not."

Sands shrugged convulsively. "Are you accusing me of having anything to do with— My God, Hite—"

Quinny shrugged. "You act like it. How's for layin' off the hysterics long enough to tell me who she is? Paula, you said. Paula who?"

Sands inhaled sharply and clenched his fists tightly.

"She's a girl I was briefly married to—about eight years ago. The marriage was annulled. I haven't seen her since." His jaw muscles tightened and relaxed spasmodically. "I—I think I'm going to be sick."

"Hold it. I want to know her name first."

"She might have changed it half a dozen times since I last saw her." Sands' green eyes flickered. "But eight years ago it was Paula Kemp."

She came to Manhattan in late '37, a shy, tawny blond girl with an overstuffed ambition to make a place in the art world. For girls like Paula Kemp, New York beckoned as Mecca to a Moslem. It promised the life she wanted, without a hint that it could also be a place to die.

PAULA KEMP CAME OUT of the little French bakery, looking amused. The old fellow who had sold her a bag of cookies was so upset about the news of Europe that he could hardly speak English. Paula couldn't see why Chamberlain's deal with Hitler should concern anyone on Third Avenue, or anywhere else this side of the Atlantic. There were a lot of things more vitally important to her than Czechoslovakia. Anton Decourré, for one, to whose studio in Stuart Mews she was now on her way.

She had been in New York almost a year. Experimentation in various art forms had convinced Paula that sculpture was her métier. Anton Decourré had been recommended to her as a competent teacher, if he could be persuaded to take her on. The man detested teaching, and only the deplorable fact that a mediocre sculptor's income was spotty, and never sufficient, caused him to accept an occasional student. With a sportsmanship matching his ability, he uniformly despised these beginners, screening his contempt behind an ill-mannered show of artistic temperament.

Paula, however, had been different from most of the young women who came to him. She was prettier, with a small-town naïveté which he found amusing. Her enchanted admiration was stimulating, too. Seeing that she was completely awed and fascinated, he had set about to make it useful. Easy success dimmed his appetite.

It was this problem of the sculptor's fading interest she was worrying over as she walked along toward Stuart Mews and his studio. She felt a vague prompting that it hadn't been very clever to let his fascination carry her away so completely. Falling in love with a genius was traditionally a hazard, of course, but she was also troubled with a swelling doubt that Anton rated that tag. Her pride resisted the insinuation.

At any rate, she thought, he might at least pretend a little appreciation when she tried so hard to please. A kind word or two, or even just a gleam of affection in his dark eyes, would have made a lot of difference. He gave neither. She had been generous with her slender supply of money, and, when the moment arrived—as it was bound to do—generous with herself, too. This hadn't helped. The more she gave, the less she received, it seemed. Her protests were answered with the lofty comment that it was not in the nature of a great artist to rest on achievement, but to go on to fresh projects.

A project, eh! Her fingers tightened on the sack of cookies she was bringing for his breakfast, then relaxed. After all, if a girl were silly enough to fall for such a man, she must expect his exasperating indifference.

Anton Decourré's studio occupied the upper floor of what had once been a two-story stable. It formed the inner end of the cobbled mews, and was reached by narrow walks along the sides of the cul-de-sac. Paula found the downstairs door unlocked, as it usually was, and entered to climb the stairs.

The sound of hard heels reached the sculptor where he sat on an old-fashioned highbacked sofa, with a morning paper spread before him on a littered table. He clutched a nearly empty bottle of tepid milk in one powerful hand, glancing across the room toward the door with irritation flaming in his dark eyes.

That girl again! he thought resentfully. Women were such damned nuisances, breaking in on a man at all hours on the pretext of worrying about his welfare. Particularly this little chit, with her unbearable idea of owning him. Hell, a man might desire a woman's warmth and beauty without intending to make a life work of it! An artist, above all, must be free.

Springing to his feet, he stalked through the cluttered studio to a dingy bedroom at the rear, still clutching the milk bottle. As he disappeared through the doorway, a key rattled in the lock and Paula pushed in from the stair landing. She stopped uncertainly while her gaze wandered around among the unfinished works of Anton Decourré, scattered about the studio. The simple, dark blue shirtwaist dress under the loose coat she wore gave her the appearance of eighteen, but she was two years older than this. The excessively high heels of her slippers were because Anton admired them.

"Yoo-hoo, Anton!" she called, moving toward the partitioned rooms at the back. "Are you up? I've brought the little cakes you like."

The sculptor came into the doorway, wrapping a frayed robe around his tall, sparse frame. His jet black hair and hawklike nose give him more the appearance of an Indian than a Frenchman. For some curious reason, this illusion pleased him, so much so that he furthered it by wearing moccasins most of the time and walking as he believed a redskin would. To the uninitiated, this interpretation of an Indian's gait more closely resembled a man walking tight-rope.

He scowled at the girl as she came toward him holding up the paper bag for him to see. Her bright smile did nothing to soften his resentment at her intrusion on his matutinal privacy—in fact, added to it.

"See!" Paula shook the bag of cookies. "Shall I make coffee?"

"I've just got up," Decourré growled hoarsely. Then, clearing his throat, "And I've drunk some milk, and I don't want anything else. Why do you have to come in at all hours of the night like this?"

"Night?" She laughed softly, but with effort. "Why, it's nearly noon. Don't be such a bear, Anton. You'll feel better when you've had breakfast."

"Damn it, I've just said I don't care for anything to eat." He slouched on out of the doorway, scuffling worn moccasins. "I am not in the humor for food. My mind was filled with plans for my work, my Narcissus at the Pool"—he waved toward a messy looking, sizable chunk of wet clay partially covered with a damp cloth—"And now you have come and destroyed it all! Of all the stupid, clumsy, silly little fools—" His voice began to shrill.

Paula had been eyeing the Narcissus with interest, feeling vaguely that it looked like a left-handed Nazi, but as Anton's voice lifted, she glanced at him in alarm.

"Oh, Anton—I'm so sorry—"

"Sorry! A fool's weak excuse. You are sorry—and my morning's work is gone. So, pouf!" He glared fiercely. "Why don't you go away and leave me alone? You are not only wasting your time trying to learn sculpture, but you are also a hindrance to my art—a Delilah, a Jezebel—"

"You didn't talk like this when you wanted me," defended Paula.

"Certainly not. The woman one desires and she whom he has loved aren't the same person," he declaimed. "Love is as the rising sun which lights our day a little while and leaves it in the darkness it found—not something which goes on forever, no fire without end. Don't you understand?"

Paula stared at him blankly.

"No," she said. "You've said it often enough, Anton, but I'll never understand. Love to me is something good, and what is good should be kept. Not thrown away because the new has worn off."

"Sentimental nonsense! One does not enjoy the same show at the theater night after night." He walked to his Narcissus at the Pool and removed the cloth, staring moodily at the wet clay, which looked more like something dropped from a steam shovel than inspired art.

"Must you always live in a make-believe world?" the girl asked soberly. "Don't you think an artist should have some feeling for reality?"

"What has that to do with anything so irrational as the sex-urge you call love?" he sneered, poking at the wet clay with a long forefinger.

"I don't care what you call it, or what it's based on. Love is real. An artist who understands emotion is that much a greater artist." Paula's breast rose and fell in a quick, deep breath as she felt the daring of her defiant speech. Now, she thought, he will be angrier than ever.

He was. Abandoning the clay, he snapped around, his eyes shining wrathfully.

"You are impertinent! A shallow little idiot with as much feeling for art as a subway guard trying to tell me—Anton Decourré—what is required of an artist."

"Oh, but I'm not—"

"Get out!" Anton took a step toward her. "Let us make an end to this nonsense, Paula—a finality. You must know that you no longer bring any fire to my blood. It is useless to try to recover a love that has vanished. Please go—and don't bother to return."

The girl's eyes that had shone with such bright earnestness were now veiled with long lashes. Her face had gone pale, spots of rouge in her cheeks joining with a mole like a beauty spot on her chin to give her pallor the look of make-up.

"I think you're just angry—because I disturbed you," she said hopefully. Somehow the words didn't please her after they were spoken.

"I'm not angry at all," Anton declares loftily. "I am just trying to convince you that this *affaire* has become distasteful and annoying to me."

She made one more try.

"If it's because you are angry, I could forgive you."

Her screened eyes were burning and she was beginning to hate herself for this persistence. Anton, however, had turned back to his potential statuary in a show of indifference, cocking his head to one side and measuring the pile of clay with half-closed eyes.

"There is nothing I wish to be forgiven for—and I insist that I am not angry," he droned. "All I want is for you to stop coming here. I don't wish to hate you, Paula, but if you insist, I shall."

The girl made no reply for a moment or two, struggling desperately to keep her prompting fury in check. When she spoke, her tone had dropped several pitches lower, but the sculptor did not catch a brittle nuance.

"Very well, Anton. Have it your way. I shan't annoy you again."

He turned his head and smiled triumphantly at her.

"Good! I knew you would be sensible, once you understood my feelings." He laughed carelessly, as though to demonstrate that he himself bore no ill will, now that the matter was settled. "You are young, Paula, and really quite good looking. The world is filled with men you can have for the flash of an eye." He nodded ratification of his judgment—and Paula trembled with a confusing abhorrence that was a new sensation. Unmindful, the sculptor continued airily, "So, good-bye, my dear—and good hunting. You may leave the cakes on the table there, as I shall presently be hungry."

There was a swish of paper and the bag of little cakes came flying through the air, breaking open as it landed full in Anton's face, cakes cascading in all directions like bursts from a skyrocket.

"You—damned—cheap—filthy pig!"

Paula retreated to the studio entrance. At the door, she half turned to look back, her face distorted with livid hate.

"Cheap—" she began throatily, then broke off. With a choking gasp she walked out into the hall, pulling the door shut behind her.

Anton Decourré stood for a moment staring at the door and listening to the sound of her feet as she went down the stairs. As the echoes died away he shrugged and smiled quite cheerfully. How consistently do women react to the same circumstances, he reflected, and then set about picking up the least damaged of the little cakes.

By evening Paula Kempt had finished with her tears and begun to organize her thoughts toward the problem of this break in her life. That it was an irreparable one was beyond question. She had been a complete fool, she realized now, to put her faith in a man of Decourré's egoism—incredibly naive to convince herself she could hold him. The thought, however, wasn't very comforting.

Too healthy to mope indefinitely in a furnished room without something to eat, by eight o'clock her appetite began to give her bitter self-recrimination considerable competition. By eight-fifteen, the urge for food had gained a substantial lead.

"*Men have died from time to time,*" she quoted with wry humor, "*and worms have eaten them, but not for love.*"

She dressed, picking out her best for nothing more exciting than dinner at the corner cafeteria. This may have been all Paula had in mind, but there was probably a subsurface impulse to rebound. The possibilities for compensating adventure would be in proportion to how well she looked.

Paula didn't go to the cafeteria. On the way she met a girl she knew, a model, who had learned the folly of letting misguided love affairs get her down. She, too, was on her way to dinner, but didn't fancy gathering it on a tray in a cafeteria. Her experience was that a girl may go to a higher grade restaurant, order a really good meal, and then, if her cafe selection had been wisely made, stand an even chance of picking up an admirer to pay the check. In all probability the pick-up would expect to turn a tidy profit by way of an interesting adventure, but, so far as Paula's friend was concerned, his investment got him nothing beyond the pleasure of her society at dinner.

Paula went along with the girl to a restaurant on Sixth Avenue, where the hunting was good and dinner not too expensive in case a girl was stuck with her own check. The play, of course, was to sit at a table and order cocktails to sip while waiting for male susceptibility to get going.

After the usual fanfare of assumed interest in how the other was getting on, Paula's companion took over, not neglecting an estimating glance or two at a couple of young men standing at the small bar nearby. These fellows were doing a spot of estimating themselves. In the model's experience, older men were a better bet, depending as they did more on cash resources than on physical attention.

"Just so-so," Paula replied to a query on the state of her world. She wasn't given to hanging her wash where anyone could see it. "Still struggling with my little people."

Paula's "little people" were the figures she carved in beeswax with a hot darning needle for the historical scenes she liked to assemble. This flair for dramatic interpretation was expressed in what looked like tiny stage settings, with characters caught in action. She had been working on a scene in miniature representing

Commodore Vanderbilt steering his small ferryboat, cornerstone of the Vanderbilt fortune, hoping to have the group exhibited at the World's Fair in Flushing Meadow.

"You and your little people," chuckled her companion. "How about giving them a rest over the week-end and going on a yachting party? Ranny Walsh is throwing it, and we're going up as far as Newport."

"I'm scared of yachting parties," responded Paula. "They get you out on a boat—and then what? Say yes, or swim home. In the water, I'm no barracuda."

"Nuts, my dear. I've been on Ranny's boat before. The staterooms have big, strong locks, and a girl who wants to sleep alone can make sure she does. I'm for the rice and Mendelssohn stuff, with flowers, and I don't intend to be bilked out of it for a cheap *affaire*."

Paula hoped her face hadn't flushed. She felt a dull glow in her cheeks that indicated it. But she laughed, and after a few moments more discussion of the yachting party, agreed to go along—if invited.

"I'll see to that," assured the girl, promptly. "There's a shortage of girls in Ranny's address book. He asked me to dig up a couple, if I could. So, you be all ready about noon tomorrow for life on the bounding billow. Who knows, you might even meet your romance!" The girl's glance returned to two young men at the bar. "Now, I guess we'd better do something about a couple of suckers to pick up our checks."

So it happened that the next afternoon as the crew of Ranny Walsh's sleek yacht, *Flying Fox*, prepared to get under way in Hempstead Harbor, Paula sat with a gay collection of the owner's friends in the smart launch as it slipped through the water to the gangway. The little ship's bell under the wheelhouse struck the triple note indicating one-thirty as they trooped aboard. It also indicated the exact moment of Paula Kemp's looking into the odd green eyes of a young man in white yachting costume.

As the green eyes met her gaze, their color seemed to change slowly to a greenish blue. For Paula, it was only a queer phenomena, but in Morgan Sands it was a sure sign that fires were kindling in his volatile being.

CHAPTER TWO

Morgan Sands stood as though glued to the bedroom rug, about halfway between the hall door and the foot of the bed, his ordinarily reddish face drained of color and his lower lip drooping open with stunned disbelief.

"I—" he began, then stopped with a nervous attempt to clear his throat and automatically fumbling for cigarettes in his jacket pocket. A fleeting glance at the dead face on the pillow cancelled the movement. "Hite, you—you aren't seriously accusing me of having done this, are you?"

"You think I kid about jobs like that?" Quinny nodded sideways toward the pitiful figure in yellow.

"I—suppose you don't," mumbled Sands. "But, it's wrong—all wrong! There isn't a reason in the world why I would have hurt Paula. She's never injured me and even if she had, I couldn't kill. I tell you, I couldn't even put a sick dog out of its misery—I know, because I tried to bring myself to it once. No—" He closed his eyes tightly and shook his head.

Quinny considered. It was natural enough for the man to be scared witless by such a situation, but this didn't go very far toward establishing his innocence. It just didn't prove anything at all.

"Okay. Maybe you did—maybe it was some other mug. Either way, you're in a tough spot, brother. The cops are going to think it was you, and they'll get the same dough for pinning it on you as anybody else. They'll give you a back room going over before they

25

even think about other possibilities. Yeah, Sands, you definitely aren't sitting pretty."

Morgan Sands recovered the use of his feet sufficiently to return to the doorway, where he leaned against the frame, eyeing the detective dispiritedly.

"You're right, of course," he said, and shifted nervously. "Could you shut off that damned radio? It's—indecent!"

Quinny reached over and snapped the switch. Sands spoke again:

"Thanks. The worst of this is that whether or not I'm cleared, just being accused will finish me with Anita—and especially her mother. They will be here Thursday." Sands scrubbed the slim fingers of one hand into the palm of the other. "If I lose Anita, I shan't care what happens to me."

Privately, Quinny considered losing a bride ran a poor second to a murder conviction. On the other hand, a man feeling as Sands declared he did ought to be a promising client, if innocent. Not for all the cash in Manhattan would the detective undertake to clear a man of whose guilt he was convinced. It simply wasn't good business. He shrugged and moved away from the bed.

"Well, I guess I better go out and phone the cops about this," he said, as though his interest was wholly concerned with his duty as a citizen. "They sort of like to keep in touch with what's going on around town."

Sands nodded, without being conscious of Quinny's words, altogether absorbed in the sinister threat to his security. A speculative flicker came into his peculiar eyes as the detective walked toward the door.

"See here, Hite," Sands exploded impetuously, "this is in your line. Suppose you notify the police and report finding . . . this . . . and keep me out of it. I would pay well for that."

Quinny grinned tightly and tugged the black derby further down on his forehead.

"So that's the set-up!" he retorted sharply. "You bring me here to stooge for you, eh? All I gotta do is to explain that while I'm prowling an empty house I come across a murdered woman—and am I surprised? What am I doin' in an empty house? Don't be a dope, Sands."

Sands colored. "Then I'll have to face it? You won't help me?"

"Look, fella," replied Quinny earnestly. "I'm a homicide man, and I ain't working. You can't hire me to ease you out—if you did it—but if you want me to crack this case no matter who it hits, I'll take it on."

"That's good enough for me," declared the harassed man, surprising the detective mildly. "If you solve this murder, that will clear me. I'll pay anything you ask without question, if you can do it before Thursday."

Quinny shook his head. "No dice. It might not be that easy. No time limit."

"Suppose I put it this way. I'll pay two thousand for the answer to this, five if you have it by Thursday noon. I don't want to bargain, Hite, but I can't stand the thought of Anita and her mother arriving and finding me caught up in a nasty business like this."

Quinny paused, staring grimly at Sands. "Anyhow, a dame that won't stick with you when the going is bad is no use. A right one will."

"Perhaps." Morgan Sands seemed skeptical of feminine loyalty. "The hell of it is that I've never told Anita of my having been married before. She had expressed herself very strongly that she would never be any man's second wife."

"This lovely you're nuts about is beginning to look more like a traffic cop than a help around the house." Quinny's hands felt around and came to rest in his hip pockets, while he teetered on his heels and grinned at his companion. "Okay, I know giving love advice ain't my job. Getting back to cases, if I'm going to take up your offer, I'll need gas for the engine." Sands looked puzzled, and Quinny prompted hastily, "Dough for expenses."

Sands got out his wallet, stripped the bills from it and held them out toward the detective. Quinny retrieved a pocketed hand to take the money. A quick riffle suggested an amount which would undoubtedly add up to a lot more than his gross receipts for the last six months.

"It's a deal, then," the detective said, stuffing the money into his pants pocket. "But get it straight—I'm not hiring out to clear you—just to crack this murder. It's the only way I work."

"That's satisfactory." Sands seemed confident, or else his shock was diminishing.

"All right. Let's go over things."

They went out and sat down side by side on the top step of the stairs, with nothing more to distract them than a view of the gloomy hallway below, visible through the interstices of the balustrade.

"Begin with the time you got to town Sunday and tell me what you did," urged Quinny, after a moment of dusty silence. "Even stuff you don't figure important."

Morgan Sands had arrived, at La Guardia Field late Saturday afternoon, he said, checking in at the Quiberon on Park Avenue. He had not gone out again, travel by plane having left him in no condition for entertainment. Besides, he hadn't wanted to run into any of the gang, Anita wouldn't approve of them. Sunday he had stayed in bed with the newspapers until noon, sent a wire to Anita, and later attended vespers with an aunt, dining with her afterwards at the Pierre.

"Yesterday—Sunday—night was the important time," observed Quinny. "I figure this girl was knocked off then, most likely. The bedlamp wouldn't have been on, if it had been in daytime."

"Mightn't it have happened Saturday night—or even longer ago than that?" queried Sands.

"Could be—but I don't think so, unless somebody else has been here and left that piece of Sunday's paper on the floor. Go on. What did you do after you left your aunt?"

He had returned to his hotel at about six and later on—he wasn't sure of the time—had gone for a long walk through Central Park, then down Broadway to Fiftieth Street, where he had cut back across town through Radio City. He had stepped into a newsreel theater, but hadn't any recollection of what he'd seen on the screen.

"This Anita gal again, I suppose."

"Yes."

"That dame is going to sit you down in the hot squat yet," grumbled Quinny. "Walkin' around all fogged up with love and not seeing anything or anybody else is a bum play for a guy needin' an alibi. You sure you didn't come here last night?"

"Of course I didn't. Why should I? Nothing could be done about getting the house in order then."

"Okay. Now give me a load about the girl in there." Quinny jerked his head toward the bedroom. "Paula, you said."

Sands stirred uneasily on the step they were sitting on. Paula Kemp was a girl he'd met on someone's yachting party back in '38, he explained. It had been one of the usual seagoing orgies and had lasted a couple of days, culminating at Newport in a liquor-inspired marriage to Paula.

"Then, when you got sober, you had it annulled? What was she, a golddigger?"

"I wouldn't describe Paula that way," Sands said thoughtfully. "We had been married for at least a month before the marriage was annulled. On the other hand, she was sensitive to money and position—"

"So'm I," Quinny declared. "I can leave out position, though."

"Paula was just a small-town girl who had come to New York to study art and make a career for herself. Like a lot of other girls, she found this wasn't a simple matter. Then she had the bad luck to fall for a sculptor who was teaching her. He was pretty much the rotter, and when he tired of her, Paula got the air. This was just before the yachting party, where I met her. But you were wrong a moment ago—it wasn't I who wanted the annulment."

"Don't tell me it was her idea?"

"No. You see, my mother was in Florida at the time of our marriage. Paula and I moved in here and then, after about a month, Mother returned. She was mad as blazes and it wasn't long until she had unearthed Paula's affair with the sculptor. I would have told her to keep her nose out of my business, if I'd had the chance. I was—and am—financially independent of her. But I guess Paula wasn't as crazy about me as I thought. She agreed—at a price, which Mother paid."

"Then what? After Paula sold her interest?"

"Nothing. This was years ago. I never saw her again, until just now. You can imagine my shock when I realized who it was on the bed in there." Sands rubbed the palms of his hands over his face as though to erase the lingering image, then murmured irrelevantly, "I was born in that room."

Sands' story had the delicate undertones of truth to the detective, trained through long experience to a fair sense of discrimination. The story was a familiar one, but for this reason not much of a guide to Paula Kemp's character.

"The next thing to do is to get a picture of what happened," Quinny said, getting up from the step and turning back toward the room. "You can stay here in the doorway while I browse around."

The suggestion wasn't intended to relieve Sands' repugnance, but because Quinny didn't want the room tracked up unnecessarily. The cops would be pretty free in their comment on that. He walked back into the room and stopped at the side of the bed, staring down at the dead woman. Her position was one natural to sleeping, her head resting on one extended arm, the other lying down across the quilt partially covering her. An ugly welt was visible on the temple, which Quinny gave careful attention. The skin had not been actually broken, but there were three parallel rows of tiny contusion marks across the swelling, about an eighth of an inch apart. The center one was more strongly defined than the other two.

Quinny straightened up and stood for several moments, just looking. There was something in the yellow silk with pastel designs she wore suggestive of a butterfly beaten to earth by a callous urchin's stick. Shifting, the detective caught the gleam of a metallic object at the edge of the quilt, partially concealed by her arm. He leaned over to inspect it more closely, but could not identify the shiny instrument. Although used to stab, it was obviously no sort of knife.

He speculated fleetingly. The stabbing had followed bludgeoning to make sure of results, and, if this were correct, it had not been an impetuous crime. Definite conclusions, however, at this stage could be misleading.

Nevertheless, since the woman had been struck on the head but once and probably afterwards stabbed in a selected vital spot, it didn't seem to have been the work of an infuriated person, but someone coolly determined on thoroughness without being messy. Sands didn't seem to be the type. Driven to kill, he probably would have struck repeatedly with the club—or whatever had been used. Didn't seem to be, but Quinny wouldn't discard the possibility.

Several tiny scratches on the woman's neck caught the detective's attention. These were at the back of the neck, scarcely more than skin abrasions, as though a chain, perhaps a necklace, had been forcefully jerked away. Another item which caught his interest was the position of the bed in relation to the door to the hall. It would have been impossible for anyone to have entered the bedroom without being seen by the victim, unless she had been asleep. The radio was no sure proof of her having been awake. It could have been turned on by the slayer afterwards, although Quinny couldn't imagine a reason for this. It was seldom that a murder was committed in these apparent circumstances by some-one unknown to the victim.

Quinny looked around for a possible object which could have served as a bludgeon. There was a fireplace a couple of yards from the bed, with a set of implements in an iron rack at the side. The poker, however, was lying in the grate. He crossed over to look at it, but didn't bother to pick it up. Used as a weapon, the poker would not have produced the three lines of contusion marks, but would have left a smudge and broken the skin as well.

Glancing at Sands, who was watching him with troubled eyes from the doorway, Quinny began a superficial inspection of the room. He was limited to what he could see without disturbing any-thing, if he was to avoid scathing criticism from the homicide men when they arrived. Luckily, this room had been swept and dusted to some extent recently, so that he could move about without leav-ing telltale signs. He had been impressed on entering the house with Sands at the appalling amount of dust which can accumulate in three years, even in a tightly closed house. Finally he returned to the hall doorway, looking faintly puzzled.

"The gal wasn't living here, like I thought at first," he said re-proachfully, as though upsetting his first impression had been a willful lack of consideration on the part of Sands' one-time wife. "There's just a couple of nighties and that sort of stuff in that bag on the chair. No clothes in the closet, except the dress she wore here, and not even any extra shoes. There's two or three hotel towels in the bathroom, a toothbrush and some make-up. A woman staying any time in a joint has the bathroom cabinet full of bottles and stuff."

"What do you make of that?" asked Sands. "I mean, if she had another place to live, why would she want to spend a night here?"

"She's been using this place to meet somebody who didn't want to risk being seen with her. Somebody important to her, too, or she wouldn't have gone to the trouble of cleaning up this room." Quinny eyed Sands speculatively. "Any idea where she might live—or hang out? I'd like to have a peek before the cops do."

Sands shook his head. "No, I don't. I couldn't even tell you where she lived at the time we were married. And she may not be known now as Paula Kemp, as I, said."

Struck by this thought, Quinny walked around the bed to a bureau, on which he had noticed a large handbag. He turned it over with the tip of his finger, revealing two large initials on its side. P.C. Nodding his head, he looked back at Sands.

"Guess you hit it, unless you spell Kemp with a 'C'," he pronounced.

He opened the bag, the catch of which was not caught, and gingerly examined the contents. He found nothing to reveal the girl's name, or anything else of helpful implication. There weren't even keys—the one thing city dwellers find it practically impossible to go without. Quinny scowled. This job was beginning to look tough. The police, of course, had better facilities for eventually learning where a person lived, such as checking store labels and laundry or dry cleaners' marks in clothing. These processes weren't fast enough for Quinny's purpose. He wanted to explore the girl's living quarters quickly, and get there first.

Nevertheless, he went back and examined the dress she had worn. It had come from a popular-price store on Fourteenth Street, where in all probability no records were kept of cash customers.

The same was true of the slip which hung on another hook, and the shoes were from the stock of a booterie which had branches all over the town. He picked up the left shoe and turned it over. She hadn't been too prosperous lately, he thought. There was a small hole in the thin sole.

Handicapped by the necessity of too cautious investigation, there didn't seem much more he could do until the arrival of the homicide squad men. He started back toward Sands, but detoured to the fireplace. On the mantel he had noticed some sort of plaque, a head molded in bas relief.

"It's General Patton," he said, interestedly. "It's got her initials in the corner—'P.C., 1943'. Why do you suppose she lugged that here from where she lived?"

"Does it matter?"

"Proves she's been comin' here for some time."

"How? She could as easily have brought it with her last night as any other time, couldn't she?" argued Sands, without much interest.

"Sure she could, but she couldn't have fixed it so it would have a thin layer of dust all over it—more'n would settle in a couple of days."

Quinny stepped back, still looking at the clay likeness of the general, a man for whom he had a great deal of admiration. The modeled head was a strikingly good piece of work, in considerable detail, even to the four tiny stars on the helmet.

"You know, Sands," he enthused. "I'd like to have that statue. Is that the only kind of—uh—sculping she did?"

"Oh, no. At the time I knew her, she liked doing figurines—"

"I didn't ask could she cook."

"You don't eat figurines," explained Sands, with the mere ghost of a smile. "Paula called them 'little people'—"

"Leave us get this straight," interrupted Quinny, who was getting confused. "You mean she made statues of midgets?"

"No. I mean she made miniature scenes, with figures of people five or six inches high—"

"Oh, I get it." Quinny wagged his head knowingly. Caught flat-footed on upper Fifth Avenue in a sudden rainstorm one day, he had ducked into the Museum of the City of New York. Once inside, he had been fascinated by the modeled street scenes of early Manhattan on display, the handiwork of that extraordinary artist, Dwight Franklin, and others. "I seen some once."

He examined the bas relief with freshened interest, wondering briefly at the error the sculptress had made and dismissing it as being probably of no importance to the matter in hand.

"Come on, Sands," he said brusquely. "Here's what you do now. Go down to the gin mill on the corner, call your lawyer, and tell him the fix you're in. I suppose you've got one?"

"I think I'll call Cecil Wayman—that's Severn, Mains and Wayman, down on Pine Street—"

"Okay. Then call the cops and tell 'em you've discovered a murdered dame in your house. Then come back. I'll be waiting for you out front. If I ain't, ring the doorbell, or stick your head in and holler."

Quinny planned to use the interval before the police arrived to do a little more poking around. He could count on at least ten minutes, if Sands called his lawyer first. The private investigator always worked under the handicap of digging up his own leads. Once the police moved in on a job, an outsider had to depend largely on hand-outs from the official in charge of the case. Some of the homicide chiefs were cooperative, but a lot of them regarded private detectives with brassy suspicion. The smart way was to get the first look when possible.

Morgan Sands left via the front door and the one in the boarded-up entrance. Quinny began an inspection of the hallway. The yellow light in the lantern overhead didn't give enough illumination for a satisfactory job, but had to do.

The hallway was only wide enough to accommodate the staircase, with a passage alongside leading to the rear of the house. Like the room upstairs, both the stairs and this hall had been swept clear of the accumulated dust, so that there were no visible marks of feet. The sweeping, however, had stopped at the arched entrance to the drawing room.

Snapping the light switch for this room, Quinny stood for a moment, sizing it up. It was, for these days, extraordinarily large, taking up more than half the floor space on this level, with a great deal of dust-sheeted furniture scattered around. Of more interest to Quinny was a row of sharply defined footprints in the thick dust, left there by a woman's feet. These began at the archway and continued straight across the room to a position behind a highbacked, cloth-shrouded chair. As nearly as he could judge from where he stood, the person had emerged again, started toward the archway and then gone back behind the chair before emerging once more on the other side of the chair and returning to the archway.

Quinny stopped for a closer inspection of the nearest footprints. They had been made by a woman with small, narrow feet and high heels. Paula Kemp, as indicated by the slipper he had inspected, had small feet, too, but wider than the ones which had made these marks. There was also no sign of the worn-through sole in the print of the left shoe.

Two women, he mused. Two women had come to this house and one remained. There was little doubt in his mind that these footprints in the drawing room were no more than twenty-four hours old, but he couldn't be entirely sure.

Turning back into the hall, Quinny went on out to the front steps, where he eased his hips down onto the lowest one to await the return of Morgan Sands.

QUINNY PULLED the last of his cigarettes from the package, lit it, then crumpled the empty container and tossed it across the sidewalk into the gutter. With time to kill, he twisted around for a more detailed inspection of the front of the house. Extending from the small stoop where he sat on a step to the other side of the house was a high fence, made of iron bars tipped with spearlike points. He could see an equally high gate at the other end, which gave access to a flight of stairs leading down to a basement entrance under the stoop.

Making a mental note to explore this stairway later, Quinny squinted toward First Avenue. The stone step he sat on was steadily getting harder and colder. He began to wonder if his green-eyed client had taken the telephone errand as an invitation to scram. If so, whoever headed the expected detail could be counted on to

deliver some pretty torrid comment on the dumbness shown in letting Sands walk away.

A gang of young hoodlums a little way down the street were
noisily engaged in that peculiar variety of football devised by them
to fit the limitations of street play. As Quinny eyed them indifferently, a red-sweatered youngster detached himself and came along
the sidewalk toward the detective. He looked about as tough and
hard as a lad of twelve can achieve in an environment offering singularly fine facilities for such development.

"Hey, bud!" Quinny called as the boy was about to pass. "Do
you live around here?"

"Naw. I live on Fi't Avenoo whadda you think?"

The urchin eyed Quinny with oblique suspicion. A boy had to
watch out for truant officers bent on rounding up victims to hustle
off to school.

"My mistake," drawled Quinny. "I thought you was a bum. A Fifth
Avenue gent couldn't tell me what I want to know about this lousy
street."

"What's your racket?" demanded the boy.

"I'm a detective. Your name wouldn't be Pete, would it?" Pete,
Quinny remembered, was the hero of the exploits inscribed in chalk
on the boarding.

"My name's Joe," the boy replied uncertainly. "Pete ain't been
around today. What's he been doing?" He picked uneasily at his
frayed red sweater.

"Ask Elsie. Or read what it says up there—I don't use such language myself."

"Funny man, ain'tcha?" It was a snarl.

Quinny grinned. "Look, I'm here on a murder job and I need to
know what's been going on in this street the last forty-eight hours
or so. If you've been hanging around here, you might have seen—"

"Chees, a murder?" exclaimed the youngster, eagerness under-
mining his insolent front. "In this block?"

"What's the matter with a murder in this street?" he demanded.
"To me, it's a natural. But you wouldn't know about that, I guess,
bein' Fifth Avenue. What are you doing here—slumming?"

"I was kiddin', mister. I hang out here most all the time, except when I see the truant officer snoopin' around. That's what I thought you were."

Quinny laughed. "Look, it would be a waste of time even to send you to kindergarten. Takes brains to get by in school."

"I ain't so dumb as you think," retorted the boy hotly.

"I hope you ain't. Feel like giving me a hand on this murder job?"

"Who got it?" The boy tried to curb his interest.

"A dame." The detective's gesture seemed to indicate that dames generally might expect to be murdered sooner or later. "I ask questions. You answer 'em, if you can. Were you in the street here last night?"

The boy shuffled his feet. "No—not last night. Me old man made me stay in."

"See anyone go in this house today?"

"Yeah—a while ago I saw a fella goin' up these steps. I guess he went in, 'cause I didn't notice him after. Slim, red-headed guy in a gray suit."

That would be Morgan Sands. "I know about that one," said Quinny.

"He's the only one I seen." The boy's eyes were disappointed.

"Well, so long's your old man improved society around here last night by making you stay home, I guess you won't be much help after all."

"Maybe I will. See the furniture works over there?" Quinny glanced at a four-story building across the street, several houses nearer Fifth Avenue. The boy continued: "They's a night watchman over there, named Gus Pilgrim. He sits up there in a second story window when he ain't punchin' his clocks. I bet he sees ever'body that goes by in this block—and most of the time that ain't many. Whyn't you buzz him?"

"What time does he come on?"

"Six o'clock."

"Okay," said Quinny. "I'll look him up tonight, maybe." He was beginning now really to be concerned about the non-returning Morgan Sands, who might not have bothered to call the police.

"Look here, Joe, how's about camping on these steps a couple minutes while I go down to the corner to phone?"

"What'll I do if some mug wants to go in?" The boy stared at the detective importantly.

"Talk to him till I get back. I'll only be a couple of minutes."

"Okay. Say, my name *is* Pete. I don't give it out till I find out what a guy wants." Pete winked knowingly.

"I thought so. Well, give my love to Elsie, when you see her."

Quinny started off toward First Avenue, ignoring Pete's retort, a word which might be found in certain of the more significant novels, but which weren't likely to have been on Pete's reading list.

Morgan Sands was not in the Golden Turtle. The bartender had noticed his coming in to use the phone, however. He complained that the man had left immediately afterward, without even buying a drink.

"He looked kind of scared when he went out," he added.

"He was scared when he came in," replied Quinny, heading for the telephone booth. He dialed police headquarters. Quinny merely announced that a dead body had been found, gave the address and hung up. This would save a lot of explanation which would only have to be repeated to the official sent to head the investigation.

Returning to Sands' house, he found Pete still faithfully guarding the premises, but plainly disappointed that no suspicious characters had shown up.

"That's the way it goes, Pete," consoled Quinny. "But, in this detectin' business, you have to cover everything. How's if you kinda snoop around and find out if any of your pals were in the street last night?"

Pete approved. His stature among, his fellows would be immeasurably heightened if he were the first to break the exciting news. He walked away toward them with a fine display of superior and cunning purpose.

Presently a white-topped squad car careened into the street from First Avenue. The car had not quite stopped at the curb before three men began to pile out. One of these was Lieutenant Madden of the Homicide Squad, with whom the detective had excellent relations. This was a break.

"Hi-ya, Madden," Quinny greeted, taking a step toward the burly, good-looking officer.

Madden grinned, looking not very surprised.

"Might've expected to see you here waiting," he said. "Damned if I don't believe you put people up to killing their friends just to keep you in work. Who, and where is it?"

Quinny jerked his head toward the house. "Inside. A dame who used to be Paula Kemp." As he reached the top step, he stopped and turned to the lieutenant. "Look, Madden, there's some foot-prints in there you won't want messed up. Keep everybody out till you've had a gander."

"All right. Stay here till I call you—you and Bill." Madden made it an order to the two men with him, although his tone was casual. Then to Quinny: "Who found the body?"

"Morgan Sands—the corpse's ex-husband." Quinny opened the door in the boarding. "That is—sort of."

"What do you mean, 'sort of?'" demanded the lieutenant, fol-lowing the detective. "Did he or didn't he?"

Quinny stopped in the amber-lighted hallway. "What I mean is, Sands came in and saw her on the bed, but thought it was some stranger sleeping there. Figured it was somebody who had moved in while he was out west working in a shipyard. He just got in town Saturday—he says."

"Where is he now?" Madden glanced about the gloomy interior as if expecting to see someone.

"I sent him down to the corner to phone headquarters and re-port the crime. He ain't back yet."

Madden laughed coarsely. "Since you got off the force, Quinny, you get more and more like a citizen all the time." The officer broke off grinning to scowl. "You know damn well you oughta held him here."

"Yeah? Since when does a private operator have authority to hold a guy, unless he actually witnessed the crime? Must be some new rules." Quinny shook his head disparagingly. "It's nothin' to get heated up about, anyway. If he don't come back, you'll pick him up sooner or later and have him behind the eight ball to start with."

"Rules or no rules, you should have held him here," dissented Madden.

Maybe so, Quinny thought, but he could see where Sands' escape might be a considerable help to getting in some private exploration while the police were busy rounding up the missing ex-husband.

"Scramming like this makes it look bad for Sands," Quinny needled guilefully.

Madden grunted. "Doesn't prove a thing," he denied. "Just makes more trouble for us. Where's this alleged body?"

"Come on. I'll show you."

On the way upstairs Quinny sketched the situation, beginning with his first encounter with Sands at the Turtle. Lieutenant Madden clumped along behind, listening attentively. At the door to the back bedroom, the detective paused.

"It's all yours from now," he said.

"You haven't been in here?" There was justified skepticism in Madden's tone.

"Sure I have. If I hadn't, I wouldn't have known whether the dame was asleep, or just dead. Sands hired me to throw some squatters out of his house, but the idea was that same were alive."

"Well, I hope you haven't messed up anything. You know damn well no one is supposed to go poking around where a murder has been committed until after the police have been called in."

"Sure, sure—I know all that, but it's just an idea some cluck of a police commissioner dreamed up fifty years ago to keep out the hoi polloi. I am not hoi polloi—and I know my way around in a murder job. Nothin's different from the way I found it. Don't be old fashioned, Madden."

"I ought to give you the heave out of here."

"But you won't."

"No, I won't. Just don't spill anything about being in here on the loose where it will reach the commissioner's ears—or you're likely to say good-bye to your license. Let's get on with it. What do you make out of the set-up?" Madden walked carefully into the room toward the bed, where he stopped.

"Love nest. Surprisin' how regular they turn out to be slaughter houses instead." Quinny came across the room to stand at Madden's side, automatically pushing his derby back and then thrusting his hands into his hip pockets. "There's some screwy angles about this job, Madden," he said.

"I suppose. Did this Mrs. Sands come east ahead of her husband?"

"You got it wrong. They ain't been married for eight years—according to him—and then only a few weeks. He claims he hadn't seen her since till today. Her name ain't Sands, either. It was Paula Kemp when Sands met her, but on her handbag over there are the initials 'P.C.' That's one of the angles. Until you find out what name she's been using, it's maybe going to be tough to learn much about her." Quinny glanced at Madden with naive candor. "How's for friskin' the bag? Might be somethin' in it with her name on it."

Having already checked, Quinny knew there was not, but felt it best to let Madden assume the bag hadn't been examined. The lieutenant went over to the bureau and spent a couple of silent minutes going through the contents of the bag.

"Not a damn thing with her name on it, or anything likely to give a lead. Hell, there must be something here to go on. Where's her baggage?"

Quinny grinned smugly. "That's all I've seen—that suitcase on the chair."

Madden opened the bag, lifted the few filmy garments and dropped them back. "She was traveling light, if this is all there is."

"I figure she wasn't living here—only using it, like I said, for a love nest. Sands don't seem to know any more than we do about what she's been doing the last seven years."

"It'll work out. The woman's friends will come forward when they hear about this." Madden returned to the bedside.

Quinny knew this to be probable, but was entirely content with the idea that it would take time. Meanwhile, he had cooked up a plan he hoped would land him in the dead girl's living quarters before the police. He was eager to get on with it, but decided to stick around in case Madden and his aids turned up something the detective hadn't had enough time to uncover.

"Yeah, yeah—it would be funny if a gal as good looking as she was didn't have friends. She had one too many." He turned around to glance down at the body in the bed. "You notice she was slugged with something that didn't break the skin. That killed her, I think, without the gadget sticking in her midriff."

Madden had noticed the unusual weapon, partially concealed by the quilt and the girl's arm. He bent over and inspected it closely.

"Looks like some kind of drawing instrument," he said. "Tell better when the medic pulls it out. Well, let's finish looking around before anybody from the D.A.'s office shows up and gets in the way. That reminds me, what's your interest in this?"

"Plenty. Sands offers me enough dough to keep my bookie all winter if I can crack the case come Thursday—"

"So that's why you let him beat it before we got here?" Madden's eyes gleamed with enlightenment; his tone was a crisp indictment.

"No. I just gave him his head—to see what he would do. Put out a radio scream for him, if you want him—or send a man to his hotel. He's probably gone to see his lawyer."

"He'll be brought in." Madden moved to a door beyond the one opening into the bath, which Quinny had noticed but supposed to be merely another closet. "What's in this room?"

"I didn't look. Ain't it a closet?"

It was not. Madden pulled the door open and disclosed a small room over a narrow extension of the house into the back garden. This room hadn't been cleaned, as had the bedroom, and the floor was a mess of footprints, none clearly defined. It contained little furniture other than a huge drawing table, with numerous shallow drawers in its base, several books on naval architecture on a shelf and a number of framed ship plans.

"This Sands guy is a naval architect," Quinny observed, "but he says he never worked at it till the war came along."

Ignoring the footprints as too blurred to be useful, Madden went on in to examine the dusty drawing board and the drawers under it. In one of the latter he found a welter of badly kept drawing instruments. Picking one up, he eyed it thoughtfully, then turned to the door where Quinny stood watching. He held up the instrument.

"This is the kind of gadget the woman was stabbed with," he said. "So it looks not so good for Sands."

"I dunno," returned Quinny doubtfully. "A guy wouldn't have to be a naval architect to know how to stab somebody with a gag like that. Madden sneezed violently. "Damned if I'm not going to open a window before I choke on this dust," he declared, snorting to free his nostrils.

"Don't see that it would hurt anything," agreed Quinny. "Here, let me do it."

Quinny opened the catch and raised the room's one big wide window. He found a pair of heavy shutters outside, built to swing out on hinges at each side of the casing and intended to be secured by a padlock when closed. All the windows in the rear of the house were similarly equipped. But the padlock on this one was missing, so that Quinny had no trouble in throwing open the shutters. He leaned out to inhale a lungful of fresh air, Madden joining him.

The garden below, not very large, was a tangle of untended and overgrown vegetation beginning to herald the approach of winter. It was surprising that anything would grow there at all, as the yard was enclosed on one side by the five-story blank wall of the tenement and on the other by the ironwork factory. At the rear was the blank wall of a huge warehouse. No sun could ever reach the garden.

"It's a sure thing nobody could get in or out of that yard, except through the house," Quinny remarked. "Not unless he had a fire ladder with him. It would be like being at the bottom of a well with the rope busted."

Madden nodded absently and his interest returned to the drawing instrument he still held in his hand. It was a ten-inch pair of proportional dividers.

"What is it, a compass?" Quinny asked interestedly. His knowledge of drawing instruments was elementary.

Madden's wasn't much better. "I think they're called dividers, but I've never seen any just like these." He dropped the instrument into the open drawer, then slammed it shut.

"Close the window and come on," Madden said over his shoulder as he started out of the room. "I want a gander at the bathroom."

The room so obviously had been slightly used that Madden saw no gain in a detailed inspection at this stage. Later, all the rooms would get a complete going over by the department experts.

"You said something about footprints," the lieutenant said, as they came out again.

"They're downstairs, in the front room. I thought you'd want to see the corpse before I showed 'em to you."

They went out to the head of the stairs, where Madden paused to tilt his head back and stare up at the space between the staircase and the floor above.

"What's up there?" he demanded.

"I didn't go up there," replied Quinny. "You can tell by the dust on this hall floor that nobody has been upstairs lately." Quinny led the way downstairs, bringing up at the entrance to the drawing room on the first floor. He snapped the wall switch, flooding the musty room with light.

"Get a load of the footprints there," he said to Madden, at his elbow. "Another dame came in here, stooped behind that high-backed chair over there, came out, ducked back, and then came back here."

"Another dame?"

"Sure. The one upstairs had short, kinda wide feet. This one had little feet, too, but narrow. I looked at the slippers in the closet upstairs." Quinny hoped that this variation of his assertion of not having poked into anything would slip by unnoticed.

It did. "Uh, hoom," Madden rubbed two fingers over his temple and nodded. "Guess you're right, Quinny. But it'll be checked."

"I figure she came here and hid while somebody else was going upstairs—or to wait till somebody did," continued the detective earnestly. "That could have been this Paula dame—or the lug who killed her—"

"The woman who was in here could have gone upstairs and put the slug on, for that matter," argued Madden. "We don't know where she went from here."

"Right," agreed Quinny. "You take your choice and hope your bet's on the winner."

"Did you see any other footprints? With dust all over the floors, no one could move around without leaving them—outside of the hall and the bedroom upstairs."

"That's why I wanted you to leave the guys outside." As Quinny spoke, new sirens were screaming in the street outside, advertising the arrival of reinforcements. "I was thinking it might be a good idea to take a gander at the basement before the place gets all tramped up."

"Then we better get at it," said Madden nervously, expecting to hear a commotion on the front stoop any moment. "What makes you think we'll find anything there?"

"Sands swears he had the lights shut off when he went to the Coast, three years ago. I want to check on that. Also, there is a basement entrance to this dump from the sidewalk. I don't suppose you noticed it."

Madden didn't admit that there was anything in all Manhattan he hadn't noticed. He said nothing, but followed the detective down the hall to the dark, narrow basement stairs. Quinny found a switch inside the entrance and snapped on the lights. At the bottom they found themselves in another hallway, directly beneath the one they'd left. A wide open door gave a view into a kitchen. Further along toward the front of the house another door opened into a furnace room, and at the end of this hall a heavy door evidently opened into a service entrance leading up to the street behind the spear-like fence. This door was locked and the key had been removed. There was also a bolt, but it was not engaged.

The furnace room, however, first held Quinny's interest. There was a partially filled coal bin extending under the service stairs outside, and the floor of the entire room was thickly overlaid with powdered coal dust. A number of overlapping footprints led across the meters, fastened to a wall. It wasn't necessary to enter the room to see that the meter had been jumped with a length of wire to provide current for the house. The marks in the coal dust had all been made by male feet.

"Makes Sands' story hold up better," Quinny observed. "Whoever moved in here with Paula Kemp didn't want the Edison Company to be bothering 'em with electric bills."

"You don't know that the man who rigged up the meter bypass ever heard of Paula Kemp," objected Madden. "That might have been done any time in the last two or three years."

"Nuts," responded Quinny impolitely. "Those footprints haven't been there long."

They found another small room between the furnace room and the kitchen at the rear, partially filled with household discard and also containing a workbench with tools scattered over its surface. The floor showed a confusion of footprints, apparently made at different times by the same feet. Avoiding these, Madden and Quinny went to the bench, where the latter spotted a padlock in the litter. The shackle of this had been sawed through.

"Somebody sawed it off the shutter to the little room upstairs where the drawing board is," observed Quinny. "Easy to dope that out."

Held in a vise was a corroded solid brass rod, about a half inch in diameter and a couple of feet long. Bright metal at one end and brass fillings on the bench made it plain that a piece had been hacksawed from it. Quinny's forehead wrinkled in thought as he stared at the rod.

"What's the idea of sawing off a chunk of that?" he asked, in the tones of a man not expecting to have his question answered.

"A len'th of it would make a pretty good club," hazarded Madden.

"Yeah—could," agreed Quinny. "But it wouldn't leave those three rows of marks like we saw on the woman's forehead. This rod is smooth."

Madden shrugged and started back to the hallway. Although he did not say so, Madden clearly was impatient to conclude his rough inspection before some ranking officer arrived and ordered the front door pushed in.

At the top of the basement stairs, at the end of the main hall, was a partly closed door. Madden pushed it open and revealed a butler's pantry, a narrow room of the same width as the hall and extending to the back of the house. They saw the same layer of settled dust and a line of male footprints going through a door to the garden.

Madden tiptoed through the pantry, keeping as far as possible from the precious footprints, with Quinny doing likewise at his heels. The pantry ended in the extension of the house and was directly beneath the small room off the bedroom upstairs. The door to the garden was secured by a spring lock with the bolt engaged.

"This is damn funny," puzzled Quinny. "This guy goes through here and out this door, but he don't come back in—not this way, anyhow. How did he get out of the yard? Figure that out for your report."

Madden unlocked the door and went out, followed by Quinny, who had no idea of permitting the lieutenant to turn up something important unless he was in on it. It didn't take much of a tour of inspection to determine that leaving the yard by way of the surrounding walls couldn't be done without considerable equipment. There was no other entrance to the house. In the center of the garden was a circular stone seat, a large cement urn in the middle forming a back rest for anyone sitting there. Someone had, and recently. The soft earth was heel scuffed, with a couple of deep, clearly defined footprints as well. There were a lot of burned matches scattered about.

"The guy must have sat here smoking quite a while," commented Quinny, picking up an exhausted match folder. "I don't see no cigarette butts, though."

Speculation on this was halted by a lusty bawl from the front of the house. Only the homicide chief, Captain Lendon, had voice enough to penetrate to the rear garden. There were those who insinuated that Bull Lendon had roared himself into his office.

"Madden! Where the hell are you, and what's the idea of keeping me outside? Who do you think you—"

Madden scurried back into the house to head off the heat Lendon was working up to, letting out a considerable bellow himself.

"All right, all right, chief! Coming."

Quinny stayed in the yard. Captain Lendon was an old acquaintance, but no pal. He hoped Madden would take the captain upstairs before showing him the rest of the house. He sat down on the circular seat to wait, listening to the babble of voices sifting from the front hall. His roving eyes caught sight of a tiny bit of black metal which seemed to be a wheel. Picking it up for closer examination didn't help to identify it. About a quarter of an inch in diameter, it seemed to be a minute gear wheel, but the corrugations on the rim weren't pronounced enough to serve as gear teeth.

Losing interest, Quinny flipped it into the dirt and then climbed up on the circular seat to see if the cement urn were hollow or just a decorative fake. There was a depression, several inches deep and about half full of water with a layer of mud at the bottom.

"Gee!" he exclaimed softly, as he saw a short section of garden hose half embedded in the mud. Protruding slightly from the tube was a piece of brass rod which had been forced three or four inches into it, leaving the rest of the hose still flexible—a crude but efficient blackjack. Quinny had no doubt of its being the murder weapon, the ridged surface of the rubber causing the three rows of contusions he'd noticed on the victim's forehead.

He didn't disturb it, but returned to the garden door. Listening a moment, he heard a tramping of feet overhead, then went on in. This, he thought, was a good place for an astute private operator to lam. He sauntered through the hall to the front door, still guarded by the men Madden had posted there—a couple of detectives Quinny knew.

"Where are you heading for?" asked the one called Bill suspiciously. He wasn't sure whether his orders about stopping anyone from entering hadn't also been intended to cover outgoing traffic as well.

Quinny stopped, automatically giving the derby an upward push with two fingers, and looked pleasantly at the guardian of the gate.

"Uptown, to run down a lead for Madden," he answered mendaciously. "Chances are, I'll be back before long."

"How come he's sending a private dick?" growled Bill. "What's the matter with us guys?"

"Can he help it, if his staff is undermanned?"

Quinny seemed deeply concerned with the war-thinned ranks of the police department. "Tell Madden to look in the cement crock out in back, will you. I forgot. See you later."

He went on down the steps. A considerable crowd had gathered in the street, with the human animal's swift response to the
morbid. There was quite a gathering of uniformed cops, and also
plainclothes men who might just as well have worn uniforms. Not
many professional detectives succeed in looking like anything else.
Just now, these fellows seemed as avidly curious as the encircling
fringe of civilians about what was going on inside the house.

"What's the lay, Quinny?" called one of the detectives.

"Front page murder—from all the signs," answered Quinny. He
wanted to get away, but these boys were frequently too helpful to
him to be ignored. "And you needn't look like a hound which has
been woke up by the smell of a rabbit. You'll be plenty sick of this
job before you get your shoes off again, Charlie. Somethin' tells
me this rabbit is goin' to take a lot of catchin'."

CHAPTER THREE

QUINNY HITE GOT HIS FOOT correctly settled on the rail of the Golden
Turtle bar and signaled the bartender, with airy souciance bred of
oblong dough in pocket, marred somewhat by a vague feeling that
wealth unaccountably lessened one's drinking zest. He glanced
about idly while waiting, but the only other customer was a mousy
little man wearing an overcoat that appeared to have doubled for a
blanket at night. Obviously, the fellow was socially inferior to a
smart homicide detective.

Quinny turned back to the bar and downed the drink the bartender had set out. Restoring the empty glass to the near-
mahogany, the detective eyed it disapprovingly.

"Y' know, Mac," Quinny commented, "you barkeeps gotta have
steady hands to pour liquor in a glass like this. Maybe you use an
eyedropper—I wasn't looking."

"And what's the matter with it, now?" demanded the bartender
bellicosely.

"Too much glass and not enough hole. A man could get a sore
arm hoisting and lowering a chunk of glass like this long before he
got a comfortable edge on."

"Why don't you try some other j'int, if you ain't satisfied?"
grated the bartender.

"Oh, don't get me wrong—I like the place okay. Anyhow, I would
if the servin's wasn't so frugal-like." Quinny emptied the glass again
and shoved it toward the bartender for a refill. "Look, Pedro, did
you know one of your neighbors got bumped off last night?"

"If you gotta get chummy, me name's Eugene—"

Quinny shook his head. "Can't be. No bartender was ever named Eugene."

"The b'ys call me Gene."

The mousy little man down the bar joined up.

"Did I understand you, sir, to say there was a homicide in this vicinity last night?" he asked, in a surprisingly well-modulated voice.

"Yeah, yeah—a dame," responded Quinny. "In the Sands house, down the block."

"The red brick which is boarded up?" demanded the bartender. "Not a bad spot for murder, at that. Who done it—or don't you know?"

"That's what I'm workin' on—finding out who. Maybe you've heard of me—I'm Quin Hite." Quinny smiled modestly at Eugene.

Eugene shook his head. "Never did. You was in here a while ago and doin' a slick job of promoting yourself a drink from the red-headed guy. Now you've promoted yourself a job of lookin' for a murderer, eh?"

"That's my regular work," Quinny replied, loftily. "Private operator, but I used to be a top hand on the Homicide Squad."

"Used to be," sneered the bartender. "I was a cop myself till they started gettin' fussy about takin' a couple extra bucks off of speakeasies. Yeah—I was a cop, but I never heard of no detective named Hite."

"Skip it," surrendered Quinny. "Fill up this doll goblet again. Look, Eugene, this murder was pulled sometime last night—I figure before midnight. Any strangers in here that you noticed?"

"I was only here till nine o'clock, but there was a guy I noticed special, not one of the regulars. Tall, skinny bloke, with a big nose and long, skinny hands. Had on Indian shoes. He sat over there at that table by the cigarette machine about an hour, suckin' on one glass of sherry. Maybe he stayed longer—he was here when I left." The bartender shrugged.

"Ever see him before?"

"Coupla times lately. Always sat in the same place and kept his nippin' to one shot of wine. That's all I can tell you about him. He never talked to anybody. Just sat there by himself and bothered nobody. If he had, I'd have given him the bum's rush in a minute."

Quinny nodded. "Probably just some bum which moved into this high-toned neighborhood lately. No reason to connect him up with this crime, I guess."

"Y' never know," debated Eugene, not liking the let-down.

Quinny tossed off the minikin of rye and gathered up his remaining change from the moist bar. "Okay, Gene. If this fella comes in again, you might get a line on him for me. Hey?"

"You do your own detectin'," growled Gene. "I'm a bartender."

The little man standing further down the bar coughed apologetically.

"Perhaps, sir, I might be of some slight assistance," he said. "It happened that I was present here last night and saw this man Gene has just described." He bobbed his head and beamed knowingly. "There was also a young lady, palpably astray from her habitual environment."

Quinny stared at the little man for a contemplative moment.

"Yeah?" he said uncertainly. "Do I get you to mean she looked like a dame which didn't belong around here?"

"Gus Pilgrim always talks highbrow," explained Gene, resting his hairy forearms on the bar and looking interested. "Knows very big word in the dictionary—an' has to make a livin' nightwatchin' the furniture works around the corner."

"I used to be a proofreader, but I find this work less contentious—"

Quinny's interest climbed like a Hellcat.

"Yeah, yeah—one of the kids told me about you a while ago. How come you saw this lug Gene mentions and also the dame in here, if you were on the job in the furniture joint?"

Mr. Pilgrim looked embarrassed.

"I slip out occasionally during the night for a cannikin of brew," he said shyly. "An excellent soporific."

"Look here, fella," said Quinny earnestly. "I had one hell of a time learnin' just the easy words in school. Do you mind talking so's I get some idea what's it about?"

"Oh, I'm so sorry," apologized Mr. Pilgrim. "I forget that erudition among the proletariat is negligible—" He coughed and pressed a thin hand to his throat. "I beg pardon, sir, but so much conversation dries the throat."

"I get you," responded Quinny tersely. "You say that so's anybody can understand. Slip Mr. Pilgrim a dish of suds, Gene. On me.

"Yeah, I'm a soft touch. You said you saw a dame in here last night. Can you describe her—in little words?"

First Mr. Pilgrim had to bury his nose in the glass of beer provided by the bartender. After two or three noisy gulps he came up from the foam, without looking in the least like Aphrodite.

"The—ah—dame was about five feet five, allowing for high heels, with dark hair and eyes. She wore a mink coat with the collar turned up."

"I can see where the beer was a good buy," commented the detective. "I understood every word. Go on."

"She was standing just inside the door while Gene was filling my bucket. She went outside as I settled my account—"

"Settled, hell," objected Gene. "You owe."

"Possibly," agreed Mr. Pilgrim, after another inhalation of beer. "To resume, as I left here I saw the girl standing on the corner across the street. Thinking perhaps I might be of assistance, I made a point of crossing over—the furniture factory is on that side, anyway—and spoke to her."

"What did she say?"

"H'm. Her answer was, shall we say, evasive."

"Never mind what we say," snapped the detective. "I'm interested in what she said."

"She said, 'Scram, bum.' Rather leaping to a conclusion, don't you think?"

"Was that all she said?" demanded Quinny.

"That's all. After this rebuff, I went on to the factory. A few minutes later, I chanced to look out from a second story window and saw this woman passing along the sidewalk across the street. She went into the old Sands house, where, I presume, she was later murdered."

The distress in Mr. Pilgrim's eyes was not for the girl's unhappy fate, but was brought about by the sudden appearance of the bottom of his beer glass. He replaced it on the bar noisily and looked hopefully at the detective, who nodded to Gene.

"I wouldn't be sure she was the one which was murdered. Outside the fur cot, what did she look like?" pursued Quinny.

"She wasn't outside the coat at all," the little man replied waggishly. "That's a good one, hey?" Seeing Gene's unappreciative scowl, he went on. "I've already described her."

"Yeah, yeah, I know, but what you said would fit forty thousand other dames in New York. Didn't you notice anything more than her hair and eyes, the coat, and how tall she was?"

"Now that I think of it, she wore a yellow orchid, a wedding ring, and had a tiny, triangular scar over her left eyebrow—very likely the result of falling from a highchair when young. She had nice even teeth and an upswept hair-do. Under her arm she carried a soft leather handbag— Of course, I really did not observe her closely."

"I can see that," interrupted Quinny again. "What kind of shoes was she wearing?"

"Brown pumps," answered the little man promptly. "Small size and fairly high heels."

Quinny finished off another rye, considering what he had learned. The night watchman had been a find indeed, as the boy, Pete, had intimated he might be. Obviously, the girl he'd seen was not Paula Kemp. This was the woman who had gone in later and hidden in the drawing room on the first floor.

"Look, Mr. Pilgrim," the detective said suddenly. "Did you see anybody come out of that house—or anybody else go in?"

"I didn't see anyone else enter, but a couple of hours later a man came out. This was after my ten o'clock round to punch my clocks. He was wearing a heavy overcoat and had his hat pulled down over his forehead. The street is badly lighted, you know, so I am not able to describe his features."

"That's all you saw last night?"

"Yes. This may have no bearing, but one evening about a month ago, on my way here for a can of beer, I met a fellow on the sidewalk—a big man with reddish hair. He looked rather Irish, I would say. Now, there isn't any place in that block where a well dressed man would be likely to go, and thinking he had mistaken his street, I asked if I could help him."

The bartender chuckled. "What'd he say? 'Scram, bum'?"

Mr. Pilgrim colored. "Not exactly. He told me to mind my own business and walked away down the street. Naturally, I watched him. I don't know where he went—he just sort of faded away in the darkness, looking up at the house numbers as he went along."

"Big fellow with red hair, eh, and wearing good clothes," mused Quinny. "A month ago."

Quinny finished his drink. Then he walked over to the telephone booths, where he looked up the number of the Museum of the City of New York in a tattered directory and entered the booth to make the call. A girl's voice answered.

"I'm tryin' to get the address of an artist named Paula Kemp," he explained for the third time as his call was shifted from one person to another. "She makes those little scenery things like you've got in the museum."

"I'll see if we have such a person on our lists," the voice replied loftily. A long silence followed, which cost the detective an additional nickel. Presently the voice came back on, "We have no Paula Kemp— K-e-m-p. But there is a Paula Camp. Perhaps she is the one—"

"Yeah, yeah! That would be her. Where did she live?" Quinny was all eagerness now. The Museum gave an address which the detective scribbled on a scrap of paper. "You see, she's been found dead," he exclaimed. "The name we had was Kemp, but there was a 'P.C.' on her handbag. We knew she was a sculp"—he wavered, uncertain of the feminine of sculptor—"that she made little scenes like you got up there. So it's probably the same dame. Goodbye."

"Oh, wait! Did you mean she has committed suicide, or—"

Quinny didn't wait. He strode out of the bar with a passing wave at Gene and Gus Pilgrim, armed with what he hoped was the address

of Paula Kemp. This promised to be difficult to find without directions—a studio located in Stuart Mews. An artists' supply store near
Forty-second Street gave the information that the mews was in the
lower Murray Hill district, extending halfway through one of the
crosstown blocks beyond First Avenue. Quinny caught a cab and
headed southward.

Mews they could call it, but to the detective it was just a blind
alley. Lining both sides were oddly contrasting specimens of stable
architecture, now made over into studios and tenanted by artists
with some claim to eccentricity themselves. One of these, a dumpy
woman wearing slacks and a piece of batik wrapped around untidy
hair, was cleaning the windows of her studio, sitting on the sill
with her feet inside. Quinny came to a halt as he reached a point
below the window where she was working. Apparently the woman
had neither seen nor heard his approach. For a moment he stood,
looking up at the buttocks squashed on the window sill.

"Hey!" he called sharply.

"*Eee-ei!*" squealed the artist, startled. She twisted around to
glare angrily down at the detective. "You scared me, you louse!"

"Didn't meant to," apologized Quinny. "Do you know which one
of these houses Paula Camp lives in?"

"The one down at the end." The woman's glare modified into
curiosity. "Collector?"

"Hell, no. Thanks."

Starting up again, Quinny strode along the narrow walk toward
the house across the inner end of the mews. This building was of
more sturdy construction than its ramshackle neighbors. It had
two entrances, one set in a new wall replacing what had formerly
been an entrance for carriages to the lower floor. The other was at
the side and evidently gave entry to the upper floor.

In small letters on the ruby glass panel he saw the name for
which he had been looking—Paula Camp. He hesitated. The chances
were better than even that he had been trailing the wrong girl.
However, he couldn't lose anything by taking the short end. He
pressed the bell button, and then several times more, but heard no

responding ring inside. Irritated, he tried the knob and discovered the door wasn't locked.

Quinny opened the door and entered. A long stairway occupied all of a narrow hall and after another hesitation the detective mounted the stairs, making remarkably little noise for one of his weight and the age of the building. At the top he found another door, with a bunch of keys hanging from the lock. He thumped vigorously with his fist, but no one came. After what he considered a suitable interval, he turned the knob and pushed the door open gingerly. The widening view disclosed a large room with a north skylight and filled with the trappings of someone who not only painted, but had a flair for sculpture and a diversity of other art forms.

A flimsily constructed wall had been erected a few feet out from and paralleling the side of the room. This had three openings set in it resembling miniature stages. In one of these was a partially completed historical group like those Quinny had once seen in the museum uptown. It was all that was needed to convince him that he had successfully solved the problem of where Paula Kemp lived. He started on an exploration to confirm it, as well as to learn what he could of the murdered girl's private life.

Before he had taken more than a couple of steps, he halted abruptly at the sight of a pair of upturned feet and spat-clad ankles sticking out of the space behind the plywood wall.

Getting into motion again, Quinny strode to the end of the wall and halted to look down at a man sprawled on his back, seemingly unconscious. Blood oozed from a wound at the edge of a thatch of dark hair, but his chest rose and fell reassuringly. Quinny flashed a quick look around and saw that the man had been dragged to his present position after having been slugged. Parts of a shattered plaster statuette were strewn on the floor.

After eyeing the injured stranger for a moment and judging that his return to consciousness wasn't imminent, the detective walked to the rear of the studio for a brief inspection of the two rooms he saw there. One, obviously a woman's bedroom, had been recently ransacked, with drawers pulled from the rickety bureau and contents dumped ruthlessly on the floor. A small bathroom opened off this, somewhat less disordered.

The other room was a kitchenette, with the appearance of having been shelled. The contents of the cabinets were littered all over the tiny room, but whoever had struck down the man in the studio wasn't hiding there. Snatching a towel from a rack, Quinny soaked it in cold water at the sink and hurried back to the injured man. Kneeling at his side, he wiped some of the blood away and laid the folded towel over the wounded forehead.

With no compunction whatever, Quinny did a quick and thorough job of going through the man's pocket's, finding a wallet with "Rush Fenton" in gold lettering on it and several letters. All but one of these were patently business communications; the other bore the name and return address of Paula Camp. There was a single Yale key in a vest pocket, made interesting because of its not being attached with others in a key container found in the man's trousers pocket.

Quinny replaced everything except the letter from Paula Camp and the key, pocketing the latter for a later checking at the Sands house. After a glance to make sure his patient wasn't likely to revive and catch him reading it, Quinny pulled the single sheet of note paper from the envelope and scanned it quickly.

> Dear Rush:
>
> I think you are being most unjust. You know that I have never loved you, or even pretended to. Perhaps, if you had been free, I should have been willing to carry on, but you aren't and there isn't any chance of it. You like young and pretty women, but I am steadily growing out of that classification and must think of the years ahead.
>
> As I have repeatedly told you, I am in love with a man who loves and wants to marry me. I would be a fool to continue my relations with you, under these circumstances, even if I could make myself do it.

Furthermore, what you have given me, I consider I have earned and certainly do not intend to return.

Why not stop acting like a silly eighteen-year-old boy, Rush, and be a good sport? You'll easily find another and younger girl to replace me, if you must have one.

Yours,
Paula

The man on the floor sighed, and, seeing that he was beginning the struggle to regain consciousness, Quinny hastily stuffed the note into the envelope and replaced it with the other letters in the coat pocket. After a little, the injured man's eyes fluttered open and he let go with a healthy if distressed groan. Then, gaining strength, he glared up at Quinny truculently.

"What was your idea in blackjacking me?" he demanded in a shaky voice.

"That was somebody else's idea," soothed the detective. "I came in a coupla minutes ago and found you here."

Rush Fenton sat up with an effort, shaking his head gingerly. Holding the towel tightly to his head, he looked about the studio and his gaze paused on the broken pieces of plaster of paris. There was a large bit of what had been a wing and the torso of the figure was still intact.

"Who the hell are you?" demanded Fenton suspiciously.

"Quin Hite, private detective. I came up here looking for Miss Camp. Know where she is?" It would be better, Quinny decided, not to show his hand until he had learned what he could.

"No. I had a lunch date with her, and she didn't show up. So I came along to see what the dickens was holding her. When she's working with her playthings, she never knows what time it is." There was a resentful expression in the man's face, but the detective caught what seemed to him to be a cagey flicker as well.

"So she socked you with a hunk of sculping for busting in on her, and lammed." Quinny eyed the fragments of plaster. "Imagine being smacked down by an angel!"

"I don't have to imagine."

"Guess you don't, at that." Quinny grinned. "Maybe she didn't want you around any more. If she had hit a little harder, that's the way it would have come out."

"She wasn't here—at least there was no one in sight when I came in. I called to her and started over to rap on her bedroom door. Then"—he grinned sourly—"the lights went out."

"Yeah?" Quinny noted that the fragments of the statue were a good fifteen feet from the bedroom. "How good do you know this dame?"

"We have been friends for some time—a couple of years or more. In fact, I have been helping her financially—as a friend interested in her progress." Fenton was recovering swiftly, although the wound still bled freely, seeping from under the towel around one eye. He shifted the cloth as though to check it. "What are you doing here?" he demanded, clearly still unconvinced that it hadn't been Quinny who had struck him.

"I'm a detective, like I said," replied Quinny shortly. "Mind telling me your name?"

The man hesitated, then spoke. "Rush Fenton. What has happened, to bring a detective here? I—I don't understand all this. If you didn't hit me—who did, and for what?"

"You said you had a date with Miss Camp—or is it Kemp?"

"It's been Camp as long as I've known her. As I told you, she was to meet me for lunch—and didn't show up. Has something happened to her?" Rush Fenton scrambled to his feet, swaying despite his widespread legs.

"Where was she going to meet you?" snapped Quinny.

Fenton hesitated again. "Why—at the, the Crillon."

He'd had to think of a place fast, Quinny decided. "When did you see her last?"

"Um—a week ago." Fenton closed his eyes tightly for a moment, as though from a stab of pain from his head. "I dropped in here last Monday afternoon. Look, I hate to keep repeating, but would you mind telling me what this is all about? You have me worried about Paula."

"You can lay off worrying," returned Quinny, his hazel eyes steady on Fenton's. "Paula Camp was found dead a while ago. Murdered."

Fenton stared a moment, but said nothing. He walked unsteadily to an easeled canvas with the beginnings of an oil painting on it, standing there in silence for a moment. Then he swung around.

"Who found her?" he demanded.

"Dead people generally get found, sooner or later," replied Quinny grimly. "Especially if they've been laying around long enough."

"Yes, but only since last night—" Fenton choked off his words.

"So you knew she was murdered—and when eh? On account of which you figured you better hurry here to prowl her studio for something you wanted. That it?" Quinny's lips tightened as he finished.

"You overlook the fact that I talked with Paula on the phone yesterday afternoon. As she was alive then, I naturally assumed that this—ah—happened last night."

"Yeah? What got you here so bright and early to frisk the place, if you didn't know she was dead? What were you looking for?" Quinny reached up and pulled his derby down with a vicious jerk.

"I've explained my reasons for coming here," retorted Fenton, with a little more spirit. "Don't forget that there was someone here before me—someone who cracked me over the head before I'd been here a minute. Doubtless the person who ransacked the place—possibly a burglar. There's a lot of that going on, you know."

"Could be." Quinny shoved the hat back up. "But I don't believe it. No burglar would be dope enough to expect to make a haul in a dump like this. Look here, how did you get out of that backyard last night, with all them high walls around it?"

"I don't know what you are talking about. What backyard?"

"Back of the house where Paula Camp was murdered, of course. You were there."

Fenton came back from the easel to face Quinny with an angry glare in his one visible eye.

"In other words, you are accusing me of murder!" he snapped. "That is pure insolence, and you have not an iota of reason for it."

"I got two or three iotas," insisted Quinny. "Take it easy, fella. So far, I haven't accused you of anything except being in the back-yard of the house. And don't kid me that you was just a nice guy helping the girl along with a little moola on account of you took an interest in her career. You were only paying off for what you got from her."

"You are entirely mistaken."

Quinny shrugged. "Okay then, I'm wrong. All you gotta do now is make the cops believe you and you're all clear. They're pretty stubborn, though—not like me."

Fenton looked uneasy. "You're not a police detective, so what's your interest in this?" His tone was noticeably less hostile.

"I specialize in murder jobs which are too tough for depart-ment men to break, when I see a piece of dough in it. At that, I've prob'bly kept more guys off the hot squat at Sing Sing than I ever put on it—fellas who didn't belong there. Maybe if you broke down and came across with what I want to know, I might do the same for you. Maybe not. You judge that—and you can figure that after the working over you'll get from the cops, you won't have any secrets left worth keeping. Like I said, I don't work for nothin', but on this job I've already got a sponsor who needs to know come Thursday who killed Paula Camp. If you see where me coming up with the right answer would also put you in the clear, this is your chance."

Quinny broke off and waited for a few seconds for Fenton to reply, but as the man merely stared at the detective, his lips tightly closed, Quinny resumed.

"That's your only chance, Fenton. Hell, can't you see it? Beautiful girl artist found murdered in love nest. Rich lover held. Rich lover arrested. Rich lover on trial. Rich lover found guilty." Quinny made a gesture of futility. "Rich lover executed—sayin' he wasn't guilty."

Fenton shivered with Quinny's cold plausibility. After a mo-ment, he spoke. "I suppose your sense of civic duty bars any sug-gestion that I might be willing to pay something to be kept out of this," said the man, frowning. "Not that I am suggesting bribery, of course. As I see it, there's nothing to be gained by you in involving an innocent man in a nasty murder case."

"No dice, mister. I don't know how innocent you are, and the cops will find out about you, anyway. I don't take jobs to clear anybody, so if you murdered the girl you'd better just keep your mouth shut and tell me nothing. That's the way I play—and no other."

Fenton sat down on a low three-legged stool. The towel was saturated with blood and the detective began to think the wound had better get proper attention without much more delay. He didn't want the man to pass out on him.

"You have very neatly put me in the position of either telling you something or being in your mind convicted of murder," Fenton grumbled.

"You started off with lying about how you stood with the dead girl, handing out a line of being just a nice guy so far as she was concerned—"

"Why do you say I lied?"

"On account of you did. I know this dame was your mistress—and that she wanted to break it up. I know a lot more which I'm not spilling. If you decide to talk, the things I already know will tip me off whether you're telling the truth or not. Either way, though, we better do something about your head."

Quinny went to the bathroom beyond the bed chamber, where he found a roll of bandage and adhesive. Returning with these and a fresh towel, he cleaned the gash and dressed the wound rather expertly, covering the ugly welt around the open wound, with bandage also.

"Now," he said, stepping back and viewing his work approvingly, "with a couple of ryes under your belt, you'd practically be a well man. Have you been doing any thinking about what I said?"

"Yes, I have," admitted Fenton. "But it seems to me, that it should be obvious that I am innocent of Paula's death. Doesn't it occur to you that whoever struck me down is very probably the person who killed Paula in much the same manner?"

"Now we're gettin' some place," enthused Quinny. "If you weren't at the house where she was killed, how do you know she was bashed over the head, too? I didn't tell you that."

Marriage had not been a part of Paula Kemp's dream of a career. It had not entered her mind as a likely result of the cruise in '38 aboard Ranny Walsh's yacht. Still less would she have recognized the wedding as another step toward final disaster.

MRS. MARGERY SANDS sat stiffly in a highbacked chair in the drawing room of her son's house and stared with the cold insolence of a wellborn lady at the wretched, jittery girl sitting opposite. This was a situation unfortunately always at the elbow of a mother with a son too well provided for in his own right. Unless the young man was constantly kept to heel—no simple matter, either—there was constant danger of his bringing home a pretty bride who in no way measured to the social yardstick of his family. Morgan had completely justified his mother's premonitory fears.

Returning from a season in Miami, she had found this beguiling little jezebel in legal residence with her son in the old Sands home. Adding to Mrs. Sands' flaming indignation, the couple had been married a month without bothering to notify her, although it was evident enough why. Morgan had, of course, known what a short shrift the marriage would receive.

"You should realize that this marriage to my son is entirely infamous," declaimed Margery Sands, in the voice of a politician substituting opinion for fact and wanting no nonsense about it. "Even though your background were all you've caused Morgan to believe, it would hardly make you acceptable to his friends."

"They seemed to like me well enough on the yacht," defended the harried girl with some spirit. "And then, it was not his friends I married."

"I am referring to family friends—not Ranny Walsh and his riffraff set," countered Mrs. Sands, loftily.

"Did I hear you speak of Ranny Walsh as riffraff, Mother?" The slight figure of Morgan Sands appeared in the hall archway, mild reproval showing in his sea-green eyes. "S'prisin' thing for you to say, considering the amount of time you spend with his mother and her gang. Nothing wrong with Ranny."

"She says our marriage must be annulled, Morgie," Paula said, with a distasteful glance at the old lady. "Seems I'm not good enough to be a Sands."

The young man came a step further into the room, looking suddenly troubled. He had feared this situation would arise sooner or later, but without making preparations to meet it.

"Not good enough? Why, I thought it was the other way round, rather. Some pretty doubtful shoots have been grafted to the Sands family tree, here and there—" Morgan's studied airiness fell flat before his mother's hard blue eyes.

"This is not a time to be amusing," interrupted the dowager. "Surely, you haven't considered the effects of this idiocy on your family."

"I don't concede my marriage as being anyone's business but my own—and Paula's." Not adjusted to what was going on, Morgan advanced into the room more boldly, bringing up at the side of Paula's chair and running his fingers through her soft tawny hair. He glanced defiantly at his mother. "Not even yours."

"Morgan!" The thin lips broke apart long enough for the exclamation, then crisped together again.

"I'm quite aware, Mother—and I really don't mean to be offensive—that, as a young lady, love wasn't permitted to interfere with your family's plans. You were—if you'll pardon the comparison—brought up and trained like a filly for the thoroughbred horse market—"

"Morgan!" This time Margery Sands' mouth opened into a squat 'O' and her sharp blue eyes sparkled. "I don't think insulting me will help the situation. I am not to be compared to a horse!"

"Merely a figure of speech, Mother. I've said I don't intend to be insulting. All I am trying to do is point out that you couldn't possibly know anything about love. It wasn't your fault, of course, to be the child of practically well-bred paupers and that your marriage had to have the financial setting which my father could and did supply." He glanced down at Paula fondly. "I suppose he loved you. I love Paula." The girl looked up at him, warmly appreciative. "Thank you, Morgie," she whispered.

"So, there we are," Morgan concluded, feeling pretty good about his speech and plainly considering that he had made his point. "I'm sorry you don't approve, but you may as well be gracious."

Margery Sands arose, pointed fingernails making dents in her soft leather handbag.

"I have no intention of being gracious," she said venomously. "Unfortunately, your fool of a father made you financially independent of me, otherwise this could not have happened. The girl married you for money and position—that's all—but I'll not accept her and I'll see to it she's not socially received. It's true that my family was not prosperous—"

"I'll say!" agreed Morgan enthusiastically. "Even now, the Morins are always broke. I've never understood how you got to be so tight with money. It certainly doesn't run in your family. Are you quite sure you weren't left on the Morin doorstep?"

"Of course, I realize you are being funny," rasped the old lady, moving toward the arched entrance to the hall.

"Funny, my eye! Only a few weeks ago Uncle Theodore put the bite on me for a grand, to keep the sheriff from setting the family out on the street. That's what he told me, but I suspect he's been experimenting with the stock market again."

"I'll attend to Theodore," responded Margery Sands—and from her expression, her brother wasn't going to enjoy the promised attention. She hesitated in the hallway, looking back with chilled intensity. "And, as you obviously intend to defy me about this designing little strumpet, I may as well go. But, I haven't given up!"

Nor did she. Armed with the perhaps not uncommon belief among the gentry that the lower classes uniformly operate with loose ideals and no morals at all, Margery Sands began the work of probing into Paula's activities previous to marriage. She would have enjoyed ferreting out the girl's suspected casuistry in person, but didn't know how to go about it. A lean, hungry-looking detective took over the active work of the investigation.

For him, this business was duck soup. He came to Margery Sands' Park Avenue apartment in less than a week with a factual report on Paula's recent intimacy with Anton Decourré. The wretched sculptor had without pressure revealed the whole unsavory episode, moved by his discovery after Paula's departure that the little money she had been generous with had played a more important part in his economy than he'd suspected. Decourré did not doubt that Paula, divorced, would return to him—probably with augmented funds. He had that sort of mind.

Margery Sands returned to her son's house, selecting a time when she knew him to be absent. With cold satisfaction, she presented her findings to Paula, with an ultimatum of handing them on to Morgan if the girl continued her unreasonable resistance.

Paula's bright new world collapsed with bewildering suddenness. That Morgan Sands might have been a great deal more tolerant of past indiscretions than his mother did not occur to her—and he would have been.

Pressing the advantage which her shrewd intuition perceived, Margery Sands executed a quick shift in tactics. She pointed out in plausible language and sugary tones that it would be best for all if Morgan were not told the true reasons for Paula's decision to end the mésalliance. Paula had not arrived at any decision, but the old lady's assumption made it seem that she had done so. Margery Sands rushed on to consolidate the victory.

"I don't wish you to consider me a selfish and interfering old woman, my dear," she said. "It's just that as an older person I realize so surely what will happen, if this marriage were allowed to stand. Morgan would soon tire of you—he's actually a fickle-minded little fool, I'm afraid—and then he would resent a wife who kept him away from lifelong friends." This was getting onto unfirm ground, Margery thought, and veered away. "Perhaps you would consider them stiff-necked, uncompromising puritans, and possibly you might be justified. Regardless of my own feelings, there would be nothing I could do to change it. As it is, I am only thinking of the future happiness of us all."

"I don't consider you a selfish and interfering old woman," Paula replied carefully. "I think that you, and your family, and your friends, are a lot of stinking fossils who should be in a museum. I can do without such people—and Morgan, too!"

Margery Sands' plump bosom rose and fell in a sigh which didn't begin to relieve her keen desire to shake this little harridan, but she kept herself in hand, lifting her thin eyebrows in resignation.

"Very well," she said. "I think I can understand your feelings, but there we are. I will make a proposal. The marriage must be annulled quickly, before it is too late. But in fairness, you shouldn't be the only sufferer from this unfortunate affair. I am going to establish a trust fund, the income from which will take care of your needs, as, shall we say, an annulment gift."

"Shall we say, a bribe?"

The aristocratic eyebrows of Sands, mater, hoisted and lowered indifferently, although she didn't feel that way.

"As you prefer, but you will need money, and are entitled to it," the old lady replied evenly. "I will instruct my attorney accordingly. Now, my dear, I may as well go. You will avoid difficulty by explaining to Morgan that this is a decision you have reached yourself."

"Thereby exculpating you," returned Paula, in an acid imitation of Mrs. Sands' precise and cultivated diction. "Okay, get out. I'll manage my part without direction."

She managed it by spending a feverish afternoon gathering and packing her belongings. When Morgan Sands returned to the city the following day the only trace of Paula was a brief note of farewell without much explanation—merely that on reconsideration she had concluded the marriage had been in haste and that she was going away to fulfill the legend of repentance. But she remained in town long enough to collect an installment on Margery Sands' promises.

Only partially solaced by money and expensive clothes, Paula visited an aunt living in an Ohio village. Then she drifted on. A year later she returned to New York, weary of glamorous resorts and the sort of people who had nothing to do but play. She was now Paula Camp, on the advice of a numerologist she had encountered at White Sulphur. The change, he promised, would improve her luck. Obviously, the man was a quack.

The urge to do things reviving, she looked around for suitable quarters in which to live and work. Learning that because of Anton Decourré's detached attitude in the matter of rent the studio of her late mentor in art and less commendable activities had become available, Paula took it over.

Aside from wanting to resume her career, her financial independence hadn't turned out to be as secure as promised. Margery Sands double-crossed her about the trust fund, substituting in place of it a monthly allowance of considerable proportions, but with the attractive feature to the old lady of not being legally collectible. She hadn't intended to keep up the payments as long as she had, but Morgan Sands lad been difficult after Paula's departure—a year passing before Margery considered the baneful influence of Paula to be safely eliminated.

The loss of income wasn't the disaster that might have been expected, once the initial impact was over. Paula still had enough to go on, not so much saved as just unspent. Money, never having been plentiful before, hadn't been something she could easily adjust herself to throwing around.

Anton Decourré had lost no time in attempting to renew their old association on her return, but to his complete bewilderment his efforts were entirely wasted. It was, to him, inconceivable that a woman who had rested in his arms might in time become so indifferent.

"You forget, Anton, that while I have been getting a little sense, you haven't changed at all. I can hardly believe that I could ever have felt as I did toward a man who isn't very clean most of the time, completely selfish and a humbug artist as well. If I owe you something, it's not something you would care to collect."

This was a shabby deal, Decourré considered. After all he had done for her, the lessons given her when anyone with half an eye would know them to be a complete waste of his talents, to send him away with a contemptible couple of dollar bills! Why, she'd even pre-empted his studio while he was temporarily deprived of occupancy! Obviously, the wealth she had taken from Sands had gone to her head. With an exercise of laudable forbearance, she would return with all the fervent adoration she had formerly expressed—and additional cash.

Anton became an intolerable nuisance, barging into his old studio at any time his twisted reasoning suggested, and, if not admitted, hanging about in the mews outside. For a place to sleep he fluctuated between Bowery flophouses and malodorous hotels tucked in here and there further uptown, according to his current funds. Sheer hunger occasionally drove him into furtive employment of his marble cutting skill in a Woodlawn tomb and memorial yard.

Paula's social life for a time was limited to avoiding or enduring Anton's visits. In a way, it was one of these which precipitated her into a new adventure. Failing to dislodge the sculptor from his carefully arranged pose on the studio divan, Paula had dressed and told him she had an important appointment.

Paula went out. After some thought, she decided to visit a girl who kept an apartment in the Sutton Place neighborhood—or, as Paula thought probable, was kept in one there. Dale Worden didn't view sin as reprehensible unless unrewarded. Paula, incidentally, had discarded her own inhibition on that score, but with the result of developing a new one. There was, she felt, nothing censurable in a casual yielding to fleshly desires, but the same surrender to a man a girl loved was an entirely different matter. In this event, only complete conformity with convention could be condoned. Marriage first, even though this insistence often lost the lover. As she felt, you lost 'em anyway, but if not in love with them, it didn't matter.

In Dale Worden's living room she found the girl and Rush Fenton engaged in cocktails and the old but always interesting fencing match between lustful male and calculating female. Fenton, discovering in his college days that his personal charm needed a salting of money to make it palatable to women, had put himself assiduously to the task of getting it. At forty, he found himself possessed of a profitable business, plus a wife of dull but solid integrity. She had added greatly to Fenton's financial success, but nothing to his long repressed yen for gaiety. There was nothing frothy in Alice Fenton's conception of a full life. Fortunately for her husband, she was tolerant of his peccadilloes, with the reservation that his extramural excursions be kept off the wave-band of Westchester gossip.

Miss Worden's profound belief was that man's only substantial interest in her sex was entirely physical—a conviction she kept to herself usually, but found useful to trot out when the current sugarman failed to be enthusiastic in giving her something she wanted.

Although Rush Fenton had given every indication of wanting to supplant her present incumbent, Dale saw no profit in making a change. Knowing that importunate lovers can't be kept dangling too long without deterioration, and in all ways hating waste, she viewed the arrival of Paula on the scene with entire approval. She wasn't at all familiar with Paula's private life, but didn't imagine any girl living alone in Manhattan would fail to appreciate the excess material another girl had on hand which could make that living easier.

The shifting of Rush Fenton's amorous direction was accomplished without difficulty. In fact, Dale Worden hadn't to do more than give opportunity for the male libido to start moving, with added stimulus from the cocktails and a breezy build-up for his presumed qualities. Since Paula was younger, prettier and less sophisticated, Dale didn't need to extend herself. Rush Fenton took the lure like a famished trout.

Paula, however, had not planned for anything like what followed. Rush Fenton had only impressed her as a potentially amusing friend. Nothing in her life had given her Dale Worden's outlook on the matter of reducing the impulses to a profit-yielding product.

Fenton's inner fires were fueled by Paula's instinctive reserve and, having gathered some benefit to his technique through trial and error in former enterprises, he spared nothing to succeed in this one. She was at once a creature of native warmth, yet thinly covered with a veneer of cool aloofness, maddeningly desirable in his eyes but with no assuring hints that she might ultimately be possessed.

In the end, Paula acquiesced.

Without compromising the quaint but useful principles which she had built up for her own guidance, absolved of any qualms through the certainty she felt of not loving Rush Fenton in the least—not even having to make any pretense of it—she accepted all that he had to give her with a complacency which had the unplanned result of never quite satisfying him and hence bringing to the liaison a continuing allure he hadn't counted on in the beginning.

Falling short of satiation, Rush Fenton fell instead into the abysmal depths of fatuous love.

This hadn't been his plan, either.

CHAPTER FOUR

Rush Fenton stirred uneasily on the three-legged stool where he sat facing Quinny Hite in the bizarre surroundings of Paula Camp's littered studio. The question the detective had just flipped at him had sent the injured man's thought processes into a spin.

"I—I don't understand you," he stalled.

"Yeah, you do, but I'll give you another shot," pressed the detective. "If you weren't in that house last night when Paula Camp was bumped off, how did you know she was slugged with something?"

"Well—" Fenton hesitated, licking dry, hot lips and looking at Quinny with harried eyes. "I suppose I may just as well admit that I went to the Sands house last night—but Paula was dead when I arrived."

"She was?" Nothing in the detective's intonation betrayed his reaction. "Why did you go there?"

Fenton sighed deeply. "I think I may as well give you an account of my relations with Paula. I am—have been terribly in love with her. If I misled you a few minutes ago, it was for good reasons."

"You didn't steer me wrong," commented Quinny. "You said just what I expected you to say. Telling the truth then woulda been, like you say, misleadin'. Go on."

Fenton continued, turning out a considerable narration of his personal contribution to the sorry career of the murdered girl. From his unconsidered fervor, Quinny was inclined to believe that it was a straightforward account.

73

"So, you see the position this puts me in, regarding Mrs. Fenton." The harassed man looked earnestly and hopefully at the listening detective from under his bandaged forehead. "I believe my wife has known something of my affair with poor Paula, but as long as it wasn't common knowledge in Pelham Manor she would take no action. Now, if my name is smeared in the newspapers, there'll be the devil to pay!"

"Devils want their money," commiserated Quinny. "Especially when they're married to you. But I don't care much about that angle—that's your baby. What I want to know is what took you to there last night, if you didn't have murder on your mind. Prob'bly got wind of the girl carrying on with some other guy, eh?"

"That's true," admitted Fenton ruefully.

"You figured it would discourage him some if you clunked him one with a piece of hardware. Then on account of you couldn't wait till he showed up, you had a trial shot at Paula, while she was in bed waiting—"

"I didn't! I told you a while ago that she was—"

"Dead on arrival. I know that's what you said, but I don't have to believe it. Some guys get kinda hasty when another lug edges in on ground they're paying rent for. Who was this new hand, she was taking on?"

"I can't help it, if you won't believe what I say," whined Fenton. "I wasn't sure that Paula was actually involved with this man—that is, I knew she was attracted to him, but I hoped it hadn't gone too far to be remedied. His name is Strohm—you may have seen it in the papers from time to time—one-time sportsman, aviator and blade among women."

"Yeah, I heard of him. But not lately."

"He was flying transports to England for the Canadian army during the war and I don't suppose he was in New York more than occasionally."

"Cased him pretty good, didn't you?"

"Paula told me what I know about him. Frankly, she was infatuated with the man, wanted to marry him, and, you wouldn't believe this—" Fenton paused, looking at Quinny with an outraged sparkle in his brooding eyes. "She wanted *me* to give her enough cash to make the marriage possible!"

Quinny chuckled. "You can never dope out a dame," he affirmed. "Well, did you see this Bill Strohm at the house when you tailed Paula there?"

"I can't answer that. I've never met Strohm—don't know what he looks like. Someone called me at my office Saturday and told me that Paula was visiting some man at that boarded up house—"

"Who? Who called you?" demanded Quinny.

"I don't know. A woman. She refused to give her name."

"I knew there was another dame mixed up in this, but I don't know who she is—yet." Quinny gave the derby a push and scowled.

"Well, I followed Paula to the place last night, getting there about eight-thirty. I found a place to keep out of sight on the basement steps of a vacant house across the street. After a while I saw a man come along the sidewalk near the house Paula had entered, but I thought he went into the tenement next door. The street is badly lighted. I decided to wait and see if anyone came out."

"Did they?" prompted Quinny, as the man paused with a curious expression flooding his face.

"I saw no one come out. But, about ten minutes later, someone else went in."

Quinny reviewed his own observations in the Sands house. "This time it was a dame."

Fenton looked mildly surprised. "Yes, it was. She was wearing an expensive fur coat."

"From where you were stashed out, you couldn't see good enough to tell whether the guy you saw went in next door or in the Sands house," observed the detective caustically. "But you could see this gal wore an expensive fur coat." Quinny shook his head reprovingly.

"I shouldn't have said expensive. But as she passed the tenement the light from the doorway made it easy to see that she had on a fur coat, with the collar pulled up around the sides of her face."

"Then you went right over and had a shot at getting in yourself. Was the front door unlocked?"

"I waited a few minutes. As the girl in the fur coat seemed to have gotten in without trouble, I assumed that the door wasn't locked, and it wasn't. A hall light was on inside. I looked into the front room, but saw no one."

"You didn't see the dame you followed in?" Quinny prompted.

"No, not then or at any time since. I went on upstairs. The door to the back room was ajar, with a light showing. I peeked in and saw Paula in the bed, with the radio going—"

"Did you notice what program was on?" This might establish the time more accurately, Quinny thought.

"Yes, I did. It was Walter Winchell. It struck me as odd, because Paula disliked his broadcast."

"He's on from nine to nine-fifteen," mused Quinny. "What next?"

"I waited a minute, then called to her. She didn't answer—didn't stir. So, I went in." Rush Fenton, looking unhappy before with his bandaged head, looked ghastly now. "She—was dead."

"How long did you stay in the room?"

"I didn't stay at all. I—I felt sick."

"You went out in back—"

"I certainly did not. I went out the way I came in."

Quinny silently contemplated what he had just heard, then eyed Fenton curiously.

"After all that, you came here today to find out why Paula had stood you up for lunch," he commented sarcastically. "Or, somethin'."

Fenton stirred uneasily and stared at the floor.

"That wasn't true, of course. I came here hoping to remove anything that would lead to my connection with Paula—the few clothes I kept here and my letters, if she hadn't destroyed them. There might have been other odds and ends—trinkets and such that might be traced to me."

Trinkets. This gave the detective a fresh thought.

"Maybe you could describe the necklace Paula Camp wore last night."

The question startled Fenton. He moistened his dry lips with his tongue before replying.

"When I saw what had happened, I was—too sick to notice any-thing like that," he hesitated, then went on impulsively. "I'll be frank—it was a necklace I most wanted to find here."

"You must have thought it was a sure lead to you, taking the risk of coming here after it. Or, maybe it was worth big dough."

"It was—but that was least important," explained Fenton. "It was a rare antique—a museum piece—in an acanthus leaf design with a pigeon's blood ruby set in the lower leaf, and once belonged to the Archduchess Marie Louise—"

"Now we got a archduchess," said Quinny impatiently. "Where does she come in?"

"Why, she was Napoleon's second wife, and later—"

"Skip Napoleon. You said the dough it was worth wasn't im-portant. What was?"

"Well—" Fenton paused, embarrassed. "You see, I had seen the thing lying around on Mrs. Fenton's dressing table. My wife has an enormous amount of cheap costume jewelry, and I thought this necklace one of the lot. I picked it up and gave it to Paula. Later, I discovered the mistake and explained to Paula. She refused to give it up."

"What a dope—tellin' a dame the present you gave her was worth dough and then expectin' to get it back." Quinny snickered, then a new angle occurred to him. "Look, who else do you suppose knew this gimmick wasn't a phony?"

"I couldn't say. After I told Paula I wanted it back, she stopped wearing it. Meanwhile, my wife has been turning the house upside down searching for it."

"I see," pondered Quinny. "When your wife finds out you glommed the pretty, she's going to raise hell about it."

"She most certainly will," affirmed Fenton. "It is the main rea-son I risked coming here. Foolishly, I suppose."

"Yeah, plain nuts as an idea, besides getting you a nasty crack on the conk with a statue of an angel."

"What do you think I should do?"

"Your best play is to skin on up to the Sands place, ask for Lieu-tenant Madden, and tell him everything you just told me. The cops'll find out anyhow, but it will look better if you hand it to 'em on a dish."

Rush Fenton considered this briefly, ending with a sigh. He got up from the stool, mumbling that he supposed Quinny's suggestion was the thing to do, and moved off toward the stairway door. The detective stayed where he was, watching Fenton until he went out. The sound of the man's feet descending the wooden treads and the bang of the closing street door aroused him to action.

After another look into the smaller rooms and deciding that sifting through Paula's scattered belongings would take more time than the prospect of finding anything pertinent was worth, Quinny came into the big studio room. He stopped to examine a cluttered workbench, where evidently the girl had assembled her miniature scenes. Paula had also experimented with modernistic sculpture in metal—with, to Quinny, entirely screwy results. A thing he wasn't sure was meant to resemble a camel or a giraffe had been made of spring wire about the thickness of pencil lead. There was a considerable coil of the wire still unused. She had also been making something from thin metal sheets that looked like, but were not, gold. Whatever this object had been wasn't revealed.

Selecting a long, elaborately carved bench near the spot where he had found Rush Fenton, Quinny sat down to organize his findings. Despite his story of having been knocked unconscious so promptly after entering, Rush Fenton was the most logical person to have ransacked the rooms. If so, he had failed to find what he'd said he most wanted—the necklace. It hadn't been in his pockets, at any rate. He had given an account of his other activities without apparent discrepancies, but the detective had no thought of accepting his unsupported story.

Nevertheless, Quinny reflected, someone had certainly skulled Fenton with the statue, and possibly without his having seen the assailant. As he had instantly accused Quinny on recovering his senses the latter seemed likely. There was still the question of the identity of the other person.

Sands? There had been time enough after the architect's departure from Turtle Bay to have come here in search of something he badly wanted. Sands had declared he had not seen Paula for years. If so, is seemed unlikely the girl had anything Sands would so desperately need to recover. Perhaps, though, it had been given abrupt importance by the fact of her death.

There was also this Bill Strohm, mentioned by Fenton, to get a line on before guessing did any good, Quinny decided. He couldn't imagine any reason why a man engaged in winning a girl from her present lover, and apparently with success, should murder the girl. It didn't make sense, but the detective knew that slayings stemming out of love were apt to disregard any rational pattern.

The wooden seat was getting harder and Quinny squiggled his hips as though to find a softer place. Then he decided he might as well get going, as there seemed nothing else immediately useful to be done here. He stood up, stretching first one leg and then the other to restore the circulation cut off by the carved molding about the edge of the bench. Evidently it hadn't been designed to be sat on, and now that this had been forced upon his attention, he saw that it wasn't a bench at all, but a long chest of dark, stained wood.

It was also about the only receptacle of any size into which the detective had failed to look. He reached for the lid, then abruptly withdrew his hand before it touched the wood, glancing swiftly around the room to locate the source of a low, rasping sound that had reached his ears. For several seconds he stood as rigid as the surrounding bits of statuary, but the sound was not repeated. Meanwhile he did a lot of fast and concentrated thinking, then took off across the studio to the stairway door.

Going on to the landing at the head of the stairs, Quinny glanced down to the street entrance. There was no one in sight. Spinning around on his heel, he re-entered the studio, kicking the door shut behind him, and then stopped, his hazel eyes darting about as he watched the room.

The ruse worked. After a few seconds, the detective saw the lid of the chest he had used for a seat slowly rise a couple of inches, to be immediately and hurriedly lowered again.

"The son of a gun!" Quinny murmured. "An' I was sittin' on it!"

Disliking the weight of a gun in his pocket (and having no confidence whatever in his marksmanship), the detective habitually went unarmed. Just now a weapon wouldn't have been a burden.

A piece of lethal hardware in his hand would have been a boon to his morals. As a substitute he laid hold of a delectably naked lady made of brass—a material Quinny had found not uncommon among livelier women he knew—and walked firmly toward the chest, swinging the brass lady by the legs to get her heft.

Arriving he rapped smartly on the chest lid with the statue and bellowed for the occupant to come out. The lid flew up without hesitancy, and an ill-kempt figure heaved into a sitting position. Quinny stared in silent amazement and the stranger returned it with slowly blinking eyes. It was practically a draw.

"My God," exclaimed Quinny, recovering. "It's alive!"

"Yes, and no thanks to you," growled the man. "I might well have smothered while you were sitting on the lid."

"How the hell would I know I was sitting on an outsize Jack-in-the-box?" demanded Quinny, amused. "Christmas ain't for two months yet. Come on, get out of that!"

The stranger glowering, climbed out awkwardly and stood up, working his shoulders and going through a little exercise of alternately lifting and lowering himself on his toes to got the blood circulating.

"*Canaille!*" he murmured under his breath.

"Can you what— Oh!" Quinny glanced at the shabby beaded moccasins the fellow wore. So this was the mug who had been hanging out in the Golden Turtle! "What are you—a bum? What's the idea of sneakin' into a lady's studio, spilling her stuff all over the place, and then skulling her boy friend? Just a lousy sneak-thief—" he broke off, glaring and belligerently swinging the brazen Diana to and fro.

The man pulled himself into a more or less dignified pose.

"I am Anton Decourré," he said. "The famous sculptor."

Sculptor, eh? Maybe, but not famous enough for Quinny ever to have heard of him. He recalled that Morgan Sands had spoke of one in connection with Paula Camp, but didn't remember exactly what had been said.

"Yeah? You look more like somethin' which snuck out of the woodwork." Quinny's lips curled in contempt. "I got a good mind to sculp you one with this naked female, but I don't like to get her all bent up. What was the idea slugging the fella I found on the floor?"

Decourré's gaze held steadily on Quinny, smoldering hate in his dark eyes.

"You are speaking in riddles," he said. "I haven't an idea of what you are talking about. I have been here since morning—and have neither seen nor heard anyone until a few moments ago."

"Do you think I'm crazy enough to believe that?" demanded the outraged detective.

"I have no opinion as to your sanity," replied Decourré, fishing in his coat pocket. Quinny watched the gesture and tightened his hold on the statue—just in case. But the sculptor's hand came out holding nothing more threatening than a small cardboard box, rather grimy. "I will explain. I suffer from insomnia, but with the aid of these barbituric tablets, I can sleep anywhere for hours without being conscious of anything that goes on around me."

"A dope, eh?" Quinny scowled distastefully. "But that don't tell me how come you've been using this studio for a flop."

"Miss Camp, the tenant, has frequently been kind to me," answered the sculptor, ignoring the insult. "I came up here this morning to see her—I have recently had reverses, due to a determination in certain quarters to deny me artistic recognition—"

"Never heard such a fancy explanation of how a guy got to be a bum," interrupted Quinny impatiently. "So you corked off in the box. A minute ago you yipped that me sittin' on the lid nearly suffocated you,"

The tall man jacknifed to pick up a bit of folded cardboard from the floor at the side of the box.

"I had placed this to keep the lid from closing tightly," he said. "When you sat down, it fell out. Could you, ah, spare a cigarette?"

"Why coop yourself up in the box when there's better places around the joint?" Quinny got out his cigarettes and held them out.

"Well, you see, I am agoraphobic—"

"Okay—okay! Skip it. You're just plain complicated. How did you get in here, if the girl wasn't home?"

Quinny recalled the bunch of keys he'd seen hanging from the lock on the outside of the door. There hadn't been any keys in Paula Camp's handbag on the bureau in the room where she had met her death. Fenton had keys in a leather container, so those in the door weren't likely his.

"Paula never locks her door," answered Decourré calmly.

"Not even the one downstairs?"

"No." The sculptor sucked in cigarette smoke and blew it out.

Quinny frowned. He wished he could think of something the man would answer with an obvious lie. There hadn't been anything in his tone, eyes or manner to give the slightest clue to whether he was telling the truth or not. In the semi-real world the sculptor lived in, one could believe what one chose, and, believing, speak without conscious mendacity. He would be a difficult witness.

"Look here," said Quinny after a moment. "A body has been found that we think might be this Camp girl. You come along with me—if you really knew her, you'll come in handy for identification of the corpse."

Decourré's sallow face seemed to go a shade lighter as Quinny, watching him narrowly, told him this, but otherwise seemed not affected particularly. His dark eyes shifted in a glance around the room, then met the detective's scrutiny.

"I hope you are mistaken—about the identity, I mean," the sculptor said, turning to walk with Quinny toward the doorway. "Miss Camp, as I said, has been kind to me. What did this girl you speak of look like?"

"Yellow hair," said Quinny promptly. "Shorter'n most girls, but good shape. Had a mole on her chin—" He indicated the location on his own face.

Decourré shook his head sadly. "It may be Paula," he said mournfully. "She had such a mole. There was a rather distinctive necklace that she sometimes wore."

"Kansas leaves," Quinny supplemented smugly.

The sculptor hoisted a shaggy eyebrow, but made no comment on Quinny's botanical erudition. "Was she wearing it?" he asked.

Quinny shrugged his shoulders indifferently. "I didn't see one," he evaded, covertly eyeing Decourré for any reaction to the statement. He caught only the barest flicker of an eyelid, not pronounced enough to indicate anything. "But I hear she hardly ever wore it—had it hid out some place."

There was no reaction to this, either. On the way to the studio exit Quinny shifted his course with the intention of restoring the brass Diana to her pedestal. It was a tactical blunder. He had hardly turned his back to the sculptor when he received a powerful shove that sent him headlong over a chair to a four-point landing on the floor beyond. By the time he had wrathfully disengaged his feet from the debris of the chair, the sculptor was in wild flight down the stairs.

Struggling back to his feet, the detective rushed after him. He abandoned the pursuit as he reached the landing outside the door and saw Decourré had reached the downstairs entrance and was dashing out into the mews. There wasn't any chance of catching the long-legged sculptor.

After thinking about it for a couple of minutes, Quinny locked the studio door, pocketed the bunch of keys and tramped down the stairs. By the time he had reached the cobbled mews, he wasn't even thinking of Anton Decourré.

Paula Camp's Sunday afternoons were usually spent going through the newspapers, dressed in a shabby sweater and old slacks. On this one, anticipation of an approaching eventful night dulled her interest in news. Apprehension might have been more in keeping.

DALE WORDEN, the girl who had introduced Rush Fenton into Paula's life, had one diversion that wasn't expensive. This was a fine appreciation of the vespers music provided by swanky East Side churches. Of course, this involved sitting through a sermon, too.

Dale endured the sermons with a vague feeling of making reasonable payment for the music.

On this Sunday, Paula Camp's lounging had been interrupted by one of Anton Decourré's unannounced visits—the only kind he had ever made. She supposed he was hungry, as usual, although he would not speak of it. In his palmier days, Anton made no bones about accepting things, taking them as no more than the due of a great artist—and without thanks. Reduced to dire poverty, however, he had shrouded himself in a sleazy shawl of pride, as though to conceal his deterioration.

Paula, wholly unsympathetic to this sophistry, usually deferred to it to save argument. It was easier to pretend that the occasional small sums she gave him were loans. Quite often she wondered why she bothered about him at all, as she had long ago ceased to have any feeling about him.

"You've come just in time to make tea," she said indifferently, returning to her newspaper. "There are cookies in the bread box and the makings of a sandwich, too, if you want one."

He would wolf anything he found in the kitchen, Paula knew, but she didn't care. The sculptor shuffled away, and, after listening to the sounds of his foraging, he faded from the girl's consciousness.

Before Anton returned, a clatter of high heels on the stairs announced another unexpected visitor. Paula struggled up from her comfortable pose on the divan and fled to her bedroom to adjust her déshabille for the critical survey of a woman. Anton hadn't mattered, of course.

"Hello-o-o! Anybody home?"

Paula peered out through the crack of her bedroom door and recognized the smartly dressed redhead. Paula had not seen Dale Worden for some time and curiosity about what had occasioned this visit brought her back into the room without any freshening up at all.

"Hello, Dale," she said, coming toward the tall girl with a cordial smile. "I didn't dream it was you coming up the stairs."

"Well, it was," said Dale practically. She looked around the disorderly studio with faint distaste. "Where does one sit?"

Paula laughed and gathered the newspapers from the divan, the only comfortable seat in the place. They sat down together.

"Anton is making tea."

"That tramp!" Dale Worden grimaced. "Why do you let him mooch on you like this? It's a wonder Rush Fenton stands for it. He's a jealous man."

"He wouldn't bother to be jealous of poor Anton," Paula assured. "Rush has more important men to worry about."

"Bill Strohm, I suppose." Dale made another face. "You have a positive genius, my dear, for picking out worthless men. You don't mean you'd seriously consider brushing off Fenton for Bill Strohm, do you? I'll admit he's big, handsome and the kind women go for, but not the sort to keep a girl in the mink. You couldn't afford him."

"I expect Rush to settle something on me," argued Paula. "After all, he can't expect me to be young and attractive to men forever—"

Dale Worden had listened to the speech with her lips sagging apart in complete astonishment. Never before had she ever heard of a kept woman suggesting that her patron finance her marriage to someone else. It was heresy.

"Paula, have you gone crazy?" she broke it. "Or, do you think Rush has? I can just see him when you spring this idea on him!"

"I already have," returned Paula, with a chuckle. "For a minute, he looked like a man who'd stepped into an open manhole. Then he got mad and stamped around, calling me the most beautiful names—"

"Finishing up with the old malarkey, about how much he loved you and how he'd marry you in a minute, if it wasn't for his wife." Dale shrugged eloquently.

"That's right." Paula laughed softly again. "But, I don't care, Dale. If he won't give me anything, there's always the necklace."

"Yes—I heard about that bauble. He said he'd filched it from Mrs. Fenton, with the idea that it had cost only a couple of bucks, and gave it to you. Now the old gal has missed it and threatens to have the police in." Dale's probing gaze held for a moment on Paula. "Going to give it back?"

"I suppose Rush has been crying on your bosom," returned Paula, deciding after a slantwise glance that Dale could provide a tempting substitution for a wailing wall. "Well, you can tell him that I'm not giving up the necklace. He gave it to me—and the thing might help to persuade him to give me what I want."

"Well, the way he feels about it, you'd better not leave it lying around." Dale eyed the jewel at Paula's throat suggestively.

"Don't worry. It's hidden where no one will find it." Paula was entirely confident. "This isn't the necklace—it's a copy I made."

"Where have you hidden the real one?"

"You'll never know. Not that I think you'd tell, of course."

Dale Worden didn't look exactly convinced of Paula's assertion of faith, but let it pass.

"Okay—play it your way," she said. "Personally, I think you're acting pretty silly. You're no high school kid, you know. I might sympathize with your wanting another man—but not a Bill Strohm. You'd better take a trip to Florida until you get over this idiotic crush. Rush will shell out what you need for that in a minute, if he gets the necklace back. Oh!" The visitor's eyes brightened. "Who do you think I saw in church this afternoon?"

"Not anyone I know. I don't know anyone who goes, except you."

"Morgan Sands!"

"You *did?*" Paula was surprised, but not particularly moved. She hadn't thought of the young millionaire for some time. "Who was he with?" she appended automatically.

"A rather striking woman, older than Morgan. Don't you ever hear from him?"

"Never." Paula's eyes became thoughtful, squinching together. "That reminds me of something. When his mother broke up our marriage, she agreed to establish a trust fund for me. She never made good."

"You were a little dope. You should have insisted on having it before you let go of Morgan," criticized Dale, nodding firmly.

"I have Mrs. Sands' agreement in writing," returned Paula slowly. "I don't suppose it would do any good now. That was a long time ago."

"Does Morgan know about her welshing on the trust fund?"

"I don't know. You see, the old lady had her lawyer mail me some money each month, as though it came from the trust. After nearly a year, I got a letter from him saying the *allowance* was to be discontinued. I went down to see him, but it didn't do any good. She had established no trust fund."

"Well, by George, if I had the paper you say you have, I'd make Morgan Sands come across. He might not object, for that matter." Dale considered this a moment. "Gee, it would be wonderful to be independent of *all* men. Except for the ones you really want, of course."

"With me, that's Bill Strohm."

"There's no use saying anything more about that." Dale sighed heavily. "But I would certainly take a crack at shaking Morgan Sands loose from the money his old lady did you out of, baby. Tell him that you intend to bring suit for, for . . . oh, something. There must be some kind of a law."

"Do you really think so? I could see a lawyer, if he refused to do anything," mused Paula, strongly attracted to the idea.

"Workmen's compensation," grinned Dale. Her eyes enlarged as she thought of something. "Sands would be scared to death of *any* kind of a suit right now!" she exclaimed. "I saw a paragraph in last Sunday's paper that he was about to be married—and it didn't say *again*. Paula, this is an opportunity! Call him up and see how he reacts before you start getting tough."

Paula frowned. "I wouldn't know where to reach him," she replied.

"Oh, nuts, dear! Try all the smart hotels. There aren't so many a man with his dough would check into. If Sands paid off, you could give Rush his old necklace."

"I won't, though. It's mine!"

The conversation was interrupted by Anton Decourré, who had assuaged an appetite some thirty hours in the making and was now ready to serve tea and the cookies still remaining. He didn't know Dale Worden, but assumed she was important, and, anyhow, what he had overheard had been fascinating. The faint outline of a dream of the riches he'd hoped to move into after the break-up of Paula's brief marriage had become vivid once more. He brought in the tray and placed it on a low table by the divan, then stepped back, with a neat little bow.

"Anton Decourré, Dale," Paula said. "You've heard of him—the sculptor."

"Yes, I've heard of him." Meant to be a drawl, it came out a rasp. Dale Worden plainly could have endured not knowing the man. "I suppose," she went on, "that it's ill-bred to mention it so soon after leaving church, but gin and bitters are definitely more attractive than tea."

"We're having tea," replied Paula firmly. "Because there isn't any gin, anyhow."

Dale Worden didn't stay long. At Rush Fenton's suggestion, she had come to persuade Paula to return the necklace and also use a little common sense about the Bill Strohm matter. Dale hadn't believed the latter project likely to be successful. Love, or even infatuation, was utterly insensible to reason, she considered, having herself been a victim several times in her less informed youth.

Dale shrugged, uttered a terse good-bye, and headed for the stairway. Echoes of her heels on the steps came back to the studio, but Paula wasn't conscious of them. She sat with chin cupped in her hands, thinking very hard about the conversation as it had concerned Morgan Sands. Dale's attempt to persuade her to return the necklace and break off with Bill Strohm hadn't moved her at all.

A little while later, having meanwhile got rid of Anton at the modest price of a dollar, she pulled the telephone directory from under a pile of old magazines and looked up the number of a Park Avenue hotel. She called several before locating Morgan Sands at the Quiberon. The sound of her ex-husband's voice sounded strange, like a once favorite phonograph record found at the bottom of a stack.

How Paula's voice sounded to Morgan Sands she had no way of knowing. He ordinarily was defensively casual, and was the sort of person who doesn't expect to be forgotten, but she sensed an undertone of misgiving.

"Well, well—how *are* you, Paula?" he asked, with a show of heartiness. "Married again—and more satisfactorily, I trust."

"Let's not go into that, Morgi," Paula was of no mind to discuss her social situation. "I'm calling about the trust fund your mother cheated me out of—or didn't you know?"

"No-o-o," lied Morgan Sands. He hadn't known what happened, but had suspected Margery Sands of pulling a fast one of some sort.

"Well, she did—a year after she succeeded in breaking us up. Now, I need the money, and I intend to have every cent she promised me, if I have to take it to court." Paula's firmness surprised herself quite as much as it did Morgan Sands.

He didn't reply at once. This was a shocking setback to his marriage plans. Anita wasn't aware that he had been married before. He had felt mention of it hazardous, considering the girl's mother's violent antipathy to profligate young men. Of course, once the wedding crisis had been safely passed, he fully intended revealing his primrose past—with sensible reservations.

"See here, Paula—you can't do this!" he demurred. "At least, not right away. You see, I'm to be married next week, and a stink like that is sure to mess up the whole thing."

"Congratulations," droned Paula. "But that doesn't mean any difference to me. I've plans of my own."

"I suppose not," returned Morgan bitterly. "But, it isn't my fault that Margery double-crossed you. If you need money, I'll be glad to hand it over—anything in reason. Later, if you want to sue Mother, I'll even give you my support. She isn't in town now, anyway."

Paula's whole inclination was to agree to let the matter slide for a time, but the years since her first adventure with Anton Decourré had built up a hard inner core. To consent to postponement probably meant getting nothing in the end.

"I can't wait," she said shortly. "I have affairs, too, Morgie, and just as important to me as yours are to you. Your mother owes me twenty-four thousand dollars, to date. Do you want to pay it?"

Anton Decourré had returned, his moccasins making no sound on the stairs. He stood at the partly opened door listening and watching Paula intently.

"That's quite a lump!" Morgan was considerably jarred. He decided it was quite enough to argue about. Even if foredoomed to lose, the total might be cut down appreciably. "Why, that's black-mail, Paula!"

"It isn't!" she returned hotly. "It is money that was promised me, and which I need badly. If your mother pays, you will get it back."

If Margery Sands paid, her son reflected gloomily, it would only be after a long court battle, with a fine chance that she would win.

"Well, suppose I give you a few thousand now and more later on as you need it?" he temporized.

"I need it now—all of it," Paula insisted, having to keep a tight grip of herself.

He was silent again for an interval. Twenty-four thousand dollars was no considerable portion of his resources, but paying out such a sum for an indiscretion of his earlier years would be unpleasant, comparable only with an invitation from the Treasury Department to discuss a tax irregularity involving seven years' accumulated penalties. Paula heard a sigh, and then once more his voice.

"Very well, Paula. I think it an outrageous demand, but I will advance you the money. The check will be in an envelope addressed to you—I'll leave it at the desk here, unless you prefer me to mail it. It—wouldn't be wise for me to see you."

"You're a good sport, Morgie," oiled the girl. Another urgent question came to mind. "I suppose you will open the house, if you're to be married."

Morgan explained that this was why he had come on ahead of his fiancée, but that there wouldn't be anything he could do about it before Monday. This was what the girl wanted to know. She had a date with Bill Strohm at the old house for later in the evening.

After she had disconnected, she remembered that in her excitement she'd forgotten to tell Morgan that her name had been changed from Kemp to Camp. She reached for the telephone to repair the omission, but was interrupted by the shuffling feet of Anton Decourré entering the studio. Paula decided that it wouldn't matter—the check would be cashable under either name.

"What do you want now, Anton?" she demanded irritably. "I do wish you would stop wandering in and out as though you lived here."

"If you had any gratitude, I should be," he returned. "After all the time I spent instructing you—"

"Time, my eye! Unless you mean teaching me the things I had no business knowing." Her resentment began to boil, as her thoughts rested more vividly on a past which had become veiled in the haze of later events. "I wish you would go and stay away! Every bit of trouble I've ever had has been because I was once fool enough to believe in you, because I was damn fool enough not to see you were a cheap, chiseling phony—" Paula broke off to laugh discordantly, then went on. "And that's just it—'chiseling phony.' Go away, will you? I've too much to do to waste time getting furious with you. You aren't worth it."

"You forget—"

"Oh, drop it. The great Decourré!" she sneered. "Carving tombstones out at Woodlawn. Oh, yes, I know about that."

The sculptor, after a long stare of bright-eyed hatred, turned and the girl heard his shuffling feet as he began the descent of the stairs. She hadn't meant to let him know she knew about his surreptitious employment, and knew that speaking of it had struck him hard. Well, she thought, once her plans with Bill Strohm had materialized, there'd be an end to Anton's visits.

She dressed. She would have dinner, then stop for the check at the Quiberon before going on to keep her assignation with Bill at the Sands house. At least, that's what other people would call it—an assignation—and she supposed the word was correct, but this would be the last time it would be. With the money from Morgan, the affair would speedily be legitimized, she believed.

Dinner wasn't a particularly successful meal, Paula's thoughts having meanwhile soared above mere appetite. She watched the last rays of sunlight fade in the west from her table at the Tavern on the Green in Central Park, where she had gone, responding with swelling emotion to the thought that this, too, was sunset for her disordered, unsatisfactory life. Tomorrow would see the beginning of a new and more contented era for herself and Bill.

Dear Bill! He'd be so elated to know that she had contrived to provide this security for them. There wasn't anything wrong with

Bill, except that he'd never learned to do anything more useful than entertain women, for whom she was sure he never had any deep feeling, really. Money had been his trouble, too, so much so that she had worried occasionally about what the lack of it might drive him into doing. He had hinted that Rush Fenton might yield to pressure, if things got worse. Men had been known to pay well to keep their wives from learning of their dalliance with other women. Paula had promptly scotched this as unwarranted blackmail, with reservations as to the application of the term to her own intentions about the necklace. She could justify that, and no matter what happened, would never go to Mrs. Fenton with a story about Rush.

She sat, some time later, on the edge of the bed in the old Sands house and thought about it for a while, and then drifted into a review of things the bedroom recalled. Once this bed had been her bridal couch, but it hadn't endured very well. Now—well, there wasn't time for this sort of dreaming, she decided abruptly, and got up. It was eight-thirty, and Bill should be along in a half hour. Gee! wouldn't he be surprised and delighted to know their troubles had vanished. She got the check from her bag and looked at it again. She would deposit it the first thing in the morning, as a precaution against Morgie's changing his mind. He had been known to do so.

In a few minutes Paula had changed into yellow pajamas and bed jacket and arranged herself in bed. She found the radio page in the paper she had brought along and started the portable going, then relaxed with a paper-backed mystery reprint to kill the remaining interval of waiting. It didn't work. She laid the book down. There was nothing between its covers half so interesting as the thoughts that flowed so easily through her mind.

Presently she heard the sound of the downstairs door. Her first impulse was to leap up and meet Bill at the bedroom door—or the head of the stairs—but she decided otherwise. Instead, she turned half on her side, and after a quick survey of her general pose, cradled her head on one arm.

"I'll pretend I'm asleep," she murmured, trying to stop the smile that quivered in the corners of her mouth.

She screwed her eyes closed, trying to modify her excited breathing as, over the sound of the radio, she heard soft footsteps approach the door. Bill walked more lightly than any man she'd ever known, considering he was so big. Anton, of course, never made much noise, either, but he wore moccasins. She almost lost control of her smile as she thought of Morgan Sands' little dancing steps.

The sound of feet stopped. She imagined that Bill had paused in the doorway, surprised to find her sleeping. It was difficult to simulate the quietness of sleep, with all this emotion running wild through her veins. Then she thought she heard the faint sound of tiptoeing in the room.

"I've fooled him!" she thought. "He really thinks I'm asleep! I'll bet he wakes me with a kiss . . ."

CHAPTER FIVE

PINE STREET WAS MILES from the corner where Quinny Hite caught a cab. It was all very well to use the subway when the bankroll is suffering from malnutrition, but with ample dough it was smarter to spend some on cab fare before some bookie got it.

A half hour later he arrived at the information desk in the offices of Severn, Mains & Wayman, asking for Cecil Wayman, the lawyer Morgan Sands had said he'd retain. Quinny was considerably distracted by the fresh good looks of the girl at the desk. It always annoyed him to see a really pretty girl tied to the dull routine of an office job.

"Do you have an appointment?" the girl asked, inspecting the detective without marked enthusiasm.

"Oh, them things—I never bother with 'em." Quinny made a lofty gesture, completing it by tilting the black derby to what he believed a debonair angle and achieving a rakish effect instead.

"Who'll I say?"

"Say Quin Hite. It's about Morgan Sands."

"Oh—just a minute." The girl manipulated the switchboard and a moment later announced that Mr. Queen High was at the desk.

"Look here, doll," growled Quinny, mildly affronted, "I said Quin Hite, clear an' distinct-like."

The girl grinned impertinently.

"Third door down the corridor," she said, snapping the gadget on the switchboard. "Go right in—Mr. Hike. Have fun!"

Quinny snorted inelegantly and turned away. This jill wouldn't get any place, anyhow, he decided as he walked on thick carpeting toward a door with "Cecil Wayman" lettered on the glass panel. Without ceremony, Quinny twisted the bronze doorknob and entered. Inside, he stopped abruptly, looking surprised.

Instead of the probably stuffy lawyer he expected, he saw a woman in unruffled possession of the office. She was tidily outfitted in a gray Mainbocher suit with a huge bunch of violets pinned on it, and her slim feet, encased in patent leather sling pumps, rested on the glass top of a couple of hundred dollars' worth of walnut desk.

"How're you, Hite?" greeted the woman. She didn't take her feet down, but passed a shapely hand through an elegant mess of red hair and then removed a coral cigarette holder from her lips.

Must be a secretary, Quinny thought, taking advantage of Wayman's absence to put on an act.

"Is the boss around?" he responded, uncertain whether to frown on this flagrant departure from office decorum, or to join the party.

"You asked for Cecil Wayman," the woman said, tilting her head and angling cool but vivid blue eyes at him. "I'm Wayman. I suppose you came to see me about my nitwitted nephew."

"Yeah, that's what I thought, too," replied Quinny. "After a gander at you, though, I've got a better idea."

"I wonder why it is men always get ideas about me?"

"Yeah—you wonder!" Quinny grunted cynically.

Mrs. Wayman laughed. "I like cute rascals," she said. "Like a drink, Hite?"

"I dunno. There's something about you makes my back hair crawl. Maybe I better stay sober."

"Oh, nuts!" Mrs. Wayman lowered her feet from the desk top to hook high heels on the pedestal of her swivel chair, then opened a drawer and came up with a bottle. From three yards away Quinny could see that it wasn't any low-proof whiskey. He moved closer to the desk, deciding the interview promised to be interesting. She placed the bottle on the desk and looked up at him. "Snag a pair of

paper cups from the cooler over there. If I'm to spend the afternoon with you, I'll need a bracer now and then."

Quinny crossed over to the water cooler in a corner of the
office, looking back uneasily over his shoulder at Mrs. Wayman.
Pulling a couple of cups from the cylinder, he returned to the desk.

"Look, sister, fun's fun, but I always figured law offices for law,
not monkey business."

"Monkey business would be definitely more amusing," the lawyer replied. "But there won't be time for play, damn it. As Morgan's
aunt, my duty is to try and keep him out of clink."

Quinny's eyebrows shot up. "You mean you place show in this
Severn, Mains & Wayman bracket? You're a lawyer?"

"What's wrong about that?"

"Nothing." The detective gallantly uncorked the bottle and
sloshed liquor into the cups. "Only, all the female lawyers I ever
saw looked more like guys in one-legged pants outfits than they
did a maybe heart interest. Water?"

"No water. There's no reason why a woman lawyer shouldn't
wear pretty clothes. I like law, but also get a kick out of looking nice."

Quinny tossed off his drink. "I can see where, in some cases,
lookin' like you do could go a good way towards helpin' a jury to
okay your client—if there wasn't any dames on it. Want another
slug?"

Cecil Wayman leaned forward on her elbows. Despite her forty
years, she looked thirty-five. She didn't need to think of trading in
her figure, either. Despite her femininity, no opposing counsel who
knew her was tempted to write her off cheaply. Ten years were
necessary, however, for her confrères to abandon the notion that
her sex was any handicap.

She shook her head. "One jolt's enough," she said, her mood
changing swiftly. "We'll get down to this nasty business. Morgan
has always been a perfect genius at getting into scrapes, and an
idiot at getting out of them, but he's the only nephew I've got. I'd
hate to lose him. He came down here a while ago with a bad dose
of shakes—quite sure he would burn for that girl's death."

"What did you do with him?"

"Sent him home to my apartment. I'm a corporation lawyer, you see, and criminal cases aren't my meat. I've got to give this mess a study before I do anything. It's nonsense, of course, to suppose he had anything to do with it. Morgan couldn't kill a mouse. He hadn't any reason, to start with," she continued, "Paula Kemp, after all these years, meant about as much to Morgan as a last week's newspaper. He'd probably forgotten she existed until he saw her dead."

Quinny shook his head dubiously.

"That's may be," he said. "But it ain't saying she didn't remember him, though. Do you know anything about a man named Bill Strohm?"

Cecil Wayman's eyes flickered, but she continued with the operation of inserting a fresh cigarette into the long coral-hued holder. She didn't look up until she finished. Quinny snapped an ornate desk lighter and held the flame until she had a light, his hazel eyes alive to any change in her expression. As she met his steady gaze, the detective felt a subtle radiation of wary challenge.

"Bill Strohm? Naturally, I know something about him—anyone should who reads the papers. He used to play around with the Long Island horsy set before the war. What about him?"

"He ties in with this deal, too," replied Quinny. "I want to have a talk with him, but first I gotta locate him."

Cecil Wayman blew out a long, thin line of smoke.

"It seems to me," she said slowly, "that I've read somewhere that Bill Strohm flew transports to England for the Canadians."

"Yeah-yeah—that's right."

Mrs. Wayman picked up her telephone and instructed the switchboard operator to call a Captain Lingard at the Aileron Club. Then she restored the instrument to its cradle and turned to the detective.

"Pour yourself another clout and soupçon for baby," she drawled. "Ed Lingard may have some idea where to find Strohm. He was in that service, too. While we're waiting, suppose you tell me what the situation is—Morgan was too excited to be intelligent."

Quinny recounted his experiences after Morgan left the house in considerable detail with only minor reservations. Cecil Wayman kept a thoughtful silence as he rambled along, only moving to re-plenish the cigarette holder from time to time.

"So there you've got it," he concluded. "Morgan don't have any alibi for last night that's good. He says he left you at the Pierre about six—and the murder took place near nine—"

"How do you know that?"

"When this Fenton came into the bedroom, he noticed Win-chell's program was on the radio. Paula Camp was no Winchell fan, so she must have been skulled before the program came on."

"That doesn't follow," disagreed Cecil Wayman. "You don't know who turned on the radio, or when. It may have been the murderer—and long before the body was seen by Fenton, assum-ing that he didn't do the job."

"Never heard of anybody so nuts about Winchell he had to lis-ten to him while beating somebody's brains out," retorted Quinny, irked at the criticism. "And you forget that the Camp dame didn't go to the place until around eight-thirty. By the time she changed into the yellow pajamas it must have been close to nine. She had a newspaper, folded to the radio page, like she had looked in it for somethin' she wanted to listen to. There was a book, open and face down on the bed, as if she'd been reading it. All this adds up to a pretty busy half hour between eight-thirty and nine."

Cecil Wayman smiled incredulously.

"It might also add up to what the murderer planned, if the crime had been committed earlier and he wanted to establish an alibi for nine o'clock."

Quinny snorted indignantly.

"Nuts," he said firmly. "That cuts out Fenton, who didn't make any play for a nine o'clock alibi. He admits being in the house about that time. But all I know about him is what he told me, and how do I know his bringing up was the kind that says lyin' is a sin? Maybe Morgan Sands never heard of George Washington, neither."

"I suppose you are trying to tell me that you doubt everybody."

"Sure, I do." Quinny's expression indicated he considered any other course to be a form of mild insanity. "Here's one thing, though, that looks like a fine bet: Whoever killed the girl meant to scram after he'd put out all the lights and locked up—but he didn't."

"So, what?" needled Mrs. Wayman, with a show of indifference.

"So I figure he heard somebody else downstairs—maybe at the door—and lammed in a hurry to the backyard."

This was a slight distortion of what Quinny had reconstructed from the evidence he had gathered. It wasn't his intention to mislead, but he didn't see any point in going into details now. He was the one who was supposed to be doing the detecting, not this Pine Street Portia.

A buzzer shrilled and Cecil Wayman picked up the telephone. She listened a second or two, then said, "Put him on, please." Glancing at Quinny, she said, "Captain Lingard."

Quinny listened attentively, but without getting much hint of the other end of the conversation. It went on for some minutes before Cecil Wayman dropped the phone onto the cradle and swiveled back to face him.

"He doesn't know where Bill Strohm lives, and personally doesn't care to know," she said. "But he suggests that we get in touch with Berte Dill."

"So, now all we gotta do is locate this Dill guy," commented Quinny sourly.

"It's a woman," corrected the lawyer. "It happens that I've met her, but she's an acquaintance I could do very well without. She's—primitive. However, under the circumstances, she can be endured. I'll put on a chapeau and we'll pay the Potts Crossing princess a visit."

"You don't need to go," countered Quinny. "I can handle it alone."

"I wouldn't trust you for a moment with Berte Dill," she said, grinning. "She'd seduce you in a minute."

"No, she wouldn't either," growled the detective. "What d'you think—I'm just a push-over for pants-happy dames? I'm a business man."

Cecil Wayman chuckled. "Business men can be had, my dear."

Quinny grinned. "How about business women?"

The lawyer's thin eyebrows raised and lowered and she laughed again. "Get my coat—and, now that we're going out, you'd better put on your hat."

Quinny looked around blankly, not seeing the derby anywhere. Then he smiled sheepishly as he realized that it was right where it had been all along—on his head.

They found the girl on the switchboard reading a late edition of a tabloid. Cecil Wayman took it away from her. The feature story was the murder, with the startling development that police had a dragnet out for Morgan Sands and, worse yet, an unnamed private detective suspected of having aided him to escape.

"The dirty lugs!" exclaimed Quinny, reading over Mrs. Wayman's shoulder and vaguely conscious of a scent from Charbert. "After all I done for 'em, they didn't even mention my name!"

"If Morgan sees this, he'll do something foolish," worried the lawyer. "I'd better get on home before he does. If the law doesn't pick you up, Hite, phone my apartment as soon as you finish with Mrs. Dill." She gave the phone number.

"*Mrs.* Dill, eh?" muttered Quinny, scribbling the number on the back of an envelope. "All the dames in this piece seem to be married and not working at it. This is a tough spot for a single guy—I better be careful."

BERTE DILL, relict of the Potts Crossing iron magnate, Gottlieb Dill, lived in Huntingdon House, one of those tall apartment hotels erected in the late 'Twenties for upper crust trade. It had not much more than pushed open its bronze doors for business when the stock market's spectacular dive broadened the management's social outlook. After this, the guest's solvency rated first importance, with mild reservations about dating strangers in the hallways or making use of windows to discard empty liquor bottles. The hotel's atmosphere of aloof snobbery nowadays required a corps of house detectives to service it.

About the time Quinny Hite left Cecil Wayman's office, Berte Dill and her mother were engaged in what to strange ears would have sounded like a family brawl. This interpretation would have been quite surprising to the two women, with a coal mining town background where a strong voice won more debates than did logic. Berte had a veneer of culture, but saw no use wasting it on her mother.

"You got no business chasin' after men who only want your money," Miriam Weber railed at her daughter.

"I can chase after anyone I want," retorted the girl. "Only I don't. Men chase me."

"You do, too!" Mrs. Weber, who had been wandering aimlessly around the room, fetched up in the doorway. "You even hired a detective to see what one of 'em was doing."

"Sure, I did that. Nothing wrong in finding out what a man you're interested in does in his spare time," defended Berte.

"I could have told you he was chasin' other women. Men always do. He only wants your money, I tell you."

Berte shrugged, eyeing her face in the mirror critically.

"Well," she drawled, "that's no way for him to get it. And you needn't worry about some fella skinning me out of my bankroll, Mama. Maybe I have got a crush on Bill, but I got my money the hard way—and I'm going to hang on to it till a man comes along who can match it."

"She don't have to take his word for it that he's got any," doubted Mrs. Weber shrilly. "Trouble with girls your age is you ain't got a lick of sense about men."

"Oh, no? When I picked out old Gottlieb and worked him into a spot where he had to marry me, was I being dumb? And, if you think being the wife of a dried herring like him for six months wasn't an education, you're crazy!" Berte Dill shuddered at the recollection of her late husband.

"So, now I'm crazy! Do you want for me to smack you with a hair brush?"

Berte Dill laughed raucously.

"In Potts Crossing, the children smack back—don't forget. Stop nagging me—I can take care of myself. If you don't leave me alone, Mama, I'll cut off your gin money. I ought to, anyway—you're getting a fanny like the back end of a Madison Avenue bus!"

With a chilling glance, Mrs. Weber stalked out, slamming the boudoir door behind her. She shuffled into the serving pantry, where she spent a little time considering the relative effects of food as against drink on hip-spread. Deciding that at her age hips weren't likely to get her anywhere anyhow, she emerged presently with a tray of refreshments.

Quinny Hite walked into the lobby downstairs, congratulating himself that, in view of the day's trend toward upper level society, he had on his good suit. This wasn't altogether chance, but the inexorable outcome of time, weather and wear on his second-string outfit. The thinned fabric of the gray number had begun to disintegrate, with the likelihood of an aperture appearing in the seat at any moment. Quinny was decidedly opposed to October breezes soughing down his pants legs.

Deciding that Cecil Wayman's suggestion of using her name when he announced himself might be useful, he picked up one of the house phones beyond the desk. But the voice answering told him to come up, with no ado about identity or purpose at all. A maid, admitting him into a small, square foyer, merely waved him through an archway and then disappeared into the serving pantry.

Quinny stopped in the opening and looked into the living room. Its size was startling, with a miscellaneous collection of expensive furniture scattered about. Doors indicated still other rooms, although this one alone appeared to take up as much space as an entire floor at the du Nord Hotel, where Quinny lived.

Then he saw Mrs. Weber sitting on a red velvet divan, with a complicated layout of solitaire spread on a coffee table. On the same table was an incongruous tin bucket and a large, thick china coffee cup. The woman didn't look up, Quinny hesitated in the archway, rather baffled, until she played a card and reached for the cup.

"Um-m-m!" he rasped loudly.

Still she didn't look up, although it seemed impracticable to drink from the cup without lifting her chin.

"Put it down," Mrs. Weber growled. Quinny started to ease his hips into the nearest chair. He didn't make it before the woman spoke again. "Fetch me my bag off the piano—" She raised her chin and the cup in one motion and broke off as she saw Quinny. "Who are you?" she barked.

"Quin Hite. I—"

"Ain't you the man from the liquor store?"

"Nope. Private detective—"

"You the man Berte hired to find out what Bill Strohm was up to?" demanded Mrs. Weber. "She won't need you any more—what you told her was all she needs to know. Anyhow, she ain't home. I'm all alone here."

Quinny caught her swift glance at a closed door beyond. "Yeah?" he temporized, "well, this time I want her to tell me somethin'." He came over to the coffee table and peered down at the contents of the tin bucket.

"She ain't in," reiterated Mrs. Weber testily.

Quinny ignored it, leaning over to sniff at the odor of the contents of the bucket. "What's this you're drinkin'?" he asked. "Looks like beer, but smells different."

"It is beer—with a stick o' gin in it," replied the old woman, with a trace of defiance in her tone. "I like it."

"It's all yours." Quinny backed away respectfully. "Don't it knock you down, or nothin'?"

"It sets me up. What'd'ya want to ask Berte? I'm her mother."

"I want to know where Bill Strohm lives. I ain't the detective she hired—I'm on another job."

"What's he done now?" Mrs. Weber eyed Quinny with fresh interest. "That man is no good, I'm telling you—"

"Tell me where he lives," interrupted Quinny.

A clacking of high heels in an adjoining room betrayed Mrs. Weber's assertion of being alone. Quinny hoped to have his question answered before a possible interruption, which would be just that much gain.

"The Maryvale Apartments on Thirty-seventh Street—"

The door beyond the grand piano opened violently and Quinny found himself staring at a dark-haired girl in a trailing blue negligée. She glared back at him with a hard glitter in her dark eyes, then shifted her attention to the woman on the couch.

"Mama," she said throatily, "all my life I've been telling you to keep your damned mouth shut—and a lot of good it does!"

Mrs. Weber shifted uneasily. "So what?" she demanded. "He ast me a civil question, didn't he?"

"You don't have to answer questions for any bum that sneaks up the service entrance!" shrilled Berte Dill. She came around the piano like a racing sloop rounding a buoy, the negligée fluttering and leaving no question of her shapeliness. She stopped a couple of yards from Quinny and eyed him malevolently. "Who the hell are you?"

"I get asked that all the time." Quinny grinned disarmingly. "How's for us starting over. If I'd seen you first, I would have forgot what I came for." He wiggled his eyebrows feverishly. "What a build! I could go for you!"

"Fresh guy," murmured Berte, but covertly assaying Quinny.

"Me? Me, fresh?" Quinny, trying to look outraged, shook his head. "Not for fifteen years. But one look at you does start my impulses impulsin'. Class oozes out of you like sweat from a doped horse!"

Berte Dill's laugh came from deep in her throat.

"That's what I like," she said. "Refined fellers. I heard you tell who you are. What do you want Bill Strohm's address for?"

"He owes on his car," improvised Quinny absently. His attention had been caught by a tri-cornered, tiny scar over her left eyebrow.

"He hasn't got a car."

"He hasn't got anything," croaked Mama Weber. "He's a bum."

"Oh, dry up, Mamie—I'm handling this!" Berte glared at her mother.

"Never mind that Mamie business," retorted the mater, who fancied the name Mariam. "Want for me to bust you one with this crock?" She fondled a Dresden china shepherdess tentatively.

"I sure like to see good feelings between a gal and her mom," commented Quinny warmly. "How's for layin' off this civil war long enough to set me straight on a matter?"

"About Bill Strohm?" asked Berte suspiciously.

"No. Not now." Quinny paused for reflection. "What I want to know is who did you see last night in that old house—"

"Hold it!" interrupted Berte, glancing at her mother. "This is a private matter, Mama. Suppose you take a walk some place—go downstairs and put away a couple of gins."

"I will not," resisted the old lady. "I'll stay right here. You can't shove me around!"

Berte Dill's gaze returned to Quinny. "All right—all right!" she exclaimed. "Sit there, then, till your hips look like a pair of buttercakes. Mr. Hite and I will go in the bedroom."

Mrs. Weber's eyes flared wrathfully. "All right, go ahead. I'm sure I do everything I can to keep you decent, but it ain't no use. You keep off my bed, though, do you hear?"

Berte Dill looked back over her shoulder haughtily. "You have a dirty mind, Mama. This is a conversation Mr. Hite and I are going to have," she said acidly.

Quinny smothered his grin as he trailed the girl into the bedroom. Berte stood aside as he entered, then shut the door violently.

"Good thing I stopped you," she said, walking across the room to sit on a chintz-covered chaise. "Spilling anything before Mama is just like putting an ad in a newspaper."

This was a large room, too, with twin beds, and not tidy. A bewildering amount of stuff was strewn around on chairs and other furniture. Berte Dill, it seemed, was an enthusiast for outdoor sports. Ski sets stood on end in a corner, with several tennis rackets and a golf bag.

"How do you get by without a ping-pong table and a pin-ball machine in here?" queried the detective, looking mildly astounded. "No tiddly-winks, neither. But I'd say a jill lookin' like you do don't need all this gear to have fun."

Quinny glanced around for something to sit on: He sat down on the foot of one of the twin beds, facing the girl and hoping he hadn't selected the one belonging to Mama Weber. Then he pushed the derby back absently and prepared for action.

"What were you saying, when I interrupted out there?" Berte jerked her head toward the living room.

"About last night—when you were hiding behind the chair in the front room of the Sands house—"

"I don't know what you're talking about." The tone was frightened.

"Yeah, you do—so let's skip the dillyin' around. Too many people saw you—and one of 'em noticed that little scar over your left eye. You don't want to get tied in on a murder job, do you?"

"Murder?" Berte Dill's eyes saucered.

"That's right. Paula Camp was bumped off in that house last night. Maybe while you were there." Quinny regarded the girl gravely. "Look, sweetheart, you better play ball. I ain't tryin' to pin anything on you, but I do know you were there and pretty much what you did."

"If you know so much, why bother asking me?"

"I ain't askin' what you did, but what you saw." Quinny tested the softness of the bed with his hand. It was a lot more yielding than the petrified hay mattresses at his hotel.

Berte Dill didn't answer right away. In the hard school of her girlhood she had learned to give due consideration to anything containing possible repercussions.

"What's your interest—who are you working for?" she demanded.

"I'm working for me," Quinny answered. "But a certain party will make it worth my time if I crack this case by Thursday. If it turns out he pulled the job himself, I'm out dough, but I can't help that. Come on, pretty—give."

"Well, I didn't see so much," Berte said slowly. Reflection had convinced her that frankness was the safe course. "You see, I've been, uh, interested in Bill Strohm."

"Interested." Quinny's nod was deadpan.

She flushed. "Yes, interested," she insisted. "But, I don't trust men—especially good-looking ones. I wanted to know what he did on nights he didn't take me out, so I hired a detective. This feller tipped me off Bill was meeting another girl in a vacant house."

"That burned you, of course." Quinny was all sympathy. He wondered why a girl with a nature palm trees could grow in would hesitate to take on a man she wanted. Then he knew. She'd been made use of at some time in the past and didn't intend having it happen again. Berte Dill both desired men and was afraid of them—or distrustful of being betrayed by her desire.

"Not the way you think," denied the girl, dark eyes showing quick hostility. "I could stand for Bill not taking me to Twenty-One and places like that, because his finances had got tied-up while he was in the war and he hadn't got them loose again—"

"*He* said," interrupted Quinny grimly. "Did he show you anything?"

Berte stared a moment before answering. "A couple of letters from his broker advising him to hold onto his securities till the price got better. But what made me mad was, this running around with another girl, when he never had any ready cash to spend taking me places. After all, if a man takes up a girl's time, he's supposed to spend some money."

"So I've heard," Quinny nodded.

"I thought I would find out who this girl was, anyway, and see what her charm was."

"Of course, not figurin' to bop her one to discourage—"

"Don't be funny. As soon as I knew where to go, I went over there a couple of times and hung around, but nothing happened. Then, last night, I tried again, except a little tramp annoyed me while I was waiting on the corner. I got rid of him. Then I saw a girl turn into the street and hurry to the house. I sneaked along after her and saw her unlock the door and go in. You see, I had to make sure somehow that Bill wasn't inside, waiting, so I went in. Funny, her leaving the door unlocked." Berte Dill's thin eyebrows came together in a puzzled frown.

"Maybe she left it open for your boy friend," suggested Quinny, who had worked this out before.

Berte shrugged indifferently. "I heard her upstairs, moving around, so I decided to hide in the big room and see what happened."

"Now you're gettin' to what I want to know. Did you hear her talking? Or anybody else?"

His curious gaze traveled to the girl's bare forearm, taking in the more than usual muscular development. Still, she evidently was quite athletic. "No. I heard her moving around for a while and then the radio was turned on. I thought I could sneak up the stairs to see what was going on, but just as I started I heard the front door open and someone come in. I hid again."

"Who came in?" Quinny questioned.

"I don't know. It was a man, but I couldn't see anything but his feet and the bottom of his pants as he went upstairs. It wasn't Bill Strohm, though."

"How could you tell it wasn't?"

"Bill wouldn't be found dead wearing spats. As soon as the man got upstairs, I scrammed. I thought it just wasn't Bill Strohm's turn with the lady." Berte's lips curled wryly.

"Did this fella say anything after he got upstairs—or did the girl?"

Berte shook her head. "I didn't hear anyone talk—but I couldn't have been more than a minute or two in leaving."

"Did you hang around outside afterwards?"

"No. I hurried over to First Avenue and caught a cab."

Her story checked with what he had heard from Rush Fenton, Quinny decided, but otherwise did nothing to eliminate the Westchester man. He had still been in the house when Berte left. There was only his word for how long he stayed.

It would still be necessary to find Strohm and see what he could get out of him. Quinny scowled with the thought that there might not be much to get. So far, he had nothing to prove that the man had been near the Sands house at the hour of the murder. Pilgrim had seen a man leave at ten. Was this Fenton?

"Did you notice what time it was when you saw the girl go in the house?" asked Quinny, jerking himself back to the present job.

"No, of course I didn't. But just before I first saw her I looked at my watch—I had a date at half-past nine and had to come home to dress. It was nearly eight-thirty then, and she must have showed up in five minutes or so."

Quinny nodded. This agreed with Fenton's estimate of the time and, if what he'd said about the Winchell program was true, the crime had been committed between eight-thirty and nine. Berte Dill, after some hesitation, told Quinny that she hadn't noticed the program but vaguely remembered music.

"Okay," said Quinny regretfully, as he rose from the bed. "I guess what you said will have to do me—for now. Thanks."

Berte swung her feet from the chaise and stood up. In a couple of steps she was standing before him, her hands clutching the lapels of his coat. Berte Dill could change faster than a chameleon and, like the small lizard, for reasons of either purpose or mood.

"You can be a good fellow, can't you, Mr. Hite?" she purred, her eyes now soft and appealing.

"Me?" Quinny seemed to be shocked at the implication.

"Yes. You—you wouldn't like to have me mixed up in this nasty business, when I really had nothing to do with it. I know you wouldn't." Syrup now supplanted the usual vinegar in her voice— and she could lay it on. Her fingers slipped from the lapel and began to twist a coat button.

"It wouldn't make any difference to me." Quinny eyed the twisting fingers with rising alarm. "Here, lay off the button. I just laid out a dime yesterday to get it stitched back on."

"Oh, sit down," ordered the girl impulsively. She gave him a push and he sat heavily on the bed. All in the same movement, she was sitting alongside—and close. "Don't you see, it would help no one for me to get messed up in this scandal? I've been trying for three years to get some standing socially in New York. Now, when I am just about to crash into the Fifth Avenue set, this has to happen." A beautifully finished hand slid up under his arm and tried to close over his biceps. It was a trifle small for the project.

"Tossing around with me won't get you anywhere socially, neither." Quinny made a half-hearted effort to shake her off and get up, but Berte clamped onto his arm with a fine, two-handed grip. "Don't forget, things got kinda spoiled for Paula Camp, too. Permanent."

"Smashing me won't do her any good—and it certainly wasn't my fault it happened. You can easily keep my name out of it, and—" The lids of her dark eyes lowered slightly and provocatively, but the exercise was a waste. Quinny wasn't looking at her. "I—I might be good to you, if you did."

"What do you mean, 'good'?" he barked. "Let me look at your stamp album, or somethin'?"

"Keep my name out of this—and good will mean whatever you want it to."

Her knee was crowding against Quinny's leg and she still clung with both hands to his arm. His head swung around and after a critical look in the girl's eyes, he laughed scornfully.

"Look, pin-up, like I said, I don't give a hoot in hell whether you make headlines in this case or not, and what you're offerin' is something which is no good when you get it at the store—if you get what I mean."

Berte Dill's face flared with resentment which she struggled to keep in check.

"Perhaps a little cash might do the trick," she said.

"That's no good, either. I ain't saying you leave me cold, or nothing like that. The trouble is I like my sin straight—and for something. So far, I only said I didn't care how much publicity you get. I also never said I was going to get you any."

Berte Dill stared for a moment at Quinny's quizzical eyes. Whether because of her beauty or the fortune she'd acquired as Gottlieb Dill's widow, she'd never needed to do anything to excite men. Just the reverse, really. Now, here was a man insultingly cool to her lure, discussing it with a detached interest. It was a jab at her self-esteem. Her stare broke into a seductive smile and before Quinny caught up with her reasoning she had squirmed against his chest, with one cool arm sliding around his neck.

"We could get chummy," she said throatily, "no matter what you do to my reputation. I'm not fooling—now."

"Believe it or not, I got a reputation, too," resisted Quinny, vaguely recalling his boast to Mrs. Wayman of his impregnability to designing women. "This will get you nothing."

"I said I'm not fooling. You"—her chic nose was just beneath his chin, and rising slowly—"you're ca-yute!"

"Ca-yute, eh!"

This all but gummed up her enterprise, and would have if the detective hadn't stopped looking into space long enough to get the full benefit of Berte's smoking upward gaze. He took a long breath. The smooth bare arm around his neck was tugging with surprising strength to bring his head down. Quinny began to see his resolution in a new light. Kinda sissy, holding out like this. A guy oughtn't to fool around when samples are being given out. Never hurts to take one. You don't have to buy anything—

Sheer sophistry! it was, all things considered, a dizzying experience in which his native caution stepped out for a minute. Berte Dill had completely forgotten her original calculations. She squirmed around in his arms like an animal making a bed in long grass, and then, as if in response to some inner warning, suddenly put her hands against Quinny's chest and pushed herself away. She looked at him with startled, brilliant eyes.

"Gee!" she exclaimed.

"Yeah—me, too," agreed Quinny nervously. He belatedly took off his hat and put it on the floor. Now that he'd had a chance to think it over, there did seem to be some point in not tossing her name to the newspapers. "Look here, bonded stuff, I better get the hell out of here while my character is still stuck together."

"No," objected Berte. Her arm once again circled his neck. "Oh, gee, I've never felt like this before when a man kissed me!"

Berte laughed nervously, then thrust her face in the hollow of Quinny's shoulder—for safety, perhaps—and the other arm came up around his neck. He snuffed delicately at her scented hair and felt her lips moved against his throat. Don't be a sucker for a dame, Hite, he cautioned himself silently, feeling a resurgence of his guiding principles. They'll get you every time, if you give 'em the least encouragement.

Berte's head dropped back and distractingly sensuous, half-open lips lifted again. Quinny struggled to keep his mind on arguments against temptation, but could only think of what a poor showing Adam had made in a similar circumstance. There was also the thought that if Adam had been a man of strong principle, nobody else would have existed to face such a test. This concluded Quinny's thinking and his mouth descended on the waiting, trembling lips like batter on a hot griddle.

Just as Quinny had begun to float away into an enchanted land he hadn't visited lately, he heard an anguished squawk from the doorway and a Dresden shepherdess crashed to an untimely end against the headboard of the bed. Quinny freed himself from the embrace to look around at the wrathful Mrs. Weber.

"See here," he admonished sternly, "this is no time to be throwing dishes around—"

"It cert'ny is, too!" snorted Mama. "I told you—not on my bed!"

"Well, we could of moved over without you wrecking the joint."

"You get out of here!" Mrs. Weber lunged toward the dressing table. "Just lemme git a hair brush—I'll show that brat of mine a couple—"

She broke off as the telephone topped her voice. Berte Dill lunged across and grabbed the instrument before Mama Weber had time to come around the bed, although the old lady had got started with remarkable speed.

"Hello . . . yes, Berte Dill speaking. Oh-h, Mrs. Wayman . . . yes, he's here—" Berte glanced at Quinny, sat up and held out the phone. "I didn't know you knew Cecil Wayman," she said, with a hitherto absent respect in her eyes. "She wants to speak to you."

"I know lots of high-class dames," bragged the detective, taking the instrument. He didn't do much talking, nor did he listen very long. "Okay," he said finally. "I'll see what's giving and call you later. . . . No. We was interrupted." He laughed and gave the receiver back to Berte, who cradled it viciously.

"What did she want?" demanded the girl, uncertainly.

"Her green-eyed nephew has taken a powder. Do you know him?"

"I didn't know she had one."

"Well, she thinks maybe I could find him. I guess, so long's I'm workin' for him, I'll have to shove along."

"Oh . . . damn—" Berte's lips were rebellious.

"Yeah, I know just how you feel." Quinny wagged his head sympathetically. "On account of I feel the same way. But we'd have to go clear back to the beginning to work up that much steam again—and right now I ain't got time."

Quinny picked his hat up from the floor and started out, with a wary glance at Mama Weber and then a half-hearted wave to Berte. "See you in Sunday school. Other times, you can get me at the Hotel du Nord."

CHAPTER SIX

THE OCTOBER DAY was fading into night as Quinny Hite strode south-ward along Madison Avenue. Leaving Berte Dill's apartment, he had decided the matter of Morgan Sands' run-out could wait. The man was a fool, trying to sneak away like that. The cops were sure to pick him up.

Turning into Thirty-seventh Street, he kept on across town until he reached Third Avenue. On the corner he stopped in front of a four-story brick, with a cheaply ornate sign reading Maryvale Apartments hanging from a bracket. A smaller one attached to the lower edge declared "no vacancies." Manhattan sure must be jammed, he thought, when dumps like this turn people away. A man in overalls and a dirty sweater was hoisting filled ash cans from a square opening in the sidewalk. Quinny sauntered up.

"Hey, Mac," he said. "Know which apartment Mr. Strohm lives in?"

"Inna annex—nex' door." The man nodded vaguely down the street.

"Thanks, pal. Don't bust your back with them cans."

Quinny went on to the indicated annex. Up three steps was a tiny vestibule, with a row of push buttons on a wall with a name over each. Quinny pressed the one under "Strohm" several times, but there was no responding click in the lock to the inner door.

About to ring one of the other bells, he heard someone coming up the steps from the street and turned to see who it was. A woman in junior miss clothes, but with a decidedly senior miss face, was entering. She opened the mail container under "D. Blake" as Quinny watched, then moved to the inner door, glancing at the detective with a friendly but restrained smile. She had a paper under her arm, the headlines screaming murder.

"Excuse me, lady," said Quinn, snapping a finger against the rim of his hat in lieu of tipping it. "I'm looking for a man named Strohm—"

"Second floor," Miss Blake cut in, holding the door open.

"Yeah, I know. But he ain't in."

The woman smiled crisply. "I'm sure I don't know when he will be, then," she chirped. "Mr. Strohm doesn't keep regular hours."

"Look, I'm Quin Hite," explained the detective. "I'm working on the Camp murder you been reading about in that paper. Maybe you can help me out. Mr. Strohm figures in the case, some way."

Miss Blake was startled, her eyes looking like robin's eggs floating around in milk. She stared a moment, her lips a frozen O, before relaxing to speak.

"You'd better come up to my apartment—it's right under Mr. Strohm's." Quinny nodded and she turned to go in. "Oh, dear, I hope he isn't involved. He's such a good-looking man."

Prob'bly figures a handsome guy is always a right guy, thought Quinny, tramping up the narrow flight of stairs behind her. And, as a joint to live in, this one didn't rate any higher than his own hotel—smelled a good deal like it. The living room she ushered him into was long and narrow, furnished with borax maple, and having three windows opening on the street side. Miss Blake bottomed herself primly on a straight chair, indicating Quinny to take the one intended for comfort. She'd hardly needed to do this.

"Might as well get right at it," he said briskly, leaning forward with hands on his knees. "Would you know if Strohm was in his apartment last night, say between eight and ten?"

Miss Blake laced and unlaced arthritic fingers.

"Yes, he was," she said after a pause. "I heard him on the stairs just before I tuned in on *The Times* news at eight."

"You only heard him?" Quinny grunted as the woman nodded. "Then you wouldn't know whether he was going or coming—or even if it was him."

"Oh, but it was him. I heard him running a bath after that—you can hear *everything* through these floors, especially when the water runs out of the tub. A little while after that he turned on his radio."

Quinny frowned. "Yeah, but how could you tell it was *his* radio? Must be other ones in the building."

"I was in the hall when he turned it on. Mr. Whitney, who lives on the top floor, gets home every night about nine and brings me a newspaper. I was at my door talking to him. Mr. Whitney was mad at our superintendent for turning out the hall lights again, as if the war weren't over. The only other tenants live on the third floor—two nurses, and they're both on night duty. It couldn't have been any other radio."

Quinny got up. "Well, thanks, Miss Blake. That gives Strohm a kinda alibi, but not good enough. Coulda been some other lug in his apartment."

"But I saw Mr. Strohm later. He came to my door in a dressing gown to see if I had aspirin. Said he'd been drinking, gone to sleep and woke up with a frightful headache. Poor man! I *don't* know why men drink."

"I do," replied Quinny. "What time was this?"

"Oh, quite a while later. I don't know exactly. I go to bed at half past ten, usually, and it was before that."

"I see," said Quinny thoughtfully. "Maybe I'll be back after a while to check on what I find out. Thanks—a lot."

Leaving Miss Blake's curiosity unslaked, he went up to the next floor and pressed the button over a bit of card with William Francis Strohm lettered on it. He wasn't hopeful of a response, and after a wait he tried the door. It was locked, and while the door was old and badly fitted, Quinny didn't think the situation justified pushing it in. He went down the narrow hall to a window he'd noticed at the rear and looked out into a singularly unattractive series of backyards. Miraculously clinging to the rear wall of this part of the Maryvale annex was a rusty iron fire-escape, which he climbed out on, hoping it would stay put.

Treading gingerly on the iron grille, he came to a window of Strohm's apartment. It was open at the bottom and, although in complete darkness, the detective fancied the room to be a kitchen. A trace of gas greeted his nose as he peered in, as though from a badly conditioned stove. He climbed in.

It was a kitchen, about six feet square. Beyond was a living room identical with Miss Blake's, dimly illuminated by street lights. Quinny headed into it, knocking over an empty bottle on the floor enroute. Seeing a door further along the living room wall, he went to see what it opened into and discovered another small room. It was pitch dark. He stood there in the doorway a moment, listening.

Now that he was in Strohm's apartment, he began to wonder why he had been so eager to get in. It was the tenant he wanted to see—not his quarters. Its cheap undesirability didn't prove Strohm couldn't afford better. Apartments of any kind were hard to find.

Quinny turned to retrace his steps, but before he took a step something long, cold and hard snapped around his neck, drawing tight like a noose. His hands flung up to free himself, but the wire had embedded itself deep into the flesh of his throat, cutting off his breath and impossible to dislodge. He kicked out savagely behind him, felt his heel crack sharply against something, and then he went spinning into the living room, crashing over some object and bringing up on the floor, desperately trying to free his throat.

It was a frantic struggle. Lights flashed in his bulging eyes, his ears roared and his chest felt as though being crushed in a tightening vise. With numbing fingers he clawed at the wire, but to no avail. Then he blacked out.

Minutes later, he began the return to sensibility, still stretched in the floor. He fumbled at his throat and found the wire loop no longer there. The living room lights were on. Little by little he began to feel the return of his strength. A pressing pain in his neck worried him until, sitting up, he saw that he had been lying on a briar pipe. Looking around for his hat, he saw it under an overturned smoking stand, well-sprinkled with ashes. Pipe tobacco from a blue jar was scattered all over the rug.

He got up and rescued the derby, without which he was never himself, then went into the bathroom for a drink of water to ease his throat. After downing the water, Quinny examined the small bathroom curiously. The Maryvale owner hadn't spent money for luxury plumbing. There was a wash basin, toilet, and an old-fashioned tub on feet. Recalling what Miss Blake had said, he turned the tub faucet and wasn't surprised at the thin trickle of water that came out. It created sounds in the pipes, though, and probably when the rubber stopper was pulled to empty the tub the noise of the drain might easily be heard downstairs. He didn't go that far in the experiment.

As the detective left the bathroom a key grated in the hall door. It opened to reveal a big man in a heavy overcoat, who appeared entirely surprised to find that he had a guest. Quinny eyed the stranger silently before speaking, taking in his clothes and general appearance.

"Strohm?" he rasped, finding it still difficult to speak.

"Yes. Who are you—and what the devil are you doing here?"

Strohm came into the room, stopping to stand with widespread feet in a pose of alertness against any overt move. He was a big lump of a man, a two-hundred pounder or more. And, as Miss Blake had reported, definitely handsome.

"I just been damn near strangled by some lug who thought I was you." Quinny replied, massaging his throat with his fingers. "A hell of a note."

Strohm could see the livid mark, but he didn't seem impressed.

"I see," he said coolly. "But that doesn't explain why you are here—or does it?"

Quinny had been working on an answer to this, with the expectancy one would be needed. He shook his head, stretching his throat to ease the constriction that still lingered—and wanting to keep the fact of it obvious.

"I came up here looking for you," he began slowly. "Y'see, I'm a private operator, workin' on a murder job—"

"Paula Camp?" asked Strohm quietly.

"Yeah, that's right. Well, I beat on your door, but didn't get any answer. So I waited for or five minutes, figuring out what to do next. Then I heard somebody movin' around inside. I went to the back window of the hall and looked out. I couldn't see any light in your windows, so I climbed out on the fire-escape for a better look. The kitchen window was open and I stood there for a minute, wondering whether I had sure-enough heard somebody. I heard the noise again. So, I climbed in."

This, Quinny considered, was one of his better jobs of embroidery.

"Climbed right into trouble for your nosiness," commented Strohm caustically. "That should teach you something. Why did you want to see me?"

"A dumb question," retorted Quinny, irritated. "Your girl found dead from a bop on the head—and you don't know why I wanted to see you. Try that one on the cops, they're kinda curious too."

Strohm went into the kitchen, where he rested a hip on the table, his face troubled and grave. He pulled a folded newspaper from his overcoat pocket and twisted it in his powerful hands. Quinny stopped in the doorway.

"Naturally, they will be," Strohm said uneasily, but composed. "This is a terrible thing, just about all that's needed to thoroughly wreck what's left of my reputation."

"That's too bad," sneered Quinny. "Funny thing, Strohm, I've talked to three people concerned in this job—and every damn one of 'em is feeling sick about how it's going to hit them. Not one gave a thought what it did to Paula Camp."

"I have," answered Strohm, his brooding eyes wandering around toward Quinny. "But, my dear man, it's understandable to think of the effects on oneself, since grief won't help her. I have been in a hell of a funk ever since I read the news this afternoon."

"Where else have you been?" asked Quinny, gaining confidence as he found speaking had loosed the tightness of his throat. "Since then?"

"After I got the paper, I came back here. I went out about an hour ago to eat something. I wasn't much of a success."

"You didn't think about showing up to give the homicide boys a hand?" Quinny pressed. "You might've saved 'em a lot of time."

"I should have reported at once, of course," admitted Strohm. "But I've been unable to decide what would be best to do. You have no idea what this can do to me. I'd got myself involved in a pretty muddy affair with Paula, meant in the beginning to be—well, just one of those things. Paula, though, went overboard—lost her head. She wanted me to marry her, although I'd always told her I was in no position to do that. I've no training for business and while I was in the service my finances were neglected. Frankly, I have been on the market for some woman with money to take me on as husband."

"Like Berte Dill," amplified Quinny.

Strohm ignored it. "Paula wasn't convinced. She could raise enough money to keep us from worry, she said."

"Yeah—I heard about that," said Quinny. "She figured she could promote dough from this other guy, Fenton. Do you know him?"

"Not personally. I knew of him, of course. It was because of the uncertainty of his visits to Paula's studio that she insisted on using the Turtle Bay house for our meetings. She had kept the keys after her marriage."

"Why did you go to her studio today?" asked Quinny flatly.

"Why did I— That's not true. I haven't been there for months."

"You say," said Quinny cynically. "Let's go back to last night. What time did you get to the Turtle Bay house last night?"

"I didn't go," returned Strohm quickly. "That's one of the things which have been depressing me all afternoon. If I had kept the date, Paula would be still alive."

"You didn't go there?" demanded Quinny, with the air of having information to the contrary he didn't possess. "What did you do, then?"

"I stopped in at the Commodore bar about seven. My date with Paula was for nine, and she usually got there ahead of me. I had no key to the house, you see." Strohm frowned, as though what he was to say was unpleasant. "Well, I'm afraid I overdid things at the Commodore—met an old flying pal, you know. Leaving, I realized that I was quite tight—one thing Paula would be very nasty about. She hated drinking. So I came on home, believing she would return to her studio when she decided I wasn't going to show up."

"You got stinko and then came back here," repeated the detective thoughtfully. "What time did you get here?"

"A few minutes before eight."

"You got to the Commodore bar and were soused in about a half hour? What kind of stuff do they serve there?" the detective snorted.

Strohm looked sheepish. "I had other drinks before that."

"But you wasn't so blotto you didn't know what time you got here?" Quinny's eyes were skeptical.

"I noticed the time by the clock in the store on the corner as I passed. I haven't said I came home staggering all over the street, you know. I was just tight enough not to want Paula raving at me."

"Who was the guy you was drinking with? We can check with him what time you left—if he noticed."

Strohm gave him a name and address, which Quinny jotted down.

"Did you stay here, all by yourself, after you came in?"

"Yes. I had a soak in the bathtub to clear my head and then sat down to wait for Paula to call me, as I thought she would after I didn't appear."

"That all you did—just sit?" pressed Quinny.

"Oh, I read the paper and listened to the radio for a while, and then, as she didn't phone, I nearly finished off that bottle on the floor there." He nodded at the bottle Quinny had knocked over. "What was left I drank this afternoon—after I heard the bad news. I guess I must have got tight again last night and fallen asleep. I woke up later with a frightful head and borrowed some aspirin from the woman in the apartment under this. Then I went to bed and didn't waken until nearly noon."

Quinny picked up the empty bottle. The label was wrinkled as though it had been wet and something had made a deep crease across it, perhaps the cord used in wrapping. He put it on the table and looked up.

"Do you always put the cork back in empty bottles?"

Strohm looked puzzled. "Why, I don't know. Perhaps unconsciously. Does that mean anything?"

"Maybe only that I'm always pryin' into people's habits," grinned Quinny. He gave the derby an upward shove and pursed his lips before continuing. "You got a lousy alibi, Strohm. Unless somebody knows you were here all night, you're sunk."

"I don't know how I can prove it," he said, spreading his hands in a helpless gesture. "Of course, it's up to the police to prove that I was elsewhere. Personally, from what I've read in the papers, I believe it was either a housebreaker who killed Paula—or Fenton.

By the way, I've seen no mention of him, although you seem to know all about him."

"So do the police," replied Quinny, walking back into the living room. Strohm followed. "But maybe they got reasons for not breaking out with his name. I wish I knew who the hell put that wire on me."

He wondered whether or not it might not have been Strohm. Quinny had seen no one—and when he recovered all the lights were on and the wire removed from his neck. His assailant had probably not wished to kill, but wanted to leave unobserved—or perhaps, turning on the lights, had discovered he had attempted to strangle the wrong man. The wire loop couldn't have been a quickly improvised weapon. If the strangler had been Strohm, it didn't seem to make much sense.

"Probably it was some prowling petty thief," surmised Strohm. "I'd better see if he made off with anything—not that there's anything of worth while value lying about."

Quinny went to look into the small room. It was a bedroom and had been as thoroughly ransacked as Paula's studio. It was furnished with a narrow bed, a small chest, and not much else. The drawers of the chest had been spilled on the floor, covers stripped from the bed and the mattress showed long gashes in the fabric.

Strohm cursed with vigor. "Look at that mattress! All slashed. Plain vandalism—"

"Nuts," cut in Quinny. "The mug was lookin' for something special. That reminds me, Strohm, Paula told you she had a way figured out to promote wedding dough. That wasn't just talking Fenton into giving it to her. She had two strikes on him about a piece of his wife's jewelry—"

"I knew of that. A rare and expensive antique necklace—"

"Made outa Kansas leaves." Quinny nodded knowingly.

Strohm looked at him curiously.

"You mean acanthus leaves," he corrected. "Yes, that was it. Fenton wanted it back. It might be called blackmail—"

"No, it couldn't. Fenton gave it to her. She didn't have to threaten to show it to his wife. All she needed to do was to stand pat until Mrs. Fenton found out it was gone."

"I guess that's right," conceded Strohm. "However, I advised her not to try to use it for extortion. I told her it was a dangerous business for a girl in her position. I may have been more correct than I thought. I assume the necklace was found on the body, since you are able to describe it."

"You better get your assumer looked at," advised Quinny. "The necklace was gone."

Strohm again spread his hands in a helpless gesture. "The motive for the murder, then."

Quinny shrugged. "Maybe—one way or another. Would you say, looking at what's been done to your room, that the mug who put the wire on me had an idea you had the necklace hid out in here?"

Strohm was silent for a minute, his eyes dead serious. "If so, this may not be a very safe place for me tonight," he said. "But I don't see how this person could have got such an idea."

"Easy. He might figure Paula gave it to you for safekeeping," suggested the detective. "Or something."

"Well, this settles it. I am going to get in touch with the police immediately."

"You'd better," agreed Quinny. "You're late as hell now. Say, maybe you can tell me this: There was a kind of statue on the mantel in the bedroom which the girl must have took to the—"

"You mean the bas relief of General Patton?"

"Yeah. Outside of that, she didn't take any more to the joint then she had to have—not even a pin cushion."

"That's curious, isn't it? I'd noticed the head, but thought nothing of it." Strohm's eyebrows knitted, but after a moment he shook his head. "Do you make something of it that I don't get?"

"Suppose she had something Sands was afraid of—a letter, or some other paper, and covered it up with a general's head when she sculped it. Not a bad hide for something flat like that."

"Why anything of Sands'? She told me she hadn't heard of or seen him for several years. If so, she wouldn't have to go to so much trouble hiding it."

"I suppose not," agreed Quinny. "Did you know Sands?"

"Slightly. We travelled in the same set before the War."

"You musta had dough, then. Look, is that the same outfit you wore last night?" Quinny eyed the gray tweed suit which came into view as Strohm began to shed the overcoat

"No. I still have two," laughed Strohm. "The other one is blue."

Quinny moved toward the living room. "Guess I might as well shove off. My name's Quin Hite, in case the department dicks want to know who you've been talkin' to. If I was you, I'd chase right up to the precinct house."

"I intend to."

Quinny left the apartment and tramped down the rickety steps. On the landing below he caught sight of the fluttery Miss Blake through the crack of her partially opened door. She came out.

"Oh, Mr. Hite!" she exclaimed. "I heard the most awful thump in Mr. Strohm's apartment."

"Nice to have interested friends," commented Quinny.

He described briefly what had happened, concluding by asking if she had heard anyone on the stairs immediately after hearing the thump above. She hadn't heard anything, but, more important, she had come to her door and opened it as far as the chain permitted to peek out. No one had gone up or down until she saw Mr. Strohm on his way up.

Quinny frowned and started downstairs, considering the implications of what Miss Blake had told him. She watched him raptly from the doorway until he disappeared.

As QUINNY HITE came down the stairs he noticed a metal refuse can tucked against the side of the staircase. He rounded the newel post to look into it, without really hoping to find anything pertinent to his quest. He was in error.

Right on top of the mess of paper, bags of garbage and other litter was a length of brass wire, like that in the coil he'd seen on Paula Camp's workbench. A small loop had been formed in one end and the other threaded through, making a large loop with a foot or so left over to serve as a handle. Quinny felt his throat tenderly as he recognized the wire as the weapon used on him. It was a vicious one.

As he coiled it up, another glint of metal caught his gaze, half hidden in the trash. Delving for it, he came up with a string of what looked like golden leaves—a necklace with an unfilled setting in the largest leaf, intended to hang at the throat. The clasp was broken. After staring at it for a moment, he dropped it with the coiled wire into his pocket. But he stood for a moment staring up at the narrow space between the stairs and the floors of the hallways above, then walked on out of the building.

On the opposite corner some fellow named George operated a lunchroom, where patrons sat chummily in a row at the counter. Quinny went in, with two purposes in mind, one being something to eat and the other to watch the entrance to the Maryvale annex. He could see the lights in Strohm's apartment and the man himself as he moved about the living room.

While waiting for George to turn out a hamburger steak, Quinny speculated on the significance of finding the wire and the necklace in the ash can.

It wasn't conclusive of anything at all. Certainly Strohm wouldn't have thrown the necklace there, where it was pretty sure to be found. More probably it had been placed there by someone planning for Strohm to take the murder rap, after removing the ruby which gave it value. On the other hand, Strohm, if guilty, might have shrewdly planned to create just this impression. Despite the scratches on the dead girl's neck, it hadn't been established that she'd worn it to the Sands house.

Quinny was half through the hamburger when he saw Strohm's lights go out. A couple of moments later he saw the man come from the entrance, turn toward Third Avenue and round the corner, disappearing in uptown. The detective kept on eating, although he was beginning to feel that George should have selected another business, if public health wasn't to suffer. The coffee had the virtue of killing the lingering taste of hamburger, but left one of its own nearly as bad.

Glancing from time to time at the Maryvale, Quinny was electrified to see the lights in Strohm's apartment flash on again. He was evidently in no hurry to act, however, for after getting up to make a telephone call, he returned to the counter and ordered a slab of pie, which he ate leisurely and meanwhile kept an eye on the Maryvale.

The lace curtains in Strohm's apartment prevented Quinny's seeing the person beyond them well enough to do more than guess who it was. The man, moving past the windows two or three times, seemed to be of at least normal height and erect carriage.

With a glance at the fly-specked dial of George's clock, Quinny got up and went out on the sidewalk. Within a short time a squad car coming from uptown made a left turn and slid up to the curb just beyond George's Place. The bulky form of Lieutenant Madden climbed out, followed by a couple of detectives.

"What've you got, Quinny?" rasped Madden, joining him.

"Th' beginnin's of a stomach ache," returned Quinny, with a hiccupy burp. "Got a slug of bicarb'?"

"What the hell—do you think I'm drivin' a rolling drugstore?" demanded Madden. "Bull Lendon wants to see you, and bad."

"Th' hell—*ic*—with Lendon. I'm busy," retorted Quinny. "I just sent a guy up to see him—Paula Camp's boy friend, Bill Strohm. That'll have to do him for a while. Now there's some other guy prowlin' Strohm's apartment over there in the Maryvale—third floor. *Ic!*"

Lieutenant Madden and his men all stared at the indicated windows.

"I figured this was goin' to happen, so I stuck around after sending Strohm up to tell what he knows to Lendon," Quinny continued, struggling to subdue an incipient hiccup. "*Ic!* Damn it to hell!"

Madden glanced at Quinny, and moved, no doubt, by compassion, suddenly dealt him a powerful smack between the shoulder blades, practically knocking Quinny right out from under his derby. By a desperate effort, he caught it in midair and restored it to his head.

"You could of busted it!" Quinny complained. "Well, what do you say we go over and round up this mug. I would have, but there are three possibles to get out of that dump—the front and back fire-escapes and the door. I couldn't cover 'em all."

Madden was already striding across the street toward the entrance of the Maryvale annex, with Quinny keeping pace and telling the police officer the building layout. One man was left on the sidewalk to watch the front fire-escape and the others went up to Miss Blake's floor. Here the other detective was detailed to climb out the rear hall window to guard that exit.

As quietly as they could, Quinny and Madden ascended the next flight. After that caution was abandoned. The lieutenant merely threw his weight against the flimsy door and it opened with a crash of splintered wood around the lock.

Anton Decourré had just started to come from the tiny bedroom. As Madden and Quinny pushed into the room, he stood frozen as any bit of statuary he had ever done.

"The sculptor bum!" exclaimed Quinny, who, however, was not surprised. The moccasined sculptor was the most likely bet for someone who could move in silence on the rickety staircase of the Maryvale. "So you're the rat who tried to croak me with a wire noose?"

"I am not a rat, nor have I ever attempted to injure anyone," disclaimed Decourré loftily. "I came here to see Mr. William Strohm, but it seems that he is not in."

"I found this guy in Paula Camp's studio this afternoon, but he got away from me," explained Quinny. "I think he skulled Fenton, too." He elaborated briefly.

"He won't lam out on me," growled Madden. He had drawn his gun before breaking in; now he moved his hand to call attention to the weapon. "Frisk him, Hite."

Quinny did a professional job of it, laying the sculptor's paltry possessions on a table. There wasn't much: a shabby pocketbook, less than a dollar in change, a pocket knife, some odd keys and a crumpled package of cigarettes. There was one thing more, a piece of dark red glass shaped to resemble a precious stone.

"This is somethin'!" Quinny exclaimed, holding the synthetic gem in the palm of his hand while he searched his own coat pocket. He brought out the necklace he had found in the garbage can and fitted the red glass to the setting. It was a perfect fit. "This will get you cooked, fella," he said, looking at Decourré. "This necklace was on the girl's neck when she was murdered."

Anton seemed unimpressed. "Then the owner of this apartment is probably your man," he said. "I found it here."

"Yeah? You didn't know it was a phony piece till you got out with it, then you threw it away. You didn't know it was junk till you pried out the stone and saw it in good light—"

"That isn't right. I didn't find the necklace—only the setting. It was in the toe of one of Strohm's shoes. I would have recognized that necklace as the one Paula made." Decourré sneered at the jewel Quinny held.

"You came here on the prowl for the real necklace then," accused Quinny. "What are you—a sculptor or a sneak-thief? How did you come to think Strohm had the good one?"

Decourré flushed angrily. "I am no thief. I had a right to that necklace. Paula was my woman—had been for years, even before she married Sands. Whatever she had was rightfully mine, just as what I owned was hers."

Quinny laughed contemptuously, Madden joining in.

"What a trade!" commented the lieutenant. "She held out on you, so you hadda bash her head in to get what was yours!"

"I see that I have been judged already," said Decourré, with forced dignity. "So there is no use answering any more questions. My attorney—"

"Your attorney!" Quinny laughed again. "Look here, bum, what made you think you'd find the real necklace here?"

"Because Strohm killed Paula. That should be clear enough. He also wanted the necklace—or the ruby. I naturally suppose he might have hidden it here. After I heard of her death, I searched her studio to make sure it wasn't there—"

"And bopped Rush Fenton when he came to look for it himself. Then hid in that long box when you heard me coming in." Quinny glanced at Madden. "Well, chief, you got plenty to hold this lug on, murder or no murder."

They were interrupted by the tramping of feet on the stairway and in a moment Captain Lendon appeared at the broken-in door, with Bill Strohm behind him.

"What's going on here?" he bellowed, glaring at the group inside.

"We was just getting ready to sit down to pigs' knuckles and beer," said Quinny. The thought brought a new twinge to his queasy stomach. "Come right in."

Bull Lendon was already in, and Strohm, too. In language more colorful than elegant, Madden brought the captain up to date. Lendon listened with growing and impatient interest.

"So, now this lousy flophouse Johnny claims Strohm killed the girl to get the necklace," concluded Madden, with a withering look at Decourré.

"Nuts," retorted Lendon. "I guess this just about cracks the job. Good work, Hite. I was ready to stick you in clink and see that you lost your license for helping Sands beat it. We found a check for twenty-four grand of his made out to Paula Kemp in the room where she was murdered. Where is he?"

"Hell, I don't know. I haven't seen him since he left me in his house," answered Quinny. "You gonna charge this mug with the murder?"

"Not until I round up Sands. But I'm going to hold him."

"I certainly hope you will, Captain," Strohm cut in. "He doesn't seem to have any scruples about assaulting people from behind. I shouldn't feel very safe with him at large."

Quinny glanced at Strohm. "I could feel the same way about you, Strohm," he said. "And I—"

"Stuff!" exclaimed Lendon. "So far as that goes, this is anybody's murder—Sands, Fenton, Strohm or this guy. My job isn't to guess who a killer is, but to get enough evidence for an indictment. Come on, Madden, bring the tramp along—and we'll see what he knows when we get him downtown."

Quinny sat down, moved by a desire to talk further with Bill Strohm and a general disinclination to disturb George's hamburger. The greasy lump of meat seemed distinctly annoyed as it was. Captain Lendon walked out of the apartment, with Madden and Decourré following.

Strohm stood in the middle of the floor, staring at Quinny with manifest hostility. "You said something about suspecting me—"

"Skip it," interrupted Quinny, pressing a hand against his uneasy stomach. "A cop suspects everybody. You get that way. Look, have you got a shot of bicarb' in the joint? I et a hamburger over in George's Place. It's putting up a fight."

Strohm walked into the bathroom and returned a moment later with a glass of water and a package of bicarbonate, handing it to Quinny. The detective shook some of the powder into the glass, swashed it around two or three times and drank it. As he finished it with a shudder, he heard the sound of someone coming up the stairs and turned his head to see who might pass the open hall door.

No one passed. Berte Dill, well-muffled in mink, came into view, stopping in the doorway. She glanced at Quinny, and then her eyes became hostile as she saw Strohm.

"Well," she said cuttingly. "Ladies' man seems to be having fun!"

"I wouldn't call it that," replied Strohm easily. "I didn't expect you here, Berte. I intended calling you, but I've been, ah, busy."

"You're always busy!" she snapped. "As long as there are women, you will be busy chasing after them. I'm through with you, Bill Strohm. It wasn't bad enough to cheat on me, so you had to get yourself mixed up in a nasty murder. All this stuff you've been handing me about your finances being tied up! Phooey! I called up the broker whose letter you showed me. He's never seen a dollar's worth of your securities, never wrote such a letter and can't imagine where you got the letterhead to write it on. You're just a cheap, money-hunting fake, Bill Strohm!"

Strohm's face was composed, but obviously taking a bit of control.

"That's all wrong, Berte," he said quietly. "It can be explained, but I hardly think this is the time for it."

"It's bad enough for me!" The girl fumbled in her bag for something to light the cigarette she had nervously stuck between luscious red lips. "And, by the way, you took my lighter Saturday night. I want it back."

"Of course." Strohm fumbled in his pockets. "It's in another suit. I'll get it for you. The sparking gadget has been lost and I intended having it repaired." He walked into the bedroom and Quinny heard him open the closet.

"Hello, pepperpot," Quinny said feebly. "How's Mama?"

Berte's lips broke into a smile and her eyes lost their frigid hostility.

"As well as can be expected," she said. "Considering she's Mama. Catch your murderer yet?"

"All I'm gonna catch tonight, anyway. Gees!" He pressed his hands against his diaphragm and beads of sweat broke out on his forehead.

Berte Dill came closer, looking anxious.

"What's the matter, Mr. Hite? Are you sick?"

"Like a dog. Like a whole poundful of dogs."

"Better take a bicarbonate."

"I've got one—an' it ain't workin'," said Quinny irascibly. "I think I must be poisoned."

Strohm came from the bedroom, juggling a small silver lighter in the palm of his hand. He stopped and looked at Quinny, whose distress was becoming very obvious.

"Do you have a bad stomach, usually?" he asked.

"I got a damn good stomach," defended Quinny. "But it's sure giving me hell now. I—I guess I better beat it home." He got up, staggered uncertainly, and sat down again. "Gees!"

"Oh, Quinny!"

Berte Dill was on her nyloned knees at the side of his chair, patting his damp forehead with a handkerchief scented for other purposes. Her dark eyes were large with distressed concern. She looked up at Strohm, standing watching them.

"Get a cab, Bill!" she snapped. "He's really sick. Don't stand there looking like a Central Park statue!"

"I'd better call a doctor," Strohm replied, starting for the hall. There was a pay phone on the wall there.

"You get a cab!" shouted Berte Dill, in a tone reminiscent of her mother. "I'm not going to have any cheap neighborhood doctor for him. I'm going to take him home. He's my man!"

CHAPTER SEVEN

Quinny Hite walked out of the smart elegance of the Huntingdon House lobby the next morning with hardly a trace remaining of his distress of the night before. In fact, after Berte Dill's selection in physicians had finished cleaning him out with a stomach pump, he had felt recovered enough to go home. Berte, though, fluttering about in the role of an angel of mercy, firmly vetoed any such idea. Quinny gave in and spent the night in comfort on a down-cushioned couch in the living room, watched over by Berte until sleep overcame her in an over-stuffed chair. He could have done very well without Mama Weber stalking in and out at intervals during the night like Lady Macbeth, though.

He walked briskly south along Madison Avenue until he reached Forty-second Street, where he stopped at the curb for traffic lights to change. Waiting, he caught sight of Lieutenant Madden in a police car, also stopped for the lights, and threaded his way through the jam of cars toward him.

"Hi-ya, Madden!" he greeted. "What's cookin'?"

The lieutenant looked at him curiously. "Did ya just crawl out of that man-hole over there?" he asked caustically. "Guess not— you look too clean."

"What did Bull Lendon do to the sculptor? Get anything out of the bum?"

Madden smiled sourly. "Not a hell of a lot. Some stuff about the Camp girl callin' Sands and demandin' dough. Decorry don't give, when it's something about him. A girl named Dale Worden showed up—friend of Camp's—and said about the same thing. She also told us that the girl was wearin' the phony necklace Sunday afternoon when this Worden dame visited her."

"What does Lendon think?"

"He picks Decorry, but he ain't charging him yet. That guy Fenton didn't go home to Pelham last night like he was supposed to, and we don't know where he did go. This burns Lendon, of course. He's having Strohm in at eleven to do some more explainin'. I'm on my way down to pick him up."

"Maybe I'll pop in at the precinct house, after a while," said Quinny, starting back to the curb as the lights changed. "Tell Bull to keep on tryin'. One of these days he'll bust a murder job all by himself."

Regaining the safety of the sidewalk, he resumed his journey southward, thinking about what Madden had told him. Fenton's disappearance was perhaps explainable in an unwillingness to face his wife, but Quinny believed Fenton an utter fool to try to run out on it. The old lady would probably stand by him.

"A dame might slap her man around plenty, but she don't want nobody else shovin' him," he murmured aloud.

"Who is shoving yuh?" snarled a hard-eyed blonde. She had mistakenly thought he had spoken to her.

"Not you." Quinny colored faintly and altered his course to turn into Thirty-seventh Street, reproaching himself for an old habit of speaking his thoughts aloud when alone and engrossed in a problem.

At the Maryvale, of course, he found that Strohm was out. He'd counted on it for a chance to do the job there which had been interrupted the night before. After examining in considerable detail the contents of the small bedroom and the clothes closet, he went to the bathroom to conduct an experiment which took a little time. Strohm's account of his activities after returning to the apartment at eight had agreed with what Quinny had learned from the woman in the rooms underneath—Miss Blake—but the detective considered additional verification would help.

He came out presently, almost colliding with a short, heavy-set man coming down the stairs.

"You Mr. Whitney—the man who lives on the top floor?" Quinny asked.

The stranger nodded.

"Miss Blake said you told her when you came in last night that the hall light was out. Which one was it?"

"That's right," said Mr. Whitney. "And, if that dope super here don't stop puttin' it out, I am goin' to bust him on the nose. A man might break a leg fallin' down these steps in the dark. It was the one on the floor below this time."

"Show me."

The man turned and walked down several steps and pointed to a light fixture in the ceiling of the second floor hall, operated by a string attached to a pull-chain socket. It contained a single, low-powered light bulb, which, judging from its covering of dust, had been there for some time.

"You're that detective Miss Blake was telling me about, ain't you?" inquired Mr. Whitney. Quinny nodded, still looking at the light bulb. "Well, I wish you luck, but I don't see how Strohm could have been mixed up in the murder. Miss Blake said he was home all that time."

"Could be she's right," said Quinny absently. "I'm just checkin'."

Mr. Whitney went on downstairs, and in a short time the detective followed. He had been intrigued by the possibilities of the light bulb, but it hadn't added much weight to his conclusions. The dust of its surface showed the smudges of fingers, but as it was within easy reaching distance of the stairway, these were to be expected.

Returning to Forty-second Street, Quinny found an unoccupied telephone booth in the Grand Central Terminal arcade and called Cecil Wayman at her office. She declared she had heard nothing from her missing nephew.

"I'm worried almost sick about him," she said. "He's such a fool, to run away like this."

"Have the cops been to see you about him?" asked Quinny.

"No. I don't suppose they know that Morgan has an aunt."

"Don't kid yourself," advised the detective. "If they don't, they damn soon will."

"Do you think so?" Cecil Wayman's voice sounded disturbed. "I've had an idea that Morgan may have gone to Chicago to meet his girl and keep her from coming on until this is over. He's afraid the scandal will upset her mother."

"He could also be afraid it's going to upset him, too," replied Quinny grimly. "I hear that hot seat up the river is plenty upsetting to a guy."

"What's happened?" demanded the woman lawyer quickly. "Has something been discovered to involve Morgan—more than already?"

"The murdered girl was blackmailing him," Quinny answered. "And he's got no alibi at all, and he's lammed. Ain't that enough?"

"The—the damned fool!" exclaimed Cecil Wayman feelingly. "But I insist that it would be physically impossible for Morgan to do a thing like that."

"It would also be pretty near as impossible for Morgan Sands to get out of town without being picked up," said Quinny. "Look, Mrs. Wayman, you are a pretty smart dame. Don't let this job make a fool outta you, too." He hung up and came out of the booth, looking slightly exasperated.

About an hour later, after giving his reconditioned innards a trial with a shot of rye followed by a steak sandwich, in a restaurant several levels above that of George's Place, he returned to Berte Dill's apartment. He walked into the big living room without formality.

"No place like home," he said, then stopped short.

Berte was sitting in the center of the red velvet couch and lounging opposite her in the overstuffed chair was Bill Strohm. Strohm's eyes did not light up with pleasure as he saw Quinny. Neither did Quinny's.

"How're you Hite?" greeted Strohm, with a curt nod.

"And you?" Quinny leaned forward, with an expression of mock anxiety. "I thought you was sitting in on Captain Lendon's investigation."

"I just came from there a few minutes ago—"

"He's been sitting here ten minutes telling me what a wonderful man he is," sneered Berte. "Always misunderstood—all that stuff."

Strohm turned to Berte. "I shan't try any further to convince you just now that everything I've told you about my financial situation is exactly true." He stood up, shooting a glowering glance at Quinny. "But, no matter what it costs me to do so, I will show you proof tomorrow that it isn't your money that interests me. It's you, darling. No matter what you have heard of me—and I've not many friends—I am sincere when I tell you that it's love that makes me want you. Tomorrow I am going to put everything of value that I own on that coffee table and you can then decide whether I've lied to you."

"I could put everything *I* own on that table right now and leave room for a bucket of Mama's spiked beer and half a ham," commented Quinny interestedly. "But that's a good idea, Strohm—put your chips on the table and see what Berte's got in her hand."

"Anybody would think I was the one who wanted to marry for money," Berte cut in caustically. "Nuts! I've already done that. It's why I'm being careful nobody takes me like I did old Gottlieb Dill. All right, Bill, show up tomorrow and bring your bait with you. You better be here, too, because I'm gettin' more than half-hearted about the boy friend here." She beamed softly at Quinny.

"I'll be here." Strohm picked up his hat and strode toward the exit door without so much as a backward glance. Quinny watched his stately retreat, then turned to Berte.

"Didn't mean to bust in on no tater-tate," he apologized.

"You didn't. I wouldn't let him come back tomorrow, except that I'm kind of curious to know if he really has any kind of bankroll. Sit down."

Quinny eased himself onto the red velvet gingerly. The thing was so soft that a man couldn't tell when it was all right to turn loose with his weight. Berte Dill, despite the yielding luxury of the divan, chose to move in close to the detective and lean against him.

"Now, see here, Berte," he said sternly. "You got lots of stuff beside moola—I can say that—but I'm strictly on the hit-and-run. I just ain't your kind of guy—"

"You are too-o," cooed the girl, getting a firm clutch on his arm. "You're my man now."

"I ain't either, I tell you." But Quinny began to realize that his resistance was running out like sand through a knothole. Next thing he would give in and kiss her red mouth—and even Mama Weber wouldn't pry him loose, if he did. "Leggo my arm before I forget I'm a business man, with work to do."

"You don't need to work, Quinny," she murmured. He determinedly shook her off and stood up, looking down at her uncertainly.

"Yes, I do need to work," he countered. "I ain't looking to be no kept guy. See?"

"You're the first man I've known since I married Gottlieb who felt like that." The way she said it made it uncertain whether this was a structural defect in Quinny's character, or a virtue.

"Let's take it easy," recommended the detective. "Or skip it altogether." He leaned over and picked up a cigarette lighter from the coffee table.

"I warn you I don't give up anything I really want without a fight."

"All right. But there's no rush, so far as I'm concerned. And this ain't going to get either one of us anything, unless maybe a piece of crockery on the bean, if Mama sneaks in on us. This the lighter Strohm was going to get fixed for you?"

Berte's eyes rested fleetingly on the bit of silver in Quinny's hand and she nodded. The question seemed to stimulate the desire for a cigarette and she fished one from a long box on the coffee table.

"You needn't worry about Mama," she said, striking a match. After a couple of puffs to get the cigarette going properly, she continued, "Mama doesn't mean it when she throws things."

"Oh, she don't!" exclaimed Quinny. "Just playin', eh? Well, I don't like it, see? A man can't keep his mind on romance with her chuckin' stuff around like that. Look, I'll get this fixed for you."

"You needn't bother. I've others."

Nevertheless, Quinny dropped it in his pocket, then clamped the derby down a little tighter, preparatory to leaving.

"I'm going over to the Sands house," he said. "Something I saw there yesterday has got important all of a sudden."

"Won't there be cops to keep people out?"

"I don't think so. The cops oughta be through working there—and the place can be locked up pretty solid. I got keys."

"I'm going with you, Quinny."

"Nix. You'd only get in the way."

"I want to be in your way all the time from now on," Berte insisted. She hurried toward the bedroom, negligee trailing behind like smoke from a destroyer.

Quinny stopped at the arched entrance to the living room, staring a moment at the bedroom door, then shrugged and went on out. This Berte Dill was a hard girl to talk out of anything, he decided.

A block away from Huntingdon House was another and even more swanky apartment building. Quinny walked in with an air of being quite accustomed to such surroundings and followed a couple of guests into an elevator. It stopped at the third floor to let them out, and, as the car started up again, the operator asked Quinny which floor he wanted.

"The Wayman apartment," he said, frowning. "Darned if I didn't forget the number—"

"Seven D," supplied the attendant briskly.

Quinny got out, tendering a ten-cent tip. It had been worth that to avoid being announced—and, anyhow, Cecil Wayman was presumably in her downtown office at the moment. He stopped and pressed the button at the side of 7-D, then waited with readied foot. He heard footsteps inside Ad the door opened a few inches, to reveal the dusky face of a maid.

"Whutta y' want? Miz Wayman ain't in," the girl shot at him quickly.

"Who said anything about Miz Wayman?" retorted Quinny, shoving his way in. "This is police business."

He walked across the foyer to the living room and looked in. As he had hoped and confidently expected, he saw the startled Morgan Sands sprawling in an easy chair, surrounded by discarded newspapers. His sprawl came to an abrupt end and he leaped up.

"Hite!" he said. "What's happened?"

"You double-crossin' jackass!" snapped Quinny. "Pullin' a sneak like you did left me in a nice spot—and you, too. If you don't want to find out what happens to guys in the back room of a police station, you better snap yourself together and hustle over to see Captain Lendon, at the precinct house. They got a dragnet out for you."

Sands looked sulky, and a little frightened. He said. "I'm paying you well to attend to my interests."

"That's just what I'm doing, kinda," retorted Quinny. "See here, you told me you hadn't seen the Camp girl for years. But you gave her a check for twenty-four grand Sunday night. The cops found it in the room where we found the body. That what you went there for—to snitch it back?"

The color drained from the architect's face and he rubbed the palm of his hand across his forehead.

"I left the check for Paula at the desk of the Quilberon," he said. "What I said was true. I had not seen her since our marriage. She called me on the phone Sunday evening and demanded the money. For that matter, it was due here. My mother did her a dirty trick years ago."

"The Sands family ain't so hot, I gather," commented Quinny. "Except Mrs. Wayman. She's okay, only for trying to hide you out here. Well, you better chase on over and see if you can square yourself with Captain Lendon. He's a tough guy to square, I warn you, but puttin' it off won't help."

Quinny walked to the door, turned there to look back. "If what I figure totes up, I'll be collecting some dough from you tomorrow," he said. "But, if I'm wrong—I'll have to write it off. You can't collect from a guy in the death house."

He went on out, leaving a pale and obviously shaken Morgan Sands standing near the chair he'd abandoned on Quinny's entrance.

It was easily more than a half-mile from where he was to Turtle Bay, but the thought of hailing a cab didn't occur to him. He could use the time needed to walk the distance for some heavy thinking. If his reconstruction of the murder of Paula Camp held together, he was moving in on the kill.

MONDAY BEERHEISTERS had pretty well evacuated the Golden Turtle by the time Quinny Hite arrived at the corner. He toyed with the thought of going in and downing a fast one, but decided against it. For once the business at hand was more interesting. Starting up again, he saw the boy, Pete, running toward him and wildly waving his hands. Quinny stopped and waited till he came up.

"They was a guy in the street a while ago," Pete said breathlessly. "He went down this side till he got to the murder house, n'en he kinda stopped an' looked up at it, n'en he got goin' again till he got to the vacant lot on th' other side of the ironworks."

"Yeah?" commented Quinny, interestedly. "What did he do then, disappear in thin air?"

"Naw—guys kin on'y do that in comics. He squeezed through the fence w'ere there was a board pulled off. I sneaked over and took a gander at 'im through a crack. He wasn't doin' nothin' but pokin' around in th' busted bricks an' stuff left w'en they tore down th' buildin'. He didn' look like no bum, though."

"What did he look like—the truant officer?"

"Naw. He had on a blue suit an' overcoat. Gray hat. Looked like just a ord'nary guy, except he had w'ite tape stuck on his forehead. Like to cover up a sore place."

Quinny crossed an arm across his stomach, rested the other elbow on it and scratched his chin thoughtfully. Rush Fenton might still be wearing a bandage on the injury he had received—and, according to Madden, he had disappeared. Deciding that this news might be of interest to the police lieutenant, he told Pete to keep an eye on the Sands house and retraced his steps to the Golden Turtle to telephone. Before he got his number, though, he had amplified his plans. It was not Madden he got on the phone, but Captain Lendon. Quinny told him that a man who might be Fenton had been seen lurking in the neighborhood.

After Captain Lendon finished a series of explosions that might have been words, ending in a lurid demand that Quinny find and hold the man until the arrival of Madden, Quinny seized the chance to make a suggestion that fitted his own ideas.

"Did Morgan Sands show up there like I told him to?" he asked in preface. He had, Lendon replied, and a damn good thing, too, because—"Hold it," interrupted Quinny impatiently. "How's for loadin' him up with Madden and sending him down here, too. He's got something I'm goin' to need."

Lendon wanted to know what it was, but Quinny was evasive. The homicide chief, exasperated, said he could send Sands with Madden, and Quinny walked out of the Golden Turtle, ignoring the bartender, Gene, and the dusty, bronzed terrapin in the window as well.

Rounding the corner into the crosstown street, Quinny had progressed only a few yards when he heard the staccato tap of high heels behind him and a feminine but throaty hail.

"Quin-nee!"

The detective turned and scowled disapprovingly as Berte Dill came charging up. Considering she had done a fast fifty yards from a parked cab on the other side of First Avenue, she was breathing quite easily, but her eyes were shining like brand new dimes.

"I told you to stay home," admonished Quinny severely. "I can't do my work with a fancy-lookin' jill tagging around after me. What's your idea?" He didn't really want to know and he was anxious to enter the house before Madden showed up with Sands.

Quinny ignored her, turned and strode away toward the Sands house. Berte Dill had to extend herself to catch up, biting her lips wrathfully. The gamin, Pete, still on guard at the curb, watched their approach with eyes bulging like a frog's.

"Keep an eye on the street, Pete," Quinny called, unlocking the grille gate to the basement steps. The boy pressed his face between the bars of the fence and watched them descend instead. This was more interesting.

The basement was in Stygian darkness, but having been there before, Quinny had no trouble locating the stairway. From her excited breathing, Berte was either thrilled or scared. She reached out to grasp Quinny's sleeve, as though to prevent being left behind. Quinny unlocked both doors to the street and then came back to the foot of the stairs, where Berte was waiting. Gruffly telling her to stay where she was, he ascended the stairs in a silence which mildly surprised the girl.

The bedroom door was open, but there was no one in sight. Quinny walked in hesitantly, his gaze darting about and his nose sampling the air. He fancied he detected smoke from recently burned aromatic tobacco. Thin fingers of light filtering through the crescent-shaped holes in the shutters did little to dispel the gloomy interior, but there were no bulky pieces of furniture to afford likely hiding places.

Crossing the room, alert to any sound, Quinny stopped at the mantel to look at the bas relief of General Patton. It had been moved slightly, as indicated by the dusty mantel, but the police might have done that. Otherwise, it had been undisturbed, which seemed to be quite satisfactory to the detective. His head whipped around at a faint rustling behind him, but it was only Berte. She was not one to restrain her curiosity and had come upstairs to the bedroom door to see what was going on.

"I told you to wait downstairs," barked Quinny.

"I didn't say I would," retorted Berte, pouting. "I keep telling you that I've got something I want to tell you—"

Quinny didn't consider the moment felicitous to romantic discussion.

"Keep it," he interrupted, walking heavily back to the door. "There ain't anything here—like I figured to find—so we might as well beat it." His voice raised irritably. "I wish you'd stayed home where you belong."

"If you're speaking to me, you don't have to yell. I can hear all right. I'm glad you've decided to leave. I, for one, do not like it here."

"Well, nobody invited you," Quinny growled. "Be quiet."

"Me be quiet!" scoffed Berte loftily. "How about you? Anybody in the house could hear you."

"That is the idea," he whispered hoarsely.

"It is?" Berte looked up at him curiously. "All right, if you don't want to listen to what I want to tell you, I'll keep my mouth shut."

"I doubt that," commented Quinny, starting down the stairs.

Berte followed in silence, which only endured until they reached the downstairs hall. Then she demanded to know where they were going next. Quinny didn't tell her, and walked back through the hall toward the basement stairway. He kept on past them, through the butler's pantry up at the rear of the house. Berte was right with him, her high and slender heels jabbing deep holes in the soft earth as she walked.

Someone had evidently lowered himself by a piece of salvaged rope to the roof of the two-story extension and then forced open the shutter of the window which overlooked it. A pane had been broken and the window opened. Quinny didn't seem surprised. He sat down on the stone steps and began scrabbling around in the scuffed soil with his fingers. Berte stood close by, watching curiously.

He didn't seem to find much. The empty match folder was still there, and also the tiny wheel he'd thrown away. After examining the folder and seeing that it had been put out by a Third Avenue tavern, he stuck both finds in a vest pocket for later consideration, if needed.

Voices suddenly floated out into the yard from the house, apparently from an upstairs room. Quinny jumped up and strode purposefully toward the garden door, Berte half-running to keep up. She was afraid to speak, although Quinny made no effort to be silent until back in the pantry once more. The voices were more clearly to be heard now.

"You cheap Romeo," a deep voice growled menacingly. "Thought you were going to get away with this, did you?"

The answering voice wasn't intelligible to the pair in the pantry. Quinny started up again, trying ineffectually to discourage Berte by giving her a backward shove. It did no good. She reached the foot of the stairs as quickly as he.

"For the love of Mike," implored the detective, with as much agony as can be put into a whisper, "will you stay here and keep out of the way? Do you want to get me killed?"

"Not especially," snapped Berte.

Her eyes showed sudden fright, nevertheless, and she fell back a step. Quinny left her standing there and ran swiftly and lightly up the carpeted treads. The voices upstairs had become louder, but more confused.

Reaching the top step, he saw Rush Fenton in the bedroom, his back against the rear wall, a bar of iron in his hand, the end of

which had been bent into a hook—the sort of implement used to
open packing cases. He did not see Quinny, but was staring intently at something still beyond the range of Quinny's view. Fenton
looked thoroughly alarmed and his face was flushed with anger. A
couple more steps brought the detective to the partly opened door
and he saw Bill Strohm standing with his back toward the fireplace.
He held a small automatic, menacing Fenton and shouting angrily.

"—didn't need to kill the girl, just to get back the stuff you stole
from your wife. Sure, you knew Paula was giving you a brush-off,
but why couldn't you take it like a man—" Strohm broke off as he
saw Quinny from the corners of his eyes. "Hite!"

"What's going on in here?" demanded Quinny, entering.

"I followed this murderous rat to the house," Strohm began.

Fenton yelled over him, "He did not! He was here when I came in."

"Put the rod away, Strohm," advised Quinny, pretty much in
the tone of offering a cigarette. "Somebody could get hurt."

Strohm's eyes flickered for a second, then he dropped the hand
holding the gun to his side, but made no move to pocket it. Quinny
walked over to Fenton and gently removed the steel bar from his hand,
turning then to the other man, his mind working like a racing engine.

"Neither one of you mugs has any business in this house," he
said sternly. "All either of you wants is the necklace—the real one.
You want it, Strohm, because you gotta show dough to Berte Dill
tomorrow, or bow out. Fenton wants it so he can go home to his
wife. Why don't you two get smart and keep out of this mess?"

"He killed Paula," insisted Strohm, glaring at Fenton.

"You're a damned liar—"

"Oh, cut it!" exclaimed Quinny impatiently. "The cops have got
Morgan Sands in the cooler for that job. Matter of fact, they're
bringing him down here right now to do some checking."

"Sands?" asked Strohm uncertainly. "He did it?"

Quinny grunted, walking away from him toward the door, then
turned to come back, bringing up an arm's length from Strohm.

"He ain't in for passin' counterfeit money," he said grimly.
"Gimme that gun, Strohm, before you do somethin' with it you
hadn't oughta. You got jitters."

"I'm keeping it," snapped Strohm.

"Okay, keep it, then," said Quinny. "Look, do either one of you fellas know where the necklace is?" There was no answer. "Well, I figured that out easy. Why did Paula Camp lug that head of General Patton over here? Why did she put the date 1943 on it, and then pull a boner by sticking four stars on his helmet? That was the tip-off. She made the thing lately and put 1943 on it, so's it would look like an old job. Patton didn't get his fourth star until last winter. Ten to one the necklace is under the head."

"You practically told me that yesterday evening," said Strohm.

Quinny smiled, rather smugly, and glanced fleetingly at the automatic in Strohm's hand, hanging loosely at his side.

"Yeah, I said I thought some paper Sands wanted was there," corrected Quinny. "The cops would be interested in something like that the girl was usin' to blackmail him with—but I don't think that's what it is. This would be a good time, if you guys are through fighting, to find out for sure what she put there when she made the statue. Do you think we could get the head off without bustin' it?"

Strohm turned to look at the bas relief on the mantel shelf behind him—and then it happened. The steel box opener in Quinny's hand swung viciously from the wrist before Strohm was aware of the movement. The heavy bar cracked against the big man's forearm and the automatic fell to the floor. As he completed the stroke, Quinny lunged against Strohm, catching him off-balance, and sent him crashing into the fireplace. Swooping, the detective grabbed the gun and straightened as Strohm began to pick himself up.

"Now that this little matter is fixed up, Strohm," Quinny said harshly, "I don't mind telling you that your goose is cooked. I got evidence no jury can turn down that you killed Paula Camp Sunday night in that bed. You sneaked in here while she was either asleep, or makin' out she was, and hit her across the head with the gag you made out of a piece of hose and brass rod. I found brass filings in the cuffs of the pants you wore Sunday, which got there when you hacksawed the rod downstairs. It was a lousy, sneakin' murder—and you'll pay for it the hard way."

Strohm was back on his feet, his face livid and one hand working convulsively. The other was still numb.

"That is a rotten lie, Hite!" he shouted. "I was nowhere near this house Sunday night. There are witnesses—"

"Nuts!" interrupted Quinny. "You was smart enough to know that a weak alibi sometimes is more convincin' then one which is airtight. But the job you cooked up is no good at all. You went home before eight o'clock, started the water runnin' slow in your bathtub, then tied the drain plug with a piece of string to a corked empty whiskey bottle. The bottle would float till the water got deep enough to pull the plug out—the one in your bathtub don't fit too tight. You had it all figured out how long this would take—maybe twenty minutes or a half hour."

"You are crazy," Strohm said, and his lips tightened.

"That ain't all. You had already put a two-way socket in the ceiling light of the floor below, which turns on and off by pullin' a string. You ran an extension wire from your radio, under the strip of carpet in the hall and down between the stairway and the floor to the two-way socket. Leaving the house, you pulled the string to put out the ceiling light. You knew that Whitney came in regular at nine o'clock—and that the nurses wouldn't be in at tall, on account of they're workin' nights. So Whitney pulls the string and turns on the ceiling light and also started your radio—at nine. You'd been gone nearly an hour by then. You got home a few minutes after ten, tore out of your clothes and then went down to chisel aspirin from Miss Blake. A slick job—but not good enough."

"Ingenious, Hite, but, fortunately for me, not true," said Strohm, having recovered something of his usual urbanity during Quinny's speech. "And even though you could prove that I was not at home—you can't prove I was here Sunday night. Since I was not, there could be no evidence of it. Fingerprints? Remember, I have been in this house often in the last couple of months."

"You were here Sunday night, all right," countered Quinny contemptuously. "And you left signs. Remember the lighter you took from Mrs. Dill last Saturday—the one you said got busted and promised to have fixed? The wheel that sparks the flint was lost out of it—and I found the wheel in the back yard, where you sat down to wait for the coast to clear so's you could make a getaway without being noticed. You hadn't figured on Fenton or anybody popping in. You didn't know Berte Dill came in ten minutes after Paula, did you?"

"How could I, not being here myself?" Strohm's eyes were uneasy, despite his suavity.

Quinny ignored him. "This job had to be done by one of four men—Sands, Decorry, Fenton, or you. It was done by whoever left the murder weapon in the big cement crock in the back yard. No moccasins made them footprints on the pantry floor goin' to the yard, so the sculptor is out. The killer sat for quite a while on the stone bench smoking. Fenton don't smoke, Decorry and Sands smoke cigarettes—and there wasn't any butts on the ground, just matches. A lot of burned matches. Pipe smokers use more matches than they do tobacco. You smoke a pipe."

Strohm's eyes were blinking slowly and his thoughts seemed to be concentrating on something other than Quinny's summing up.

"Another thing. Fenton had never been in this house before and after getting locked out in the back wouldn't have known he could climb back through the window into the room where Sands did his drawin'. It was dark out there, and no light in that room, so he couldn't have seen the shutters wasn't fastened. He's no athlete—I doubt he could have climbed in anyhow. No, Strohm, it was you—and you'll cook for it. I never turned in a murderer before who made me feel so good about it. Usually I'm kinda sorry for 'em."

"You haven't turned me in—yet," grated Strohm. He started to walk past Quinny, who brought up the automatic, pointing it at Strohm's midriff. The red-headed man glanced at it contemptuously. "Go ahead, pull the trigger, Hite. I never carry a loaded weapon."

Quinny wasn't disposed to test the assertion by pulling the trigger. He hated guns. That Strohm was bluffing seemed unlikely, too. The steel bar was more appealing to Quinny as a means to dissuade Strohm from leaving. He swung it back.

"You'll stay right here, Strohm, or have your head cracked open," Quinny threatened earnestly.

He took a step backward to gain room for the swing. As he did so, Strohm's hand shot out like a ball-carrier fending off a tackle. Quinny landed violently against the end of the bed, and before he could regain his balance, Strohm was leaping for the door. Quinny threw the bar at him, and missing, dashed in pursuit. Fenton watched dumbly from his place by the windows.

The bar clanged against the wall and fell to the floor. Strohm almost stopped to snatch it up, but, changing his mind swiftly, kept on. This slight hesitation gave Quinny opportunity to make a flying tackle as the big man reached the head of the stairs. Strohm staggered against the wall, then grabbed the detective in his powerful arms with the intention of throwing him down the stairs. No novice at rough and tumble, Quinny kept his hold on his adversary's legs and heaved upward. In a second, both men were rolling down the steps to the front hall, each savagely clutching the other.

As they reached the bottom, Strohm, heavier and stronger than the detective, twisted to gain the upper position and successfully freed one hand. His fingers closed over Quinny's throat and contracted in a viselike grip. Helpless on his back, Strohm's knee pinning one arm to the floor, Quinny struggled and kicked to free himself, pounding Strohm's face with his free hand. It was a losing fight, with things going black and his ears roaring. With a final vicious shake, Strohm eased the pressure on Quinny's throat and started to get up. He didn't get very far.

A slim figure in a mink coat had darted from the living room and the flat side of a battle-axe came down on the big man's head, accompanied by a wild, hysterical shriek. Strohm grunted and collapsed on the rug. Berte stood over him uncertainly, trying to decide whether another blow was necessary to complete victory. Still debating, she heard the tramp of feet on the steps of the porch outside. Madden and Captain Lendon pushed in, followed by a scared looking Morgan Sands.

"Well, for—" Bull Lendon's amazement choked him off.

Berte dropped to her knees, sat back on her heels, and pulled Quinny's head into her lap, murmuring words that Lendon would not have understood. The detective, however, had not passed out completely, although he was much too occupied in drawing deep gulps of air into his lungs to consider talking.

"They should put a sign over this dump—'Murder House',", cracked Madden. "Who slugged who—and what for?"

"I hit Bill Strohm," said Berte defiantly. "He was trying to choke Quinny."

"That's the kind of girl I always wanted," replied Madden. "One who would keep big lugs from pushin' me around. What started this brawl?"

Quinny cleared his throat and sat up.

"Me," he said succinctly. "Put the cuffs on this guy Strohm. It would be okay with me if this clip Berte gave him with that pick thing had kayo'd him for keeps. The bastard killed Paula Camp."

Rush Fenton appeared at the top of the stairs, looking pale and more haggard then he had when the fight started, which Quinny didn't appreciate, as the Westchester man had kept safely away from the struggle. The group in the reception hall watched him as he slowly descended the stairs.

"You were right, Mr. Hite," he said as he joined them. "I pried the general's head from the base and found Mrs. Fenton's necklace there. I hope I shall be allowed to return it to her."

"I don't know why not," replied Quinny. "It won't be needed as evidence. That's up to Captain Lendon, though. Did you find anything else?"

"Only this." Fenton handed a folded sheet of paper to Quinny.

It was an agreement signed by Margery Sands to provide a trust fund for Paula Kemp. Aside from its dubious legality, it could have small significance now. Quinny handed the paper to Lendon.

"May I go now?" asked Fenton uncertainly.

"Sure, scram," said Lendon contemptuously. "Take the jewelry back to mama—but be ready to produce it if I need it, see."

Fenton went out and Quinny began a ten minutes' recital of the same things he had explained to Strohm after getting possession of the gun. He added some details. Strohm, after getting home with the necklace torn from Paula's throat, had discovered it worthless and next morning had gone to her studio, for which he had taken her keys after the murder. His search for the real jewel had been interrupted by Fenton, with sad results for the latter.

Strohm recovered consciousness during the narration, but made no comment or denial. He sat on the floor, propped against the wall, and dully eyeing the handcuffs securing his wrists.

"After Strohm found out the ruby was phony, he probably stuck it in a shoe, like the sculptor-bum said, and threw the rest of the necklace in the ash can. It was pretty far down in the trash, and I just happened to see it when I picked up the wire Decorry used on me. That mug, after taking the noose off me—I think he figured I was Strohm till he turned on the lights—lammed upstairs, dropping the wire down to the ash can through the space between the stairs and the different floors.

"This louse"—Quinny glared contemptuously at Strohm— "wanted to get rid of Paula Camp and at the same time get dough enough to marry this girl, who has got plenty. He is a big, attractive guy and all covered with flyin' glamour besides—"

"He isn't either," interrupted Berte, with a glare of her own at Strohm. "That's what I've been trying to tell you, Quinny. Cecil Wayman called me right after you left, trying to get in touch with you. She said she had learned from Captain Lingard, who was in the Canadian transport command, too, that Bill Strohm was kicked from the service three days after he joined. They believed he was sabotaging planes. They couldn't quite prove it, but he made no squawk when they threw him out. He was no more war hero than I am."

Captain Lendon nodded, and there was a gleam in his eyes as he looked at Berte Dill that didn't stem from having rounded up a murderer, either.

"Okay," he said, putting the lighter and the striking wheel in his vest pocket. "The rest can come up at the trial. My job is done. Say, Hite, why did you want me to drag Morgan Sands down here?"

Quinny grinned. "On account of I didn't want him wigglin' out of paying me what he promised by claimin' I didn't crack the case. But get me right, Captain, I don't want no publicity—it's bad for private detectives. You and Madden split the glory between you—cops get fat on it."

"You needn't have worried about your money, Hite," said Morgan Sands. "I'm only too happy to pay. Come by my hotel and pick it up."

"And how!" replied Quinny Hite. "This jill you see here is prob'bly goin' to cost me heavy dough. I can see it in her eyes—both of 'em."

"How do you like that!" exclaimed the Potts Crossing princess. "With a bankful of my late husband's dough, I can pay my own way, Quinny Hite. Come on, let's get out of here. The show's over, and I have something personal to say."

They walked toward First Avenue, Berte clinging to the detective's arm possessively.

"What's on your mind?" asked Quinny warily.

"This. Meeting you has given me a good look at myself," the girl returned firmly. "I see now that I don't react to Park Avenue stuff. I'm your kind. We're just a couple of grown-up brats. It's you for me, Quinny, and whether you like it or not, I'm telling the world that you're my man."

Quinny chuckled.

"Yeah, tell the world," he said. "The world can take it. But there's one thing you better figure on doing when you tell your mother."

"What?" demanded Berte Dill.

"Duck," he answered.

SINISTER
STREET

1
LOLA HAD TWIN DAGGERS

WHOEVER, OR WHATEVER, is responsible for the variation in human faces and figures had certainly turned out a stuffy job in Henry Page. His face was quite round and normally pale, punctuated in the center by a wispy black mustache over liverish red lips, and topped off with closely trimmed black hair, parted precisely in the middle. At the moment, he had on a velvet smoking jacket and striped morning trousers, which took nothing away from his air of complacency.

The room had been designed as a library in the old Riverside Drive mansion, put up in the early years of the century by Franklyn Page, Henry's father. Nowadays it was usually referred to by the household as the "study"—particularly by Henry, who'd appropriated it for his private use following the old man's passing. It was spacious, with ceiling-high bookcases forming the walls and poorly lighted by two rose windows.

Henry Page, in his forties, was standing behind an ornately carved mahogany table, set diagonally across a corner, reading a typewritten sheet which he held against the polished wood with a stubby forefinger. A long ivory cigarette holder was held loosely between the fingers of the other hand.

Out in the hall, Arthur, the butler, rapped discreetly, and, on command, entered. "A Mr. Hite is calling," he said stiffly.

"I've been expecting him. Show him in at once." Henry Page dropped the sheet he was studying into a drawer of the table. The ordinarily genteel superiority his manner expressed showed an underlying concern. This discomposure increased noticeably as he

155

looked at Quinny Hite, in the doorway. The detective occasionally had this effect on people.

"How do you do, Mr. Hite?" greeted Page. "I—ah—had expected someone answering to a rather different description."

"Yeah?" Quinny eyed him composedly. "Well, when you phoned, all you said was you wanted a man to crack a burglary job. You didn't say what he had to look like."

Page smiled with attempted affability. "Have a seat, Mr. Hite, while I explain. It was not a conventional housebreaking and robbery which caused me to send for you," he said pompously. "It is, shall I say, a rather extraordinary work of thievery."

Quinny dropped his hips into a deep leather chair near the table. "Call it anything you want, Mr. Page," he said graciously. "It's your cookie, ain't it? If you want me to work on it, give with the details."

A baffled expression came into Henry Page's black eyes. They were like small buttons, set under half-moon eyebrows which had the look of having been painted on. He took a few steps the length of the table, then stopped and stabbed the air toward Quinny with the long cigarette holder. "I find your locution a little difficult," he complained. "Naturally, I suppose, as I've not been thrown among the lower classes."

Quinny's back hair bristled. He wasn't exactly clear about it, but he felt his prospective employer was making with the insult. This crack about the lower classes, now . . . "You don't know your luck," he fumed. "Not bein' thrown in with low-class people. They'd toss you right back. How's for layin' off showing me how big time you are and spilling the dope on this matter?"

Henry Page apologized, his face flushing into something like salmon pink. "I'm sorry, Mr. Hite," he said, "I—ah—was engrossed—"

"Get unengrossed and stay on the beam, if you expect me to handle this job."

"I stand reproved." Henry Page bowed formally and hurried on. "As I've just stated, this isn't an ordinary burglary. You see, Mr. Hite, I happen to be a wealthy man."

"Only a dumb crook picks out a poor guy to rob," commented Quinny. He reflected that the take for his own efforts stacked up higher where his employer was well-heeled, and decided to forget about being touchy.

"I have an expensive hobby," expanded Page.

"Women or horses?"

Page shook his head, frowned a little. "Famous jewels. My collection includes such rare items as the sunburst given Catherine the Great." Henry Page wriggled his eyebrows significantly.

"The great what?"

"Empress of Russia. The sunburst was given her by Joseph the Second of Austria. There are also a pair of jeweled daggers, presented to Lola Montez by Ludwig of Bavaria; and many other pieces of like historical value."

"Any cash-in value? I mean for some bum who don't know about hist'ry."

"Of course, but at a much less figure. The jewel settings alone are worth thousands of dollars. There are, for instance, thirteen rubies set in the hilt of each of the daggers I mentioned."

"Okay. Tell me what happened."

Henry Page jabbed the cigarette holder toward a heavy Gothic door, set in the bookcases to his left. "The next room, there, is where the collection is kept. Night before last—Wednesday—it was broken into and many of the choicest pieces stolen." The man scowled with recollection. "I might add that the thief—or thieves—made his selections with the eye of a connoisseur."

"Picked out the good stuff," interpreted Quinny. "Could be he was tipped off."

"Precisely." Henry Page took a turn up and down the length of the table. "It is a disturbing possibility. Therefore, instead of going to the police, I made inquiry for a good private operator. You were highly recommended."

"Cops can handle jobs like this—they do it all the time," Quinny asserted. The conventional idea that police were inefficient always irritated him, perhaps because he had formerly been one of them.

Still—no sense in talking yourself out of what might be thick dough. "Not that I ain't willing to take it on," he added hastily.

"I daresay the police are quite effective," agreed Page. "However, I wanted a confidential investigation—without publicity. I'll explain my reasons after I've shown you the thief's handiwork." He stepped briskly to the Gothic door and rapped his knuckles against it. "This door is deceptive. It appears to be of solid oak, but actually has a core of drill-proof steel. It cost a pretty penny, I assure you."

"It also did not do no good." Quinny grinned and reluctantly hoisted his bulk up from the comfortable chair.

He came over and watched while Page unlocked the strong-room door and opened it, revealing an oblong chamber containing several flat, glass-topped cases. He followed the man inside, noticing that the door swung back unaided, the lock engaging with a snap. There were three windows, one facing an air well at the side and two at the back. An iron grating had been set in each, but in one of the rear windows this had obviously been cut out with a hacksaw. Only a narrow strip had been left around the edges.

"These cases contained upwards of fifty thousand dollars in historical jewelry—for the most part collected by my late father, Franklyn Page. You may have heard his name." Henry Page's round face went smug again. "He was one of the originators of the chain drugstore idea."

"Nope. Never did. I don't hang around drugstores, much." Quinny leaned over for a closer look into the nearest case. There were still a number of old-fashioned pieces of jewelry in it, but vacant places above descriptive cards indicated some had been removed. "You mean these souvenirs was worth all that moola on account of they had history, or scrapped for a hock-shop?"

"The intrinsic value might—probably would—be something less, but the gems set in them would bring a small fortune—perhaps twenty or thirty thousand." The words rolled unctuously from his tongue.

"What'd'y' mean, small?" demanded Quinny, twisting around, glowering at Page. "Even twenty grand is considered not marbles where I hang out. You had 'em insured, didn't you?" If so, there was going to be strong competition from the insurance dicks.

Henry Page shook his head sadly and twitched his half-moon eyebrows resignedly. "No. With the precautions I have taken, it seemed unnecessary, even if it were possible to insure the jewelry beyond the intrinsic value."

"You should of, anyway. Whatever dough you got would be better'n a kick in the pants."

Henry Page shrugged and walked to the rear window, his strides longer than his short legs were designed to span. "The entry was made through this window, after the grating had been cut from it."

"Yeah-yeah—I see that soon's we came in here." Quinny joined Page for a closer look at the sawed-off edges. Then he moved to the other window to study the frame there. It was composed of about three-quarter-inch iron bars which had been welded together to make a grating, with square apertures through which only an unusually small hand could pass. There was very little space between the grille and the window itself. Quinny returned to the other window, looking out at the yard beyond, a floor below.

There wasn't much of it. A space the width of the property, ten or twelve feet deep to a high wall which had an unbroken layer of dingy snow from the last storm lining the top. A two-foot hedge, also bearing a mantle of snow, extended along the base of the wall. Barred windows in the buildings abutting the Page lot offered no access into the yard. Deciding to go down for a look later, the detective turned back into the room.

"Anybody been in here since the robbery—except you?"

"No one," asserted Page confidently. "As a matter of fact, aside from you, no one knows about it—and the thief, of course."

"Not even Mrs. Page?"

Henry Page pursed his red lips and frowned. "I am—unmarried," he said. "If you refer to my mother, her professional name is Dr. Mary Linden. She has never used either of her married names."

"Why not?" queried the detective indifferently.

"I suppose you'd call it an idiosyncrasy—"

"The hell I would!" Quinny broke in feelingly.

"Mother graduated in medicine and practiced for a year or two as Dr. Mary Linden. When she married my father, Franklyn Page, who—"

"Yeah, I know—ran a drugstore."

"Well, she chose to retain the name she had established, although retiring from the practice of medicine. Later, she married Ernest Bain, but still preserved her identity." Page smiled crisply. "Despite his views on Lucy Stone."

"You mean your stepdaddy was giving this Lucy the eye when he married your mother—?"

"Don't be ridiculous," complained Page wearily. "Lucy Stone was a woman who believed a girl should retain her own name when she married."

"Never heard of her." Quinny shook his head. "Save a girl a lot of bother these days, when they figure they rate a divorce ever' two years. Okay—you and the doc the whole family?"

"No. A sister, Glory Bain—a stepsister, actually. Ernest Bain's daughter."

"Neither one of 'em knows about this robbery, eh?"

"My mother doesn't. I only hope that Glory doesn't, either."

"How come?"

"I'd be worried," answered Page reluctantly. "I've been troubled with the idea that the robbery may have been a result of Glory's careless talk. I wouldn't imagine that knowledge of my collection would ordinarily be found among crooks."

"What makes you think this stepsister might of tipped off some crook?"

"I didn't mean to imply she had done so deliberately," defended Page. "But, you see, Glory is a comparatively young woman—and you know how they chatter."

"I get it. You didn't tell her the junk was stolen. So, if you find out she knows about it, it won't look so good."

"I suppose that's the gist of it." Henry Page brooded a moment. "But, really, I've not the faintest reason to think she knows. I don't know what prompted me to say what I did just now—that I hoped Glory did not know. Perhaps a subconscious dread, without substance in fact."

"Skip it," suggested the detective, but marking down mentally that the idea was worth a look later on. "You cracked about her bein' a loose talker. Where does she do this poppin' off—so's it could be picked up by anybody liable to pull this kind of job?"

Henry Page walked across the room and back before he replied, hands clasped behind him. "Frankly, Hite, Glory has a regrettable flair for night club life. I understand that criminals frequent such places to obtain information useful to their—ah—enterprises."

"You don't bat around the nighteries yourself, I s'pose?" probed Quinny.

"You are correct," nodded Page. "I abhor the places, mixing with all manner of riffraff and suffering vulgar entertainment. Glory, however, does enjoy them."

"How about the old lady—Dr. Linden? Does she okay these kinds of sport for your stepsister?"

"Glory has her own income from my stepfather's estate," explained Page irritably. "Mother doesn't approve, but cannot forbid the girl from doing what she pleases—as long as she doesn't involve us all in scandal."

"What if she did, this last?"

"Mother has the disposition of the bulk of the Bain estate—a very substantial fortune in realty holdings. Whether the threat of disinheritance would influence Glory's attitude toward indiscretion or not, I frankly don't know. She's headstrong, and perhaps sufficiently wealthy to ignore Mother's strict ideas of propriety. That, however, is not a matter of worry to me."

"What is?" prompted Quinny.

"The fear that she may become involved in a scandal of some sort without intending it. It's simply that she seems to enjoy flirting with potentially dangerous situations." Henry Page scowled. "I think enough has been said on this."

"Us old guys like to dish the dirt—just like a couple of dames," laughed the detective. "Okay. This is all the family, eh? How about servants?"

"There are four. Arthur, the butler who let you in. He has been in the family for almost as long as I can remember. His wife takes care of the upstairs, with the help of a girl named Dody—whether it's her given or family name, I really don't know. She's some sort of a cousin of Arthur's, and lives with them—they live elsewhere, by the way. Then there's the downstairs woman—Maura—who also has been with us many years."

"What does this one do—stoke the furnace?" Quinny, still in his overcoat, shivered expressively. "She sure goes easy on the coal. Okay. You say nobody in the house knows about the robbery, so far as you know. You said this room was busted into night before last. Any idea what time?"

"None. I was in Washington on Wednesday and didn't return until yesterday afternoon. Glory attended the theater Wednesday night and, she tells me, got home about two. I assume the burglary took place between six—when she left for dinner at the Orizaba Club—and her return after the theater. Cutting the grille from the window must have been a noisy operation, which she probably would have heard, if at home."

Cutting that grating would have taken a lot of time, too, the detective mused. Not an easy piece of work.

"How about your mother? Was she home?"

"Mother's rooms face the street at the other end of the house, on the floor above this. Since her illness, her suite has been sound-proofed—"

"Anything serious—her bein' sick?" interrupted Quinny, with a show of sympathetic concern.

"Quite serious—an incurable organic trouble. She rarely comes downstairs, and retires early. The sedatives she uses make it very unlikely for her to be disturbed by any noise at this end of the house—together with the soundproofing." Henry Page smiled grimly. "If she'd heard anything, I should certainly have been told. Mother's illness has not made her, well—diffident."

"When was the last time you were in here before you found out you had been robbed?"

"Wednesday morning, just before I left for Washington. Every-thing was in order."

"Then that sets it for Wednesday night," commented Quinny. "I was just wonderin' if it couldn't of been done before. How about the window—did you look at it, then?"

"I closed it tightly when I left. As you see, the catch is an old-fashioned one, and, with the grating removed, easily disengaged with a knife blade."

"Okay. We'll settle for Wednesday night, between six and two." The detective struggled with mental arithmetic and came up with an interval of eight hours. A good man could cut his way into a bank vault and be out of the state in that time, he reflected. But this was no bank vault. "Le's take a close gander at the yard," he suggested. Seeing Page's bewilderment, he interpreted, "I mean, leave us go down there and see what gives."

They returned to the study, Page meticulously trying the jewelry room doorknob, then leading the way to basement stairs which came up at the rear of the hall. Reaching the yard, Quinny poked around, examining the cement surface under the window and squinting up at the building. It was evident that entry into the area could only be made from the basement door, or over the back wall, where he had noticed from the window another similar space behind the building which faced on the other street.

Quinny suddenly frowned. "Where's the piece which was sawed out?" he demanded. "Don't tell me the crooks carried that away, too?"

"No. I brought it back upstairs, after seeing what had happened, and locked it in the study closet. Finding it here would have aroused the curiosity of anyone in the household."

"Where did you find it?"

"There—under the window." Henry Page pointed to a section of the cement. "You can see the marks on the cement where it struck after being dropped."

Quinny eyed the scarred surface, wondering how much racket the falling grille could have made. He straightened up, pulled his derby down over his forehead and stuck his hands deep into his overcoat pocket. It was cold out in the yard, with stray flakes of snow in the air threatening a storm.

"You didn't get back from Washington until yesterday afternoon," he said. "So the sawed-off chunk was here nearly all day. You don't know whether anybody in the house saw it or not. So, you can't be so sure nobody but us knows what happened."

"I'm sure, if anyone of the household had seen it, it would have been mentioned," Page replied, confidently.

It sounded reasonable. "Yeah—most likely," commented the detective. "Le's go back, before our insides freeze." Page, who hadn't bothered to don an overcoat, was willing. They returned to the study, which Quinny had already noted wasn't exactly tropical, but felt warm in comparison with outdoors. Page unlocked a small closet to show the detective the grille. Quinny displayed little interest.

"I've prepared a list of the stolen articles," Page said, going around the table and taking two typewritten sheets from a drawer. "Here's a copy for you."

Quinny ran his gaze over the two carbon copies. It read more like biographical data on some of the more profligate European wastrels of the last century or so. He sat down on the grateful softness of the overstuffed chair for a more thorough reading. Finishing, he folded the sheets and put them in his inner coat pocket. "You said a while ago you wanted this to be confidential," he said. "How confidential did you mean?"

"Completely between us," Henry Page replied promptly. "I don't want a word of it to get out—not even to the family, and particularly my servants."

"Why?" demanded the detective. "That's the hard way—an', besides, makes duck soup out of the job of peddling the stuff. Nobody who might buy the junk will be on the lookout for it."

"As the thief so obviously knew the extrinsic—the museum value—of this 'junk,' as you choose to name it, I have a fancy that in due course it will be offered to me for redemption intact. I don't care to risk frightening the thief into breaking up the pieces for easier disposal of the gems."

"I get it. He might dope out that selling it back to you was a safe play, at that." Quinny's hazel eyes shone with a new appreciation of the man behind the table. He wasn't as big a chowderhead as people might think. "Okay. We'll let it ride like you say. Any ideas where I might pick up a lead on this?"

Henry Page hesitated, his pale skin showing a trace of pink. "I dislike the suggestion I am about to make, Hite, but surely you will understand," he said slowly. He fitted a cigarette to the ivory holder and reached for a desk lighter. "But, of course, I've already mentioned Glory's taste in amusement. She favors two of these night clubs—the Living Room and the Orizaba Club—both on Fifty-second Street off—"

Quinny interrupted impatiently. "Yeah-yeah, I know where they are." Both were upper level nighteries.

"The crowd she consorts with more often gathers at the Living Room, I understand. Lately, she has spoken of a man named Maestring quite often. The fellow seems to be a playwright. Also an actor, James Nailton; and she seems to have developed a friendship with the owner of the Living Room. A man named—"

"Phil Silburn. I know him—kinda."

Quinny was hardly a member of café society in good standing, but had nodding acquaintance with most of the operators of the cocktail lounges in which it disported.

"I'm not saying anything is wrong with these men, mind you," cautioned Page. "But you might make inquiry there. From what I've heard Glory drop, I assume that Maestring—the playwright—hasn't been particularly successful with his writing."

"He'd be one in ten thousand, if he was," commented Quinny. "Well, Mr. Page, I'll see what I can pick up there. Which reminds me—it takes moola to circulate around in them parlors."

"Moola?" Henry Page's eyebrows shot up into more perfect half circles.

"Jack." Quinny lifted a hand and rubbed the tips of his fingers against the ball of his thumb. "You know—green stuff. Dough."

"Oh—you mean money!"

"That's close enough."

"I have planned to pay twenty-five hundred, if the jewelry is recovered intact. Roughly, that's ten per cent of the basic value." Henry Page rubbed his hands together. "For expenses, say a hundred a week."

"Easy to see you never hung around night clubs much," grumbled the detective. "You give out that much to get your hat back. Fifty bucks a day and a week in advance is what it'll take.

Otherwise, I have to spend my own dough nightclubbin', which it would hurt me to do."

Page nodded and got out his wallet. He counted off several bills and shoved them across the satiny surface of the table toward the detective.

"There's three hundred," he said. "I don't mean to spare expense in this matter, so come to me when you've exhausted this. If you are successful, you will save me a considerable sum in redeeming my property—if I have that chance."

"And, if I flop, I don't make." Quinny struggled up from his chair and came to the table, picked up the money and stuffed it into his pants' pocket. "All right. I'll keep in touch."

"Now that business matters are settled, Hite," said Page expansively, coming around from behind the table, "may I suggest we enjoy a drink in the drawing room before you go?"

"If you do, I'll sure say yes." Quinny brightened appreciably. "Not that I am a drinking man, y' understand, but I hear a slug or so is good to keep pneumonia off a guy in this kind of weather."

Page chuckled, his stuffiness diminishing as he took the detective's arm and walked with him toward the study door. "You're quite a fellow, Hite," he said warmly. "Quite."

"That's what my girl tells me," returned Quinny modestly. "And who am I to argue?"

"Ha ha!" Mr. Page sounded suspiciously like the clown in *Il Pagliacci*. "When I've less on my mind, I should enjoy the study of your crisp, pungent speech mannerisms."

Quinny glanced uncertainly at a large frame of pinned-up specimens of butterflies on the wall across from the entrance to Page's study. Am I bein' ribbed by this mug, he pondered, or is he figurin' to pin me on a board like them butterflies? As they reached the foot of the staircase to the upper floors, his thoughts were diverted.

A dark-haired girl coming down had almost reached the bottom step. Reddish-brown eyes, alive with curiosity, flicked from one man to the other.

"Ah, there, Henry. Going out?" Her voice had the low resonance of woodwinds, well played.

"Oh, no. No." Page glanced doubtfully at Quinny, staring at the girl with lively interest. "Ah . . . This is Mr. Hite, Glory. My sister—Miss Bain."

Quinny promptly reached for his hat, tipped it and condescendingly kept it off. "Pleased t' meet you," he said.

Glory Bain was amused. "Don't mention it," she returned, bobbing her head.

"Oh, yes I will! Ever' place I go—except my girl's house." He chuckled with appreciation of his joke. Class she had but plenty! From two yards, you could feel heat waves like at Jones Beach in August.

The girl's high cheekbones and slightly flaring nostrils lent a somewhat Oriental look, augmented by thin eyebrows slanting upward. Liking it, she had skillfully accentuated this with make-up. The cleft in her oval chin alone could pry an unwary gent out of hard-earned dough, Quinny decided. She was older, though, than he had assumed—twenty-four or twenty-five, anyhow.

"Could I use your knife a moment, Henry?" she asked. "I've a loose thread." Page detached a small knife from a gold chain and handed it to her. Occupied with cutting the thread end from a sleeve, she went on, "I'm going out to dinner. Kyle Maestring is reading his play later at his apartment. I shan't be terribly late."

"There will be others there?" queried Page sharply.

"Naturally. Several, including a producer who may be interested. I'd better tell Arthur I shan't be having dinner here. Where is he?"

"Downstairs, I suppose."

The reddish-brown eyes shifted to Quinny. "Nice to have met you," she said in a stylish drawl. She started away toward the back stairway, looking back.

Quinny lifted a deprecating hand and grinned. "Don't mention it."

Page escorted him to the drawing room, where he mixed a rye and soda for Quinny at a portable bar and poured brandy for himself.

"By the way, Hite," he said, "you'll find a telephone number on the list I gave you. It's a private line to my study. It can be used without risk of someone listening on other instruments in the house."

"Okay." Quinny swallowed the first instalment of his drink.

A few minutes later Page went with the detective to the front door to let him out, carrying the brandy glass close to his side at the waist, so far untouched. Quinny had noticed the same pose in movies, but hadn't been impressed. He wasn't now, and suspected his host would funnel the brandy back into the decanter as soon as he was alone.

The detective descended the worn sandstone steps, set between a pair of horrific animals of the same material, pulling his kelly down to shield his eyes from the snow, now driving in thick, feathery flakes. He paused on the sidewalk, peering down Riverside Drive for a cab. Then a voice called from somewhere behind him. It had an unmistakable quality.

"Hello there, Mr. Hite!"

Quinny turned and saw Glory Bain, shrouded in sable, standing outside the grilled basement door. She was pulling on a pair of gloves. She was also smiling winsomely. Quinny hardly noticed the gloves.

"Going my way?" she asked brightly. "Could I drop you somewhere?"

2

THE LIVING ROOM

Quinny Hite grinned affably at Glory Bain through the veil of swirling snow, which was already showing like popcorn on the shoulders and turned-up collar of her sable wrap.

"I been dropped by worse looking dames," he replied. "Lots of 'em." He flashed a glance along the stretch of curb, seeing nothing parked there but the beaten remains of a '29 Ford. No squiffy limousine. "What am I goin' to be dropped out of?" he inquired, nodding at the jalopy. "That?"

"I'm taking the cab I phoned for. There it is now—I hope."

Quinny saw it, too, and moved to the curb to flag it down. As it plowed through a snowdrift to a stop opposite him, the girl came cautiously across the treacherous footing. He opened the door of the cab and helped her in, then followed.

"A gal oughta wear gooloshes in weather like this," he chided.

"I hate 'em." Glory Bain lifted her foot, frowned at the clinging snow, and wiggled it tentatively. The snow stuck. Her smouldering, red-brown eyes turned to the detective with a piquant glint. "You could wipe it off."

Quinny pulled a handkerchief from his overcoat pocket and went to work, admiration for the finely made, tall-heeled sandal mixed with wonderment that even foot-proud women could endure the discomfort of wearing them in blizzard weather. Glory crossed the other foot over for treatment, of course arching the instep for most advantageous display.

"Okay," said Quinny, finishing the assignment. He straightened up, eyeing the foot with the professional detachment of a professional bootblack. "Guess that'll have to do."

"Thanks. That's swell."

The cabby, who had been watching the performance with interest through the glass partition, decided the show was over. "Where to, folks?" he called.

"The Living Room, on Fifty-second," returned Glory.

The cabby knew where it was and the roar of the starting car drowned the rest of her directions. He turned at the next intersection toward West End Avenue. Glory Bain was silent until the cab rounded the corner and headed downtown. Dully conscious of pleasantly pungent perfume, Quinny watched for the building back of the Page residence. It was next to a tall hotel, making it easy to locate. Formerly a single, large dwelling, it had been refaced and remodeled into a four-story apartment. Quinny got a fleeting glimpse of a narrow passage along one side, barred from the street by an ironwork gate.

"Interested in real estate, Mr. Hite—or just looking for a flat to live in?"

"Used to know a girl who lived somewhere along here," replied Quinny, carelessly.

"I didn't really think you were a real estate man," drawled Glory Bain.

Quinny thought that there must be things on West End Avenue more interesting to look at than himself, but his companion ignored them. Huddled in the sable, eyes that contrasted with the fur kept steadily on him.

"What kind of business did you think I was in?" he asked uneasily.

"I don't go for quiz programs. Couldn't you just tell me?"

"Sure," he replied, putting his inventive power to work. "Right now my job is locatin' one of these hist'ry jewelry pieces which was lifted from the Metropolitan Museum."

He hoped she wouldn't be curious about the mythical object. If she were, he was stuck. The only person he could think of in connection with jewels was Queen Isabella, who'd hocked hers to stake Columbus to boat fare. He felt this was pretty far back. But the girl responded with disconcerting promptness.

"What sort of a jewel is it?"

Quinny flashed a saturnine glance at the face peeping out from the dark fur. "Sorry. Can't give on that," he said firmly. "It's confidential."

"Is Henry suspected of having it?"

"Certainly not. He collects this kind of goods, so we figured the thief might try to peddle it to him. I guess he's already loaded up with the stuff—a pile of dough laid out in it already."

Glory Bain laughed disparagingly. "Trash," she said surprisingly. "Paste and brass."

"You mean, his is phonies?" demanded Quinny.

"I wouldn't wear them on an election bet—unless to a Hallowe'en brawl. If they have any real value, it would be only to a museum."

Quinny was mildly shocked. It wasn't the way he'd heard it from Henry Page, and didn't harmonize with the substantial reward offered. Then he wondered if Glory Bain wasn't doing a smooth job of putting something over. Could be. He chuckled.

"Mr. Page would be hurt, if he heard you say that," he said. "He figures his stuff is worth plenty. Well, if not, that's his worry—not ours. Look, is this cocktail sippin' you're headed for strictly a two-party job, or can anybody buy a drink?"

"You can buy me one; I'm going to be early," she replied. "If you do, I'll buy you two."

Quinny shook his head vigorously. "No, you won't. I don't gigolo."

The girl shrugged. "All right, then. You know, I wish I could have listened in while you and Henry were talking. I can just see him looking all bewildered. I doubt that he's ever heard anyone speak as you do."

"Likely, likely," conceded Quinny indifferently. "How about your date? Does he go for third wheels on his bicycle?"

"I'm to meet Jimmie Nailton, the actor. Jimmie doesn't care a hoot how many other men join his party. The more the merrier."

"That way, there's a better chance somebody else will grab the check," retorted the detective cynically. "Him bein' an actor."

"You have a low, commercial mind, Mr. Hite."

"That's how come I have cocktail dough, now an' then."

"Is that boasting—or do I hear a wolf call?" Glory Bain tilted her chin, with a rippling smile and flash of perfect teeth. "Something tells me Little Red Riding Hood better watch out!"

"That's what I tell the dame I find myself goin' with practically steady." He grinned chummily, thinking that giving this girl a chase would be an interesting experience, if he could depend on Berte Dill not finding out about it.

"You're going steady, eh?" quizzed Glory Bain. "Who is the fortunate damozel?"

Quinny frowned, shaking his head reprovingly. "Easy there, my friend," he cautioned. "This Jill I refer to is respectable. Dames can be lucky without bein' called anything like that."

"Damozel? Oh, I'm sorry—a slip of the tongue. I meant, who is the fortunate lady?"

"Okay, then," forgave Quinny, mollified. "Her name is Berte Dill—"

"Why, I know her!" exclaimed his companion. "Lives at Huntingdon House, doesn't she?"

"Yeah. She and her old lady."

Glory Bain stared at him with freshened interest—not that it had shown signs of flagging. "So Berte Dill is the woman who claims you! I thought the Potts Crossing princess picked her males from Park Avenue."

"That was before she met up with me," explained Quinny smugly. "Knowin' a guy like me give her a new idea about Park Avenue clunks. Now she claims I am just the cookie she always woke up dreamin' about, and, the way it looks, I have been taken over."

The cab turned into Fifty-second Street and pulled up at a marquee in front of one of those brownstone hangovers from the 'Eighties, a few of which are still scattered around mid-Manhattan. This one was now a small night club named the Living Room. The idea

had been to attract an exclusive clientele from among café society—exclusive insofar as financial resources were concerned. Phil
Silburn, who operated it, didn't bar anyone whose personality or
fame brought spenders to the place, however.

Paying off the taximan, Quinny walked with the girl into the
foyer, where he surrendered his overcoat and iron hat to a pretty
girl whose smile was designed for later profit. Then they went on
through an arched opening into what had originally been the drawing room of the old mansion, not greatly altered in the conversion
into a cocktail lounge. A wide, red leather seat had been constructed
around the walls, with a row of tables lined up before it, and others inside the horseshoe so formed. Another similar but smaller
room was behind this, having a large fireplace at the back and a
service bar in an alcove at the side.

This fireplace was set in a space a step down from the level of
the rest of the room, railed off and furnished with two love seats.
Words of love too tender for the ears of whoever sat in the other
seat would need to be spoken in an undertone—a contingency seldom of concern to a Fifty-second Street clientele which had other
facilities for romance. But these seats were prized by Living Room
patrons who came only to drink and chatter.

By grace of either the hour or the storm outside, Glory Bain
and Quinny found the love seats unoccupied and moved in. The
warmth from the burning chestnut logs was grateful to both. The
girl wanted a sidecar, but Quinny remained faithful to rye and soda.

"This is okay, eh?" he enthused, rubbing his hands together to
drive out the remaining chill. "Nothin' like a roarin' fire and a
couple o' drinks on a snowy night."

Glory Bain smiled faintly, staring absently at the silver-sandaled feet she had crossed and extended toward the fire. Her mood
seemed to have changed, her eyes were graver than Quinny had
yet seen them.

"And a handsome man with a pretty girl to enjoy it."

"Well, I wouldn't say I measure up," disclaimed Quinny. "But
you sure do."

"I didn't mean you. I . . . was just thinking."

"Um," grunted the detective, let down. "What about?"

"Men."

"I might of known that. Anybody special—or just runnin' over the entries?"

"Just men. All men, and the things they do."

"That sounds to me like a full night's work," Quinny commented. He took a sip of his highball before continuing. "I suppose they been giving you trouble lately."

"Lately?" Glory Bain's laugh was softly explosive. "They began early—when I was about fifteen."

Quinny lifted her drink from the cocktail table and handed it to her. "That would be about five or six years back."

"Nine. I'm twenty-four." She touched the rim of the glass to her lips and sipped a little.

"Yeah? Well, I'm no good at guessin' dames' ages. The ones between twenty and thirty just look young to me. Fifteen, though—that's too young to get tangled up with a guy."

"I didn't get tangled up. But from that time on I had to watch pretty sharply to avoid it." Glory Bain's eyes angled up at him from under sheltering lashes. "Now more than ever. Can you read palms?"

She dropped her hand over Quinny's crossed knee, palm up. He picked it up, admiring its satiny, shell-pink skin.

"I don't see no writin'," he said, putting it back across his knee. "And they don't teach fortunetellin' in policemen's college."

She withdrew the hand. "I wouldn't believe you, anyhow. Fortunetellers are the bunk, aren't they?"

"Yeah—and some kinds have fleas, besides."

"Just the same, I'm worried. I feel a premonition that something terrible is about to happen to me."

"Like gettin' a letter with U. S. Treasury Department up in the corner of the envelope. I know." He sighed and abandoned the light tone as he continued. "What's goin' on? If I could help . . ."

"I don't know." A thin frown marred the smoothness of the girl's forehead and the red-brown eyes brooded morosely.

Quinny hitched around on the love seat to face her, resting his arm on the upper part of the couch and bringing the hand under the back of his head for additional support. Probing curiosity burned in his eyes. "Come clean, baby. You're not worried. You're scared. What of?"

"If I only knew! It's just as I said, a feeling that I'm threatened with something." She recrossed the silver-sandaled feet restlessly. "Something hanging over me like the sword of Damocles."

"Sounds like some Greek."

"Damocles?" Glory shot a glance at him. "The man who had a sword suspended over him by a hair."

"A hell of a way to hang up a sword," criticized Quinny. "But there's got to be somebody—or somethin'—which means you no good, to get you all jittered up like this."

"It's just intuition," Glory reiterated. "And I needed someone I could talk to about it. That's why I was glad you suggested we have a drink together here."

"An' I thought it was my oomph!" Quinny pulled down the corners of his mouth wryly.

He wasn't greatly impressed with intuitive fears, although sensitive enough to the occasional hunches he had. To him, these weren't the same thing—a point he'd debated with both Berte Dill and her mother frequently.

"See here," he went on abruptly, taking down his arm and leaning forward. "Only two things bring on these kind of jitters, Miss Page. One's somethin' you've pulled in the past—maybe somethin' you don't still have in the front of your mind. You can't put a finger on it, but it's floatin' around loose-like in your subconscience . . ."

"I suppose you mean subconscious."

"Yeah-yeah! I always get them two mixed up." Quinny grimaced disconcertedly. "The other is that you've got somethin' you don't want to lose. Maybe if you trace back through all the people you've mixed with close, you'll turn up a face card you can connect with somethin' which is hollerin' in your subconscious now. Best time to work on this is after you go to bed. You can also run over what you've got to lose. This last would take me, personal, about five minutes."

"I think I'll try that, Mr. Hite," Glory said slowly. Her eyes indicated there was more in mind than she wanted to bring out, something to consider under a cover of talk. "Your insight into the workings of the mind would have surprised me a while ago. You might even work up a profitable practice among smart-set women!" She laughed lightly, but without mirth. "If you spoke English."

"Learning the kind you mean wouldn't have left over time enough to figure out how people's brains work," he retorted crossly. "In my business, that's the most important."

The girl didn't comment. She sipped a little of the sidecar, gazing moodily at the cheerful fire, her eyelids drooping. Quinny watched her covertly. She would spill what was eating her, if he let her think it out. He was certain she had been holding something back. He saw her breasts rise and heard the sibilance of a sigh as her head lifted and turned toward him.

"I think I will trust you," she said. "There's—something about you . . . or, maybe it's because I must talk to someone."

"Shoot," Quinny urged. "If you're ridin' a horse you can't handle, I'll help you get off—if I can. And, you can always get me at the Hotel du Nord."

A warm light wavered in the veiled brooding in her red-brown eyes and she smiled tremulously, like a child who has just finished crying.

"You're—somehow reassuring," she said. "Thanks. There have been some queer happenings lately. Strange telephone calls. Five or six weeks ago someone phoned at four in the morning. 'Miss Bain,' the voice said. 'Europe is calling you.' I first thought it was a transatlantic call and got all excited, then realized that the operator would have named a city—not Europe. I asked, 'What do you mean?' The voice said, 'It means you'll be happier the other side of the Atlantic.'" Glory Bain swallowed nervously. "Then whoever it was hung up."

"Sounds like the gags my pals pull when they get playful stinko," commented the detective soberly.

"That's exactly what I thought—then. But, it didn't stop with that. The next time, it was a man's voice—I think disguised. He said, 'Better go, while the going is good,' and disconnected."

"The first time, it was a dame, eh?"

"And the last two. Four calls, altogether, all saying about the same thing—urging me to leave the country." Glory Bain looked at Quinny with bewilderment. "Mr. Hite, believe me, I've done nothing to hurt anyone. Why should someone want me to run away?"

"You're going to be the one which figures that out—after you've done like I said. Take it to bed with you. Is this all which has happened? The phone calls?"

"No. Two weeks ago a message was left for me at Orizaba Club, by someone who isn't known there." The girl picked up a beaded bag and opened it. "I have it here." She searched, a tiny frown gathering as she poked around inside the small bag. She looked up. "It's gone!"

"Maybe you stuck it some place else—or lost it."

"No. It was in this bag when I dressed to come downtown. I haven't opened it since. Oh, but I did! I've come away with Henry's knife." Her lips twitched with anxiety. "But, I couldn't have dropped it then."

Quinny wasn't convinced, but let it go at that. A woman might open her bag a half dozen times and not remember anything about it. She had probably dropped the note in her room, if not while stowing the knife away.

"Do you remember what it said? I mean exactly?"

"I certainly do. 'Be stubborn and lose everything. Europe is calling, but there's room for you in Woodlawn, if you must have it.'

It was Quinny's turn to frown, and he did. This was a definite threat. "No name on it, of course," he said. "What kind of writin' an' paper?"

"It was printed in lead pencil—like children do who don't write well. The paper was plain white, with the top torn off, as though it had been written on a letterhead. There was a watermark—part of one, I mean. Three letters—'OGA.'"

"Sounds like somethin' from Washin'ton." Quinny's lips pursed thoughtfully. He would have liked very much to clamp on the derby, to facilitate his thinking, but that baby-faced checkroom hussy had it. "Well, even if you don't find it, that's something to go on," he said. "Did you show it to anybody?"

"No. I was afraid."

"Why? I should of thought you would—to the doc. Or Henry Page."

"Oh, I couldn't worry Dr. Linden. She's ill, you know—and this might still be someone's grotesque idea of humor. As for Henry . . ." The girl managed a disdainful laugh. "What good would that have done? You've met him. He's a dear in some ways, but hardly a person to be any help in this sort of thing."

"That the only reason you didn't go to him?" prodded the detective.

"Not . . . altogether. Henry and I don't see eye to eye in a good many things. He'd immediately decide I'd got mixed up in some sort of scandal. He worries about that, anyhow."

"On account of you likin' night club hoppin' and him not?"

The girl met his questioning scrutiny curiously. "I suppose you mean that Henry doesn't care for that sort of fun. That's wrong. He would—but he can't afford it."

Quinny shrugged. "He talks like a man who has night club dough, if he wanted to spend it that way."

Glory Bain laughed softly. "It isn't that. Henry really doesn't have as much money as he would like, but that isn't the reason. He's afraid of Dr. Linden. He got into a mess with a night club entertainer a few years ago and he's still on his mother's blacklist. You see, she controls the family fortune and, if Henry doesn't watch out, he won't get any of the estate when she passes on. Another affair like the other and he would probably lose his soft job as manager of her real estate."

"How about you?"

"I probably should lose out, too, if I succeeded in getting notorious. Dr. Linden doesn't take the modern view toward that sort of thing, you know." The girl shook her head emphatically. "My, no! But it wouldn't make so much difference to me. You see, when my daddy died, he left me more than a comfortable income, aside from the main bequest—left to the discretion of Dr. Linden."

"So you can kick up your heels all you want, without bein' left holdin' a empty bag." Quinny wagged his head, thinking that this was as nice a spot to be in as anyone could want. "How about Mr. Page—didn't the old man hand him a cut, like he did you?"

"You forget that Henry and I hadn't the same parents."

"That's right, you didn't. So he didn't rate for somethin' separate—on'y if the doc cuts him in when she conks out. I mean, like you said—passes on." Quinny smiled apologetically. "I forget I'm talkin' to a high caliber doll. And how I do it, sittin' here looking right at you, I don't know. Well, that's all cleared up and now I see it's not any of my business, anyway. Interestin', though."

"How did we ever get off onto that?" Glory's tiny frown returned fleetingly. "Oh, we were speaking of things Henry and I didn't agree on."

"Yeah-yeah! Look, I gotta hunch that I maybe better look over this dame Henry was married to. Or did he marry the gal?"

"Yes, but I don't see what she could have had to do with the telephone messages—or the written one. Henry is divorced from her, anyway. What could she gain by frightening me this way? I've never even seen her."

"You got me there, Miss Bain," admitted Quinny reluctantly. "But you can never tell about dames. They get sore about somethin' an' they don't care who they hurt—or whether it does 'em any good or not."

"Julia Page wouldn't bother. I've more than a suspicion that Henry sees that she is provided for, besides what he gave her at the time they separated. I'm sure he's still rather infatuated. He doesn't let go of an idea easily, and doesn't seem interested in other women."

"Just the same, I'd like a gander at this dame," said Quinny insistently. "I never pass up anything because it don't look promisin' and there just could be something come out of this angle. Any idea where I might locate this Julia Page?"

Glory shook her head. "Not the slightest. And I'm sure it would be a waste of time."

"Like I said, I wouldn't get anywhere, if I only picked out sure-thing leads. Don't worry about it, but if you happen to find out where she lives, or anything, phone me at the du Nord."

"I will," she said, without enthusiasm. "I don't suppose he'd know, but you might ask Phil Silburn while you're here. I think he knew her. He seems to know nearly everyone in his business."

"Okay—I'll do that." Quinny slumped down further on his spine. "You know somethin'?"

"What?" Glory Bain's eyes swept around to him, enlarging as though she expected something surprising.

"You're a honey," he replied, grinning. He was trying to divert her mind from the things they had been talking over for the last half hour. "You sure would go good with my mornin' toast."

The girl laughed, now with a touch of music. "You will say that once too often one of these days, Mr. Hite," she said. "You'll look over the top of your *Times* some morning and discover some girl has taken you seriously. Perhaps a dashing little widow named Berte Dill."

Quinny chuckled. "In that case, it'll be *Racing Form* I look over—an' what I see will likely be Berte Dill's old lady. Berte don't get up mornings." On second thought, he added hurriedly, "I hear."

Glory Bain looked back at something in the room beyond the railing. "I wonder if Berte would appreciate your saying such nice things to another woman?" she murmured.

"She would not." Quinny was sure on this point.

"Well, she's just this minute come in—with a man who looks as though he expects to be paid for his time."

Quinny wasted no time switching around for a look. Glory Bain wasn't kidding. Coming into the room behind the headwaiter, he saw Berte and a dinner-jacketed barracuda who wore the drawn expression commonly the result of irregular eating habits. They were headed for the fireplace nook.

Quinny got up. "Excuse me a minute," he said, moving out belligerently to intercept the approaching couple.

"Nice going!" exclaimed Berte as he came up. "All afternoon, I've been calling you—and now I find you having a chummy little fireside chat with another girl—"

"Okay, okay!" Quinny broke in. "So what? I'm a businessman—like you been insistin' on the last two months. I'm 'tendin' strictly to business—workin' on a matter—and here you come rompin' in with this hired Toto, all set for a big evenin' at maybe fifty bucks a throw." He turned wrathful eyes on the Sinatra-thin specimen slightly behind Berte. "Lam, you!" he finished.

The gentleman lammed. It was a situation he had met before.

"You know this jill, Glory Bain, Berte," said Quinny, his fire abating. "I took on a job this afternoon—from her brother. Right now I'm probin' possibilities—an' gettin' nowhere fast. If you don't think so—come on back with me. Remember, luscious, you gotta act like a lady. No makin' cracks at Miss Bain, see?"

"Me? I'm always a lady," declared Berte meekly. She added in a murmur, "But not always wanting to be."

"Well, come on."

Quinny seized her arm and walked her into the nook, watched by Glory Bain with badly hidden amusement.

"Hel-*lo*, Berte!" the girl greeted. "So-o glad to see you."

Quinny grinned, feeling he had done a smooth job handling the situation. Berte sat down beside Glory on the love seat and Quinny violated the decorum of the Living Room by bringing a gilt chair over the top of the railing for himself. A waiter scowled, but might as well have saved it.

"Nice to see you, Glory," said Berte, not meaning a syllable of it.

Glory Bain thought she'd better add an explanation. "I found your man on the sidewalk in front of my house. He very kindly offered to bring me here."

"He very often kindly does things like that," responded Berte, glancing darkly at Quinny.

This misinterpretation of his knight-errantry needed a bit of correction.

"I was waitin' for one of them Saint Bernard dogs," he said.

3

THE STRIPPER

QUINNY HITE, SITTING FACING Glory Bain and Berte Dill with his back to the agreeable warmth of the fireplace, saw the headwaiter crossing the rear dining room toward them, escorting a sallow-faced, dark-haired man in a brown suit that needed a bit of pressing. He carried a thick bundle of paper under his arm. Soft, dark eyes, with disproportionate whites, lighted up as the newcomer saw the group in the fireplace nook.

"Here comes your date," Quinny said, glancing at Glory. She turned to look. "It's Kyle Maestring," she said. "He seems to have brought his play along."

The playwright came down into the nook, smiling with cultured urbanity. Glory made introductions, but neither Berte or Quinny seemed to rate more than casual nods of acknowledgment.

"Am I late, Glory?" he asked, with synthetic concern. "My watch is at my jeweler's."

I lay good odds his jeweler's got the three-ball sign hangin' over the front of his store, mused the detective.

"No, Kyle. It's that I got here early. We're to have dinner with Phil Silburn and Jimmie, then go on to your apartment for the reading," explained Glory Bain. She sent an exploring glance back into the dining rooms. "I haven't seen Phil yet, or Jimmie either."

"Nailton should be along soon." Maestring looked at Quinny and Berte coolly, as if seeking a reason for their presence. "I shan't be able to take dinner with you," he added reluctantly. "I'm to pick up Leverring and bring him to the apartment. Jimmie has my key to the apartment, so he can take you over after dinner."

"Your reading is set for nine o'clock," demurred the girl. "I could stay here with Jimmie Nailton until then."

Maestring frowned. "Nine? I thought it was eight. I never seem to keep time straight." He thought a moment, then spoke again. "That leaves me in a predicament. I've invited some others to be there at eight. Would you mind going there with Jimmie, to let them in? With Leverring to contend with, I might not be able to make it."

"Perhaps Phil will be able to get away and come with us," said Glory. It was evident that she did not relish the thought of going to an apartment alone with the actor.

"Yes, of course." Maestring brightened. "You know, if there were something for me to sit on, I could stay for a drink or so. Couldn't we move to a table in one of the other rooms?"

The actor, Jimmie Nailton, joined them shortly after they'd got settled at a round table in the center of the room. He was a tall, rather slight man, with light, wavy hair and pale-blue eyes. Quinny had seen dozens of men just like him in Times Square theatrical centers. The type seemed irresistibly drawn to the stage.

Kyle Maestring launched into the subject which was nearest his heart—the play.

"I've made an important change in the second act, Glory," he said. "Instead of having Andolev coming to the tower room unaware of Perdita's treachery, he has become suspicious of it. The act now ends with his entrance, heart filled with vengeance and his sword drawn. Perdita is standing at the window, but Preme is nowhere in sight."

"Prob'ly in the bathroom," suggested Quinny helpfully.

Maestring glared. "The scene, my friend, is laid in a medieval castle in the Maritime Alps," he said loftily. "In 1634, there were no bathrooms."

"No?" Quinny considered this serious architectural oversight. "Well, there had to be someplace, didn't they?"

Maestring glowered. "It would be an appreciated courtesy if you saved your comments until I've finished," he said crisply.

"In which case, me and Berte ought to bow out," retorted the detective. "Fellas which write plays can go on about 'em for hours, so long as somebody else is buyin' drinks. Personally, I go for shows when they're done on the stage—not in a barroom."

Maestring flushed and got to his feet. "I'm sure you could be excused," he snapped.

Quinny grinned, undisturbed. One of the best devices for getting the real low-down on anybody was to prod him into getting mad. There could be stuff he would like to know about the playwright—and Jimmie Nailton, too. Or anyone else among Glory Bain's intimates.

"Oh, sit down, Mr. Maestring," he said. "I was kidding."

Maestring slowly resumed his seat, looking at Glory as if for an inkling of her reaction. She seemed not to be listening, her head bowed and a long, pointed fingernail creasing a design into the tablecloth. Nailton, though, seemed quite interested in the verbal exchange between the playwright and the detective.

"I'm afraid I must agree with Mr. Hite, Kyle," he said gravely. "After all, don't you think we should wait until after the reading tonight to go into the revisions? It isn't constructive to discuss the changes piecemeal."

Nailton, Quinny saw, was a smoother individual—a man who would always try to steer a conversation into untroubled waters.

"I think Berte and me oughta leave you people fight it out," said Quinny. "I'm no expert on this stuff. The on'y time I go to a play is when it's for free, anyhow."

"What's your line?" queried Nailton, glad to get the conversation off onto something possibly less contentious.

"He's a detective," Berte put in brightly. "Couldn't you tell? A cop wearing a ballet skirt would still look like one."

"Okay-okay!" exclaimed Quinny, furious. "So I'm a detective! Anything wrong about that?"

"Not if you're like those I read about in mystery books." Nailton smiled graciously. "Are you working on something interesting now?"

"Mr. Hite is working on the theft of a historical jewel from the Metropolitan collection. He came to see my brother, who is interested in similar pieces." Glory turned her warm but faintly skeptical eyes on Quinny.

"All I need is to get what I'm doin' on the front page of *The Times* now to gum the works right," growled the detective. "In my racket, ever'body ain't supposed to know what I'm doing."

"Oh, I'm sorry!" Glory exclaimed contritely.

"I shouldn't suppose that Henry Page would be interested in stolen goods," commented Maestring sourly. "Hardly that sort of man, I should say."

"He could be plenty interested," denied Quinny. "And I don't mean buyin' anything hot, either."

"Then what do you mean?" asked Maestring superciliously. "Or, do you intend being ambiguous?"

"A guy which collects fiddles is interested in fiddles. Is that easy enough for you?" There was a hint of contempt in Quinny's bland look, to match Maestring's expression. "He could give me a steer to other collectors."

Maestring flushed. "You could have said in the first place that Henry Page would be interested in historical jewelry, per se."

"My front name is Quin," corrected the detective coldly. "You go around callin' fellas Percy and you prob'bly'll wind up back of a sore nose. Did you ever get a look at Mr. Page's stuff?"

Maestring shook his head, glancing at Glory Bain. He chuckled. "No. I'm not on Mr. Page's social calendar. As a matter of fact, we've not met."

Glory cut in. "Henry doesn't very often show his collection to anyone except other collectors. Did he show it to you?"

Quinny shrugged. "Why should he? I'm only interested in collectin' this piece which was snitched at the Metropolitan."

Berte Dill started to say something, but changed her mind. A trifle belatedly, the thought struck her that it might be smart to stop talking until she had some idea what this was all about.

Maestring got up out of his chair. "I'll have to run along," he said, smiling apologetically at Glory Bain. "Sorry to leave such charming company, but I mustn't risk missing Sol Leverring. I'll see you at the apartment."

"We're leavin', too," said Quinny, with a sharp glance at Berte, designed to check any objection. He brought out the money Henry Page had paid him and stripped off a five-dollar bill. "Here, Nailton, take care of my part of the check out of this. That oughta cover it."

Berte Dill got up obediently, curiosity about this unexplained enterprise of Quinny's gnawing insistently. Maestring and the detective stopped to reclaim their hats and coats from the checkroom chick, then the trio moved out to the sidewalk. It was still snowing heavily.

"Where you goin' to pick up Leverring, Maestring?" asked Quinny. "Maybe we could drop you off—if we're lucky enough to get a cab. What a night!"

"At the theater," replied Maestring. He shivered involuntarily. The topcoat he was wearing hadn't been intended for this sort of weather. "I don't mind walking."

"Well, I would. This stuff's gettin' deep." Quinny frowned at the snow accumulating on the sidewalk on each side of the marquee.

"There comes a cab!" shrilled Berte. "Oh, goody, it's someone coming to the Living Room."

A yellow taxi lunged through the snow piled in the gutter and stopped at the marquee. A couple got out and the trio climbed in.

"Haymarket Theater," Maestring called to the taximan.

"An' keep your flag down," supplemented Quinny. "We ain't all gettin' out there."

The Haymarket was one of the oldest theaters north of Forty-second Street and had borne a succession of names. Sol Leverring, the present lessee, had offices upstairs over the lobby.

"Thanks, old man," said Maestring, getting out before the Haymarket entrance. "Sorry, if I appeared sharp with you a while ago."

Quinny lifted a hand magnanimously. "No hard feelin's," he said. "Give an' take keeps Jack from bein' a dull boy. Be seein' you."

"You've been reading books again," said Berte accusingly. "But, that isn't the way it goes. 'All work and no play keeps your bookies in hay.'"

"Well, the lugs gotta eat, don't they?" defended Quinny. He was watching Maestring. The playwright hadn't gone into the theater lobby, but had stopped on the sidewalk to talk to a woman. As Quinny watched, Maestring took her arm and started down Broadway. "Which reminds me," he continued, "we oughta put on the feed bag ourselves. Go around to the Hotel Maywood, on Fiftieth, driver."

"We're not having dinner in Times Square, are we?" objected the girl. "There isn't a decent restaurant in this neighborhood."

Quinny eyed her reproachfully. "Look, sugarfoot, in Times Square you can do anything you can anywhere in New York—except ride a roller coaster. They'll put one of them up, any day now. If you want to eat little or eat big, carry your own or get waited on, there's both kinds of places. We can put it on big—I'm packin' a bundle of expense dough. I guess the best place is Johnny Broad's Steak House." He thought for a minute. "Yeah, soon's I stop at the Maywood to see a fella."

"Make it snappy," grumbled Berte. "I'm hungry. Broad's better be good, too."

"Only the best people go there," assured Quinny. "But they'll let us in, all right. Hold the cab when we get to the hotel."

Arriving at the Maywood, Berte admonished him again to hurry back. "This neighborhood doesn't smell nice," she complained.

Quinny eased out of the cab onto the sidewalk. "Yeah-yeah!" he chuckled, looking back at the girl. "And, besides bein' stinky, it's no good for getting chummy with strange lugs which wants to make with talk. You could kinda pull your dress down, too, before you start gettin' pneumonia in the gams."

He entered the hotel lobby, ignoring the clerk to pass on to the elevator. The clerk also ignored him. A dwarf usually ran the car in daytime, but he was nowhere in sight. As Quinny stopped before the cage, a man came from the basement stairway. He opened the door and the detective followed him in. The fellow's weaving stance at the controls indicated there was a bar downstairs. The car started with a jerk.

"Take it easy, fella!" cautioned Quinny. "Fourth."

"Fort'," affirmed the operator. The elevator came to a clanking stop. "All out for de Fort'—acrobats, dog acts, burlesque dolls—an' 'cessories. Urrp!"

"Hold it!" admonished Quinny, deciding he'd walk down when he left.

He went up the hallway toward the front of the building, wrinkling his nose at the odor of stewing cabbage. There were signs posted in the rooms forbidding culinary operations, but it was probably too much to expect that all Maywood guests knew how to read. At the door of 400, he stopped and rapped smartly on the panel.

The inmate of the room seemed not eager for company. It was some moments before the detective heard the drag of slippers on the carpet inside. Then the door opened as far as it could without removing the chain. A round, florid face appeared in the slit. "What d'you want?"

"'Lo, Abe," greeted Quinny. "I ain't collectin', or servin' processes, or tryin' to sell subscriptions to put me in college. Open up."

Munch unfastened the chain and Quinny went in. This was a fairly large room, overlooking the street—the parlor of a suite in the hotel's palmier days. It had been furnished with whatever was at hand—a mission table, one soiled purple upholstered chair, a pair of maple straight ones and a wooden bed with a pomegranate design machine-carved on the towering headboard.

Abe Munch was a theatrical agent who at one time had taken his 10 per cent from a considerable list of high-grade flesh. His best stars had either disintegrated with time or ditched him for the longer grass of Hollywood. And Quinny Hite, at Berte Dill's urging for a better front than provided by the old du Nord, now had Munch's impressive suite of offices in Times Square on a sub-lease which permitted the agent to use it occasionally.

"Cozy little joint," enthused Quinny, looking around. He sniffed indelicately at the musty atmosphere, suffused with the odor of insecticide. "You oughta be careful about lettin' in all this fresh air, though. Anybody knows it ain't healthy."

Munch sat down on the purple chair and ran his fingers through what was left of his hair. It was mostly a memory. "I suppose you've moved to the Waldorf," he sneered.

Quinny ignored it. "Look, Abe, I'm tryin' to pick up information about a couple of guys. One of 'em's an actor. The other writes plays, but I never heard of him. I figure you'll know about these mugs, if anybody does. The actor is Jimmie Nailton."

"That one I know. He's been in dozens of shows the last ten years, but I don't think he ever had more'n a ten-side part in his life. Works cheap—or don't work." Munch grinned reminiscently. "I've spotted Jimmie in a couple of turkeys. Nice fella—lousy actor."

"Where does he live?"

"Right across the hall. Him and his missus. She's got looks—an' I guess she dopes it out that if she's goin' to cash in on 'em, she'd better take a waiver on Jimmie."

"Yeah?" commented the detective, without much interest. "Then, there's this other fella—the playwritin' guy. Kyle Maestring. Know him?"

After some hesitation, Munch shook his head. "Couldn't of had anything done on Broadway, or I would of," he said. He picked up a half-smoked cigarette from an ash tray and lit it. "A hundred fellows write plays to one that gets produced, you know."

"More'n that, probably. Maestring's reading his opera to Sol Leverring tonight, though."

"Nuts, Quinny. Leverring's in Boston."

"You sure about that?"

"Natch'. Left this morning with a play doctor—Conlon—to fix up *Pearl River*. That Chinese thing. I tried to sell him Wu Su Tu for the piece." Munch scowled. "No dice—the cheapskate!"

Quinny speculated silently on Maestring's reasons for lying about the appointment. The guy might just have been putting on an act to impress Glory Bain, of course.

"What's this fella Nailton live on when he ain't workin'?"

"Like anybody else, he chisels. When a man is broke, he has to chisel." There was a defensive tone in Munch's voice.

"Would he go for a piece of easy dough an' no questions?"

"If you mean, would Jimmie sit in on a hot deal, I wouldn't know." Munch shook his head. "When a man gets hungry, you can't tell what he'll do. So far's I know, Nailton is on the up and up. He probably would take on a piece of gigoloing, if he could get the work—and, brother, so would I, only women don't go for fat slobs who can get a haircut without taking off the hat. Show business is terrible. Yes, and ten more years of the kind of government we're getting . . ."

Abe Munch, expressing his convictions concerning the administration, wasn't to be stopped. After listening for a couple of minutes, Quinny walked out, leaving the agent somewhere between OPA and the Wagner Act.

As he closed the door behind him, he saw a nicely filled-out specimen of womanhood, with dark eyes and hair and a rose-petal mouth, about to open the door opposite. Quinny halted, looking her over curiously. If this was Nailton's little helpmate, she was, as Munch had pronounced, a looker. The girl leaned against the door jamb and returned his gaze, unabashed.

"Well?" she queried.

"Hi, babe!" Quinny grinned pleasantly. "That you, cookin' cabbage? What's the matter—your company ain't showed up yet?"

The woman wrinkled her nose distastefully. "Not my cabbage," she said, looking resentfully at the detective. "What are you, the house dick?"

Quinny was amused at the idea of a small, careless hotel like the Maywood bothering to employ a house detective.

"Sure," he said. He moved his head to one side as though to see past the woman into her room.

"Well, you won't find anyone in my room," she asserted brashly. "Except Minsky."

"Minsky?"

"And Gypsy Rose Lee."

"It's gettin' crowded. When's the first show go on?"

"Don't undo your necktie—Minsky and Gyp are my two kittens. Brother and sister—but I'm beginning to suspect that doesn't mean much to cats. Couldn't use a kitten, could you, mister?"

"It's all I need. Put me down for one." He paused as she shifted her pose, red silk pajamas slithering over her figure distractingly. "What's your racket, cat girl?"

"I'm Nana Lester—said to be an actress. You'd say stripper."

"Burlesque, eh?" This didn't sound as though she were Nailton's wife. "How long've you been livin' in this bug-trap?"

"Ages. Three weeks."

"Workin'?"

"Not this week. Come up to Bridgeport next week, if you want a good look. The Gaiety. You'll see all of me then." She laughed shortly. "Practically," she added.

"I'm lookin' forward to it already. Look, I was kidding when I said I was the house dick. They don't even have one in this joint."

"I know." She smiled crisply. "I can see that you're big-time."

"I was in seein' Abe Munch—about a matter. He said it was a married dame lived in this room, named . . ." Quinny scowled as though trying to remember.

"Sure, I'm married, but not for long. Don't let that stop you." She turned back into the room. "I'll see you in Bridgeport, yes? Bring your Cadillac and we'll drive back." The door closed on her derisive laugh.

Quinny hustled toward the iron stairway, reflecting that any change in Jimmie Nailton's marital status couldn't help being an improvement. Nana Lester clearly had her sights on personal advantage.

About to start down, he saw a door further along the hall open. A heavy-set man, lantern-jawed, and with close-set dark eyes, appeared. He took a couple of steps and then retreated into the room.

"So, that's why Phil Silburn wasn't at the Livin' Room, like Miss Bain thought he would be," chuckled Quinny, clumping down the steps. "I'm bettin' a doughnut the guy's been a-dallyin'!"

4

BEYOND THE SCREEN

GLORY BAIN SAT IN A DEEP, yielding chair, pulling off her gloves and
looking curiously around the large living room. She hadn't removed
the enveloping sable coat. For one reason, the room was not particularly warm; the other—well, she was alone in the apartment
with Jimmie Nailton. It would seem better, she thought, to pre-
serve the appearance of having just come in when the other guests
arrived. Some of those invited to the reading of Kyle Maestring's
play should be arriving any minute. The gloves removed and laid
beside her bag on a table at the side of the chair, she glanced at
her wrist watch to see the time. It lacked several minutes of eight.

She heard Jimmie whistling in the kitchenette, off the short
hall between the living room and the rest of the apartment. This
would be a bedroom, she thought, but a black, silver-traced screen
across the opening at that end barred the view from where Glory
sat. The refrigerator door slammed and she heard the clatter of ice
trays in the sink. Jimmie was preparing for the party.

Glory recoiled at the thought of a highball. Tea, or something
else hot, would have been more attractive. She wondered if the chill
in her fingers and feet might not merely be another token of the
uneasy dread which had been troubling her. Recollection of the
detective's advice to take her forebodings to bed and think them
out flitted across her mind. The suggestion had been sound, she
thought, but would it be that simple? She wondered if he had
really believed what she had told him about strange messages.
Mr. Hite, she decided, kept his true reactions effectively screened

192

behind apparently bland candor. She sensed, rather than saw, shrewd appraisal in his casual eyes. Nevertheless, he gave her a warming impression of dependability.

The reddish-brown eyes resumed their wandering inspection of the surroundings. The apartment was a surprisingly lavish job of modern interior decoration, considering the three flights of dingy, sour-smelling stairs leading up to it from the street. This wasn't at all her conception of a struggling playwright's quarters. Perhaps hastily, she had assumed from Maestring's clothes that he wasn't in healthy financial circumstances. His apartment should scotch that thought.

But, prosperous or not, the room hadn't the look of a writer's place. She saw no typewriter, no desk or table suitable for such work. The books in the ultramodern end-table bookshelves were bright and new in dust jackets. No dictionaries or other reference works that a playwright would need. She frowned slightly, then dismissed the impression. She hadn't seen into the room beyond the black screen at the other end of the hall, which she had supposed to be a bedchamber.

The actor was still whistling and making a clatter in the kitchenette. Her thoughts drifted to Kyle Maestring and his play, into wonderment of her pretense of interest in either. She quite well realized it was sheer humbuggery. What she'd heard read of the play—bits and pieces—was wretchedly written, clinquant and stilted, a charade which even the Lunts couldn't successfully interpret. She knew that Maestring had hopes of listing her among potential backers and wondered if she were being quite fair. Strange, the devices a girl will resort to, when she's mildly bored, for amusement. Well, she was in for it! Now she would have to listen to the whole play.

She shivered involuntarily. A slight movement of the drapery over one of the French doors to the terrace caught her eye. She got up and walked over to it, now feeling a cold draft of air from outside. The catch was unfastened and the door open a couple of inches. She closed it tightly, latching it, seeing then that one of the small panes of glass had been broken out near the catch. Cold air still came in, but not so much.

Glory sauntered into the hall, stopping at the kitchenette door to look in. Nailton was polishing glasses with a dish towel, awkwardly, as though unfamiliar with that sort of work.

"How are you doing?" asked the girl carelessly.

"Oh, very well indeed!" he returned over his shoulder. "Whoever last cleaned these glasses did a dishonest job. I'll be with you in a moment. I'm thinking a set of hot toddies would be more in order than highballs."

"They certainly would," agreed Glory. "I'm freezing. One of the French doors was open."

She walked on up the hall to peek into the front room beyond the screen. The furnishings matched the living room in luxury. Between two narrow windows in one wall was an exquisitely appointed vanity, with an amazing collection of toiletries on the glass shelf. At the other end of the room she saw a wide bed on a low dais, the headboard a sunburst of delicate pink-and-white rays.

Glory turned back toward the living room, with an expression of amused disdain. Kyle Maestring, it seemed, slept in a room as devoid of anything masculine as a Madison Avenue lingerie shop, which was rather odd, too, as he certainly revealed no feminine traits. There was nothing in the bedroom to indicate that it was also used for his writing, either.

Nailton came out of the kitchenette as she reached the door, carrying a silver tray with two old-fashioned glasses filled with a steaming concoction.

"I've mixed up something special in toddies," he said brightly. "Found a bottle of Demerara rum on the shelf. These'll drive the chill from the body and warm the heart, too."

He followed the girl into the living room, where he placed the tray on a cocktail table in the angle of an ell-shaped couch. Then he sat down, patting the down cushion at his side invitingly.

"I'd rather stand," demurred Glory, smiling. She reached over and picked up one of the glasses.

The actor raised and lowered his eyebrows and shrugged. He picked up the other glass. "Drink it while it's hot," he advised.

Glory had no need for urging, draining half of it. Then, impetuously, she went to the overstuffed chair she had been sitting in and sat down. "The others should be here soon," she said, glancing at the door to the stairway hall.

"And they'll think I'm a very bad host," said Nailton, getting up again. He returned the glass to the cocktail table and came over to her. "Won't you let me take your coat and make you comfortable? You look so, well, impermanent—as if you were leaving at any moment."

She shook her head. "I'm cold, Jimmie," she objected. Adding to her uneasiness, he sat down on the arm of her chair and placed his arm along the back, slightly over her head. Putting the tips of his fingers under her wrist, he lifted the hand holding the toddy to her lips.

"Get it down, and if it doesn't do the trick, I'll fix you another." The windowpanes back of them rattled as the driving storm pressed against them. "In fact, that's an excellent idea. How did I ever come to think of it? After two or three of those, we could easily imagine we were sitting under waving palms on a tropical island, and wouldn't care if the others didn't show up."

"That's the trouble," drawled the girl, a little warmed by the toddy. "I've had experience with waving palms before—and not on an island more tropical than Manhattan."

"Those were the wrong kind," he said, with a nervous laugh. "Now, I have some very fine ones. Soothing. See?"

The arm dropped from the chair back across her shoulders, invading the warm spot between the sable collar and her neck. She leaned forward and got out of the chair swiftly, the empty glass splintering on the floor.

"Behave, Jimmie," she said simply. "I—"

He jumped up and unexpectedly she found herself close in his arms. At first too surprised to do more than press her hands against his chest to hold him off, she found herself struggling to free herself of his embrace. For a man giving a visual impression of slightness, he was astonishingly muscular.

"Oh, do stop, Jimmie!" she exclaimed, keeping her head down to avoid his mouth.

He didn't answer and she became aware that his hands were trying to pull the coat down over her arms. She made another desperate effort to free herself, then found herself helpless, hands made useless under the shackling fur. She lifted her head defiantly. The actor was looking toward the stair hall door, but without relaxing his encircling grip. "Are the others coming?" she asked sharply.

Nailton shook his head. "No, I imagined I heard something," he said. He grinned down at her. "We've plenty of time."

His confident tone convinced her she'd been made the victim of a trick. Eight o'clock, Maestring had said. The whole episode now had the look of prearrangement between the actor and the playwright, to give Nailton an hour alone with her. It was, she decided swiftly, the moment for using a bit of guile herself, if she were to get out of this satisfactorily.

"Well, you said something about mixing fresh toddies," she said, leaning away from him. "Do you have to be so precipitate about this?"

He searched her eyes, but saw only gleaming amusement and sultry promise dancing in them. He laughed, releasing her. "Quite right," he replied briskly. "Another drink might help adjust your viewpoint. I might also phone the Living Room and make sure Phil Silburn hasn't left yet."

"How much time did Kyle agree to give you?" she asked, having difficulty with her smile. "The 'others,' I suppose, were just some of his fiction."

Nailton laughed. "Of course, darling—and Kyle isn't to come before nine. No doubt a shabby trick to play on you, but 'all's fair in love and war.' This is love. I've been crazy about you ever since we met."

This is war, the girl refuted silently, until I can get away from here.

"And I never knew!" she exclaimed, wonderingly.

He walked away jauntily, his shoulders very erect and his hands swinging just so at his sides. Glory's expression faded from ingenuous admiration into vivid repugnance as she saw him disappear around the screen into the bedroom. She stood watching until she heard the faint sound of a telephone receiver lifted from its cradle. With a glance toward the door to the stairs, she turned and started toward the table where her gloves and bag were lying.

As she reached it, she heard the rasp of the telephone being dialed in the front room. Then she changed her mind and walked in swift silence over the soft carpeting into the hall, keeping on toward the black-and-silver screen. Before quite reaching that end of the hall, she stopped and looked back, her arched eyebrows drawn together. From somewhere came a dull, heavy thump, followed by the click of a closing door. She listened intently for a moment, as if she thought the noises had come from the outside hall, then turned and went on, disappearing beyond the barrier screen.

Something fell to the floor in the bedchamber with a sharp crash and then a shrill cry, as of a hurt child, echoed back into the hall. "No! Jimmie . . . no!"

The cry trailed off into hideous silence. Presently Glory Bain reappeared at the end of the hall, weaving uncertainly for a few steps and then falling to her hands and knees, her head hanging down. With a prodigious effort, she raised it, devastating horror shining in her eyes. She pushed herself back on her heels and stared dumbly at one of her hands.

It was covered with blood. There was more on the front of her white dinner dress where the fur coat hung open. Shocked realization slowly seemed to steady her. Staggering to her feet, revolted and sick, she moved to the wall, supporting herself against it with the bloody hand, desperately trying to repel assailing waves of blackness.

You mustn't—you mustn't . . . faint. You've got to carry on—got to keep your chin up! Get out of here—get out—do you hear? Pull yourself together—that's it—that's the girl—get out—hurry . . .

She started down the hall, leaving a bloody trail on the delicately traced wallpaper with the sustaining hand. Presently she found herself at the living-room end of the hall, without awareness of the passage. The first shock, receding slightly, no longer crippled her progress, but she could not think clearly. She could only envision as in a dream that Nailton lay dead in the bedroom—that she must leave the apartment, and quickly.

Reaching the stair hall door, she fumbled for the knob. As her cold hand grasped it, she chilled and went rigid. There were footsteps outside, someone toiling up the creaking old stairs. She tried to focus her eyes on the dial of her watch, but couldn't. A fresh wave of terror sent her flying across the living room to the French door she had latched earlier. Groping frantically for the catch, she cut her hand on the broken glass, but wasn't aware of it. The wind from the terrace blew the door inward and she staggered out, knee deep in drifted snow. The footsteps on the stairs continued on to one of the upper floors, but she did not hear.

Through the haze of falling snow, she saw the dim outline of the wall between the terrace and the roof beyond. Still farther away, lights shone in some of the windows of a hotel. Making her way through the drifts toward the wall, she tried to scrub the nauseating stickiness from her hand with scooped-up snow. At the wall, she saw that the roof beyond was a flat expanse of wind-swirled white, but thought it might be possible to cross to the lighted windows. What she would do then, she didn't know. Of dire and first necessity, she must get away from the terrace.

She climbed awkwardly over the slippery top of the wall, landing on all fours. Getting up, she plunged forward, zigzagging unsteadily as her high heels slipped and skidded in the difficult going. Lights flashing in alternation from a sign she could not see, instead of helping, added to her confusion. She tripped over the coping of a small skylight and fell sprawling. Choking back convulsive sobs thrusting upward in her throat, she got back to her feet, wiping blobs of snow from her face, and started on.

A shrill laugh came from the direction of the hotel. She stopped, cowering, until she realized that it had not been directed at her. Shaking with cold and the effort to stifle the throb of terror she felt in her breast, she crossed the remaining distance to the brick wall of the hotel. For a time, she stood there, peering back over her shoulder. The lights in the apartment showed only as luminous squares through the snow-filled air.

Resisting the temptation of dropping into the snow and resting for a moment, she began to consider what she was to do now. There was a lighted window a couple of feet from where she leaned against the wall. She felt her way toward it, not hoping to escape the roof that way, but because she felt vaguely that the sight of an ordinary, unthreatening human being might help to restore her vanishing courage. She peered in, between the drawn shade and window frame. A woman was pulling on a squirrel coat and speaking to someone Glory could not see.

"All right," the voice sifted out. "I'd better pick up Ju and go on. This is one party I'd hate to miss." A telephone receiver clicked on its hook. The lights in the room went out and Glory heard the closing of the door. For minutes she stood there, trembling and shivering, then, calling on her last reserves of resolution, she tried the window. It was unlocked, but she broke fingernails and started the small cut on her hand bleeding before she succeeded in raising the sash to crawl into the room.

The room was warm, but Glory did not notice it immediately. She stood listening until the passing moments reassured her that the occupant of the room would not return. Then she brushed off the remaining snow and did what she could to her hair, with still shaking fingers. She wanted to wash the bloodstains from her hand and perhaps find something to stop the bleeding from the cut, but thought it better to go on. Her hands could be easily hidden in the sable sleeves.

Opening the door a couple of inches, she peered out into the hall and saw no one. A deep sigh relieved some of the pressure on her chest, but as she started out she thought of someone else. This, it occurred to her, was a matter for the man with the derby—Mr. Hite. He'd promised to help her, if ever she needed it.

Closing the door again, she went to the rickety table at the side of the bed and pulled the telephone directory from its lower shelf. Finding the number of the Hotel du Nord, she gave it to the switchboard operator downstairs. Presently the voice of the du Nord clerk, replying to her hoarse query, said that Mr. Hite was not in. Might catch him at Huntingdon House—ask for Dill. She put the receiver down and started looking up the number. Before she found it, the scream of the telephone bell almost ripped her heart from her bosom. It rang insistently.

Glory hurried to the door, thinking that perhaps the hotel switchboard operator had noticed the voice was nothing like that of the tenant of the room—and possibly the woman had stopped at the desk on her way out.

Halfway down the hall, she found stairs and turned to descend them. Although she had shaken herself free from some of the clinging snow, the sable coat was wet and her silver sandals sopping. That she would be noticed when she reached the lobby was certain. The best she could hope for was that no one would feel impelled to intercept her with a demand for explanation. On the second floor a misshapen dwarf caught sight of her and stopped, his small feet firmly planted, to ogle interestedly. She controlled a shiver and kept on down to the main floor.

There were few persons in the shabby lobby and, to her relief, these seemed utterly uninterested. She saw the woman in the squirrel coat ahead of her, going out with a man—or so she supposed— who had already passed beyond the small portico and was going cautiously down the steps, pulling his overcoat collar up around his ears.

She was not afraid of them now, at least not so much as she feared a peremptory hail from the clerk behind the desk. Creeping down the steps, she crossed to the curb, hoping to sight a vacant cab. Several cars passed and her nerves began to assert themselves again before she saw a taxi. It was impossible to see whether it carried a passenger or not. She lifted her arm and waved frantically, then started violently.

"Hey, you!" someone called from behind.

She resisted the impulse to turn her head and plunged out knee deep into the pile of snow lining the curb, the fur coat dragging behind her over the surface. The cab veered toward her, slowing to a stop. Glory reached for the door handle and twisted it furiously, and then, somehow surprised that the door opened, climbed in.

The cab driver looked back at her curiously through the sliding partition as she fell back into the seat.

"Huntingdon House, please!" she gasped. "And—hurry!"

5
SANCTUARY

MRS. MIRIAM WEBER, mother of Berte Dill, finished the exhausting process of becoming enveloped in an evening dress of brown net. There was a lot of it, but also a lot of Miriam. She eyed herself disapprovingly in the mirror and sighed. This was risky, considering how closely the fabric fitted around her ample bosom. It was no use, she thought darkly, when a healthy woman starts gettin' old she'd better quit caring how fat she gets or stop eatin'. After all the trouble of getting inside the net creation, Miriam felt uneasily that she looked like a freshly caught sturgeon.

Dressing for dinner was one of Berte Dill's New York notions. Back home in Potts Crossing, folks ate in whatever clothes they happened to be wearing when suppertime came around. But this folderol had to be put up with. Berte was her sole gift to the world, although it was doubtful old Gottlieb Dill had thought of the girl in this light. He had paid plenty. Mr. Dill was the wealthy old codger Berte had helped to the altar with a view of inheriting his estate. May and December—with December happily turning out to be an uncommonly short month.

Berte and Quinny Hite were waiting in what Miriam insisted on referring to as the parlor. Sitting in a cold cab in front of the Maywood, Berte had developed an appetite it would have been criminal to waste on any Times Square eating place. Besides, if they'd given up the cab, heaven might know where they'd have got another, but Berte didn't. The prospect of arriving home looking like a polar bear wasn't her dish. A girl paying four hundred a month for an apartment in the ultra-smart Huntingdon House, with room service from the equally swank Chez Ninon downstairs, shouldn't be batting around through a blizzard in a taxi looking for a place to eat.

Quinny hadn't argued. There was an advantage in the idea he didn't bring up. Once he got Berte home, he wouldn't need to bother about her for the rest of the night. He might get some work done, although he wasn't too hopeful of turning up anything so soon.

Mrs. Weber moved out into view from the bedroom, stopping by the grand piano and looking expectantly at the couple on the red velvet divan. Busy scanning a menu which Quinny was holding, neither noticed her at once. Berte, moving to pull one foot under her, saw Miriam first.

"Oh, looky, Mama in her new dress!" she exclaimed.

Quinny lifted his eyes, restraining the impulse to blink. "Wonderful!" he echoed hollowly.

"Miss Fish Market!" Berte shouted.

Mrs. Weber picked up a porcelain dachshund from the piano and started heavily toward the divan. Chill purpose gleamed in her eyes. "Do you want for me to smack you with this crockery pup?" she demanded threateningly.

"Oh, lay it down, Mama," soothed Quinny. "Don't let Berte kid you. You look fine—kinda like pictures I seen of Lillian Russell."

"She'd make two Lillian Russells, with some left over," disagreed Berte.

"Nix, nix!" cautioned Quinny. "She can't *always* miss."

"Oh, all right, Mama dear. Can't you take a joke? At ease, pet— we're ordering dinner."

Miriam put the porcelain dog on the top of a secretary and came on toward the divan, with an angling glance at a solemn-faced waiter she hadn't previously noticed. This was evidently all right with him. He gazed stolidly at a framed abstraction in oil that no one else understood either.

"What're you goin' to eat?" Mrs. Weber asked, with interest.

Quinny marked his place on the menu and looked at Berte. She was sort of draped on his shoulder.

"It says here they got a double sirloin," he suggested. "Would you go for that?"

"Like a starved alley cat," responded the girl promptly. "Order it for me. What are you going to have?"

"Does it say they got any tripe?" asked Mrs. Weber hopefully.

"Of course not, Mama! Chez Ninon doesn't serve anything like that."

Miriam looked grieved. "I don't see why not," she said. "There ain't nothing better."

Berte got her mother straightened out on the matter of high-priced food while Quinny brooded over the menu.

"Le's see," he murmured. "What else?—um-m—musherrooms—"

The order finally given, Quinny summarized for Berte's benefit the project on which he had become engaged. Mrs. Weber went off to the kitchenette for a bottle of whiskey and one of gin for herself. Problems of detection left her cold.

"I suppose Henry Page thinks Glory is in on the robbery," commented Berte, as he finished. "Maybe she is."

Quinny was annoyed. "Where do you get off to make cracks like that?" he asked coldly. "Page only thinks she maybe popped-off too loud some place about his collection. That's happened often enough. Look, babe, in this business it don't pay to make up your mind before the dope is in. When you do, you can't help tryin' to make it come out that way."

Berte digested this short homily on the science of criminal investigation, without being remarkably impressed. She'd trade fact for intuition any time.

"I know." She lifted her eyes for a deprecatory glance. "You just think Glory Bain's too good-looking and highfalutin to do anything wrong!"

Quinny frowned. "You read my mind," he growled. "But the difference is that my mind works both ways from the middle. Yours don't—it's a one-way street."

"Oh, yeah?" retorted Berte crushingly.

Mrs. Weber returned with her load of bottles and glasses. Disdainful of trays, she carried the liquor held against her with one

ham-like arm, and the glasses in her hand. Peace and some measure of tranquility descended on the little party until dinner had
been disposed of, and then Quinny began turning over in his mind the
project of a graceful exit. Before he'd finished working this out, there
came an interruption—the prolonged sound of the door buzzer.

"It's the waiter coming for the dishes," said Berte, getting up.
"I'll go."

She went across to the foyer entrance and disappeared from
the view of Mrs. Weber and Quinny. The old lady's eyes, which
usually wavered between hostility and wary defense, rested on the
detective. She started to say something, when an astonished exclamation of greeting came from Berte in the foyer. "Glory Bain!
What on earth—"

"Mr. Hite—is he here?" came a shaken response.

It was a strange Glory that Quinny saw as he hurried to the
entrance of the suite. The magnificent sable coat was saturated;
loose, wet ends of hair plastered against the girl's pallid face; and
her lips were quivering, blue with cold.

Berte, too dumbfounded to move, stood staring.

"What's the matter?" demanded Quinny. "What's happened to
you?"

"Not me—Mr. Nailton," replied Glory, her usually musical
speech tight and strained. "He—he's dead! And—I'm freezing!"

She put out her hands and stumbled toward Quinny with her
remaining strength. Abruptly aware of her condition, he thrust
supporting arms under hers, shocked at the convulsive trembling
he felt through the fur coat. Mrs. Weber, her eyes bulging with
excited curiosity, came into the living room entrance and stopped.

"The poor kid," commiserated Berte, snapping out of her dazed
immobility. "Bring her in, Quinny. She's soaking!"

"Put that girl to bed—an' give her whiskey!" exploded Mrs.
Weber. "She'll have her death of pneumonia, she will."

Glory sagged heavily on Quinny's supporting arms. He stooped,
gathering her up in a swift movement, then strode toward the bedroom, Berte running ahead. Mrs. Weber, with a detour to snatch
up the liquor bottle and a glass, hurried after them. She found the

detective supporting Glory while Berte got her out of the dripping coat. The white dinner dress under it clung soddenly to her legs, the silver sandals mere soggy leather.

Mrs. Weber took charge in small-town tradition, peremptorily ordering Quinny from the room. Glory had to be stripped, rubbed vigorously, and put to bed under warm blankets, she asserted.

"Berte, you see'f you can get a doctor," she concluded.

Quinny went out into the living room, anxious and still flaming with curiosity about what had happened to Nailton. He listened to the sounds from the bedroom, mostly sharply voiced directions to Berte from Mrs. Weber. Presently Berte opened the door and looked out.

"We've got her in bed," she said. "She insists she must see you. Something terrible has happened, I think."

She'd been looking for it, the detective reflected as he went in. He hardly recognized the vivid face he'd seen at the Living Room only a couple of hours before. The blue pallor which had alarmed him when he carried her to the bedroom was now succeeded by a dull flush. Her eyes, shifting restlessly to look at him as he entered, were brightly feverish. But she tried to smile.

"Did you call a doctor?" Quinny asked Berte.

"He'll come in a few minutes."

"I'm goin' to fix her somethin' hot," said Mrs. Weber, walking heavily out of the room. Berte trotted along after her.

"Mr. Hite," called Glory, softly. "I must tell you— I've got to tell you, quick."

Quinny came around to stand at the side of the bed, looking down with concern showing in his hazel eyes. "Maybe you better hold it," he suggested. "Till you feel better."

"No. I must tell you now." Her voice was low, like wind-ruffled leaves, and the red-brown eyes were liquid with introspective fear. "Jimmie Nailton—someone killed him in Kyle's apartment—with a knife—and I saw no one. We thought we were alone—waiting for the others. They will think I did it! That's why I—came here—to see if you will help me? Will you?" She looked up at Quinny, timidly, as though reluctant to hear an answer that might be refusal.

"Sure, babe—if I can."

She went on, in fitful sentences, to describe her terrifying experience. The telling seemed to relieve some sort of mental congestion, so that as she went on she gained coherence—sufficiently as to give the detective a reasonable idea of what had happened. He realized, if the account hadn't been colored protectively, that Glory Bain was in a frightening situation. If she had killed the man, of course, her position was the same and his was worse. He would never enter into any suborned scheme to aid a guilty person to escape punishment.

Mrs. Weber came back with something steaming in a cup. Quinny bent over and touched the girl's moist, dark hair.

"Okay, sister—I'll take over. Don't worry about it now. But you'll need family help as much as you need me. I'm goin' to call Henry Page," he said firmly. "What's the number?"

He stepped back out of Mrs. Weber's way and picked up the telephone from a bedside table. Glory whispered the number and he dialed it. Listening intently, he watched Berte Dill, who had returned with her mother. She was standing at the foot of the bed, looking uncommonly upset.

"What's the matter with you?" he asked.

Berte shook her head. "I—don't know. Nervous, I guess."

"*You* should be nervous!" he exclaimed. His expression changed as he spoke into the transmitter, asking for Henry Page. "He ain't? When do you expect him?" Quinny listened briefly, a scowl appearing between his eyebrows. "Well, tell him to call Huntingdon House—the Dill apartment—the minute he comes in. It's very damned important. This is Quin Hite speaking." He glanced at Glory Bain, who was watching him. "Hold on a minute." Covering the mouthpiece with his hand, he spoke to the girl. "How's if I talk to Dr. Linden?" he asked.

Glory Bain sat up with an abruptness that almost spilled the contents of the cup in Mrs. Weber's hand. "Oh, no!" she exclaimed. "She mustn't be told. She can't stand a shock—it would kill her!"

Quinny shrugged and put the phone down. Glory relaxed weakly into the pillows. The effort of sitting had started beads of perspiration on her forehead.

In the kitchenette off the living room the door buzzer began a squawking which promised the probable arrival of the physician Berte had summoned. She started out to answer and Quinny followed, with a wave at the girl in bed and an admonition to hold everything.

He caught up with Berte on the way to the door. "Look, babe," he said quickly, "I got to lam over to this Maestring's place and give the set-up a gander. When Page calls, tell him to burn his britches gettin' down here—tell him all about it before he starts. Glory Bain's goin' to need the best lawyer he can get for her, if she keeps out of either the jug or Bellevue. See?"

"Do you think she killed that fella?"

"I don't know anything about it," he snapped. "Anyhow, I don't guess. That is a very bum way to crack a murder job."

Berte slipped her hand up under his arm and pinched it affectionately. "I suppose it is," she said. "But it's interesting to think about."

"Here's somethin' else. If you get hold of Henry Page, tell him I said it would be a good play to rush Glory to a hospital. She looks like a plenty sick dame to me. When I tell whoever the Homicide Squad sends to Maestring's apartment what I know—an' I have to do that, see?—it's a hunnerd to one they're goin' to want to take her away—if what happened is anything like she said. Gettin' her out of a hospital will be tougher." He put his arm around Berte's waist and surprised her with an impulsive kiss.

She looked up at him searchingly as he turned loose and reached for the doorknob. "What was that for?" she asked.

"Just to hold you till I get time for a real smack," he grinned.

He pulled the door open and admitted a heavy-set man with kindly eyes, carrying a medical bag.

"Dr. Stokes," the man said. "You sent for a physician, I believe?"

"Show him in, Berte," said Quinny. "I'll see you—or phone—later."

Leaving the elevator downstairs, Quinny went to the phone booths near the desk, where he called Homicide headquarters and asked for Lieutenant Madden. Presently Tracy Madden's brusque voice greeted him. Quinny explained that he'd heard there had been a killing in the Fiftieth Street apartment and suggested meeting him there.

Madden cursed. "On a night like this, with N' York up to your neck in snow, you have to go an' turn up a murder!" he went on. "All right—all right! But if I get up there an' fin' out some lug's been takin' you for a gag well, I got a brand-new sap which needs loosenin' up and you'll do as good as the next one."

Fastening his overcoat around him, with collar pulled up to his ears, Quinny went out to the street. The snow had moderated somewhat, and the spectacular doorman of Huntingdon House whistled down a cab for him without too much delay.

"Say," said Quinny suddenly, "a lady came to the Dill apartment a while ago, wearin' a black fur coat which prob'bly had snow all over it. Did you see her?"

"Yes, sir. She explained that she'd had an accident and lost her purse. I paid her cab. She said she would send the money down."

Quinny fished out a couple of dollar bills and handed them over. "Guess she forgot," he said, and climbed into the cab.

Now that he thought of it, he remembered Glory Bain had carried no bag when she came in and wondered if she had lost it en route or left it in the apartment. He shook his head. Anyway you looked at it, the girl was in for tough going, he thought. He sternly kept his thoughts from speculation on the truth of her story.

But it was going to need a lot of substantiation.

6

THE RUBY ON THE FLOOR

IT WAS A SLOW PASSAGE across town, through heavy going. Gangs of men were struggling to widen the lanes in the snow-clogged streets, but without having made notable progress. Fortunately, the tide of theater-bound traffic had ceased and the hour was too early for the return flow. Reaching his destination, Quinny took shelter from the icy wind in the box-like vestibule to wait for the men from the Homicide Squad and his old friend, Lieutenant Madden. In two or three minutes he heard the wailing of a siren and then saw a squad car turning into the street toward him.

Madden and a couple of department detectives squashed through the deep snow in the gutters. The Lieutenant kicked his feet savagely against the side of the door frame to knock the clinging stuff from his shoes. "Why didn't you clean off a path while you were hanging around waitin'?" he demanded loudly.

"Y'know, I never thought of that," returned Quinny mildly. "I just love to play in snow. Don't you, Trace?"

"Nuts to that," commented the official. "Well, where is this alleged corpse?"

"Up here."

Quinny opened the inner door of the vestibule and started up the narrow stairway. Madden and his men clumped along behind. At the third-floor landing Quinny saw a group at the top of the next flight—two women and, surprisingly to him, Abe Munch. The younger of the women was the one he'd talked to in the Maywood, who'd said she was Nana Lester, Nailton's wife.

"Playin' games?" he asked cheerfully, as he neared the top of the flight. "Ever'body have to go out in the hall?"

"I'm this girl's sister," declared the woman Quinny hadn't seen before. "Her husband is in this apartment with another woman—and is afraid to answer the bell."

"If that's his reason, I can see he's no dope," commented Quinny, measuring the speaker. "How about you, Abe? Cousin, or somethin'?"

"I just came along for the ride," returned the agent, half sheepishly. "What're you doing here?" He glanced at Madden and the other men, coming up the stairs behind Quinny.

"We got some business in there, too." He crossed to the door of the apartment and tried the knob, then glanced back at Madden. "What do we do, Chief? Push it in?"

Madden nodded. "You know these people?" he demanded.

"I know Munch. Looks like a divorce frame."

"Hmph! Okay. Kelly, keep this gang here. Push the door in, Greenbaum. You're the biggest." Madden and Quinny stepped back to make room for the bulky Greenbaum's lunge.

"What's the lay, Quinny?" asked Munch, uneasily.

"We think it's murder."

Greenbaum's weight hit the door heavily. Once was enough. There was the crackle of tearing wood and the door swung inward, all but throwing the big detective to the floor inside. Madden, Quinny and the dick named Kelly went in. Sirens shrieking in the street indicated the arrival of reinforcements. The three men stopped automatically to stare around the lush living room.

Quinny, having advance information, knew what to look for, but Madden did not. The Lieutenant, however, was a man with too many years at this sort of thing to go charging in at the risk of destroying evidence not seen at first sight. Quinny saw the shattered glass near the chair where Glory Bain had sat; saw the small beaded bag and gloves on the table under the lamp. Madden hunched his burly shoulders as the cold of the room penetrated.

"Th' place is as cold as a Morgue icebox!" he exclaimed resentfully. "The dead guy—if there is one—prob'bly froze to death!"

"There's a glass door open over there." Quinny nodded toward the French window, which Glory had not closed in her flight. "This corpse we're lookin' for oughta be in th' front room."

He walked to the entrance of the short hall gingerly. Madden came along, and after a long scrutiny of the scene as far as the black-and-silver screen blocking the view at the other end, both men entered the hall. All the lights were on, including those in the kitchenette which they passed with only casual glances into it.

Reaching the screen, Quinny saw part of the luckless Nailton's body beyond its edge. He moved forward for a more comprehensive view and stopped, Madden crowding against him.

"There it is," said Quinny. "Like I told you on the phone."

Madden grunted and pushed past Quinny into the room, where he stood looking down at the body, one arm folded across his stomach supporting the elbow of the other. He rubbed the stubble on his chin thoughtfully, then glanced at Quinny. "Well, here we go again," growled the Lieutenant. "The old merry-go-round."

"You could be drivin' a truck," suggested Quinny critically.

"Sure, but that ain't what I meant," returned Tracy Madden. "It's just the old round-and-round—cheeseheaded people thinkin' they can settle anything by killin' somebody. All they do is put us to a lot of trouble takin' *them* out of circulation. It don't make sense. Nobody makes."

"No, they don't," agreed Quinny restlessly. "Neither does a cop standin' around makin' like Hamlet. Let's get going."

Nailton, it appeared, had fallen on his side on the step of the dais on which the bed rested, and, in the agony of dying, had slipped from this to the floor, where he now lay face down. Glory had not described the position of the body, although she'd told Quinny about trying to help the actor up and getting her hands bloodied. Nailton, who still clutched the telephone receiver in his left hand, had capsized the stand as he fell. Then the detective's roving inspection took in the weapon.

It answered exactly to the description he had of the twin daggers of Lola Montez! Recognition was shattering to his subconscious inclination to believe in Glory's account. But, the knife! If she had realized where it came from, she hadn't said so, merely saying Nailton had been stabbed. Page's reluctant forebodings of the girl's unwitting cooperation in the robbery seemed verified. As Madden would see it, the weapon would be ample evidence to convict Glory Bain. If he went further than this, it would be merely to learn whether anyone else was accessory to the crime.

"Fancy lookin' shiv," observed Tracy Madden, leaning over the body for a closer look.

Only the handle, of course, was visible. There was a small crown, set with rubies, on the end of this, the grip composed of black varnished cord, tightly wound. The guard was a filigree of what seemed a coat of arms.

"It did the job," mumbled Quinny, debating whether or not to tell what he knew of it. He decided to withhold this until he'd had time to consider it more thoroughly. "You know, Trace, I'd like to know if he got the number he was callin' before he got this. The thing ain't buzzin'."

"They disconnect after a while," answered Madden, straightening. "But, that's something to keep in mind. If the call went through, maybe I can get a check on it."

Madden went to the wall, now interested in the smears of blood Glory had left. Quinny, noticing that the door to a closet in the same wall about a yard from the telephone table stood ajar, opened it. He saw what appeared to be three negligees hanging there, still wrapped in tissue as they had come from a cleaner's. The closet was bare of any other clothing.

"The lug which lives here thinks of everything, Trace," he said, glancing toward the Lieutenant. "Look what he's put in for lady visitors!" He lifted an indicating hand and it brushed against the tissue. It was wet to his touch. He glanced at the floor and saw several damp spots there.

"What did you say the guy's name was that owns this joint?" queried Madden, joining him at the open door and peering in.

"The name I got is Maestring," said Quinny doubtfully. "But there's something phony about it. This don't look like a place a half-starved playwright could keep up." He hesitated a second, then went on. "Look here, Trace, somebody hid in this closet tonight. A wet coat rubbed against the tissue paper them passion pajamas is in—and the floor shows where wet feet stood. See?"

"Yeah," commented Madden sagely. "The dame prob'bly hid in here before she stuck him. Hell, this job's a cinch! Nailton was foolin' around with another dame. This one you told me about gets wind of it, so she stashes herself in the closet. When he comes in, leaving the new gal out in the other room while he makes a phone call, the Bain woman lets him have it. A flattie could handle this job!"

"That the way it was?" asked Quinny blandly. "How do you know it wasn't the other way around? Works out the same way."

Madden scowled, recognizing the logic. "Could be," he admitted gruffly.

"The set-up looks better to me this way," Quinny abandoned the closet, turning around to size up every detail on this side of the bed. "The story the Bain girl handed me didn't have any holes in it, so far's I can see. She did just what you'd expect, if she was sitting out there when this thing happened. She run away as fast as she could—which couldn't of been quick, neither, across the roof next door and through the hotel."

"Well, where's the other dame, then—and who?"

"I wouldn't say we knew there was another dame, Tracy. We ain't turned up any signs that prove it was. How about the woman out on the stairs, the one who says she's this guy's wife?"

Madden nodded with slow grimness. "I'll have a little chat with her—now," he said, walking away toward the connecting hall.

Quinny grinned with smug satisfaction. He didn't want Tracy Madden to bear down on Glory Bain while there was an outside chance of her innocence. If subsequent weight of evidence destroyed this, there wasn't anything to be done about it, but he felt nothing would be lost in giving the girl a chance.

He opened the closet door again for a more thorough examination, even getting down on his knees for a minute inspection of the floor there. Aside from the moist smears, the varnished surface was scrupulously clean. About to get up, he saw a small red spot near the back wall. His first impression that it was a spot of spattered blood was instantly revised. Blood wouldn't congeal into little round spheres. It was a red stone, like those in the crown on the dagger in Nailton's back.

Picking it up, he compared the gem with those set in the knife used to kill. The match was practically perfect, but no stone was missing from the tiny crown. He frowned, disappointed, and absently thrust his find into a vest pocket.

Crossing the room, he inspected the dressing-table top. There was a variety of perfumes and cosmetics, none of which seemed to have been used except a lipstick in a gold container. A crumpled piece of tissue showed lipstick smears. He saw a set of silver boxes and toilet implements, with a racing greyhound embossed in the metal. All pretty fancy, he thought.

Hearing acrimonious debate in the living room, he sauntered back through the hall to see what was happening. He found Madden with the three people they'd found in the outer hall. Abe Munch stood away from the others, green about the gills and uneasy. The older woman faced Madden, glaring frigidly. He didn't mind. His attention was on the burlesque doll—Nana Lester.

"I knew Jimmie was playing around—and I knew who with!" she was saying bitterly. "Tonight I learned that he was coming here with Glory Bain. I was determined to put a stop to it. I didn't care, if he wanted someone else—but I didn't intend to be made a fool of by any cheap, glamour tramp like—"

"You didn't need to get rough about it," sneered Madden, in fine form. "Didn't have to hide in a closet and knife the guy."

Nana Lester wasn't even slightly fazed. "Oh, nuts, cop! I've never set foot in this apartment," she declared. "When I heard they were coming here tonight, I got my sister and Abe to come with me as witnesses, so that I could get a divorce out of it, that's all. We rang and rang—but no one came to the door. So, there we were—stuck out in the hall. I simply determined to wait until they came out."

"How did you know they were coming here?" demanded Quinny, moving into the scene.

Nana Lester gave him the benefit of a sultry, ill-tempered glance. "Because my room happens to be in the hotel across the roof. I can see into this apartment from my window."

"Yeah-yeah—but you just said you 'heard' they were coming here. Who told you?" pressed Quinny relentlessly.

The girl's eyes flickered sullenly. "I didn't mean I heard they were coming *here*," she corrected. "I got it out of Jimmie—that he was seeing her—and I knew this is where they came. I was watching my window and saw them after they got here."

Quinny didn't believe this. He didn't think it would have been possible for anyone to see clearly enough through the snow-filled space between the buildings to identify anyone. Perhaps she had merely assumed that Glory Bain and Nailton were in the apartment when she saw the lights come on.

"All right," said Tracy Madden. "That'll do for right now. But you stick around—all three of you. I ain't done with you yet. Take 'em back out in the hall, Greenbaum—an' keep 'em there."

Greenbaum shepherded them out. There were a lot more of Madden's men there, but the Lieutenant told them to stay there until he called them in. Too many feet tramping around would be no help.

"Take a gander in Miss Bain's bag, Chief," suggested Quinny as they turned back into the living room. "I'm kind of curious if she packed a key to this joint. Might be other things, too."

"Who's runnin' this show, Quinny?" growled Madden, not liking it. "You finished your job when you gave me the tip-off about the murder. I don't need your help. It'll be busted wide open in time for the mornin' papers."

"Wanna bet?" needled Quinny, unflustered by the Lieutenant's baleful glare. "I got idle money which says it won't. One will get you ten that you ain't even started yet. Know what a smart horse don't ever do? *Never?*"

"What?" Madden picked up the beaded bag and opened it.

"He never throws his jockey." Quinny chuckled noisily. "Don't go forgettin', Trace, that I've rode you to four or five wins before this."

Madden glared stonily at Quinny Hite for a moment, then grinned wryly. "Guess you're right, Quinny," he said. "Of course, I would have cracked those jobs, anyway. You just made it easier— maybe. Tell you what I'm gonna do—I'm gonna let you stick around. I don't know where it's goin' to get you anything, though, except a work-out to keep in practice."

"I always come out all right," assured Quinny. "See anything in the bag? Is there a lipstick? Or a small knife?"

"A couple of keys, but not the kind for a lock like on the door there. That's a Corbin. These are Yale." Madden pursed his big mouth and shook the contents of the bag on the table. "Just the junk a dame usually packs around. No lipstick, though. No knife, either."

Quinny had abandoned interest in the bag already, moving over to the open French window to stare out at the gray murk of the terrace, lessened intermittently by the reflected light of advertising signs atop buildings facing Broadway. He had no difficulty in seeing the broad trail through the snow left by Glory Bain on her way to the terrace wall. But he also saw another, leading to a different part of the same wall.

"Look here, Trace!" he called sharply. "This Bain gal told me she lammed across the roof to the hotel. So did somebody else— or, maybe, it was another person comin' from there. There's been too much snow since to tell which way that one was goin'."

Madden joined him, staring out at the terrace. "How can you tell which would be her trail and which one somebody else's?" he demanded.

"From here, you can't," admitted Quinny. "We'll have to go out there and see where they go—or come from. I think I can pick out hers from what she told me."

There was a commotion at the living room door. Looking around, Quinny saw the burly Greenbaum towing Kyle Maestring in by the elbow. The playwright looked scared.

"Here's another guy comes snoopin' around," rasped Greenbaum. "Seems to know all them other mugs out in the hall, too."

"Maestring," said Quinny, coming back into the room. He eyed the playwright with open contempt. "Late, ain't you? You told Glory Bain over in the Livin' Room you'd be here soon's you picked up Sol Leverring. You lied about that, too. You knew Leverring was in Boston."

"I did not!" shouted Maestring. "I only learned it when I stopped at the Haymarket."

"Yeah?" sneered Quinny. "So, what did you do for the next hour an' a half—or so?"

Maestring's eyes became sullen, his fingers clenching into fists and relaxing nervously. "What have my movements to do with you?" he demanded.

"Plenty." Quinny glanced at Lieutenant Madden, who was taking it all in with none too much grace. "Trace, could we have those other lugs back in?"

Madden nodded to the detective, Kelly, who went out into the stair hall and returned with Munch and the two women. Quinny resumed.

"I want to tell you bums just what you did," he began. "You had a big idea of pullin' a divorce frame tonight. You picked out Miss Bain because you figured she would come across heavy to keep out of it—"

"That's a damned lie!" shouted Maestring.

"Shut up, before I forget steppin' on cocker-roaches always makes me sick!" snorted Quinny. "You fix up ever'thing pretty so's Glory Bain is goin' to be caught alone here with Nailton. She didn't want to come until she knew there were other people here. I heard her say so—before she left the Livin' Room. You talk her into it, on the stall you got to pick up Sol Leverring to hear you read your lousy play. I know Leverring. Might surprise you to know he can read himself. If he's interested enough in a play to hear somebody spiel it off, it would be after he'd read it—or somebody in his office had. You couldn't of dragged Sol here to listen to this one—from what I heard of it."

"Are you such an authority on theater?" sneered Maestring, looking Quinny up and down contemptuously.

"I don't have to be to know that one stinks. Okay. You talk Miss Bain into coming here with a gag that you expect some other people at eight. Who did you expect?"

"A couple of my friends," muttered Maestring.

"What's all this got to do with the stiff in there?" growled Madden impatiently.

"Maybe a lot, Trace." Quinny's attention flipped back to Maestring. "Give these couple of friends' names," he snapped.

Maestring's eyes wavered uneasily, angling for a swift look at Nana Lester. "I'm not bringing them into this," he declared.

"All right. I don't think you've got that many friends," observed Quinny. "So, you stall around for couple hours, waiting for Nailton to get in his licks." He noticed Maestring's empty hands. "Where's the play?"

"My feet were wet, so I went home for dry shoes and rubbers," muttered the playwright defensively. "I—I guess I left the play there."

"You went home. The gag was that this was your apartment. Whose is it?"

"It belongs to Phil Silburn—the man who owns the Living Room," answered Maestring. "Naturally, I wanted to impress Leverring, and my apartment isn't suitable. Phil very kindly agreed to let me use his."

Quinny made an unpleasant noise with his lips. "Okay. But it don't take all that time for a guy to change his shoes and put on rubbers."

"I stopped for something to eat. As you may remember, I didn't have dinner with the others at the Living Room."

Quinny turned to Tracy Madden, with a shrug. "You see how it is, Trace," he said. "This bunch of crooks wasn't just pullin' a divorce frame. Looks like a blackmail racket, to me. If this G-string jessie was on the level, there's a whole hotel full of jills where she lives which could be hired for a sawbuck to sit for a divorce raid. Am I right, Abe?" He eyed Munch speculatively.

The agent shuffled his feet uneasily. It was obvious that he would have been quite happy to have been left out of the proceedings. "Sure," he agreed throatily.

"Yeah, an', by the way, how come I find you workin' this kind of racket?"

Abe Munch examined the rug vacuously. "I could use a saw-buck myself," he answered, glancing up. "Look here, Quinny—all I know about this is that Nana Lester propositioned me to come along as a witness. I didn't know there was goin' to be any trouble."

"Now you do," retorted Quinny grimly. He looked at Madden again. "So there you are, Trace. You see what's been goin' on. I ain't sayin' any of these bums killed Jimmie Nailton, but they set him up for it. I am also not sayin' none of 'em stuck him with that fancy shiv. Don't forget we know there was somebody else crossed that roof out there besides Glory Bain."

"You alibin' her?" asked Madden curiously. "Of course, seein's she has dough—"

"It might s'prise you, Trace," retorted Quinny coldly, "but what I'm tryin' to do is crack a murder. All you're lookin' for is some-body to pin it on—guilty or not." He walked over to examine the lock on the door Greenbaum had crushed open. "Here's somethin' right here you prob'bly would of missed, Trace," he said conde-scendingly. "The top lock, which was put on by the guy which lives here, is a Corbin—like you said. But th' reg'lar one worked by the doorknob is a Yale."

Madden clumped across to the door, scowling, and twisted the doorknob to and fro. His face lightened and he laughed. "Yeah, smart guy," he crowed. "But the regular lock don't work. See?"

"What?" Quinny stooped over, glaring resentfully as he tried the knob and saw that the bolt failed to respond. He straightened up reluctantly, seething with words he didn't even want to hear himself. He needed a goat and, looking around, his eyes fell on Maestring, who seemed to be having trouble with his nose.

"Le's see the key you got, Maestring!" he barked.

The playwright shook his head and snuffled noisily. "I gave the one I had to Nailton," he replied. "See here, officer, I wish you'd let me go home. I'm catching cold."

"You don't say?" answered Madden shortly.

"Yes, I am—" Maestring broke off and explored his side top-coat pocket for a handkerchief. As he whisked it out and applied it to his moist nose, something fell on the floor.

Quinny pounced on it, coming up with a flat key. He examined it closely, seeing "5-D" stamped in the handle part. "So you didn' have the key?" he triumphed.

The playwright stared at the bit of metal in Quinny's hand. "That's the key to my own apartment at the Goldman Court on Fifty-third," he said. He held out his hand. "I'll take it, please."

"You just wait!"

Quinny tried the key in the upper lock, but it failed to operate it. He glanced at the door panel and saw that it bore the letter A instead of a number. Swinging back into the room, he tossed the key to Maestring. "Wrong number," he growled, disappointed. "Excuse it, please."

7

THE SPIDER

Ordering Maestring, Munch and the two women to be held in the hallway outside the living room until he was ready to take up with them again, Madden returned to the French window, Quinny with him.

"Look, Quinny—there's one of those little square panes of glass busted out," said the Lieutenant. "Right near the lock."

Quinny glanced at the floor and saw fragments of glass. "Busted in," he corrected. "That kind of fixes it the other set of tracks out there was made by somebody comin'—not goin'. Check?"

Madden nodded, still staring at the wintry scene out on the terrace. "Damned if I'm goin' wading in all that stuff, just to see where the tracks go," he murmured. "Greenbaum!" he roared suddenly.

Quinny winced at the bull-like voice. "Easy, Trace!" he cautioned. "Greenbaum couldn't of got clear down to the Battery this quick. You could bust somebody's eardrums, yellin' like that—when they ain't set."

Greenbaum reappeared. He was a big man, with a permanent expression of anxiety in his eyes. He had been promoted to detective status following a feat of rare heroism, inadvertently having stepped through a skylight and fallen on an unsuspecting gunman in the room beneath. It was Greenbaum luck that the ratty gangster was a man long sought by the police. It was also Greenbaum luck that there had been anyone there at all to fall on.

"Callin' me, Chief?" he asked, coming across the room. Madden searched the big fellow's eyes as he stopped.

"How's your guts, Greenbaum?" he asked solicitously.

"Okay."

"Well, here's a job I can't trust to just any chowderhead," said Madden. "So, I'm pickin' you. I want you to go out on the roof and see where those two sets of tracks in the snow go. On the off chance the murderer might be hidin' out there, keep your eyes open. He might take a pot shot at you, see?"

Greenbaum immediately produced his service revolver and brandished it menacingly. "Leave him just try it!" he threatened. "I guess I can take care of the lousy rat!"

Quinny restrained a grin. "Look, Greenbaum, see if one set of them tracks shows where somebody fell over a skylight, and notice special where that set goes."

Greenbaum eyed Quinny, suspicious of being ribbed. His comrades on the force never had accepted his version of having deliberately dived through the skylight in the line of duty. He nodded, satisfied that Quinny wasn't kidding, and went out on the terrace.

"I'm turnin' the joint over to the department experts," Madden said. He walked toward Detective Kelly—a good man—who was standing inside the hall door. "Kelly, take this Maestring to the precinct house and hold him for Lendon. Get names and addresses of the other three and let 'em go."

"Where you goin', Trace?" asked Quinny.

"I'm goin' over to Huntingdon House an' have a talk with this Bain woman," answered Madden. "I'm pickin' up a warrant on my way. See?"

"You better go easy, Trace," urged Quinny. "You don't have no sure-thing case—an' a girl like her can't run away."

Madden grunted. "She's guilty, all right. Couldn't of been none of those mugs out in the hall. What could they make?"

"We don't know, but that ain't sayin' there couldn't be somethin'," argued Quinny. "Far's that goes, what could Glory Bain make? She's got plenty."

"Okay-okay! But I ain't goin' off half-cocked, Quinny. I'm passin' the decision to Captain Lendon, of course. I'm bettin' he says bring her in."

Quinny shrugged. This was what he'd expected and tried to avert by planting legitimate doubt in Madden's mind of Glory Bain's apparent guilt. The conviction was growing in his own mind that the girl was a victim of circumstance, resulting in a situation primarily created by Maestring, Nailton and the two women. The weapon used to kill the actor was of singular menace to the girl as well. She alone of this group had more or less legitimate access to it.

He followed Tracy Madden out of the apartment and down the stairs, thinking deeply of all this. One thing was certain: Henry Page would be forced to reveal the robbery to the police. It would be short work for them to trace such a historical piece to his collection. Tracing it to the murderer's hand might not be so easy, but Quinny was faced with this, if he hoped to solve the riddle. He thought about it, with a queasy realization that doing so might implicate the girl in the theft, even if removing the implication of more violent crime. That would be unpleasant, too, but less tragic.

He left Tracy Madden at the building entrance, turning along the slippery, snow-covered sidewalk toward Broadway. Reaching the steps to the small barroom under the Hotel Maywood, he went down them and entered. A stiff slug of rye might drive the chill from his blood. First, though, it would be a good idea to warn Berte Dill of the impending visit of Tracy Madden and, in all probability, Captain Bull Lendon, the homicide chief. There was a phone booth just inside the doors to the dingy bistro.

"Berte ain't here," responded the voice of Mrs. Weber to his query. "She went along to the hospital with that girl and her brother. Dr. Stokes says she's maybe got the pneumony. Ain't that just awful?"

"Sure is," replied Quinny glumly. Nevertheless, he was glad that Glory Bain was safely out of the clutches of the law, at least in a fashion. "Where'd they take her?"

"Babtis' Hospital—and her prob'bly Episcopalian!" exclaimed Mrs. Weber, disapprovingly. "I guess if a pers'n is sick enough, it don't make much diff'rence, though. You'd never guess where I had Berte."

"I ain't interested," Quinny said hurriedly. "Did you say Mr. Page went to the hospital, too?"

"Yes, I did," answered Mrs. Weber shortly, peeved at not having been permitted to reveal an interesting detail in the career of Berte Dill. "He said to tell you to call him up there—right away—if you called up here. You know, he's a right interestin'-lookin' man. How old d'you s'pose he is?"

"Forget it, Mamie—he ain't your type," advised Quinny. "If Berte comes home, tell her I'll be phonin' later."

Quinny called the hospital and, after some delay, succeeded in getting a connection with Henry Page. The man's voice sounded worried.

"This is a terrible thing, Hite," said Page. "I'm all confused about what to do—"

"Never mind about you," Quinny cut in. "How about Miss Bain? Has she really got pneumonia, like Mrs. Weber told me?"

"She very definitely has. An oxygen tent has been ordered."

"That's bad," Quinny's expression was solemn. "Now, look, I think we better have a talk, Mr. Page."

"I was going to suggest it. Could you come to my house? There's nothing I can do here."

"Yeah. I'll be along after a while. Somethin' I want to look into first—won't take long. How about Miss Dill, is she still there?"

"No," returned the worried voice. "She's just left for home. I had the very devil of a time convincing her it would serve no useful purpose for her to sit in the reception room here. She's a stubborn young woman."

"You're tellin' me! All right, Mr. Page—I'll get up as soon's I can. So long."

Quinny emerged from the smelly telephone booth and walked over to the bar. A hold-over from the speakeasy era, it hadn't been changed to any extent and, from the sour odor, hadn't been cleaned since repeal. Only a couple of patrons were present—a dwarf and a dumpy, flat-nosed, tin-eared palooka who probably made hooch money letting himself be slugged about in some Eighth Avenue training gym. The dwarf, Quinny knew, ran the hotel elevator. He answered, when not in a sullen mood, to Sneezy.

"Hello, sneaky-foot," he called, in a surprisingly booming bass.

"Hi, Sneezy," returned the detective, settling a foot on the rail. "Where's Snow-White? Slip me a quick rye an' soda, barkeep—an' a couple o' beers for my friends here."

"I like rye all right," suggested the palooka in a reedy tenor.

"Aw, shut up, Kid," growled the dwarf. "Nobody ast you what you like. You're lucky to get even suds offa dick—an' you wouldn', on'y you're with me. See?" He grinned insolently at Quinny and waved his baby-like hand toward his companion. "Kid Gunk," he introduced.

The battered pugilist bobbed his head a half inch or so, his watery blue eyes not wavering from Quinny.

"Who'd you ever lick?" asked the detective carelessly, coiling his fingers around the highball glass.

Kid Glink dropped his eyes and shuffled his feet. "Nobody, yet," he said apologetically. "But, I keep on tryin'. They can't hang a guy fer that. I nearly kayo's Benny Fogarty coupla years back. I got him hangin' on th' ropes, see, but whilst I'm makin' up me mind which han' to slug 'im with, the rat hangs a haymaker on me chin. Was I s'prised when I comes to on the canvas!" He shook his head glumly.

The dwarf climbed up on the rung of a bar stool. "Like this?" he asked, and swung his pudgy fist to Kid Glink's jaw.

"Hey, youse! Lay off," piped the Kid shrilly. "That hoit!"

"Behave, Sneezy. I want to ask you something," Quinny said. "Were you on the elevator couple of hours ago?"

"I was off duty at eight." Sneezy showed instant reluctance to talk.

"I was wonderin' if you happened to get a look at a dame in a black fur coat about that time. She might of got on at the fourth floor." Quinny frowned. "I guess it would have been after eight, at that," he added.

"What's the racket?" demanded the dwarf, belligerently. "You oughta know I don't go shootin' off my mouth about women in the hotel."

"This one don't live here," amplified Quinny. "She wouldn't be anybody you ever saw before, neither. She ain't wanted for anything. I'm just checkin'—on an angle, see?"

Sneezy examined Quinny narrowly, then seemed reassured. "Sure, I see this dame—if it's th' same one," he said. "I was off duty then, an' up on th' second floor. I see a woman walkin' down—like you say, wearin' a black fur coat. She was drippin' water like she'd fell in a bathtub, clothes an' all."

"That's what I wanted to know. Same one, okay." Quinny eyed the little man for a speculative moment. He knew it would be useless to try to get any information about anyone living in the hotel from him. That is, in any ordinary way. "You know Nana Lester?" he asked sharply.

"She's a burlesque dame," replied the dwarf. "An' that's all I got to tell about her."

Quinny grinned. "Push-over for a skirt, ain't you?" he needled. "She had plenty to tell me about you, kid. But plentee!"

"What'd'yu mean?"

"Numbers."

Sneezy's eyelids flickered uneasily. He found the numbers game a distinctly profitable sideline to the business of running an elevator—and Quinny knew that it was a rare bellboy or elevator operator in the Times Square district that wasn't an agent for the racket.

"That stripper's full of—"

"She's sore at you about—somethin'," cut in the detective, adding salt to the dwarf's injured ego. "Skip it. You wouldn't know anything about Nana Lester. She's too smooth a worker for a dumb mutt like you. I gotta go—"

"Don't be so sure I don't know nothin' about her," growled the little man, his eyes flaming. "What'd'yu wanta know?"

"How long has she been split up with Jimmie Nailton?"

Sneezy made a reprehensible noise. "They ain't split," he asserted. "Where did'yu get that bull? They sleep together, an' if they ever throw a fight, I never hear 'em. I would."

"You wouldn't be no help gettin' the divorce she says she wants," observed Quinny.

"No? For a finif I could get her any dame in th' joint for that kind of job," retorted Sneezy. "What'd'yu think these jills live on—hay? But I ain't been ast. Jimmie don't want no divorce, neither, fr'm either Lester or that front room they live in. 'Specially the room. She pays the rent."

"Okay, kid." Quinny threw a coin on the bar. "Give 'em another beer, Ed. I gotta travel."

"Wait a minute, Hite. What's all this guff about?" demanded the little man.

"Nothin' much." Quinny grinned tolerantly. "You better go back. Kid Gunk is movin' in on that beer dough I left."

Quinny went to the back stairs which led up at the side of the elevator shaft to the lobby, mulling over what he had learned about Nailton and his wife. More and more the odor of fish came over the story told by Nana Lester. Firmly convinced now that the whole episode was a blackmail job, with the jewel robbery somewhere in the, as yet, unpenetrated background, he climbed the stairway to the fourth floor.

He went into the public bathroom, which had a window facing out over the roof traversed by Glory Bain in escaping the apartment. The catch was fastened tightly, indicating that the window had not been used for any outgoing traffic toward the Silburn apartment. Quinny unfastened it and raised the window, recoiling against the cold blast of air that swept in. Then he climbed out, trusting that Greenbaum had finished his mission and gone back to the apartment. It wouldn't be fun for the detective to find himself dodging a fusillade from the startled homicide squad man.

He turned toward the rear of the hotel, walking with difficulty through the deep drift along the wall. Passing a couple of windows which obviously no one had climbed from, he came to another which marked the end of one of the trails. As Glory had left the roof via a window nearer the front of the building (which Quinny thought likely had been the room occupied by Nana Lester from what Glory had told him), this must be the trail of the unknown visitor to Silburn's apartment.

For a few minutes he studied the marks in the snow, both on the roof at his feet and the ledge itself. Some yards away, in the flashing light from the advertising signs, he saw other marks which he presumed had been left by the bulky Greenbaum. There was nothing to give him a hint of which direction the person had been going, so he tried the window. It opened easily. He didn't consider this particularly significant. Even though the catch had been engaged, it would have proved nothing, as this could have been set by someone else, after the window had been used for an exit.

Quinny climbed in. Not worried greatly at being discovered in the room, he crossed to the door to switch on the lights. Then he returned to the window to inspect the floor under it. Except for the snow he had brought along climbing in, the floor was quite dry. This settled the question of direction of the trail across the snow-covered roof. Someone had gone from this room to the Silburn apartment.

Closing the window, Quinny gave the room a casual inspection. It had the look of being occupied on a "permanent" basis. Bookshelves had been put in, well filled with works that would have been dull going to a typical guest of the hotel. The furniture was in better condition than that to be found in other rooms of the Maywood, with two or three lamps and a comfortable easy chair. Quinny picked up an envelope from a desk in the corner. It was addressed to Robert Enstey, care of a real estate firm on Seventy-second Street.

The one closet revealed nothing of interest. Thinking it likely the room had merely been used as a passage to the roof, without knowledge of the legitimate tenant, Quinny didn't feel justified in a thorough search. He went to the hall door, which was held with a spring lock needing no key to operate it from inside. In the corridor, he stopped to make sure the lock had not been tampered with from that side.

He found the night clerk downstairs working on his books behind the grilled-off section of the desk. Quinny stopped, drumming his fingertips on the blotter, to wait until the clerk showed signs of finishing with the column of figures he was adding. One of the guests came to the counter to look across at the pigeonholes on the back wall, and, seeing a letter in his box, pushed through the wicket to go and get it. The clerk seemed hardly conscious of the unorthodox procedure, but presently lifted his head and nodded.

"Hello, Hite," he greeted. "What brings you here? I don't see any bodies on the housekeeper's check list."

"You're short a guest, just th' same," returned Quinny. He gave the deeply interested clerk a brief résumé of events. "You got a fella named Enstey here. Who is he?"

"Works for some real estate outfit, uptown. He's lived here for years. He's out of town now—left for Boston last Monday. What's wrong? Enstey's a right guy, Quinny." The clerk twirked humorous eyebrows. "That's more'n I would say for most of our guests."

"You're sayin' to me," grinned the detective. "Well, I ain't got anything on him. Look, pal, do people have to pick up their own keys and letters out of the rack there—like I saw a fella do a minute ago?"

"Sometimes, if I'm busy. What the hell—saves me jumping up and down, don't it?"

"Yeah." Quinny frowned, giving the iron hat a backward push. "Look, I want a gander at Nailton's room before his widow comes back from the precinct station. How about lendin' me the key?"

"That's asking a lot, brother," resisted the clerk. "It's against the rules."

"So's murder. I'd hate to have to tell Captain Lendon you turned me down." He had no intention of telling Bull Lendon about it—or anything else concerning the case. They weren't chums.

The clerk reached around and plucked a key, attached to a metal disk, from a pigeonhole and dropped it on the counter. "I hope you get out of the room before Nana Lester gets back here," he said. "That stripper's got a temper you could fry eggs on."

"This I have noticed myself," agreed the detective. "But I like my eggs scrambled. I'll take a chance."

Quinny sauntered to the elevator, hoping to find the operator who had taken him up earlier still sober enough to stop the car somewhere short of the roof. The man was still pretty high, but functioning.

Unlocking the door to Nana Lester's room, the detective went in. He stood for a moment, surveying the interior, an architectural replica of Abe Munch's quarters across the hall. The furniture was different without being any better, used mostly as handy objects on which to toss odds and ends of feminine frippery and costumes. Some of the latter were of singularly violent color and design and provided with long zippers at strategic points. A couple of brilliant-studded G-strings hanging at the side of a bureau mirror would have made a Cartier showcase look like a boxful of coke.

Crossing the littered room, Quinny looked into the closets, finding them packed with stage costumes and other clothing. A lonely looking suit squeezed between silks was Jimmie Nailton's sole contribution, as far as the detective could see. There were several bags and an animal carrier on the floor, all emptied of contents.

It would take a couple of men all night to sift through this stuff, he decided, and he had no idea how long Madden would keep Nana Lester at the station. This would have to wait. He abandoned the closet and walked to the side window, to check on what Glory Bain had said about her entrance into the hotel. It opened stiffly, but with not too much difficulty.

An agonized wail abruptly ripped the silence of the room behind him. He whirled around, his scalp crawling. At first look he saw nothing capable of such a howl, then spotted a little black face and earnest blue eyes staring at him from the floor under the edge of the bedspread. He relaxed, grinning sheepishly. "One o' them Synamese cats," he muttered. "Shut up, Minsky!" The animal came timidly from under the bed and squawked again, less noisily. On more comprehensive evidence, Quinny revised his guess. "No—you must be Gypsy Rose Lee."

Glory Bain had climbed in from outside through this window, as shown by the disturbed snow. He closed the window and transferred his attention to bureau drawers. The bottom ones were stuffed with finery, which would need to be gone through carefully, if he wished to avoid leaving certain evidence of his visit. He did not, private operators having no leeway at all in such an unauthorized search. The two top drawers were more rewarding. One was filled with garish and theatrical costume jewelry.

He sifted through the stuff casually, having little confidence in his judgment in the matter of jewelry. Good stuff and well-made phonies looked pretty much alike to his unpracticed eye. But most of this wasn't well-designed, mainly accenting glitter. He picked up a piece having slightly less abandon than the others. It was a brooch, in the form of a large spider, set with green stones. With a cynical smile, he started to drop it back into the drawer, when recollection sent his hand diving into his inner coat pocket for the list given him by Henry Page. His gaze ran down the items and stopped.

> Brooch. Spider design. Eight small emeralds each leg, one large on back. Marquise de Montespan, mistress Louis XIV of France.

"Bingo!" exulted Quinny. Now he was getting somewhere! He studied the jewel, even counting up on the emeralds on the legs. There could hardly be any question of the identity of the bauble. He returned it to the drawer and closed it, deciding that it would be more useful where it was. Pretty slick, hiding it in with a lot of junk so it wouldn't be noticed! If he had only been sure of time for uninterrupted search, he might find some more of Page's stuff in the room.

There wasn't going to be time. Not even enough to leave the room unobserved. He heard the rapid succession of clacking high heels in the hall, then the door was shoved in forcefully to reveal Nana Lester, seething with anger.

Miss Lester's introductory remarks were colorful and rendered with fine emotion, but distressingly lacking in elegance. Their only novelty, however, to the detective was in such a maledictory blast coming from a piquantly pretty face. Finally she stopped for lack of breath—not ammunition.

"Well?" she demanded.

Quinny nodded, then pushed up his hat a little. "Yeah-yeah," he said. "Pretty good. Your papa must of been a dockwalloper, baby."

"I asked you what you were doing in my room!" she flamed afresh.

"Was *that* what you was sayin'?" Quinny's eyebrows shot up as if hitched to rubber bands. "I didn't get it. I sort of got an idea you was speakin' about my folks, which you seem to know real good—even better'n me."

"I should call a cop and have you thrown in the can!" Nana Lester added a couple more descriptive words.

"Look, you!" snapped Quinny sternly. "There's a little cat under the bed, which is full of littler cats, seems if. Is that any kind of talk to be throwin' around in front of a expectin' mother? I ask you, as man to woman."

Nana Lester's sensuous face blazed with fury as she choked over a few more expressions calculated to raise blisters on an alligator. Quinny listened, with approving nods, till she finished.

"Okay," he said as she paused. "That last took you clear through the deck, I guess. Now listen, stripper, you ask me what I've been doing in your room. I been lookin' around, see, and I found somethin' here which will take you off the burlesque wheels quite a while. Where this will send you, G-strings ain't fashionable. You might get a harp, though, if you're a good girl an', like Father Moynihan says, get your soul cleaned up in time."

The raging glitter in the girl's eyes wavered into uneasy speculation. Quinny sauntered toward her. She was still in the doorway.

"You just dare to take anything from this room! I'm calling a cop, right now!" She came from the door in a sudden movement, bringing up at the rickety bedside table, on which the telephone sat.

"Don't bother—they'll be comin' here, anyway. After you." The detective's mask of affability faded. "What I found can stay where it is. You won't dope out what it means, on account of you're a lame-brain body-waver which couldn't even think straight long enough to keep out of a stinkin' blackmail racket. Now you're tied in on a murder, baby. Strip-tease out of that, if you can!"

Nana Lester, her hand on the phone, showed more resentment than alarm. Nevertheless, there was a flutter of agitation in her torrid eyes. "What blackmail racket?" she demanded throatily. "Are you crazy?"

"You wouldn't know." Quinny's gaze swept over her contemptuously. "That clunk playwright, Maestring, an' the dame which says she's your sister, fix up a deal with you and your husband to shake Glory Bain from thick dough. Smart guys! You see what you collect, don't you? Nailton dead like a herring on account of a doublecross somewhere. Cops fixin' for the rest of you to take the rap for killin' him. You like?"

Nana Lester gasped sharply. She sat down heavily on the bed. "It's not true! I wanted a divorce. That's all."

"Well, you got one—kind of."

Watching her narrowly, Quinny thought he saw signs of slipping control. She was fighting to overcome spasmodic breathing, betrayed by the throbbing movements of her breasts, and her eyes were enlarging.

"You—rotten tramp!" she exploded.

"Don't worry about me, kid," Quinny advised. "You could think about that poor mug, Jimmie Nailton—prob'ly stretched out in a Morgue icebox by now. Awful cold." He came over to stand close in front of the girl, and, catching sight of a well-smoked pipe in an ash tray on the bedside table, picked it up. "I bet he loved this pipe," he continued morosely, smacking the bowl against his palm. "Guys do, don't they?"

Nana Lester stared at the blackened briar as though at a ghost in which she didn't quite believe. Her eyes swelled moistly and long fingernails bit savagely into her palms. An uncontrollable, choking sob thrust upward from her throat and, turning abruptly, she threw herself face down across the bed, no longer able to stifle her wracked emotions.

"Jimmie . . . Jimmie . . . Jimmie—!"

Crazy about the guy, like Sneezy said, exulted Quinny. He didn't like what he was doing, but he had to know the truth of the divorce set-up. Knowing it to be a phony frame made a difference.

"Take it easy, babe," he said soothingly, putting the pipe back in the ash tray and dusting his hands together. "You ain't the first dough-dizzy jill to pull a bust."

The burlesque girl twisted on the bed to glare up at Quinny with freshened hate. She mumbled something the detective didn't catch, but got enough for the gist.

"Okay—I know how you feel, but what will that get you? If it was me, I'd want to make sure the guy who fixed me up helped pay off." He paused, watching her intently, then went on. "Of course, though, he gets off free. Prob'bly won't even kick in on Jimmie's funeral expenses—"

"Don't!" the girl whimpered. "Please."

"—not even a handful of crumby, second-hand daisies to lay on the coffin lid," the detective pressed relentlessly. "I know the kind o' guy he is. Smooth worker—knows how to get people to stooge for him . . ." He paused, seeing that the girl was staring at something behind him.

"Phil!" she wailed.

Quinny swung around and saw the owner of the Living Room, Phil Silburn, standing in the open doorway.

"What's going on here?" demanded Silburn. His lantern jaw clamped shut again and small, closely set eyes under shaggy brows gleamed belligerently.

"This guy's a lousy private dick, Phil!" shouted the girl. "Throw him out!"

"That will be a pleasure," growled Silburn. He lowered his pugnacious head and stepped toward Quinny.

8

MR. SILBURN INTERVENES

Quinny Hite, shifting his feet for a more fluid defense, watched the approach of the night club man with the alert caution of a prize-fighter. A rugged bringing-up in the turbulent environs of Hudson Street had long ago conditioned him to any sort of rough and tumble as well as more forthright slugging matches.

"Do I throw you out, or do you scram on your own?" growled Silburn, slowing down. He didn't care for the detective's unruffled readiness. "I should slug you one, anyhow."

"Go ahead—throw it," taunted Quinny. "That cowcatcher jaw you got needs pushin' back, and I wouldn't charge you a dime for doin' it. Maybe, though, while you can still wag it, you better tell me where you stand in this blackmail racket."

"Blackmail?" Silburn stopped, safely more than an arm's length away. "What are you talking about, Hite?"

"Thanks. Didn't think you remembered me." Quinny grinned sourly. "I'm talkin' about the job to collect dough off of Glory Bain—kind of a new style badger-game play. Do you hold cards—or on'y takin' a cut for lendin' your love-hideout for the frame-up?"

"Hit him, Phil!" enthused the girl. She swung her feet from the bed to the floor and sat upright.

"That would be a good way to keep from answerin', wouldn't it?" jeered Quinny.

"Let me handle this, Nana," snapped Silburn. "See here, smart guy, I don't get this at all."

236

"You didn't know this bubble dancer's husband got knocked off by somebody in your apartment a while ago, either, did you?" prodded Quinny. "If you did, you sure didn't lose no time in runnin' in to call on the widda."

Silburn flicked an uneasy glance at the girl sitting on the edge of the bed, then back to the detective. "Certainly, I heard about the murder, but your crack about blackmail is news."

"Nuts! You're the mug who planned it out." Quinny laughed insultingly. "The stripper here gives me this item before you came in."

Silburn faced the burlesque doll. "Why, you little—"

"That's a lie, Phil!" shrieked Nana Lester. "I never said such a thing! He's just trying to trick you."

"She didn't spill it in words. But she gave with it, just th' same." Quinny improved his strategic position by moving sidewards a step. "You saw a chance to grab safe dough an' a chance maybe to move in on Nailton's territory here. Yeah, big shot—you are standin' pretty to take the murder rap."

Silburn gurgled wrathfully. "Why, you lousy, stinking—"

"Now, wait a minute." Quinny held up his hand like a traffic cop. "Remember, you're s'posed to be refined. Anyhow, when it comes to callin' names, you can't compete with this burlesque jill. She knows 'em all—an' she just said 'em. An' I didn't say you killed Nailton. But, if you don't want to sit for that picture, you better go to work on a good alibi."

"I was at the restaurant until a short while ago."

"Unless you can prove you were there till after eight o'clock, old pal, you better not pull that when you start explainin' to Bull Lendon. Here's somethin' else he's goin' to want to know—and this hits you, too, sister"—Nana Lester came under the detective's prob- ing stare—"Bull is goin' to be awful curious how many people knew that they could crash into that apartment by goin' across the roof from this hotel. You did and she did." Quinny chuckled humor- lessly. He was trying a fast ball, without much confidence in where it would land. "I oughtn't to tip you off like this, Silburn, but this murder ain't what I'm workin' on."

Silburn's shaggy eyebrows were a continuous black line across his forehead and his lantern jaw stuck out further than ever. "Give me one sane reason why I should be mixed up with what happened to Jimmie Nailton, or Glory Bain, or any of this!" he roared.

"Killin' somebody don't always have a sane reason," replied Quinny. "Sittin' in on the Bain deal is different. You're the only one I've come across that's in a spot to put a gang o' crooks in contact with her. How'd she meet up with Nailton, Maestring and this beetle, if you didn't put it over? They ain't Living Room types."

"Are you referring to me as a beetle?" demanded the girl haughtily. "You'd better use more choice in your words, you bum!"

"I pick 'em out careful," assured Quinny earnestly. "How about giving me the low-down on this dame which was with you a while ago over in Silburn's apartment. She said she was your sister."

He saw a certain resemblance between the two women, but this one's disposition showed more alley cat wariness and hair-trigger bellicosity, he thought.

"Her name is Melford, and so, what?" retorted Nana Lester defiantly. "If you want anything more than that, you'll have to get it from her. And, believe it or not, she *is* my sister!"

"Okay. What's that make her to you, Silburn?"

"No more than we've been friends for years," replied Silburn, looking confused. "Has that anything to do with you?"

"Nope," returned Quinny cheerfully. "I could see she's been around. I go for younger models, myself."

"Never mind cracks," grated Nana Lester. "Finish your business and get out."

Quinny nodded. "It's an idea," he drawled. "I don't seem to be helpin' anybody, stayin' here. I'll ankle along." He passed around Silburn, heading for the door.

"You wait a minute!" exclaimed Silburn. "I want to set you straight on a couple of things."

"Shoot." Quinny stopped, reaching up to reset the iron hat.

"You got it wrong, thinking blackmail was behind what happened in my apartment," said Silburn. "Jimmie Nailton has been playing around too fast with dames. Nana wanted to catch him—short. See?"

"She didn't want no divorce." Quinny eyed the girl on the bed. "On account of she's nuts about him. Don't hand me that."

Silburn paused for a fleeting glance at Nana Lester, then answered. "I didn't say she did. What she wanted was to get Jimmie in a spot he couldn't wiggle out of—"

"She done that, okay."

"Shut up, will you? She knew that if he was alone any time in an apartment with a good-looking woman, he'd make passes. So, we fixed it up to have the play reading there and for the rest of us to be late. That's all there was to it. I offered my place for the reading because there wasn't a chance that Glory Bain would go to the dump on Fifty-third Street where Kyle Maestring lives—and because he wanted to impress Sol Leverring." Silburn's undershot jaw clicked shut.

"Was Maestring tipped off to stay away till late, too?"

"Naturally."

Quinny scowled, and shot a question at Nana Lester. "If this was all just nice, clean fun, why did you have to slip Abe Munch ten bucks?"

"I didn't. He owes me ten, and I suppose he thought this would square it. It won't!"

"Right." Quinny's attention switched back to Silburn. "So, Maestring shows at the party more'n an hour late—an' you don't show at all. What kept you?"

"I didn't want to hear that stinking play again," explained Silburn. "I can stand just so much of that sort of goo. And I was at the apartment a few minutes ago—before coming here."

Quinny thought the reason offered for the night club man's delayed arrival was the most logical he'd heard yet, even if it didn't stand up later.

"You probably never did anything in your life for nothin', Silburn," he observed. "Where did you figure to make on the play readin'?"

"I didn't figure. I was doing Maestring a favor, that's all."

"You're slippin'. Sure you weren't settin' pins for the girl friend there?"

"What do you mean?" demanded Silburn restlessly.

"I mean this play readin' stunt was rigged to get Glory Bain in your apartment. I still have my own ideas why—an' catchin' Jimmie Nailton in fragrant delicious ain't part of 'em." Quinny rubbed his chin between his fingers and thumb a moment, then shifted his gaze to Nana Lester. "Where did you pick up the notion Glory Bain was interested in your husband?"

"Because he talked about her all the time, that's why," retorted the girl. "Jimmie never could keep his trap shut about a woman he was chasing."

"You said you called Glory Bain a couple o' times—to warn her off."

"Sure, I—" Nana Lester broke off, lips still parted. Then she shrilled, "Why, I never said any such thing!"

Quinny laughed. "But you did call her—told her she better lam for Europe, or some place. You also wrote her an anon'mous letter—"

"I did not!" The denial had a vaguely hollow ring. "Why should I? With Jimmie, if it wasn't one woman, it was another."

Quinny turned to the night club man again. "From what I know, this frame looks like the stripper wanted a chance either to get rough with Glory Bain—or shake her down. I ain't had a good reason yet. Do you have one?"

Silburn shrugged. "I don't know any more than you do. I've given you what I understood about it."

"Uh-huh," doubted Quinny. "Look, do you know a man named Robert Enstey?"

"Enstey?" Silburn's expression faded from blank surprise into a gleam of recollection. "A man of that name works for the firm handling the Living Room property. He comes in occasionally to look over the premises. What about him?"

"Just askin'," replied the detective laconically. "Do you know him, Miss Lester? He lives here—on this floor."

The girl shook her head.

"Well, I guess I might as well leave this little gatherin'. Captain Lendon's hands will prob'bly be comin' to drag you back to clink, soon's he gets through addin' up what he knows. No use me bein' there—I can read about it in the papers, after." He snapped a finger formally against the rim of his derby. "Good-night, all."

Closing the door after him, Quinny walked heavily some steps down the hall toward the elevator. In a moment, he was back, listening intently outside the door. He heard Phil Silburn running through a discourse on Quinny Hite, his immediate family, plus some ancestors Quinny himself didn't know about. This finished, the voice calmed down.

"What did you tell that louse, Nana? You must have said something, or he wouldn't have made all those cracks."

"He got no ideas from me," insisted the burlesquer's voice. "He brought 'em with him."

"Somebody's been popping off," Silburn retorted. "And I wouldn't trust Maestring in a pinch. He gets hysterical."

"Ju likes him. Maybe he's got more guts than you think. When it comes to action, I notice you keep somewhere in the back."

"Okay-okay! It seems to me that Ju's showing bad judgment, falling for a guy like Maestring—if she is. He's got nothing on the ball at all," argued Silburn. "Well, it looks like we've got to call the thing off, Nana. You can see that, can't you? It's too hot, now."

"You certainly don't expect me to do any more." Quinny heard a quick sob. "Haven't I lost Jimmie, as it is?"

"That was a tough break," soothed the night club man. "I didn't know he meant so much to you. But it won't be easy to get Ju to drop this. She'll insist that the set-up is perfect to cash in—that nobody's got a thing on us that will stick. I'm going to the club now. I'll call you tomorrow, Nana." A brief pause, then, "You poor kid! I know how you feel, but you better hold together for a while longer. It won't help Jimmie for you to go to pieces—and it might hurt us."

"I'm not staying here alone. Take me over to Ju's apartment."

Silburn seemed unenthusiastic. "How about the cats?"

"They'll be all right. Your car's out in front, I suppose."

"Sure. I brought Ju home a minute ago."

"Well, wait till I put my coat back on."

Quinny tiptoed away from the door, grousing inwardly that the conversation he had listened to hadn't been more illuminating. The best thing to do was to let them play out the string, if they would. The woman, Ju Melford, seemed to be high card of the outfit, instead of Silburn, as he had first thought. At least the two inside the room foresaw difficulty in persuading her to abandon the enterprise—whatever it was.

On the way downstairs, his thoughts shifted to the spider brooch he'd found in Nana Lester's bureau. There should be a quick search of the room for more of the loot, but Madden's lads could take care of that. Leaving the brooch might have been a gamble, but one worthwhile if it paid off. There existed a regrettable tendency to doubt a private operator's unsupported testimony. Yeah, better to let Tracy Madden find the pretty.

On the face of it, this precious group had certainly engineered the robbery, but, if so, there was still someone else in on it, he thought. Someone who had cased the job and made known the best time to pull it. Not necessarily Glory Bain. There were servants in the house as yet uninvestigated. Quinny couldn't see any gain in the theft for Henry Page's stepsister.

Meanwhile, Maestring's lodgings should have a going-over before the fellow had a chance to dispose of anything incriminating. Quinny decided to phone Madden and suggest the search, hopeful that the playwright was still being detained. The Lieutenant didn't know about the stolen stuff, of course, so Quinny would have to give him a steer on what to look for—and Page couldn't hope to keep the robbery secret now, anyway. If the department men located some of the stolen stuff in Maestring's place, it would serve as well as having done it himself.

Passing on to Nailton's murder, the more he considered it, the more curious it became why Nailton had been murdered at all. It didn't seem to Quinny that his death could have been useful to the crooks who had stolen Henry Page's jewelry—and yet, as a piece from the loot had been used, the killer's connection with them was plain enough. Thinking it over, his random shot at Silburn—insinuating that the night club man had plans to take over the widow—gained in plausibility. But the same situation could have existed for Kyle Maestring.

Coming out into the hotel lobby, Quinny saw the night clerk staring at him curiously. The detective grinned, lifted a hand palm upward, and shook his head, then went into a phone booth near the elevator. Madden, he learned, had not returned to the precinct station. But Quinny's hope that Maestring had been kept there was sustained.

"Look," he said. "I s'pose you guys have somebody out to frisk his apartment, ain't you?" The officer replied that they had not, as they were waiting for either Captain Lendon or Madden to show up. "Well, buddy," Quinny counseled, "it might turn out a good idea, see? If you do, tell 'em to look out special for jewelry. It could have something to do with the murder."

Quinny left the hotel. He caught a cab on Broadway and settled back in the cushions, his hands thrust deep into over-coat pockets. The cab headed across town, and his thoughts returned to the murder. He had an annoyingly unsubstantiated feeling that the killing was more than an accidental inclusion in a plan to besmirch Glory Bain. On the surface, the idea of collecting blackmail from someone locked up on a murder rap seemed fantastic. Ju Melford might not think so, Quinny reflected as the cab jolted eastward over the hardened lumps of snow. She might consider that Glory Bain was in a spot to pay heavily for anything which would get her out of it.

Quinny shook his head. This was sheer guesswork, something he rarely engaged in without some sort of lead. He felt he was being moved by the plight of Glory Bain—and that wouldn't do. A man in the business of homicide investigation never made any progress trying to prove someone's innocence. He had to dig out the truth, no matter whom it hurt, and truth was easier to recognize where sympathy had not interposed its veil.

QUINNY HITE LOUNGED in a deep chair in Berte Dill's luxurious living room and waited for the girl to come out of her bedroom. She'd returned from the hospital only a few minutes before, Mrs. Weber had told him, and was changing into a more comfortable outfit.

The old woman wandered about, making a poor pretense of inspecting various objects scattered around the room. Quinny watched her, with faint amusement. Her eyes were gleaming with unsatisfied curiosity about what was happening. Mrs. Weber, he knew, would stand this just so long. She picked up a limp leather volume of *Plutarch's Lives*, parked ostentatiously on a small table, and put it down again.

"Looky here, Quinny!" she exclaimed suddenly. "I been readin' about murderers all my live-long days. But this is the very first time I ever seen one."

"Don't be so sure you have yet," replied the detective acidly.

"Well, maybe no," defended Mamie Weber. "What I mean is that I never even seen anybody who might have been."

"You could put on your specs and look around sometime," commented Quinny. "Anybody could kill somebody. You, too. The way you heave bric-a-brac an' stuff at people when you get mad."

"But I don't ever aim to kill nobody," insisted Mrs. Weber, sheepishly. "I been doin' that since I was big enough to hold my rattle, but I never hit nobody. Except Sam Weber, who don't count nohow. He was my husband. I got him with a ketchup bottle an' th' stuff came out all over him. Sam thought it was him bleedin' an'

244

fainted dead away!" Mrs. Weber chuckled reminiscently. "He died right soon after that, anyway."

"He did?" Quinny looked stern. "Why, I oughta run you in, right away—"

"Oh, Sam didn't die on account of that!" corrected Mrs. Weber hastily. "A coal mine fell in on him."

Berte Dill came out of the bedroom, stopping in the doorway. "Who did a coal mine fall on?" she asked.

"Sam Weber," said Quinny.

"Oh, on Papa," said Berte. "Yeah, I remember that, kinda. I was four years old. The funeral, too. There were twelve automobiles, wasn't there, Mama?"

Mamie Weber nodded. "From his lodge. Some of 'em had people in 'em, too."

Berte, now in flame-red pajamas and robe, clattered across the floor in red satin mules, to plump down on the red velvet couch. Quinny watched her progress from his comfortable chair.

"You look like an ad for a tomater," he commented. He pulled himself up and went to sit on the couch at her side.

"Yeah?" replied Berte. "Well, what do you think you are, a head of lettuce?"

"Skip it," said Quinny. "Tell me about Glory Bain—is she going to be all right?"

"With pneumonia, you never can tell. I rode to the hospital in the ambulance, but they wouldn't let her talk. I guess she didn't want to, for that matter. You know, Quinny, I feel awful sorry for the kid."

"I guess Mr. Page didn't get to talk to her, either, then," mused Quinny. "I s'pose you gave him some idea what happened?"

"Not very much. When he got here, they were already taking Glory down to the ambulance. I told him that somebody had got killed at Maestring's apartment and that she was in a jam and that you said he'd better get the best lawyer he could to keep her out of clink. That was about all I knew anyhow, Quinny."

"Well, I told him that much on the phone a while ago." Quinny got up and rescued his overcoat from the radiator where it had been warming. "I better scram on up to his house," he continued. "The guy's prob'bly wonderin' why I ain't showed there already. I told him I'd be up. I wanted to find out how she was doin' first, though. From you, I learn about as much as I already know."

"What did you expect? Glory wouldn't see any use telling me about it—if she'd been able to."

"I s'pose not." Quinny, struggling into his overcoat, thought of something else that had brought him to Huntingdon House. "Say, do you know a canary named Ju Melford?"

"I know who she is. She used to sing at Club Orizaba—oh, quite a while ago."

"That all you know? What I want to know is what she didn't do in public."

"I wouldn't have been there, so how would I know?" snapped Berte. "And if I had, I wouldn't tell you. I don't use such language."

"When did you start gettin' ladylike and all?" scoffed the detective. "Never mind."

"What has she got to do with Glory Bain?" demanded Berte.

"This," replied Quinny, "is just what I want to know myself. She and her sister showed up at the apartment where Nailton was killed, with a phony story about catchin' the guy with another dame. To me, there was some other reason which I ain't figured out."

"You're going to help Glory?" Berte's warm eyes inspected him gravely.

"If it helps her any for me to crack the Nailton killin'," replied Quinny evasively.

"That wouldn't be because you could go for her, would it?" Berte's eyes grew a little hard. "Don't forget, sweetie pie, that I'm number one girl friend and there better not be any number two— or three!"

"I will bear this in mind," replied Quinny. "Don't get up," he said politely. "I can kiss you sittin' down just as easy."

Kissing Berte wouldn't make leaving her any easier, but otherwise was a refreshing experience. From the sultry expression that flamed in her eyes, it wasn't one which she found precisely boring, either. Not so for Mrs. Weber, who made a funny noise with her lips and stalked out of the room.

THE CAB VEERED from the lane between banks of snow on Riverside Drive, crushing through to the curb line like a destroyer bucking heavy seas, and stopped. Quinny Hite paid the driver and got out, grateful to find the worn steps to the portico of Henry Page's house had been swept. The cold wind from the river seemed to be blowing right through the fabric of his overcoat by the time someone came to answer his ring. It was Page.

"Sorry if I kept you waiting out here, Hite," he apologized. "My butler has gone home, of course."

"It's all right," said the detective, shivering and resisting the impulse to back up against the small radiator in the octagonal reception hall. "I ain't much stiffer'n a billiard cue."

"Come on back to the study. I've a fire in there."

The prospect of heat was alluring. Page led the way down the hall. Quinny trailed along, working on a nice, polite way to get himself invited to a couple of stiff jolts of rye. This time, he could skip the soda and ice. Entering the room behind Page, he circled around to stand close to the crackling flames. He shivered violently, but his host didn't seem to notice. He tried it again, adding to the gesture by blowing warm breath on his icy fingers. Page, who had taken up his standard position of standing behind the long table, persisted in muffing Quinny's sign language and seemed about to launch into one of his long, precise sentences.

"I read somewhere once," began the detective hurriedly, "that people which has been exposed to bitter cold and is liable to have their ears start fallin' off any minute is sometimes saved by a good slug of whiskey. S'pose there's anything in the idea?"

Henry Page produced a decanter and a glass from a stand in the corner behind him, put them on the table and shoved them across to the detective. "I hope you will excuse my lack of hospitality, Hite," he said. "I'm so worried and upset about what has happened"—he paused, swallowing nervously—"that I scarcely am aware of my actions. Help yourself."

"I know." Quinny filled the glass and downed it as though taking a pill. "I'm kind of worried myself. A girl like Miss Bain oughtn't to get loused up in this kind of deal. How is she? Did you get to talk to her?"

"Not a word. They were taking her down to the ambulance when I reached the hotel. The little I know I learned from Miss Dill." Page sighed heavily. "No details at all."

Quinny nodded. "Berte was standin' too far away to hear what Miss Bain said. Wasn't much more'n a whisper. I'll give you the whole picture—"

"It's sickening," Page cut in. "I would have given everything I possess to prevent it, not because of Glory alone, but for what may be the effect on my mother. She's a sick woman—with a rheumatic heart. The shock of this may very possibly . . . bring on the end. Although Glory is not her own child, she is devoted to her."

"Do you have to tell her right off? When we're sure about things, you might kind of break it to her easy-like."

Page shook his head. "I'm afraid not," he said morosely. "Newspapers and radio are her sole amusements now. If I cut them off, she will surely suspect something. Mother is an intelligent woman, you know."

"Well, what can you do?"

Page's usually bright eyes lifted to gaze dully at the detective. "I have been hoping that you might have developed something," he said. "I suppose I should have said 'wishing.' Perhaps this is something for which I should have been prepared, in view of the fears I expressed to you this afternoon concerning Glory's unwise choice of associates. Despite that, the news seems to have dazed me with shock. I can't think clearly at all."

Quinny was about to say something, when the telephone on the table shrilled.

"I'll take it!" he said sharply, reaching for the instrument. "I'm expecting a call. Hello?"

It was Lieutenant Madden, calling from the hospital, and obviously in a bad humor. He had called the precinct station and got Quinny's message to call the Page number.

"Hop in your prowl car—or whatever you're ridin'—and come over here," said Quinny. He gave Page's address. "Right away, see?"

Madden saw, but resisted.

"Well, you better, Trace," argued Quinny. "You ain't goin' to get anything hangin' around the hospital, unless it's a disease some mug's got. Look, I called you at the precinct, an', on account of you wasn't there, I told the cop who answered it would be a smart idea to give Maestring's flat a frisk before you turn him loose. I don't know whether your gang'll work on the tip-off or not. You could call and get 'em goin', if not. Then hightail it over here. Maybe you'll learn somethin'."

"I'll come—but I don't need to learn nothin' from you, you bum. Anybody'd think I was just out of high school, to hear you go on."

"Not if they knew you like I do, chowderpot. They'd settle for kindergarten, though." Quinny laughed hollowly, and disconnected. He looked at Page. "Gotta keep that guy in line," he explained.

Refilling his glass from the decanter, the detective carried it to the fireplace and sat down, stretching his feet toward the flames. He sipped a little of the whiskey, then looked over his shoulder at Page. "You said a minute ago you hoped maybe I had turned up something," he said. "Well, I have, but I don't see where it's goin' to make you feel any easier. Here's the main thing right now: nobody cut that gratin' out of the back window from outside."

Henry Page's eyes enlarged with surprise and he came back the length of the table toward Quinny. "Why, it must have been," he demurred. "There would be no other way to get into the jewel room."

"That's wrong," insisted Quinny. "There's a door, you know."

Page smiled with smug confidence, for the first time since the detective arrived in the house. "No one has a key to that door except myself."

"Did you have that lock put in?" Page nodded. "Generally, when you buy a lock, you get two keys," Quinny suggested.

"Yes. I have the other securely hidden."

"Maybe you only think so," argued the detective. "Seen this other key since the robbery?"

Some of Page's assurance faded. After short reflection, he picked up a leather-backed blotter holder from the table. The blotting side was curved, with a short, turned handle on the other. Page shook it and the thing gave forth a rattle. His expression lightened. "The blotter holder is hollow," he explained. "The other key is inside. No one would think of looking for it there."

Quinny wasn't convinced. "Open it up and leave us see if it's really the key."

Page pried the top off with the blade of his knife. In the shallow space under it Quinny saw a Yale key. Page dumped it from the holder into his free hand. "This is it," he said triumphantly. "So, you see, the thief must have come in through the window. Besides, Hite, why should the thief go to the trouble of sawing that heavy frame from the window, if there were an easier access to the room?"

"On account of he'd want you to think it was an outside job," drawled the detective, thinking that was obvious enough. He held out his hand. "Le's see the key."

Page handed it over and Quinny inspected it casually. It hadn't the shiny appearance of an unused key. Deciding there was no point in merely looking at it, he got up and went to the door to the jewel room. The key fit readily, but would not operate the lock. He glanced back at Page, who was watching him interestedly. "No dice," he said. "Le's compare it with the other one, Mr. Page."

Henry Page got out his key container and separated one from the others, coming over to the door. A brief comparison showed that the two keys had been cut for different locks. The detective tried the one Page had selected from the container. The bolt turned. Page looked chagrined.

"You are a thorough man, Hite," he said, sheepishly. "As long as I knew, from shaking the blotter holder, that a key was in it, a substitution wouldn't have occurred to me."

"You don't take anything for granted, in my business," replied Quinny unctuously. "Look, this key which was in the blotter has got a 'B' stamped on the handle end. Mean anything to you?"

Page looked startled. "Yes-s," he hesitated. "The basement keys to the house are marked that way. Oh!"

"Oh, what?" Quinny raised his eyes from the bit of brass he was studying.

Henry Page's black eyes shifted their direction toward the fire. "I'm afraid to speak of it," he said slowly. "Glory, of course, has one of these keys to the basement." He brightened slightly. "But, so has Arthur and his wife, as well as Dody—the girl—and Maura, the downstairs woman. So, there are four keys other than the one Glory carries."

"How about you?"

"I don't have one. I never use the basement entrance."

"Miss Bain does?"

"When she comes in late," explained Page. "Which is fairly often. By using that entrance, she can reach her room by the back stairway and avoid the chance of disturbing Mother."

"Well, I hope she's still got it," said Quinny. Then he remembered her bag, with a pair of keys in it, was in possession of the police.

"We can't check on the servants' keys until morning," observed Page, looking as though he wanted to rush right out and attend to this immediately.

"That will be time enough."

"I suppose." Page returned to his spot behind the long table. "This puzzles me, Hite: how did you come to the conclusion that the iron grating had not been cut from outside the house?"

"Because there ain't enough space between the window glass an' th' iron grating to work a hacksaw back an' forth. The window couldn't be opened from outside till the grating was off. Of course, it *could* of been sawed, but on'y with little, short strokes an' it would of taken four or five hours."

Henry Page nodded slowly, his black eyes speculative. "Shrewd, Mr. Hite. I hadn't thought of that, but then, I'd hardly qualify in your field. However, aren't you ignoring the fact that the thief had somewhere around eight hours for the work?"

"Nope." Quinny finished his drink, feeling the gratifying glow stealing through his veins. "What dopey crook would stand on a ladder or somethin' on a cold night that long doin' a job? Windows on all sides where neighbors, hearin' the noise, could take a gander at him. Nuts! Besides, nobody could of got over the back wall, bringin' somethin' to stand on—I didn't see no ladder or anything in the yard—without knockin' off some of the snow. I looked at the top of the wall. Not a mark on it—or those bushes right under it, either. This was inside work, Mr. Page."

"The deduction seems conclusive, Hite—even though my natural inclination is to rebel against it." He paced to the other end of the table, hands tightly clasped behind him and his head bowed in thought. "You can readily see the further implication against Glory. The police will believe, logically, that she had best access to the Montez dagger."

"Sure, but nothin' can be done about that. We got to spill about the robbery now, because the cops will get onto where the shiv come from, anyhow." Quinny frowned as he felt the vague prodding of his inner consciousness, but wasn't able to give it shape. He glanced sharply at Page. "You done anything about gettin' her a lawyer? She's goin' to need a good one, bad."

"I've phoned Rachelmeyer—"

"Tops—if he'll take on the job," Quinny cut in. Rachelmeyer was a criminal lawyer who would take on a case of this sort mainly for the promised publicity. He was not, however, averse to being paid. "When you goin' to see him?"

The front door buzzer echoed from somewhere in the back hall.

"That may be him now," said Page. "He's driving over from Brooklyn."

Page walked out of the study, leaving the detective settling in the comfortable chair by the fire. He listened dully to the faint, distant sounds of Page opening the front door, still trying to recapture the thought which had escaped him. It still eluded him, and then he heard Tracy Madden's hearty voice inquiring for him. Page brought the Lieutenant back to the study.

"You turn up in th' damndest places, Quinny!" Madden said accusingly. "Didn't take you long to find out where th' home plate was, did it?"

"Why should it?" asked Quinny mildly. "Ain't that where you start off from, too? I cut corners gettin' back, if I can."

Madden crossed the room and backed up against the fire, rubbing his hands behind him. "Well," he growled, "what you got to tell me? Come on—I ain't got all night."

"I have," needled the detective. "Me and Mr. Page here have got stuff to tell you which is goin' to make it look worse'n before for that girl in th' hospital, but you got to know about it. What's the set-up there?"

"At the hospital? The girl is in an oxygen tent, that's all. We'll have to leave her there till she's well enough to be moved to the clink. Under guard, o' course."

"Bull Lendon goin' to ask for an indictment on what he's got?"

"Certainly. It's open an' shut." Madden made a gesture with it.

"Then what the hell are you wanderin' around in this kind of weather for, Trace? If Bull's satisfied he's got a case, why don't you go home to bed?" Quinny shook his head. "No use me tryin' to tell you anything, then."

"Give!" snorted Madden. "Think I plowed snow all the way over here to hear you yap smart?"

"Okay-okay! Help yourself to a slug of Mr. Page's best—which is too good for you—and listen." He went into a long but tersely rendered account of what he knew that Madden didn't. The big Lieutenant listened attentively, occasionally intruding a sharp question.

"So," concluded Quinny, "now you got as much dope on this job as I have. What you are goin' to do with it is up to you."

"I don't see where it changes anything," commented Madden. "Like you said, Quinny, it just helps tie the girl into a bag she can't get out of."

"Maybe *she* can't," retorted Quinny. "Look, did you hear whether your boys turned up anything at Maestring's place? I s'pose not—there ain't been enough time."

"I've got 'em friskin' the joint, but what they find can't change anything," said Madden. "Suppose they do find some of Mr. Page's stuff? We found all we're interested in—stickin' out of Nailton's back. That dagger is the pay-off."

Quinny shook his head. "Not *that* one, Trace. There was two of them daggers—just alike." He fumbled in his vest pocket.

"So what? Suppose there was a dozen of 'em? Only the one we found means anything," debated Madden. But there was an uneasy expression in his eyes as he scrutinized Quinny.

The detective brought out the small red stone he had found in the closet at Silburn's apartment. "Take a squint at this, Trace," he said. "I picked it up in the closet where signs said somebody had hid out."

Madden inspected the ruby carefully, then shook his head. "It don't talk to me," he said. "What was the idea of holding it out?"

"I stuck it in my pocket and then forgot all about it till we left the apartment," explained Quinny. "Keep it, Trace. It might come in handy."

"What is it?" asked Page curiously, coming over from the table.

"Probably one of Hite's brainstorms," replied Madden, not bothering to show it. "Piece o' glass."

"Say, did you see Phil Silburn?" demanded Quinny abruptly. "There's a guy who maybe couldn't stand too close a lookin' over, Trace. It was his apartment where the murder was pulled, you know. And he was expected to show up there. Did he? After we left?"

"Not so far as I know. Probably didn't hear yet about the killin'."

"You're damned anxious not to tie-in anybody else to this job, ain't you, Trace? How come?"

"What's the use?" Madden made a skeptical gesture. "The case is busted. We can't prove anybody else was in the apartment when the guy got it. That water you saw in the closet don't mean a thing, Quinny. Nailton could of got it there hangin' up his coat—or somebody who came in and went out again before he showed up with Miss Bain."

"Nailton's coat wasn't in that closet," Quinny pointed out. "And, if somebody else was in the apartment before they came, you better find out who it was before you go asking for an indictment. Because I know—and so do you—that there was. That other trail across the roof, Trace, wasn't made by no sleepwalker from the Maywood."

"We don't know when he—or it, or whatever it was—was in the apartment."

"And so you're going to let it ride like that!" sneered Quinny. "Too bad, Trace. You used to be a smart dick. Now that the Commissioner has touched you with the brass, you hunt for easy outs."

"You are flirtin' with a bop on the nose, dick!"

"Go on—bop, if you think it'll help you any. There's maybe five or six thousand flatties on the force that can beat me up, but no bottletop lieutenants I can't think circles around!" raged Quinny. "Go ahead, pal—louse it up, and later on I'll give you the right answer—like I've done before."

"I suppose you've got it all doped out right now," taunted Madden. "Got your killer all taped, an' all."

"Sure," returned Quinny. "It's a natural. Want to know who he is?"

"Go ahead—spill it." Tracy Madden looked just a little less sure.

Quinny laughed. "A skull named Ludwig. It was his knife."

Madden glanced around at Henry Page. "I thought this shiv belonged to you," he complained. "Who's this Ludwig guy? Not you—unless that's your middle name."

Page smiled crisply, without humor. "I assume Mr. Hite meant to say that the dagger once belonged to Ludwig of Bavaria. It was presented by him to Lola Montez."

Lieutenant Madden's glare of suspicion swept around to Quinny. "Where do all these people come in?" he demanded. "You didn't tell me about any Ludwigs or Lolas."

"I keep tellin' you, Trace, you won't get anywhere bein' nasty with me," retorted Quinny, his flare-up of temper easing. "There you are—you never even heard of Ludwig and Lola."

"I certain'y haven't!" roared Madden. "You been holdin' out again. Where do I dig for this couple?"

"Forty-second and Fifth Avenue's the best place," said Quinny. "In a hist'ry book."

"Yeah? I could poke you one and feel good about it," growled Madden. "An' now I'm leaving for downtown. You can either stay here and tell jokes or break a trail through the snow to Broadway. I would have busted the rules an' given you a lift in the squad car, only for the cracks. Goodnight!" Madden stalked angrily into the hall and presently the sound of a slammed front door floated back into the study.

Page shifted his gaze to Quinny Hite. "Do you think it is wise to antagonize a police official?" he asked pointedly.

"You're expectin' Rachelmeyer, ain't you?" returned the detective. "He wouldn't appreciate havin' anybody hangin' around while he's talkin' things over with a client. Not even me. He'll take me on later—tomorrow prob'ly."

"I see," mused Henry Page. He filled his long cigarette holder, then tapped it tentatively against his teeth. "I wish you could be present, though. I'm at a loss what to tell Rachelmeyer."

"You needn't worry about that. He'll tell you. About all he can do right now is to keep the cops from botherin' Miss Bain till she can take it." Quinny buttoned his coat and adjusted the iron hat. "They prob'bly won't ask for an indictment yet, anyway. Madden ain't half as sure as he lets on—"

The front door buzzer interrupted with its wasp-like singing.

"I'll let him in," said Quinny. "An' I'll get in touch with you tomorrow. If what I got in mind works out, Miss Bain won't need a lawyer." He headed for the study door, looking back. "*If* it works out."

10

THE GLOVE BOX

Quinny led Lew Rachelmeyer down the hall and ushered him into the study. He wasn't interested in what transpired between the lawyer and Henry Page, but felt assured that the latter's resources were in for a generous carving. The lawyer, after Page's greeting, walked to the fireplace, holding pudgy hands to the fire. A big diamond flashed from a finger.

"See you tomorrow, Mr. Page," Quinny said, withdrawing.

Returning to the front door, he opened and closed it noisily, without leaving the reception hall. A moment later he was silently ascending the stairs to the second floor, hoping to locate Glory Bain's room and have a look into it before anyone else did. Reaching the head of the stairs, he stopped to case the layout.

Page's mother, Dr. Linden, he knew, occupied the front rooms. Opposite where he stood, he saw a closed door, which might be either the girl's or Page's room. He thought about it a moment, then recalled what Page had said about Glory's use of the back stairs when coming in late. Her room, then, was probably at the rear, too. He went down the wide hall, which turned off to the right further back.

The first door in the rear wall of the ell opened into the back stairway. Grateful that the old doctor's suite had been sound-proofed, he went to the next door and cautiously tried the knob. It turned easily and he pushed the door open a couple of inches, applying his eye to the crack to see what was beyond. It showed indisputable signs of being an unlighted boudoir.

Thrusting the door open, he went in and felt for the light switch. As he snapped it, at least ten lamps scattered about the room came on. He looked about him curiously. The architecture was Victorian, but the furnishings ultramodern. The dominant piece, a huge, square bed, had a covering with impressionistic animals woven into the fabric. The species would never be encountered in the Bronx Zoo, a circumstance Quinny would have thought all to the good.

So far as he was concerned, trends in decor were of moderate interest. More so was the fact that the room obviously had not been straightened since its occupant left. Glory Bain was no slave to the precept that discarded garments must be immediately put away. Quinny began a swift inspection of every drawer in the room, then, finding nothing pertinent, continued the search in a closet which extended clear across one end of the room to a bathroom—both evidently later additions to the house. The floors were several inches higher than in the chamber.

Thinking there was enough clothing in the closet to outfit a convent (one with uncommonly liberal views on costume, however), Quinny pushed the trailing garments back to examine the floor beneath. That space between this and the original floor would make an attractive hiding place to someone who didn't realize it would be one of the first things to catch the attention of an expert. But, without shifting a lot of piled luggage, Quinny couldn't be thorough and if there were such a cache he saw no signs of it.

He decided to abandon the search and take it up again in the morning, under less risky conditions. Rachelmeyer, he thought, might not spend much time with Page at this point in the case, and it might occur to Page to look into this room. After a glance into the pink-and-white bathroom, Quinny came out, and, extinguishing the lights, went out into the hall.

At the head of the stairway, he paused to listen. He could hear the murmur of voices in the study, and then, as a door opened below, the words became audible. Evidently the specialist in criminal defense was leaving.

"We can't do a damn thing, Page, till we know there's going to be an indictment," Rachelmeyer was saying. "We won't beat this case before it comes to trial, anyhow. Miss Bain was on the scene when the fellow was killed, a knife belonging to you was used, and, from what you tell me, the cops haven't any evidence that anyone else was in the apartment at the time—if anybody was."

"It is impossible to believe that Glory could have done such a thing!" argued Page.

"I wouldn't say that," retorted Rachelmeyer. "But that isn't the question. My work will be to get an acquittal, whether she did or not—and, my friend, that's going to be no simple matter. Don't worry about it. I'll beat this with fireworks, not evidence, if it comes to a showdown. I've licked tougher set-ups."

"Meanwhile, my mother will die of shock," said Page bitterly.

"Never count on what a woman will do, Page," comforted Rachelmeyer. "Dr. Linden may surprise you. Well, I'll toddle along. Boy, what a night! Only a deep sense of responsibility to those in trouble could have got me out!"

He ought to get one of his hired brains to write him a new line, reflected the waiting detective. He heard the front door open and close, then Henry Page returning to his study. Quinny went silently down the stairs and on into the octagonal reception hall. With great caution, he opened the heavy front door and went out.

With seeming irresolution, he tramped around in the drifted snow at the side of the stoop, picking up a handful to sprinkle on his shoulders and derby. Quinny could be thorough, when there was reason. This done, he pressed a cold finger against the button at the side of the door. Waiting for the response, he noticed that the snow blown into the basement entry bore no signs that anyone had entered the house that way since the storm began.

Henry Page opened the door. He looked disturbed, his black eyes examining the detective anxiously. "Come in, Hite. I didn't expect to see you again tonight. What's happened?"

Quinny came in, with a realistic shiver. "Good thing you was up an' handy to the door," he said. "Seems as if the North Pole is movin' down on New York. Rachelmeyer still here?"

Page closed the door. "He left a few minutes ago."

"I got to thinkin' about that key business an' came back," explained Quinny. "S'pose you lock up that back room where you keep your collection—where you *did* keep it, anyway—an' leave me have the key. I want to check it with the ones which was in Miss Bain's bag."

"I presume that is an excellent idea," returned Page doubtfully. He turned to go to the study, adding ruefully, "If you don't find Glory has its mate."

"It's a good idea, anyway," defended Quinny, trailing along after Page—and hoping the decanter hadn't been put away. "Trace Madden is goin' to think of it, sooner or later —an' I'd like to beat him to it. See?"

The decanter of whiskey was still on the table. Quinny made a beeline for it. "Mind if I have a snort?" he asked, sloshing some into a glass. "I'm prob'bly goin' to land in a oxygen tent along with Miss Bain, trampin' around in a blizzard like I been doin'."

"Can't have you taken down," replied Page absently. "In fact, I shall join you in what you refer to as a snort. I'm not cold, but my morale certainly is at a low ebb."

Quinny filled another glass and handed it to Page, who looked at the size of the potion with mild alarm. Quinny tossed the whisky down and shuddered delectably, but Page took his time and then consumed less than half the contents of his glass. He got out his key container and removed the wanted key, handing it to the detective.

"I shan't need it, of course," Page said. "But, you won't be able to make your verification before tomorrow, will you? It's getting quite late." He pulled his sleeve back and glanced at his watch, frowning.

"One thing about police stations—they stay open all night," said Quinny. "But I won't go around there till mornin', anyhow. This can keep, an' a man has to sleep sometime. I was just savin' a trip up in the mornin'."

"That's what I was thinking. If you like, I could put you up here."

"Well, I don't know," equivocated Quinny. "I could sure do with some shut-eye, but I'll have to get goin' early. Maybe I better scram on home—if I can get a cab. They're awful scarce up here on a night like this, I notice."

"Nonsense. We have plenty of unoccupied bedrooms here," insisted Page, to Quinny's relief. The fella might of said okay, I can get you a cab by phonin'. "Take off your coat and hat—and have another drink by the fire, if you like."

Quinny acquiesced, moving the decanter along the table to within reaching distance of the comfortable chair, and then sitting down to warm his recently exposed feet. "How'd you make out with Rachelmeyer?" he asked idly.

"He promises to do something, as quickly as he learns that Glory has been indicted."

Page went on with a comprehensive account of the conference, which got dull and then duller to the detective. Himself pretty well up on the procedure of a criminal lawyer like Rachelmeyer, the subject lacked novelty. Guys like him were only interested in beating the prosecution's case, not proving their client was innocent. Rachelmeyer would be a lot keener about getting a bunch of softies in the jury box, mugs whose insides he could get at and turn over with a show which ought to be in a theater instead of a court room.

And, if Glory Bain came to trial, she would never be the same girl afterwards, whether she beat the rap or not. She'd be headlined and sobsister'd and gossip-columned into a tattered effigy of her former self. Freed only through Rachelmeyer's undoubted eloquence, she wouldn't be exonerated in the public mind. The public still remembered Lizzie Borden, mainly for unexplained details of the crime of which they had not acquitted her, although the court had done so.

Quinny suddenly became conscious that Henry Page was asking a question. He rolled his head around and looked blankly at the other man, who had pulled a chair to the other side of the fireplace. "What did you say?" Quinny asked. He grinned self-consciously. "I guess the fire's makin' me dopey."

Page smiled understandingly. "I asked if you consider, as the situation stands, whether there's hope that Rachelmeyer will succeed in clearing Glory of this terrible charge?"

"He's pretty good," acknowledged Quinny. "But, he won't clear her. All he can do is beat the D.A.'s case—which is all he'll try to do. Gettin' her clear's my job—if she ain't guilty."

"I hope you accomplish it," said Page. "If so, the twenty-five hundred I promised will be doubled—whether my property is retrieved or not. I somehow have a great deal of confidence in you, Mr. Hite."

"Thanks." Quinny stretched luxuriously, smugly considering that there were certain advantages in handling jobs for people with dough. "Y' know," he said, "the screwy thing in this is the killer usin' that dagger at all. Proves somethin' to me."

"What is that?"

"Unless it was meant to be draped on Miss Bain, the murder wasn't planned. She wouldn't be dope enough to take that fancy shiv along, knowin' it would be traced right back here. And I can't see her packin' the thing around just because she thought it was pretty. Can you?"

"It doesn't seem at all probable," agreed Page.

"So, if she killed Nailton with it, the shiv was already there—an' handy," continued the detective. "Anybody else wouldn't care whether the knife was traced here or not—an' this could also be why it was used. See?"

Page nodded slowly. "You imply using the dagger might be a deliberate attempt to implicate Glory," he commented.

"You put it soft. But, if it was blackmail, I still can't figure how the mugs expect to collect from a girl which is in clink on a murder rap. They could on'y get her out by gettin' themselves in—I mean, if they propositioned you or Dr. Linden for smoky dough. They would not care for this."

"It is a baffling situation."

"You're sayin' to me." Quinny hoisted himself out of the chair. "Guess maybe you better show me that bed, if these brains I'm s'posed to be luggin' around are goin' to be any use tomorrow."

They went upstairs, single file, to the second floor. Page, arriving first, stopped to wait for Quinny.

"Dr. Linden has a suite there in the front," he said, pointing. "My quarters are here, and Glory has the large room to the rear. I can put you in a room on the next floor—and Arthur will be in early enough to serve your breakfast whenever you want it."

"Okay. I ain't fussy when I'm sleepy."

Page hesitated. "Do you suppose we should examine Glory's room, on the chance of satisfying ourselves that nothing is there which shouldn't be?"

"Mean to tell me you didn't already?" Quinny asked, looking surprised.

"No, I haven't," replied Page. "It did not occur to me to do so. Frankly, Hite, had I made such a discovery, I don't believe I should have admitted it."

"You hadn't oughta be like that, Mr. Page," reproved the detective. "Findin' somethin' and not sayin' anything could easy be coverin' evidence which would clear her. See? That happens—somebody tryin' to help an' gumming things up instead."

"Very well. We'll look into it."

Page walked into the transverse hall and opened the door to Glory's room, switching on the lights. He sat down on the hassock in front of the dressing table, to watch the detective's explorations. Quinny, of course, had to make a show of going through the same things he had previously examined, but his real concentration was on less likely places of concealment—behind paintings hanging at angles from the wall, under furniture with no apparent space beneath, and particularly the bed. Mattresses, he knew, have singular appeal for those who wish to hide things.

"This was my room, until I married," Page observed nostalgically.

"Yeah?" Quinny, on his knees at the side of the bed, looked back over his shoulder. Glory Bain had spoken of Page's marriage, but the detective was interested nevertheless. "You didn't tell me about a wife."

Page smiled lugubriously. "A youthful folly," he said. "Since repaired. The woman was hardly suitable to the Page social orbit. During that episode, I lived elsewhere, because of Mother's antagonism. Meanwhile, Glory returned from college and took this room. Of course, I didn't mind. A man doesn't spend as much time in his quarters as does a girl."

"How did this Mrs. Page take gettin' th' air?" quizzed Quinny. "Or, did she take a powder on *you?*"

"A powder?"

"Yeah. Who ditched who?"

"I see what you mean." Page's half-moon eyebrows lifted. "The separation was mutually agreeable."

"I don't want to get pers'nal, but do you have any trouble now with this dame?" persisted Quinny. "Like her hollerin' for extra dough? An', if she didn't get it, could she be interested in a shake-down for smoky moola? That's what I'm gettin' at."

Henry Page looked entirely baffled. "I haven't the dimmest idea what you mean," he said. "What, for instance, is smoky moola?"

"Dark money—blackmail dough. Looks to me like this Silburn outfit is on the make like that."

Page shook his head firmly. "Mrs. Page has the feminine trait of demanding money, but I'd not suspect her of going to that length to get it."

"Sizin' you up, I'd say you ain't a first class suspecter, anyhow." Quinny grinned tolerantly. "I am. Fact is, I'm wonderin' whether or not this burlesque flora's sister could be your ex-wife. Her name, she says, is Ju Melford."

Page's small black eyes enlarged abruptly. "My former wife's name was Julia Bensch at the time of the marriage. If she's as-sumed another since, I've not heard of it."

"Does she put the bee on you for dough?"

Page smiled grimly. "She telephones me occasionally for funds."

"Who does she say she is then?"

"Mrs. Page—more often simply Julia."

"I see." Quinny frowned. "What does she do for a livin', out-side of what you donate? Or, before you took her on?"

"Julia was singing at Club Orizaba before the marriage. I don't keep up with what she's doing now—if anything."

Quinny pondered a minute. "Then, I'm bettin' even, this Ju Melford is the same dame, Mr. Page. Has she called lately, askin' for a handout—extra dough?"

Page laughed. "She does that fairly regularly, but I've always told her flatly that the alimony I pay should be ample for her needs."

"If you think that's goin' to satisfy a jill, you're crazy. Okay. I'll do some checkin' on her. Where does she live?"

"I really don't know, Hite. My only contact, aside from her telephone calls, is through my attorneys. I can find out, of course."

"Do that. It can't hurt anything." Quinny straightened up after looking under a bedside table. "Well, there don't seem to be nothin' here which don't belong—except us."

Page eyed him tentatively. "As I told you, Hite, this was formerly my quarters—for years, in fact. As a boy, I had the usual flair for secret hiding places and that sort of thing. I went to a great deal of work to make a cache for my trivia in the floor of that closet. It is still there."

Quinny was puzzled. "What does a kid use a trivia for?" he asked. "I never had nothin' called that when I was a kid."

"I mean the trifles such as a boy collects," Page said. He got up and went to the long closet, sliding one of its mirror doors open. "The hiding place is still here. I'm not sure that Glory knows of it. Would you care to see it?"

Quinny nodded. Page reached into the closet and shifted the bags stacked in a corner. Quinny came over to watch, reflecting that he would have done a more thorough job himself, if there'd been time on his first visit to the room.

The flooring was of polished hardwood and tightly fitted. Page, however, pressed a hand firmly against the baseboard, which yielded slightly and exposed the ends of the flooring. Using the thin blade of his knife, he pried up a section two boards wide at the extreme rear of the closet. A shallow box had been built in the space between the floor.

"Hell," exclaimed Quinny, disappointed. "They ain't anything in it!"

"For which I am duly thankful," said Page heartily. He replaced the boards and stood up. "To tell the truth, I hesitated to show this to you—for what it might reveal."

Quinny walked back to the dressing table, not thinking about the cache's lack of incriminating contents. The hiding place had revealed something equally suggestive, he thought, if he could get it straightened out in his mind. He stared abstractedly down at the amazing amount of stuff a woman can collect in the upkeep of beauty. Page, over by the closet, watched him with restrained curiosity.

"I wasn't hopin' much to find anything here," Quinny mused, glancing at Page. "But, findin' nothin' don't always prove nothin'."

Finding nothing could also be the result of an inadequate search. Quinny's gaze, traveling over the objects scattered on the dressing table, came to an automatic stop, then lighted with quickened interest. He picked up a silver glove box. "Hey, wait a minute!" he exclaimed. "Here's somethin'."

"What is it?" Page hurried to the dressing table. "The glove box?"

"Yeah. All the other silver stuff here's got fancy 'G's' on it," Quinny pointed out. "The junk on the dressin' table in Phil Silburn's hide-out has got dogs on it, just like this box."

Page studied the glove container, the lines around his black eyes intensified in a puzzled squint. The box was of plain, highly polished silver, with a racing greyhound embossed on the cover. The detective opened it. Inside was a long, flat leather case, with a crest stamped on the upper side. It wasn't anything Quinny had ever seen or heard described before.

"Oh!" grunted Page.

Quinny glanced at him, then opened the case. A grunt echoing that of his companion's escaped his lips as he saw the missing twin dagger of Lola Montez. He eyed the weapon thoughtfully, rubbing his chin between the fingers and thumb of his disengaged hand. A ruby was missing from the miniature crown on the handle, but how the glove box and its contents had reached Glory Bain's dressing table was more prominent in his thoughts.

"What do you think, Mr. Page?" he asked, after a considerable silence.

Henry Page was still staring. "I don't know," he answered dully. "This—is staggering. I don't know what to think."

"Yeah, you do, but maybe you can't face it," commented the detective laconically. "Might as well, though. You figure that findin' this sinks any chance of springin' Miss Bain from the murder rap, don't you?"

Page shook his head despondently. "What do you think?" he asked.

"I don't," replied Quinny positively. "Chances are, this will show that she didn't kill the guy."

"Would you explain, Hite? I—don't follow your thought."

Quinny put the glove box back on the table and tapped it with a fingernail, his eyes slanted around toward Page.

"It's odds on, this box came from Silburn's apartment tonight," he said. "Miss Bain ain't been here since the murder, unless she came before she showed up at Huntingdon House—an' that don't add up. If she'd of come home, she'd of stayed here—feelin' like she did."

Page nodded eagerly. "I should imagine so. But, this box may not have come from Silburn's place. The design is not so unusual."

Quinny grunted dissent. "What would be is findin' one here just like the stuff on his dressin' table. Th' percentage is against it."

"It does seem too much of a coincidence to be likely," agreed Page. "But, there's another possibility: Silburn may have given this to Glory some time ago."

"With daggers in it?" Quinny shook his head. "That's somethin' else. This dagger an' the case it's in was in the apartment at the time of the murder. We can tell that on account of the ruby I found on the floor."

Page pursed his liverish lips and rubbed the tip of his forefinger over his wispy black mustache. "I don't like to appear arguing against you, Hite, since if you are correct, it would clear Glory. I'm trying to find loopholes in your reasoning—and hoping that I shan't—to avoid being let down later. But, does the ruby alone prove the dagger and case were there? Couldn't the stone have fallen from the murderer's pocket?"

"Look at it this way," said Quinny patiently. "Whoever had a hate on for this Nailton fish wouldn't need to pack two shivs around loose in his pocket to knock him off with, when he got the chance. He was killed with the other one, so this ruby wouldn't have been there to fall out of his pocket. The way it looks to me, it came loose while this dagger was still in the case, and fell out when the killer opened it to take the other one out. Like I said a while ago, the killin' wasn't planned an' the shiv was used on account of it was handy—or because somebody wanted to pin the job on Glory Bain. If I knew which—an' a couple of other things—I could bust this case in half an hour, now."

"You sound encouraging," commented Page, looking pleased. The expression quickly faded. "But, how are you going to find out?"

"What I need to prove is whether this dog box came from Silburn's after the murder, like I think maybe. Then find out how it got here." Quinny pushed his derby back from his forehead and nodded. "It could have been planted any time after about half past eight—an' any dumb crook could have got in to do it."

Page didn't think so. "Perhaps not so easily," he ventured. "Arthur, his wife, and the girl Dody, were here much later than that. In fact, Arthur left only a few minutes before you came. He had volunteered to stay until I returned from Huntingdon House, after I got the news."

"Yeah-yeah, but maybe this butler mug couldn't take a goin' over, either," dissented Quinny. "What time did you leave here to go downtown?"

"I didn't notice, but I arrived at your friend's apartment at about nine-thirty. It probably took me a half hour at least to get there."

"That leaves Arthur an' Dody the only ones in the house till you got back," mused Quinny. "Except Dr. Linden. She don't get around much, if she's sick like you an' Miss Bain says."

"Mother is able to move around, so long as she avoids exertion likely to strain her heart. As a rule, though, she keeps close to her rooms."

Quinny nodded impatiently. He hadn't considered the old doctor as figuring in the case, but now made a mental note to get a look at her in the morning, if possible.

"Well, with on'y the help around, it mightn't have been much of a trick to get in." Quinny sat down on the hassock, elbows on his knees and hands folded together. "Did you ever know this play-wright—Maestring? Or Phil Silburn?"

Page shook his head. "Not personally."

"Maestring showed up at the apartment about an hour after the murder. Silburn, so far as I know, didn't show up there at all. In that time, maybe one of 'em could have knifed Nailton and had time to run up here and back."

"Meaning . . . ?"

"To drop off this silver box with the shiv in it. They wouldn't know then that Glory Bain didn't streak for home—that she went hunting for me instead." Quinny got up. "You can think it over. I'm going to bed, if you'll show me where."

Sitting on the edge of the bed in the room where Page had shown him, Quinny lit a cigarette and thought some more on the finding of the silver box. This recalled the lipstick he had noticed on the dressing table in Silburn's apartment. There had been none in Glory Bain's bag—and no girl who gave as much attention to her looks as she did was at all likely not to carry one.

At Berte Dill's, Glory had declared she had not entered the bed chamber until she went in and discovered Nailton dying or dead on the floor. If she had told the truth, someone obviously had taken the lipstick from her bag after her departure and laid a herring on the dressing table.

Quinny didn't believe she had lied. Finding the lipstick seemed to fit with the discovery in her room here of the silver glove box.

11

CONFESSION

THE BLACK DARKNESS of the room in which Quinny Hite slept began to yield to the gray light of winter morning. In the old but lively Hotel du Nord, he was adjusted to the noises created by the exercises of its nocturnally minded guests. The tomblike hush of the Page mansion, coupled with a temperature more agreeable to polar bears than slumbering sleuths, aroused him. After some experimental moves in search of a warmer location under the covers, and finding only colder ones, he disgustedly threw them off and got out of bed.

Blinking sleepily and shivering, he got into his clothes in front of the radiator, discovering wrathfully as he finished that the thing wasn't turned on. Whether or not this would have made any difference, he went out into the hall, which was darker but no warmer. He started downstairs, wondering if Arthur was doing any butling at so early an hour. About to pass Henry Page's room, he saw light under the door and paused. Listening intently, he decided the series of thuds coming through the panel were being made by someone pacing the floor. Quinny rapped lightly.

A moment passed before the knob rattled metallically and Henry Page appeared in the doorway, shrouded in a blue velvet dressing gown.

"Oh—Hite!" he greeted dully. "Come in, please. You are an early riser."

Quinny entered and Page closed the door.

"Yeah, when I wake up an' see my breath hangin' like icicles on the ceilin', I rise," growled the detective. "I was goin' outdoors to get warm."

Page nodded absently. "The fires die down during the night."

"They must of died dead," returned Quinny. "Livin' in an ice-box like this joint, you'd think Glory Bain wouldn't go down with pneumonia just from wadin' around in a little blizzard. She oughta be used to it."

Page glanced at a clock on a table by the bed. "Arthur must be downstairs—it's eight o'clock. I'll tell him to bring coffee." He walked to the same table and picked up the phone.

"Tell Arthur also to put a slug of brandy in it," suggested Quinny, hopefully.

He noticed now that the bed—a huge, heavy affair with an over-hanging, semi-circular canopy at one end, a type commonly found in some of the older New Orleans houses—had not been slept in. From what he could see of the man's clothes under the dressing gown, he thought he had not undressed during the night. There were puffy circles under his small eyes and his round face was drawn. He finished giving directions to the butler and replaced the instrument. "There is brandy in the tabouret by the chair," he said. "Napoleon."

"It could be Mussolini and okay with me. You ain't been to bed, Mr. Page."

"It should be obvious that I have not slept," replied Page, heavily. He got up, turning slowly toward Quinny, his chest swelling in a deep sigh. "Hite, after a night of indecision, I am prepared to make a confession."

Quinny's senses leaped like a startled animal. His hazel eyes, ordinarily either covertly suspicious or blandly indicative of nothing, flared with eager expectancy. "Shoot!" he said.

Page passed the palm of his chubby hand over his eyes and forehead then went unsteadily to an easy chair and sat down. He waved limply at another opposite the one he had chosen. "Do sit down, Hite," he said. "Arthur should be along in a moment with coffee. After he goes."

They sat there silently until the butler came in with a silver tray bearing an ornate coffee set of the same material. He put it down on a chair, then moved the tray to a folding serving table which he had carried on his arm and set up between the men.

"You needn't trouble about bringing anything else, Arthur," said Page. "We'll be down presently for breakfast."

Arthur executed a slight bow and withdrew. Funny mugs, these butlers, thought the detective. Don't even look curious when somethin's goin' on they don't get. He poured coffee into the cups and sloshed some of the rare brandy into one.

"This had oughta take some o' the chill off," he said, swallowing a mouthful. He straightened up, still holding the cup, watching Page as he sipped the hot liquid. "You can start shootin' when you're ready, Mr. Page, like Dewey said to somebody. The other Dewey—not Tom."

Page appeared to be more concerned with his thoughts than listening. He closed his eyes and rested his head on the back of the chair, then opened them to stare fixedly at the line of plaster ornamentation around the edges of the ceiling. "What I have to tell you now is with the full knowledge that it hopelessly involves me in a debasing and sordid situation, which has culminated in murder. One which will spell death for my mother as well. However, I am now reconciled to whatever may be the consequence—and to the realization that, having told you, I expose myself to whatever penalty the law may exact."

Spillin' the works to one guy, in private, don't mean a thing, Quinny reflected, if the mug wants to deny it later on. He nodded gravely, nevertheless wanting to listen while the man wanted to talk. There was always the chance of a useful lead, even though he later recanted. "Okay. That's off your mind," he said. "Keep goin'."

Page cleared his throat, then sipped another mouthful of coffee before going on.

"I am aware of what you suspect, even though you have not put it in words," he said slowly. "So, now, I shall start at the beginning and tell you everything.

"At the time we met and married, Julia Bensch was a night club entertainer. Unfortunately, she was not a character acceptable to my mother, nor perhaps, in a less infatuated state, to myself. Within a few weeks Mother refused to tolerate Julia in this house. It was necessary for us to move into an apartment. I believed that in time Mother's resentment would soften and reconciliation follow. Instead, it steadily increased.

"Mother then insisted that I divorce Julia." A faintly humorous gleam crept into Henry Page's distracted stare. "By that time, I had begun to feel similar promptings. But, it wasn't a simple undertaking. You see, Hite, Julia was possessed with the idea that, on Dr. Linden's passing, I would come into a fortune, despite explanations that defiance of Mother could only result in my complete disinheritance.

"As a matter of fact, Mother did change her will to provide that practically all of both estates would pass to Glory. You see, the Bain estate—much the larger—for some reason of Mother's has always been maintained separately. The original will disposed of the Page estate to me and that of Ernest Bain to Glory—a considerable proportion of which had been put in trust for her, anyhow. In the revised will, my share was divided among other relatives and, in part, to Glory. On my divorce from Julia, Mother agreed to restore the provisions of the original.

"You see, Hite, I am completely dependent. My only income now is from my position as manager to Mother's realty holdings—rather a sinecure, and like most sinecures, paying little." Page shook his head. "Mother threatened to take this away, too, if I continued to refuse her demand.

"I compromised with truth. I announced that the divorce had been consummated. This was Julia's suggestion, and, having done so, I found myself entirely in that unscrupulous woman's hands. Julia, you see, is the author of all my troubles. She began demanding money which I did not have, on the threat of going to Mother, who would never forgive my deception. Adding to my worry, Mother's heart ailment steadily became worse. Her physicians informed me that any shock would spell the end, although in any event there's little hope of her living very long. Meanwhile, she had not changed the will, saying that she would when convinced of my return to—ah—stability."

"So you get worried she will conk off and leave you outside lookin' in," remarked Quinny. His affability increased as brandy-spiked coffee got in its work.

"A future as Glory's pensioner wasn't attractive, much as I like the girl," said Page. "That was the situation, however, and Julia was becoming more and more pressing in her demands for money. Finally she suggested that, as it was merely a question of time before the end for Mother, that involving Glory in a mild scandal might hasten the writing of a new will. Mother's code of morality is decidedly Victorian, so this wouldn't need to be anything considered censurable nowadays. Glory's amusements had already brought Mother's disapproval to some extent.

"Julia's suggestion seemed both harmless and effective. She agreed to take over all details. She enlisted this man Silburn in her plot, and then came the first step toward disaster. She told me that the others concerned—I wasn't aware of their identity until recently—refused to help unless they were secured for payment. Julia demanded ten thousand dollars."

"Ten grand for that kind of frame-up!" ejaculated Quinny, amazed. "An' Times Square full of mugs who'd work it out for coffee money. You oughta smelt somethin', brother."

Page shrugged. "It wouldn't have mattered. I was powerless—and incidentally could not raise that sum. Then Julia suggested the robbery. She would keep the jewelry until I inherited my share of the estate—which, of course, would not be too long deferred. The theft was necessary to account for the missing pieces when Mother discovered it. Again I agreed.

"I shall pass over the robbery, as it was substantially as you have so shrewdly deduced." Page's eyelids lowered as he contemplated what he had been saying. "I sawed the bars myself, from the inside—and thereby committed a stupid act. I cut the bars from time to time through an interval of several days and did not realize how long it had taken me—which, I suppose, helped you—"

"You're right about that," broke in Quinny complacently.

"I gave the jewelry to Julia last Saturday. She called me Thursday and told me the party planned for Glory was all arranged for the apartment in the Stern building—"

"*Stern* building?"

"Yes. Oddly enough, it is a property on the lists of the real estate firm where I keep my office as manager of the Page estate."

"It *is?* Look, is there a fella workin' there named Enstey?"

"Enstey?" Page's eyes screwed up. "Why, I believe there is. An outside man."

"Okay. Go on."

"Well, by Friday morning—yesterday—after a night spent more in thinking about this affair than in sleeping, I became worried about Julia's plans. You see, I couldn't put much faith in her. She hated Glory, imagining her responsible for Mother's attitude. I don't believe that Glory really gave my marriage a moment's thought. She wouldn't have considered that it affected her."

"Just th' same," commented Quinny, "you let this Ju—or Julia—Melford put Glory on a spot."

"I did—and, I say, worried later. So, I decided on a move of my own which might clear me of Julia's threats. I sent for you, hoping that my suggestions about Glory's supposed indiscretions and acquaintances would lead you to trace the jewelry to Julia's possession. Then, with the threat of prosecution for theft, I could break her hold on me completely."

Quinny's bland gaze was marred by a trace of contempt as he stared at Page. "You damned fool!" he exclaimed involuntarily.

Page dropped his eyes. "Quite," he agreed. "But yesterday morning, it seemed a clever answer to my problem. I suppose you mean that, as my legal wife, she would have defied me."

Quinny nodded. "Sure. What could she lose? Exceptin' that the stink of havin' her jugged would be to kiss good-by any chance of gettin' the will fixed up."

Page sighed. "It is clear enough now, but in my foggy, depressed state of mind yesterday, the prospect seemed bright. Well, after launching you on the project, I decided to interfere with the proposed party—enough to cause a postponement, at least. I went downtown last night, expecting to arrive in time to save Glory the embarrassment planned."

"I'll take it from there," said Quinny coldly. "You got there ahead of the others and thought it would be a smart trick to hide

in the bedroom closet till the goin' got ripe. You got in by crossin'
th' roof from this fella's room I mentioned—Enstey—an' bustin' a
pane of glass out of the French door. I know all about that, Page—
but I don't get th' idea of knifin' Jimmie Nailton."

Page's black eyes swung around, half-moon eyebrows lifting.
"But, I didn't!" he exclaimed wonderingly. "I crossed no roofs—
indeed, I didn't know there was one available, then. I came up the
stairs through the building and entered the apartment in the ordinary way."

"Oh, you did!" sneered Quinny. "I suppose the apartment door
was standin' open an' it said welcome on th' mat."

"No, the door was locked. I had stopped at the realty office on
my way downtown to pick up a passkey to the building." He fumbled
in a trouser pocket, brought out a key attached to a crumpled tag and
threw it on the coffee tray. "This opens the downstairs door as well."

Quinny picked up the key and studied it. Smoothing the tag, he
saw "Stern Bldg.—Pass" written on it in faded ink, then stuck it
in his pocket. "I'll check," he said indifferently. "Who was there,
after you let yourself in?"

"Only the dead man—Nailton—on the floor in the bedroom."

Quinny felt let down. All through Page's long account he had
felt the man was leading up to confession of having committed the
crime. The detective had been strongly drawn to this conviction
by the time he had gone upstairs to bed from Glory Bain's boudoir. The intimation had come when Page first spoke of the Montez
dagger. Quinny had not mentioned its use up to then, and Page
could not have learned the identity of the weapon from Glory Bain.
The man's story now accounted for it.

There was also the matter of the pocketknife he had loaned
Glory just before she went out. Glory had taken it with her, but it
had not been in the beaded bag she'd left at the Silburn apartment.
Later, Henry Page had used it to open the blotter holder, and then
again to pry up the boards in the girl's closet. It had seemed definite proof to Quinny that Page had been in the Silburn apartment,
and therefore no mystery how the silver box had got to Glory Bain's
dressing table.

Quinny looked at Page and his tone was harsh. "You will have one hell of a time convincin' anybody that you didn't kill Nailton," he accused. "There ain't one single thing to show there was anybody else in the apartment but you, Glory Bain, and Nailton. That knife you picked up out of her bag an' put back on your chain shows you were there—not mentionin' the silver box with a greyhound on it. She couldn't have brought those things back here. I'll come clean, Page—I had it doped out you killed the man. The only reason I ain't turned in what I know is that up to now I didn't have jury-proof stuff to show.

"When I called you up from Berte Dill's last night, you hadn't got home. I didn't know where you were, but I was goin' into that today. Now I don't have to. You better get Rachelmeyer back here. You're goin' to need him, but this is another case he's goin' to lose. Mr. Page, you ain't cooked yet, but you're goin' to know what a 'lectric light bulb feels like—an' not too far off."

Page's black eyes burned in contrast to the pallor of his round face. Surprising Quinny, he nodded. "I am resigned to an inevitable trial for murder," he said slowly. "But, if I am . . . to die, it will be for my stupidity, not for the death of Nailton. Last night it seemed a less degrading fate to do away with myself. Only the thought that it would be construed as a confession restrained me— or perhaps the human response to hope, no matter how thin, that something might yet save me."

"Could be you didn't have the guts," scoffed Quinny.

Page shook his head. "I don't believe it was that, Hite. Actually more courage is needed to face the ordeal of trial—and the fact that it condemns my mother to death as well."

While there's life, there's hope, reflected the detective. "Okay," he said. "Well, le's run over things. What time did you go downtown last night?"

"A short while before eight—right after dinner, in fact, which I had in my study. Dr. Linden had decided to take hers in her rooms, you see. Arthur will probably recall the time he served me."

"You said you went to your office to get the key. What time did you get there—an' did you see anybody who'd remember seein' you?"

Page shook his head despondently. "I saw no one. The office closes at five. It took me some time to get there from here, as no cabs were available and I had to wait for a bus to Seventy-second Street. I got the key and then took the Seventh Avenue subway down to Fiftieth Street, which probably took six or seven minutes. The station, of course, is only a half block from the Stern building. I walked there through the storm. It was really snowing hard then."

"You don't see anybody you know durin' all this travelin'," prompted Quinny. "Or anybody who would remember seein' you— whether they knew you or not?"

"That is correct," affirmed Page. "I reached the Stern building and went up the stairs—Oh, wait!" His eyes lighted excitedly. "I met a man coming down to the Street! I'd completely forgotten."

"Somebody you know, no doubt." Quinny's lips curled derisively. This was the old alibi malarkey.

"No—not exactly, that is. Seeing him in this building recalled to me that I'd noticed him several days before in the realty office. I'm fairly sure of this, although I doubt I should have remembered him had I encountered him elsewhere. I presume he is a tenant of one of the apartments." Pausing, Page stroked the fingers of one hand with those of the other, then continued. "This fellow asked me something about the weather, I seem to remember."

"Don't prove a thing," commented Quinny. "It don't say what time you got there, unless I find this guy an' he knows. We figure— an' we could be wrong—that the murder come off within a few minutes of eight, maybe five minutes either way. All we got to go on is what Miss Bain said—an' the last time she remembered lookin' at her watch before the killin', it wasn't quite eight. You will have to prove that you didn't get there till after she and Nailton. What you said, don't—not yet, anyhow."

Page nodded agreement. "But, I don't see how I could have got there before eight o'clock," he said. "Even with the unprecedented luck of catching a cab the moment I left here. You know what the streets were like."

"You are not the one which has to be convinced," objected Quinny. After a pause, he got up from his chair, deciding something more solid than brandy-spiked coffee might be a help to thought. "Your only bet is the fella you claim you met on the stairway, if he remembers what time it was. I'll check on 'im—if I can find him. And—if he exists. If he don't—well . . ." The gesture was expressive.

"I understand," said Page. His fingers groped in the dressing gown pocket and he cleared his throat nervously. "I . . . shall try to be prepared for any eventuality." He raised his eyes and saw that Quinny was watching him with a speculative stare. His eyes flickered and his hand slipped from the robe pocket with a cigarette lighter held in his fingers.

12
A VISIT FROM MRS. PAGE

QUINNY HITE LOOKED into the dining room of the Page house and saw Arthur arranging the table in the sepulchral, mahogany-wainscoted gloom. For his money, he'd take the brightly lighted, nickel-in-the-slot cafeterias of Times Square any time. The butler, after a moment, caught sight of the detective in the doorway.

"How about eats?" inquired Quinny politely.

"Breakfast is ready, sir," answered the fellow crustily. "If you will be seated, I will serve you."

Quinny pulled out a chair and sat down, studying the imperturbable face of the butler. He was an oldster, probably had been in the Page service for many years, the detective thought—a circumstance likely to be a hindrance in getting information from him. Quinny reached for a folded newspaper lying on the table and spread it out.

"Read the papers this mornin'?"

"Certainly, sir," the butler replied shortly, as though to discourage further talk.

Quinny ignored his reserve. "Looks pretty bad for Miss Bain," he said, reading a three-column headline. "What do you think?"

"I think it is not my place to discuss my employer—or her family," retorted Arthur chillingly. He added, belatedly, "Sir."

Quinny glanced up at him. "That ain't th' way hired hands play ball nowadays," he said. "They got plenty to say. Look, did you notice what time Mr. Page left here last night?"

"I assume that you are a detective, but are you employed by Mr. Page?"

"Sure—ever'body *always* knows what I do. Nothin' up th' cuff," grumbled Quinny. He downed the orange juice. "Remember when he left? It could be important, see?"

"Mr. Page should be able to inform you . . . *sir*."

"I'm askin' you. If you're smart, quit stallin'." Quinny scowled belligerently. "You can also keep that 'sir' in th' can. I am not a duke or somethin'."

"Mr. Page left immediately after dinner." Arthur came from the buffet and stood behind Quinny's left shoulder. "It is the custom here to serve it at seven."

"Yeah?" Quinny looked at the platter from which the butler had lifted the cover to expose an omelet of loaf-like proportions. "Okay, put it down, but I can't eat all that. You got enough—"

"If you would serve yourself . . ." suggested Arthur. He stared meaningly at the empty plate in front of the detective. Quinny got the idea and transferred some of the omelet. "Mr. Page had his dinner in the study, as Dr. Linden did not wish to come downstairs. Later, when I went to her rooms to get the dishes, I tuned in a radio program she wanted. This went on at a quarter of eight. Mr. Page left just at that time."

"Did you see him go out?"

"I heard the front door close after him. Then, when I came down, I got the tray from the study."

"Might have been somebody else went out."

"Only the household staff was here. None of us left until later."

Quinny relapsed into silence, skimming through the lead to the murder story in the paper. There was nothing in it he didn't already know. Finishing his breakfast, he returned to the room on the third floor to get his overcoat. Having pressed it into service as auxiliary covering during the night, he had to unsnarl it from the heap of quilts and blankets. He struggled into it, making a note that he'd have to get it pressed the next warm day, and went back down the stairs.

About to pass Page's room, he noticed light still showed under the door, although he heard nothing. He stood still a moment, and then his curiosity prevailed. He tried the knob and, as it yielded with silent ease, turned it and slowly pushed the door open a few inches. The huge bed came into view and he saw Page stretched out on it, face down and unmoving. The hair on the back of Quinny's neck bristled. He thrust the door open and entered.

"Yes?"

The barking demand startled the detective into an abrupt halt. Henry Page moved, twisting to glare stonily at Quinny. "What do you want?" he asked throatily. "I should like to be alone for a while."

"Okay," replied Quinny meekly. "Just checkin' to see if you was . . . all right."

Page's liverish lips smiled cynically. "I suspect you wanted to assure yourself of exactly the reverse," he said. "You rather hoped to find that I had gathered the courage to make an end to it."

Quinny didn't say anything immediately, unconsciously reaching up to adjust his derby. "That's wrong, Mr. Page," he said earnestly. "My dough was on what you said about human bein's figurin' a bet stands till th' numbers go up. This is okay. Tearin' up a ticket before that is a sucker trick. See what I mean?"

Page grunted. "Vaguely. But I don't get much comfort from it."

"Well, put it this way, then," Quinny argued. "You made plenty dumb plays already. Pass this hand and wait for another deal. I'm goin' downtown an' see if I can locate the guy you said you met on the stairs. I'll phone you back."

"Very well," agreed Page, indifferently. He swung his feet to the floor and sat up, rubbing his hand through his disordered hair.

"Take a bath an' go get somethin' besides coffee in your belly," advised the detective, returning to the still open door. "It'll buck you up. This is why they always give a guy they're goin' to electrocute what he wants for a last meal. A guy don't start for Kingdom Come easy on a empty stomach."

"You're very encouraging," commented Henry Page, looking worse, if anything.

Quinny started to back out of the room, wondering if he was really being smart to leave the man unobserved. He all but staged a collision with the butler, who had chosen that moment to come in. Dexterously avoiding it, the butler ignored the detective.

"I beg your pardon, sir," he said to Page. "But could I have a word with you—alone?"

"Whatever you have to say, Arthur, I prefer this man to hear. He is in my confidence."

The butler glanced doubtfully at Quinny, then back to his employer. "Very well, sir," he said. "I have just learned from Dody that Mrs. Henry Page was in last evening while you were out."

"What?" bellowed the amazed Quinny. "You mean Ju Melford?"

"The same, of course." Page nodded at Quinny. "What did she come here for? You know how Dr. Linden would feel about it."

"I don't know, sir. Dody admitted her while I was cleaning silver in the kitchen pantry. Dody tells me she told Mrs. Page that you were not at home, but she insisted on waiting. Dody put her in the drawing room and then forgot she was there."

"This Dody, I take it, is a first-class dope," commented Quinny.

"Young girls are apt to be flighty," agreed Arthur, reservedly. "Dr. Linden didn't mention it this morning, when I took her breakfast up, so I assume she was not aware of the visit."

"You say Dody put the dame in the drawrin' room an' then forgot she was there? How long did she stay—an' did she stay put in the front room?" demanded Quinny.

"No one seems to know, sir," replied Arthur. "Dody, it seems, had an engagement, and she slipped out without telling me, or my wife."

"This is all you know about it, then?" asked Page.

"Yes, sir."

"Thank you for telling me." Page's expression dismissed him.

Arthur went out, with another disparaging look at Quinny. This Quinny missed, having turned to Henry Page.

"You see what I mean about not tearin' up your ticket till the numbers go up," he said. "I think it would be a bright idea if I see this Dody gal right away. From what the butler says, though, she has been all the help she's goin' to be."

Going downstairs, Quinny saw a young girl working with a dustcloth in the hall. She wore a wrinkled brown dress, a piece of sleazy material bound around her hair; and she would never be Miss America.

"Hi, buttercup!" Quinny greeted as he came from the stairs.

The girl glanced anglingly across the hall at him. "Nuts to you," she replied pleasantly.

"You're Dody, ain't you?"

"Yeah—wanta make somethin' of it? Who'd you think—Lana Turner?"

"I did for a minute. You look kind of like her, around the ankles—which is always where I look first at a dame." He glanced at the sloppy moccasins the girl wore.

"You ain't no Errol Flynn yourself. What d'you want?"

"Nothin' much," Quinny deprecated. "I'm a detective, see?"

"Then you don't get it," Dody replied firmly. "I've heard about you guys."

"You heard about the wrong ones. I'm diff'rent. Anyhow, I'll tell you what I want to know, which is not a pers'nal matter."

As he brought out his questions, Dody's resistance melted before her curiosity. But she had little to add to the butler's report. She had been lurking around in the hall, she said, hoping to be on hand when her boy friend came. Arthur, it appeared, had a low opinion of Dody's selections. Seeing someone through the frosted glass of the front door, she had opened it before the buzzer sounded.

It was Henry Page's wife she had let in, and it was evident the girl held the woman somewhat in awe. Mrs. Page had asked for her husband, and, told he was not in, said she would wait in the drawing room for his return. Not long afterwards, catching sight of her Romeo in front of the house, Dody had hurried out and gone away with him.

"Gee, an' did I get a t'rill!" she exclaimed. "Standin' in front of the next house was a bee-yoo-tiful red automobile. I thought for a minute Eeric had a surprise for me, but he didn'—it wasn't his. We hadda walk all th' way to Broadway an' it snowin' hard. Eeric didn't care—he's a Scandy."

Quinny gave up. How long Mrs. Page had remained and whether she had stayed in the drawing room were questions it seemed that she alone could answer, which was of no value. Her mere presence for an unobserved interval had a deteriorating effect on the discovery of the silver box and the other Montez dagger.

He went out to the street, where he stood hopefully waiting for a cab, but otherwise feeling baffled. Page, without apparently having realized it, might have a substantial alibi. A cab came along and, settled against the cold leather cushions, Quinny resumed his study. He noted the time, wanting to confirm his idea of how long it would take to reach Fiftieth Street. Of course, it wasn't snowing now, but speed over the ice-cluttered highway wasn't feasible.

He thought it probable that Glory Bain and Nailton had reached Silburn's apartment about a quarter of eight, in which case Henry Page could not have got in without having been seen by her—if he had not started downtown earlier than Arthur's account indicated. Quinny wasn't assured of the butler's accuracy, but, if possible, Glory's movements would have to be checked. It would be days before he could take it up with her.

It required exactly twenty-five minutes for the cab to reach the Hotel Maywood. Henry Page's journey, as he had told of it, would have taken much longer, but this hadn't been definitely proved. That story of having met an unknown on the stairway of the Stern building might be difficult to verify. Murder suspects had a uniform tendency of mentioning people who didn't exist or weren't to be found. Madden's boys, as a matter of routine, had gone through the building the night before to make inquiries, but the only sure way for Quinny to learn what they had found out, if anything, was to have a try himself.

He got out of the cab and walked to the apartment house. In the small vestibule, he stopped to examine the names on the mailboxes. His eyes lighted as he saw "Bensch" under 5-D. That would be something to take up later. There was no response to his ring at the two apartments on the second floor, but on the third he struck pay dirt. An overweight man with a bloated face and sleepy expression answered with a surly demand to know what was wanted. And, whatever it was, he didn't need any.

"I'm on the murder job—upstairs," explained Quinny. "I—"

"What murder job?" interrupted the man, the drowsiness fading.

"Why," replied the surprised Quinny, "there was a fella killed in the apartment over yours last night. Didn' you hear?"

"No. I'm a bartender. I work nights. I didn't get in till five."

"That let's you out, then," said Quinny reluctantly. "You wouldn' know nothin'. Y' see, a man we suspect says he met a fella comin' out of this joint when he was comin' in. The time this could of happened is important."

"Yeah?" The big fellow considered, scowling. "Well, look, I go out o' here last night on my way to work an' I meets a guy comin' upstairs. Could this be him?"

"What did he look like?"

"I didn' take much of a gander. I kinda remember black eyes an' a black mustache—one o' them dinky kinds—"

"Adds up. You wouldn' know what time this was, would you?"

"Sure. I leave here ever' night at half past eight to show up on the job. Las' night, on account of it was snowin', I leave five minutes sooner."

Eight twenty-five. That settled any possibility of Henry Page's arrival before Glory Bain and Nailton.

"Did he say anythin'?"

"I ast him how was the streets an' he said turrible. That's all."

Quinny wagged his head thoughtfully. "Say, you went up to the landlord's office last week for somethin', didn't you?" asked Quinny.

"Yeah. Th' way they don't heat up this joint is a crime."

"This fella I mention said he'd seen you there."

The bartender shrugged. "Could be. I wouldn't remember. He ain't the guy I hollered at about the heat, though."

"Yeah-yeah," Quinny cut in. "He didn't say that. You maybe save this egg from the hot seat, though."

"If he lived in this icebox, he'd love it."

Quinny walked slowly downstairs, chagrined at having let himself get out on a limb. He ordinarily withheld decision on anyone's guilt until what he learned left no other possibility.

Leaving the building, he trudged along the sidewalk toward the Maywood, with the sensations of a man who, after a long, exhausting swim, finds the turning tide sweeping him away from a goal almost attained. A suspicion that he had perhaps been seduced by the beauty and charm of Glory Bain pricked at his ego like a swallowed tack. He began to wonder if he hadn't overrated his prowess in detection all these years. Maybe he had just been lucky before, and now that he faced Grade A pitching, he might find himself walking back to the bench without even having hit a pop foul. These thoughts were not comforting.

Entering the Maywood, he stopped at the desk. The day clerk was on duty, but Quinny saw the dwarf, Sneezy, standing by the elevator. This was a minor miracle, as usually he kept out of sight as a work saver. If the clerk couldn't help him, Quinny thought the little man might do so. He turned to the clerk, who seemed to be making out bills with little optimism about collecting them.

"What time did you go off duty last night?" Quinny inquired.

The clerk looked up. "Late. I got stuck—the night man didn't show till nine."

"Yeah? Look, did you see a dame goin' out after eight, wearin' a black fur coat, which was all wet?"

"I sure did. I knew she wasn't checked in here, either. Good looker, but, boy, was she soppin'! Who was she?"

"I ain't found out yet," lied Quinny. "Notice what time it was?"

"No, but probably around half past eight. Here's something funny, which happened then. About five minutes before, the burlesque dame in 401 came down. She was standing here when a call came from her room. Some woman asking for a number. I dialed it and then asked Miss Lester who was calling from her room. She said there wasn't anyone there. I went back to the switchboard, but whoever had made the call had disconnected. I rang the room, and got no answer." The clerk shrugged thin shoulders, rounded from years over hotel bookkeeping. "I dunno. But Lester's stuck with the call."

"Very interestin'," said Quinny, turning away. "But, no point."

Nevertheless, an idea came to him which might reveal the time of Glory Bain's presence in the hotel. He went to the phone booth by the elevator and called his own hotel. The clerk there answered and Quinny asked if there had been any messages for him.

"A couple, Quinny," answered the voice at the du Nord. "One a while ago, from a fellow named Lucky—"

"Never mind that one. He's one of the bookies I keep. What was the other one?"

"A Miss Bain, it looks like. Called last night at eight-fifteen—"

"Okay. Be seein' you." Quinny hung up and came out of the booth, frowning.

He saw Sneezy regarding him with the usual impertinent, wise gleam in his beady eyes. Well, Quinny reflected, no use checkin' with him. Glory was in the hotel right about the time Henry Page was goin' in the Stern building. And the murder was a finished job, by then. Just the same, a word with the dwarf might be rewarding. He walked over.

"Hi, kid," he said affably "You know Phil Silburn?"

"Sure. The night club guy. Great sport—give me a quarter last Fourt' of July." Sneezy's lips screwed into an expression of immoderate distaste.

"Must of been for somethin' big—like sneakin' him into a room where he didn't belong," prodded Quinny.

"For two-bits I wouldn' show a guy to th' public bathroom. Nope—I guess the mug was just drunk an' careless wit' the dough."

"Yeah-yeah!" chuckled Quinny heartily. Sneezy liked having his witticisms appreciated. "Look, this Silburn's got a crush on Nana Lester—"

"You're tellin' me!" interrupted Sneezy. "Hangs around up there on the fourt' floor all th' time. Got a key to Enstey's room an' uses it when the man is out o' town—sometimes when he's here."

"I saw him come out of there last night," said Quinny. "Ducked back in when he saw me. Did you see him, between seven an' eight?"

"Yeah. I saw you go out of the hotel an' then Silburn came down right afterwards. I saw 'im get in his car an' drive off."

This shattered Quinny's half-formed theory that it might have been Silburn who took the short cut across the roof to the apartment. It would require serious business to wade through deep snow like that, some imperative need not to be seen entering the building from the street. Silburn had apparently been indifferent to who saw him, once he had left the room to go to his car.

Quinny went out toward the street entrance, thinking this over and deciding it might be well to talk to Tracy Madden. The Homicide Lieutenant, Quinny reflected wryly, might not be so far behind as imagined. He could be out in front, for that matter.

Passing through the doorway, his face brightened as he saw Nana Lester climbing the steps. It was her sister he wanted to see most, though. A glance beyond the woman revealed that she was alone. Her vindictive eyes slued around at him.

"Hi, smart guy!" she greeted nastily.

13
MAESTRING'S ERRAND

She wore a squirrel coat, with the collar turned up around her face and a white scarf covering her hair, but nothing more than slightly reddened eyes indicated grief for her murdered husband. Having shot her caustic greeting at Quinny, she attempted to brush on past. The detective blocked her way.

"Wait a minute, stripper," he said. "I want a talk with you."

"I can do without it," she snarled viciously. "It gets me nothing."

"This time it might," Quinny hinted darkly. "Don't forget, they took the 'Men Only' sign off of the death house door a long time ago."

"What d' you mean, dick?"

"Come along with me to the bar downstairs. I'll buy you a drink an' tell you what I mean—all at th' same time."

Nana Lester scrutinized the detective suspiciously, then nodded in assent. They went down the steps to the dingy bistro under the hotel. As usual so early in the day, the bartender was a lonely man. Times Square alcoholics seldom reached the serious drinking stage before dark. Quinny and the girl perched on high stools at the end of the bar and ordered beer, which neither wanted.

"What's on your mind?" drawled the burlesquer.

"You remember I told you last night about findin' somethin' in your room liable to take you out of town for a long, long time?"

"Sure—but you didn't say what it was."

"You had a look for it?"

"I did not. I left right after you did." The girl's eyes wandered coolly around over Quinny's face. "Your crack didn't worry me. What did you find?"

"A big spider, with emeralds all over the legs—in your bureau." Quinny's eyes narrowed accusingly.

The girl laughed. "That thing! Worth 89 cents in any dime store."

"Where did you get it?"

Nana Lester pondered. "Oh, I know. I snitched it from Ju's dressing table Sunday. I use a lot of that junk with my costumes."

Girls whose art consists wholly in provocatively getting out of clothes piece by piece seldom rise to higher dramatic talents. What Nana Lester was saying obviously was what she believed.

"Okay," Quinny said. "On'y it just happens this spider is part of a lot of hot jewelry snagged from a fella named Henry Page lately. Know him?"

"I know who he is," answered Nana, looking less confident. "My sister's husband. I've never met him. What's this yarn about a robbery?"

"You wouldn' know," returned Quinny, with rasping sarcasm. "Well, skip that. I've got the dope on the racket you and your sister, Nailton, Maestring and Silburn was workin' on. It wasn't blackmail, like I thought, but somethin' just as crooked. It adds up to a murder."

"I don't know what you're talking about," retorted the girl coldly. There was, however, an uneasy movement of her eyes and she fidgeted with the gloves she had taken off.

"Yeah, you do. I know all about it, see. So don't hand me that." Quinny tasted the beer and grimaced. Unless to soften a hangover, beer was poison before noon. "What I want to know from you is this: what time did you see Jimmie an' Miss Bain across the roof last night from your window?"

The girl's eyes were instantly wary. "I didn't really see them. I just knew they were going there." She paused, glancing at the detective appraisingly.

"Yeah-yeah, I knew you couldn't see through all that snow. Go on."

"What I meant was that I saw the lights go on, so I thought they had got there."

Quinny nodded. "That's more like it. What time was this?"

"Half past seven."

"How do you know?"

"Because I looked at my clock. I was to meet Abe Munch downstairs."

"You see the lights in the apartment an' figure it's time to go." Quinny pulled the corners of his mouth down and lifted his eyebrows disparagingly. "Well, baby, it wasn't them."

"How do you know?"

"They didn't get there that soon. I left Miss Bain an' your husband at the Living Room about seven, an' they hadn't started eatin' dinner yet."

"Someone was in the apartment," insisted Nana stubbornly.

"Sure. Where was Phil Silburn, about that time?"

"Ask him."

"I will." Quinny rested his elbow on the bar, cupped his jaw in his hand and regarded the girl earnestly. "Look, stripper, you wouldn't want to land in a worse mess than you're in, would you? Don't forget—this is murder. I see a chance Phil Silburn killed Jimmie, see? Coverin' for him is a bum play, even if you did kind of go for him."

"That's a lie! Phil means nothing to me—that way!"

"She says!" Quinny grunted. "I saw you comin' out of a room down th' hall from yours last night—an' right after Phil Silburn comes out—"

"Stop it!" wailed Nana Lester. The bartender, doing something at the other end of the bar, glanced curiously in their direction. "I swear Phil is nothing to me! I—I have been trying to promote him for a night club job. I'm sick of burlesque—grind and bump and strip, do it again, three times a night—"

"An' matinees ever' day. I know—but that's got nothin' to do with what we're talkin' about. Where was Silburn at half past seven?"

Nana Lester recovered her slipping control. "He was in 405— down the hall—earlier. I don't know where he was at seven-thirty." She shot a defiant glance. "He said he would be at the apartment about nine. That's all I can tell you."

"How would you feel, if it turned out he killed Jimmie?" Quinny softened his voice.

"I'd want to cut his throat! Jimmie was the only man I will ever care for. And . . . he's gone."

"How did he stack up with your sister?"

Nana's trembling lips distorted petulantly. "Oh, they didn't get along. Ju thought I was wasting my time. Jimmie wasn't much, in a lot of ways, but he understood me. He's the only man I ever knew who treated me as though I were something more than a body." The dark eyes were getting wet. "But, I don't believe Phil did it. Yes, I know—Phil has a yen for me, but not killing bad."

"How about Maestring? Ever make passes?"

Nana's rose-petal mouth sneered. "That tramp! Say, mister, I'd slap his head off for trying. He wouldn't. All he ever thinks of is his lousy play."

"Ju Melford thinks diff'rent."

Nana smiled sourly. "Ju gets crushes. I'm not so sure on this one. She uses people, too."

"She talked you into settin' Jimmie up for a clay pigeon, eh?"

The girl's eyes dropped. "Yes . . . damn her!"

"Why didn't she use Maestring for that part of the job?"

"Kyle isn't married. It had to be someone with a wife."

"I see." Quinny thought he had covered everything he needed to know at the moment. "Okay, babe—maybe you better lam upstairs an' see how your animals are holdin' out."

"Thanks." Nana Lester slid off the stool. She hesitated, then said, "You won't believe anything I say that I can't prove, but if you think I had any idea that Jimmie—" She turned around abruptly and walked away toward the back stairs, stilted heels clacking noisily on the tile floor.

Quinny shrugged, glancing at Charlie, the bartender, who had stopped his work to watch the departing girl. As she disappeared into the stairway, he swung his head around and winked at the detective. "Hot little number!" he called familiarly.

"Know her?"

"Seen her around." Charlie put down his towel and shuffled along behind the bar to a spot opposite Quinny. "In here last night a while before I knocked off, with another dame an' Abe Munch. You know him, I guess."

"Yeah?" returned Quinny interestedly. "What time was this?"

"About eight—maybe after. You might's well lay off. Them burlesque dames are hot like ice cubes—"

"I ain't on the make," Quinny broke in impatiently. "I'm workin' on the Nailton murder job. This dame's his wife. How long did she hang around last night?"

"Well, le's see now." Charlie scratched his head where hair presumably had once grown. "Abe an' the dames come in off the sidewalk. They have a couple of snorts—which the oldest jane pays for. They're workin' up to a second one when another guy comes in from outside an' joins 'em."

"Know this last one?"

"Nope. He sure has the shakes! 'Course, he's only wearin' a thin topcoat, an' it's cold as hell outside. Seems as if another man is supposed to show up. This fella in th' topcoat asks where Phil is."

"Did he find out?" Quinny had been wondering himself.

"The dame which is buyin' says he's waitin' some place else. She hands this topcoat guy a package to take to him, an' he lams. The two dames an' Abe Munch scram, too, couple minutes after. I notice 'em while I'm puttin' on me coat back there to beat it home."

"What did th' package look like?" asked Quinny, thinking it might have been Maestring's play.

"Like—like maybe a shoe box, wrapped up in brown paper."

This didn't describe the manuscript Maestring had with him at the Living Room.

"Guess maybe I better run upstairs an' see what Abe knows about it. He oughta be able to take from where you leave off."

Quinny found the agent sitting in the lobby talking big to a pair of song-and-dancers who hadn't worked lately. They were holding out for eight bucks to show their act in South Brooklyn. They weren't going to get it.

"Now, see here, Quinny," Abe complained. "How do I know what I'm gettin' inta when I tell Lester I'll go along on the divorce business? Th' way things are, with alphabet soup runnin' th' gov'ment, ten bucks comes in handy—"

"Lester says she didn't promise you the sawbuck."

"This she is payin' anyhow, out o' th' ten which I owe her," said Abe positively. "But, about this murder I don't know from nothin'."

"What was the idea tellin' me you didn't know Maestring?"

"On account of then I didn't. First time I see him was last night."

"Did you see Glory Bain when she went out of the hotel?"

"I see a dame in a fur coat, soakin' wet, come out. Lester an' me was goin' down the outside steps to the bar. Lester bawls, 'Hey, you!' at her, but she don't stop. Goes wadin' through knee-deep snow to a cab." Abe searched the detective's face. "That the one?"

"Maybe." Quinny frowned in concentration. "Look, if Nana Lester saw her, she oughta known the frame at Silburn's apartment was off."

"If that was the Bain whimsy, I'd say Nana didn't know it," offered Abe. "The clerk said some dame used Nana's phone after she come downstairs. Lester thinks this could be the same one. She was sore—like usual."

"Right. You stayed with th' stripper an' her sister till we found you outside Silburn's apartment. Correct?"

"Yeah." Abe pushed out his lips and pulled them back again. "An' this is all which I have to do with this business. See?"

"Where did Maestring go, after you saw him downstairs?"

"I dunno. Understood he was goin' somewhere to see Phil Silburn." Abe hunched his shoulders. "He went out an' I didn't see him again till he showed over there." He jerked his head toward the building containing Silburn's place.

"Did anybody say where Silburn was?" pressed Quinny.

"I wasn't listenin' close. If somebody did, I didn't hear it."

Quinny inspected the agent's shifty eyes, without much reward. "Ju Melford gave Maestring a package. Did she say what was in it?"

"Looked like a shoe box," said Abe. "But she didn't say what was inside. Just told Maestring to give it to Silburn to put in the safe." He spat expertly at a cuspidor nearby, but the pitch was high and outside.

Quinny, watching, grunted. "Ball one," he said irrelevantly. A new line of thought struck him. "Say, where did these jills go after the cops turned 'em loose next door?"

"I dunno. They went away towards Eighth Avenue. I came back here. Pretty soon after Lester comes in by herself an' goes upstairs."

And that was that. The song-and-dance team, who had been discussing terms with Abe, returned from a conference over by the pin-ball machine. "We will take seven-fifty," one of them announced.

"You will take six bucks," answered Munch firmly. "With sixty cents out for my commission."

Grinning absently, Quinny started for the street. Ju Melford had lost no time in starting uptown to the Page house, he decided, and wondered briefly why Nana Lester hadn't gone along. Something clicked in his mental prodder and he turned back. Sneezy was standing outside the elevator, talking to another man, who walked away as the detective approached.

"Look, Sneezy," Quinny said. "What kind of car does Silburn drive?"

"I don't know what kind," returned the dwarf. "It's d' size of a box car, wit' chromerum all over. Painted red—an' red is what I mean, brother!"

Quinny left the hotel. So Phil Silburn had taken Ju Melford to Page's house! His was the red sedan Dody had spoken of seeing. There were lots of red cars, but the coincidence would be too strong, he thought—and, besides, Silburn had brought Ju back to her apartment later.

The thing to do, if he wanted to find out what she had sent to the Living Room by Maestring, was to go there and demand to be told. Silburn was yellow enough to come through, with a little bullyragging.

After a brisk but chilling walk eastward to Fifty-second Street, Quinny entered the Living Room. It was too early for business, but there was plenty of activity going on. Waiters were arranging tables for lunch and men from stores were bringing in supplies. Quinny found Silburn at the service bar in the rear dining room.

"What do you want?" he demanded as he saw the detective.

"Thanks, pal," returned Quinny happily. "Rye an' soda, I guess."

"Give him one, Mike," snapped Silburn. "But what I meant was what's the idea of dogging me around?"

"Oh, *more* things!" exclaimed Quinny. "Maybe we better go somewhere private to talk. After I get this slug you kindly donates."

Silburn jerked his head around to the bartender. "Make that two, Mike, and send 'em in to my office."

The office was a small room off the foyer. A stairway ran up one side, with a checkroom under it, and to the right of this was a door marked "private." Silburn twisted the knob and ushered Quinny in by the simple expedient of entering first. "All right, dick," he said, dropping into the swivel chair at a modern desk. "Shoot. I'm getting pretty sick of this business."

"So'm I," agreed Quinny promptly. He went around the desk and sat in the only other chair. "I like summertime better. This wadin' around—

"Oh, cut it! You didn't come here to gossip about the weather."

"I didn't come here to tell you anything, either," replied Quinny. "You're tellin' me. Last night, you picked up Ju Melford over on Eighth an' drove her up to Page's house on Riverside Drive. Where did Nana Lester go? She left your apartment with Ju, after th' cops said scram."

"Back to the hotel, I guess. Where did you get the idea I drove Ju uptown?"

"Because you did, an' I don't need to explain. How long was you parked up there waitin' for Melford? Keep in mind, brother, I know what time you got back to the hotel."

Silburn rocked back in the chair, regarded the ceiling for a thoughtful moment, then tilted forward. "Ju couldn't have been in the house more than twenty minutes," he said. A waiter rapped, then came in with the two drinks on a tray, put them down and went out. Silburn looked at Quinny curiously. "Well, do you make something out of that? She wanted to see Page."

Quinny snared one of the glasses. "There's funny business ever' time you turn around on this job," he grumbled. He downed a swallow and brightened perceptibly. "She was in a hurry to collect, wasn't she?"

"Collect for what?"

"Don't stall. For dough, you frame Glory Bain for Henry Page, so she gets kicked off Dr. Linden's will—"

"Who's Dr. Linden?" Silburn's mystification was hardly assumed.

"Page's mother. See here, Silburn, this would go faster if you come clean now an' spill your part in the shakedown. Page broke down last night and told me all about it. Now I want to hear your version."

Silburn finished most of his drink rashly, and almost choked. He sputtered, then cleared his throat. "All right," he said. "Here it is. Ju told me she needed some help. She wanted to stay married to Henry Page, on the chance of his coming into important dough. Naturally, if he didn't get back in the old lady's will before she died, Ju wouldn't cash her bet."

"I know all this, but keep goin'," commented the detective.

Phil Silburn kept going—for some time. But, for the most part, he added nothing to what Quinny already knew, with minor alterations tending toward modification of the club owner's implication in the sordid plot. In fact, one would have gathered that Phil Silburn had acted with remarkably altruistic motives.

"It didn't strike me as anything criminal," he concluded. "Miss Bain has money of her own, but plenty. And all I agreed to do was to furnish the apartment—and also all I had to do with it."

"I can see where you learned a lot at Sunday school," observed Quinny skeptically. "Okay. I think you're in deeper'n you say, but let it go. Ju Melford sent Maestring here last night with a package—about so by so." Quinny roughly indicated the proportions of a shoe box with his hands. "He brought it here about eight-thirty. What was in it?"

Silburn seemed entirely astonished. "Why, that's ridiculous, Hite! I haven't seen Maestring since he left here yesterday evening—when you were here."

"You didn't see him then, either. You were down at the Maywood makin' a play for Nana Lester."

Silburn's eyes wavered evasively. "All right," he growled. "I said I hadn't seen him since you were here last night. I didn't say I saw him then. But, he brought nothing here last night. I'll call in Maurice and make sure about it, if you want." Maurice was Silburn's right-hand man, taking charge of the Living Room in Silburn's absence.

"Call him in." Quinny pinned no faith to what Maurice might say. The man had a job to protect.

Silburn went to the door to send for his assistant, but, opening it, halted abruptly, his expression shifting into mild surprise. "Why, Ju! I didn't expect you here," he said. "Come in."

Ju Melford swept in, storm signals flying. She didn't notice Quinny, sitting on the further side of the desk. "Have you seen Kyle?" she demanded throatily. "Has he called, or anything?"

"Of course not," replied Silburn uneasily. "I've just come in a little while ago. What's wrong?"

"He's disappeared. I went to his apartment a few minutes ago. The man he lives with said he had packed up and lammed."

"Good riddance," commented Silburn. "That lame brain—"

"All right, but did he bring the package here last night I sent him with?" demanded Ju, still in the doorway. "I'm scared to ask you." She caught Silburn's glance at Quinny, following his eyes. She gasped. "What's that cheap dick doing here?"

Silburn laughed mirthlessly. "Same thing you are—asking me about a package. If Kyle was here with one last night, I haven't been told."

"What do you know about it?" Glaring at Quinny, Ju came into the room, closed the door and leaned against it.

"Nothin' much," the detective replied. "Me an' Silburn was just talkin' about it. Go ahead, Silburn, get your man in here and see what gives."

Ju Melford abandoned the door to let Silburn look out into the foyer. He called to the checkroom girl to round up Maurice and send him in.

"What is all this, Ju?" he asked, closing the door again. "You didn't tell me you were sending something here."

"Somebody is getting the doublecross," she answered, looking doubtfully at Quinny. "What does this dick know?"

"Everything," asserted Quinny. "Me an' Henry Page had a heart-to-heart talk. So, say anything you want. It won't be news."

Ju Melford had a flash of alarm, shifting her gaze to Silburn as if to conceal it. "I was looking over the stuff Henry gave me to keep for him"—she flicked a glance at Quinny to gauge the effect of what she was saying—"and I discovered one piece missing. It was a spider brooch—" She broke off at the sound of a raucous snort from Quinny. "What's that for?" she demanded.

"This show you're puttin' on," returned the detective mildly. "I was gettin' set to laugh when you got to th' joke. This is it, I guess. Your sister snitched this spider gag, thinkin' it was cheap costume stuff, an' took it home. Is this where we all laugh—or just me?"

The woman's face lost some of its grimness. "I'll wring her neck," she threatened wryly. "Just the same, it's good news. I'm responsible to Henry for that stuff—and I was afraid petty larceny's been going on where I live. That's why I wanted it locked up in your safe, Phil."

A rap sounded on the door panel and Silburn admitted Maurice.

"You know Kyle Maestring," the club owner said. "Did he bring a package here last night while I was out?"

"Yes, Phil. I locked it up in the safe."

Silburn fumed. "You might keep me informed on what goes on around here when I'm away. The package happens to be valuable."

"I thought you knew all about it," answered Maurice, undisturbed.

"Well, I didn't. All right—that's all." Silburn practically shoved his assistant out of the doorway and closed the door. He turned to Ju. "Okay. That settles that."

"It doesn't, either. I want to know where Kyle is."

Silburn went to the safe, where he began working the dial. "Maestring scares easy," he said. "After the cops turned him loose last night, he probably decided to take a powder. I'll get the package out for you, Ju. I don't want it here."

He swung the heavy safe door open and Quinny saw a package inside wrapped in brown paper. Picking it up, Silburn carried it to the desk. "You better get a safety deposit box for it, Ju," he said.

She pulled at the string, which had been tied in a bow. It came loose and she peeled the paper from a white shoe box. Then she removed the lid and stepped back, her face draining of natural color.

"Look!" she gasped.

Quinny got up to peer into the box.

It contained a pair of soggy and well-worn men's shoes.

14
SINISTER STREET

Ju Melford sat down heavily in Silburn's swivel chair, her fingers clawing her palms as rage surmounted the shock of discovery that the box contained only a pair of shoes.

Quinny chuckled irritatingly. "Looks like Maestring has figured out a way to promote dough for his show. An' you thought he was dumb!"

"If—if that half-wit is pulling a fast one and tries to get away with that stuff, I'll—I'll cut his heart out!" stormed Ju Melford.

"How many markers would this put on your tote sheet?" asked the detective.

"What do you mean by that?" demanded the woman.

"You figure it out, canary," returned Quinny. "A man was killed last night, with a dagger from that collection. You was holdin' this stuff—an' you live right over the room where it happened. You will be very interestin' to the Homicide Squad."

Ju Melford lost color again, glancing swiftly at Silburn and then back to Quinny. "You are accusing me of—of murder? Oh, no!"

"You're a possible. You didn't like the guy. You were handy. You were anxious to see Henry Page's name back in Dr. Linden's will—"

"You—you dirty crook!" exclaimed Ju. "You're trying to rig me, but you can't get away with it! I wasn't anywhere near Phil's apartment, or mine either, when Jimmie was killed."

"Can you say where you was—an' prove it? You met Maestring outside the Haymarket about seven. The next time I know anything about is when you show up in the Maywood bar with your sister an' Abe Munch—maybe twenty minutes after the murder."

"I was up in my sister's room at the hotel."

Quinny shook his head. "No, you weren't. Nana Lester an' Abe picked you up in the bar. Want to try the question over again?"

Ju brooded hesitantly, then spoke rapidly. "All right, I met Kyle at the Haymarket. I took him to dinner and he left me there. I didn't see him again until he came to the Maywood bar."

"That don't say where you was between, but why did he leave you in the restaurant?"

"He said he wanted to go home for dry shoes and to put on rubbers."

Maestring had said the same thing when questioned by Tracy Madden. Quinny thought the woman might have remembered this in answering. She was thinking hard now. Quinny waited for her to speak.

"I'll tell you where I was," she said suddenly. "In my apartment in the Stern building. I went there to get the box of Henry's stuff to send here, and put on another dress. And, I'll tell you something else: someone came to my door while I was there and tried to get in."

"Yeah?" Quinny's interest took a sharp upturn. "Who?"

"I don't know. I heard someone try a key in the lock. I called out, 'Who's there?' No one answered, and I heard steps going downstairs."

"You didn't take a look?"

"I had no dress on—was right in the middle of changing. By the time I could throw something around me and open the door, whoever it was had gone out of sight."

"Good story," commented Quinny laconically. "On'y it don't end right. Ought of been blood on th' doorknob, or somethin'. Did you look inside the box before you wrapped it up? If the jewelry was in it then, it's a cinch Maestring has 'em now."

"No. I had already wrapped it, a couple of days ago."

"Then how did Nana Lester get hold of the spider she snitched?"

"It must have been left out when I packed the things in the box. I had them spread out on my bureau Sunday, looking at them."

Quinny rubbed the side of his face with the palm of his hand, then scratched the tip of his nose. "The switch could have been made any time since Sunday. Yeah?"

Ju Melford nodded ruefully. She got up from the chair as though discovering she was sitting on a pin. "Yes—and I'm going to find Kyle Maestring!" she announced. From her expression, it wouldn't be to the playwright's best interests if she succeeded. "The rat. He's the only one who could have taken the jewelry. He left a package of shoes in my apartment one day. He said he was taking them to be fixed—and then went off without them."

Quinny picked up one of the shoes, holding it up distastefully and turning it over. After staring at it a moment, he shook his head. "That's no good," he said. "If it was before last night, the shoes wouldn't be all wet like this. And they don't need fixin'." He glanced at Silburn's feet. They were at least two sizes larger than those in the box. "Oh, I get it. Maestring had a key on him marked 5-D, last night."

"Looks to me," said Silburn, who had been listening attentively, "as though you have the answer to the murder. Who else but Kyle could have had the Montez daggers?"

"You," said Quinny shortly. "Or Homicide Hannah, here. The daggers didn't have to be in the box when Maestring lifted the stuff—if he did. Get right down to it, Silburn, you had as good a chance as anybody—an' a reason, too. Nailton was in your way. You could get in an' out of the apartment whenever you liked. And"—he paused impressively—"you ain't said where you was when Nailton got stabbed."

"You—" Silburn exploded, his fists balling menacingly, and his lantern jaw stuck out. He broke off.

Quinny ignored him, turning to the woman. "Gettin' back to you; you also fit pretty good. You had the shivs, you had a hate on for Nailton, too, and nobody knows where you were, either, except what you say. Okay, kids—standin' around tradin' theories with you mugs gets me nowhere. See you later—maybe in court."

"Where are you going?" demanded Silburn, moving to intercept the detective.

Quinny kept on going. "I'm lookin' up this pal of yours, Maestring," he said. "I ain't heard his story yet, an' he might have somethin' interestin' to tell me—if I locate him. Specially when I tell him you two are trying to make him the fall guy."

THE AFTERNOON SUN was getting well down over Jersey City before Quinny decided that finding a nondescript person in the numerous hideouts around Times Square, with which Kyle Maestring no doubt was familiar, was a hopeless task. Police had better facilities for such a search. He stopped in at the Maywood to phone Henry Page and check on events up there, not at all sure that Page hadn't succumbed to a rash impulse. The butler answered.

"Mr. Page is not available, sir," Arthur said, his usual stiff formality fading as Quinny identified himself. "I . . . I'm rather worried about him. There has been more misfortune."

"Yeah? What now?"

"Dr. Linden passed away this afternoon."

"Oh! Well, gosh—I mean that's too bad," mumbled Quinny, surprisingly jolted by the news. "He told me he was afraid that would happen."

"He is taking it very badly, Mr. Hite—has locked himself in the study and refuses to see anyone."

"He figures it's kinda his fault. I wish you would tell him that I found the man he met on the Stern building stairway and the time was eight twenty-five. This might make him feel a little better."

"I shall try, sir, but I don't believe he will listen. A few minutes ago I went to the door, but he did not answer my rap. I'm at a loss, sir . . ."

"Well, you can't break the door down," said Quinny. "Better leave him alone, I guess. For a while, anyway."

He stood in the telephone booth for a few seconds, thinking about Arthur's news, then got out the list of stolen jewelry to check on Page's private number. Dialing it, he listened to the rhythmic buzz at the other end for some time before he decided that the man had no intention of answering. He restored the receiver to the hook, retrieved his nickel and came out. Abe Munch, sitting in a dilapidated leather chair across the lobby, was watching the detective curiously. Quinny strolled over to him.

"Gettin' anywhere on the Nailton case, Quinny?" Abe queried.

"Cleanin' up odds an' ends," replied the detective. "No pinch yet. I've been hunting for that egg, Maestring, all afternoon. He's lammed."

Abe grunted. "I saw him a while ago in Cheery's fish an' chips joint—over on Eighth. Staked him to half a buck, which shows what a soft touch I am." He sighed dolorously. "I'll never have a dime!"

Quinny frowned as he thought of all the walking he had done, while Munch had found the playwright without even looking for him.

"Did he talk?" asked Quinny. "I mean, besides puttin' you on for chow money?"

Abe nodded. "Some. Said Silburn an' Ju Melford were out to spot him for the murder. Said he was sure one of 'em did the work, and he wasn't goin' to be made no goat of."

"Lammin' like he did won't help him any," commented Quinny.

"He said he didn't want to be picked up before he had a shot at Ju an' Silburn," explained Abe. "I told 'im if he knew anythin', he better go to the cops with it, instead of tryin' to outsmart anybody. I think the guy is nuts enough to take a crack at 'em. He's got a mean eye."

"This I have noticed myself," agreed Quinny, wagging his head. "I don't give him guts enough to tackle Silburn, but he might give Ju a workin' over which would not improve her singin' any."

Abe made a derisive sound. "Or hurt it, either. Ju is washed up as an entertainer, unless she goes in for a strip act, like Nana Lester."

Quinny grinned absently. "Could be she peels pretty," he said.

An idea beginning to shape up, he walked away toward the hotel entrance, where he stopped at the top of the steps to the sidewalk. He felt an impulse to phone Silburn and tell him to watch out for a crazy playwright, but quickly abandoned it. He should worry about the night club man.

Despite day-long efforts of gangs of men and machines, the street was still a clutter of frozen snow, a low barricade of broken-up pieces lining the curbs. At best, this block of the crosstown thoroughfare was not gay. Now it was merely a bleak and murky channel from Broadway to the Garden at Eighth Avenue. Quinny hesitated in the scant shelter of one of the columns flanking the worn steps, reluctant to leave.

Watching the few pedestrians picking their way along the sidewalks, his attention was caught by the flare of a match in the entrance of a dark store building across the street. Peering through the gloom, he saw a vague shape standing there. At first, Quinny took it for granted it was someone who had stopped to light a cigarette out of the wind, but the figure stayed in the doorway. In this weather, a man wouldn't hang around purposelessly in such an exposed spot, he thought. Nobody, that is, but a lug who was dope enough to be a detective in the wintertime.

While he was watching the figure across the street, he saw a cab climb over the piled snow to the curb in front of the Stern building. A woman got out, hurried across the messy sidewalk and went into the apartment entrance. There wasn't light enough to be sure, but Quinny imagined the contours were much like those of Ju Melford.

His attention whipped back to the man in the doorway. A passing crosstown bus cut off the view for a few seconds, and meanwhile the dark figure moved somewhat further down the street. He was now standing at the curb, holding to his hat, his overcoat flapping about his legs in the chill wind from the river. After a couple of false starts, he plunged over the piles of dirty snow, dodging a couple of cars—risky business on the treacherous footing—and successfully reached the other side. Quinny saw him disappear into the same building as had the woman.

Galvanized into action, Quinny came down the steps and walked briskly to the Stern building. Letting himself in quietly, he stood listening to someone climbing the stairs. Hearing a door close on one of the upper floors and no more footsteps, he started up himself.

At the fourth floor he paused to examine the door to the Silburn apartment, speculating on the likelihood of the man he followed having gone there. He tried the knob to see if the lock had been fixed. It hadn't, but Quinny didn't go in. The man he had heard could easily have been a tenant of another apartment. The echo of voices from above started him on up. He heard Ju Melford's strident voice as he gained the fifth floor landing.

"That's just plain nuts!" she was arguing. "Why should I do anything like that? Why should I try to doublecross anyone?" There was an abrupt movement inside the room, the scrape of a piece of furniture on the floor followed by the sound of something soft which thudded against the wall. "Stop it!" screamed Ju's voice. "I tell you, no one's trying to . . . stop it!"

Sounds of a furious struggle came through the thin wall, followed by a choking scream, almost instantly cut off. Quinny didn't bother with the doorknob, but threw his shoulder against the flimsy panel with all his weight. The door, not being locked as he supposed, flew open, sending him charging into the room badly off balance.

Bringing up, he saw a pair of nyloned legs kicking on the couch beyond the back of a man struggling with their owner. Then Quinny saw Ju Melford's head against a pillow, her eyes bulging and hands clawing at fingers crushing her flabby throat. Her assailant seemed unaware of the detective's precipitate entrance.

With hardly a pause, Quinny swung his hard right fist, landing with a sharp smack against the man's ear. He didn't pull the punch, and Ju's attacker went spinning to the floor at the side of the couch, turning onto his back, with the agonized scream of a shell-torn horse. The face was a caricature of Kyle Maestring.

Quinny eyed the sprawling figure frostily. "What is the general idea of this brawl?" he asked, shifting his gaze to the woman on the couch.

"He's trying to kill me!" moaned Ju, sitting up and feeling her bruised throat tenderly. "The dirty rat stole Henry's jewelry—and now he wants to kill me . . . like he did poor Jimmie!"

Maestring pushed himself up into a sitting position, holding one hand against his damaged ear with his head cocked over on that side. "Filthy liar!" he exclaimed. "Made a fool of me—she and that . . . cheap night club man, Silburn." He broke off with a moan of pain, and then went on. "They killed Nailton, and now they're trying to make me the goat for it! The rotten, dirty . . ." He lowered his head into both hands and gave vent to choking sobs. "My play . . ."

"Now it's hysterics," growled Quinny. "You can get anything in this joint. Shut up, guy, before I dump a load of water on you!"

"Hit him again—the bum!" urged Ju vindictively.

Quinny eyed her contemptuously. "I oughta slug you one," he snapped. "An' I would, if you wore th' same kind of britches he does. Maybe you won't burn for it, but you ought to, for killin' that old lady—"

"What old lady?" Ju cut in sharply. "Is Dr. Linden dead?"

"Yeah."

"Did she make a new will?" demanded Ju impetuously, then bit her lip.

"I wouldn' know, an' I wouldn' even be interested," replied Quinny. "By the time you get back out of clink, you'll be too old to need fancy cash, anyway."

"You haven't anything on me!"

"Leave us wait an' find out." Quinny watched Maestring, struggling to his feet. "How long's this guy been here visitin'?"

"He was here when I came in," said Ju sullenly. "I caught him going through my bureau drawers."

"Lookin' for Henry Page's stuff, eh?"

"Only to make sure she had the jewels," answered Maestring shakily. "They aren't here."

Quinny's attention returned to the woman. "Did Mr. Page give you a list when he handed the stuff over?" he asked tentatively.

"Yes." Ju picked up her bag and opened it. After a quick search, she brought out a folded sheet of paper and gave it to the detective. "Here it is."

Quinny opened it up, then got out his own list to compare. There was a difference of one item. Folding the sheets together, he put them away in a pocket and looked at Maestring. "So you didn't find anything," he said.

Maestring shook his head, still seeming dazed.

Quinny turned again to Ju. "Silburn?"

The woman's face shifted chameleon-like into a flush of swift wrath. "If this tramp hasn't them, Phil has. The rat!"

Quinny grinned. "Y' know, somethin's goin' to have to be done about all these rats runnin' around loose. Maybe I better call the Sanitary Department. I think I will, at that."

He walked around Maestring and picked up the phone from a stand at the end of the couch. Ju Melford and the playwright watched him in bewilderment as he dialed a number.

"Hello," he said, after a short wait. "Tracy Madden around? Oh, I didn't reco'nize your voice, Trace. Who stuck you on th' switchboard? Say, button up good an' run over to 5-D in th' buildin' Nailton got knocked off in. Never mind why—I got a surprise for you." He slapped the receiver back on the cradle.

Maestring edged toward the open door.

"Where you goin', fella?" asked Quinny mildly. "Stick around an' catch what's goin' to happen to this jill. Should be interestin'."

Maestring halted uncertainly. Quinny moved toward Ju Melford.

"That was the police you called," the playwright accused.

"Sure. They'll be here before you can get downstairs." With a swift change in his direction, Quinny gained a position between Maestring and the doorway. Reaching behind him, he closed the door and released the lock catch. Ju Melford stared, obviously puzzled and disturbed. Maestring's eyes flickered uneasily.

Minutes passed, with no sound save that from a cheap alarm clock on the telephone stand. Ju Melford's nerves began to get out of control.

"What the—"

"Shut up!" The tense expression in Quinny's eyes became that of listening. Then he moved quietly from the door and flattened himself against the wall.

Now comes the pay-off, he thought swiftly. He could hear someone climbing stairs, but, from their faces, the other two hadn't heard. Gradually Ju Melford showed she had become aware of the creaking stair treads. She started to speak, but kept silent as she caught Quinny's warning look.

The footsteps reached the landing outside, where there was a carpet to deaden the noise. Quinny heard only a faint shuffling, then a sharp, metallic clicking indicated a key was being inserted in the lock of Ju Melford's door. The woman caught her breath and pressed the back of her hand against her lips. There was panic in her eyes.

The door swung slowly inward.

"Henry!" she gasped.

15
TOTE SHEET

"I TRUST I AM not intruding."

Only because it was the voice he expected to hear did Quinny recognize Henry Page's taut, anxiety-strained tone. The door was pushed open, swinging around and partially concealing the detective. Page came two or three steps into the room, hands deep in overcoat pockets, not seeing Quinny at all. A brief, ominous silence followed, broken by Ju Melford.

"There's trouble," she said obscurely.

"Where you are concerned, there's always trouble," retorted Page grimly, his cold eyes swinging to Maestring. The playwright had retreated toward the further end of the couch. "Who is this fellow?"

"Kyle Maestring," wavered Ju.

"Good! I may as well be thorough."

"What do you mean, Henry?"

"You and your wretched companions have brought about the death of my mother," accused Page bitterly. "You planned by killing Nailton to make certain that Glory would be eliminated from her inheritance and put me completely in your hands. The subterfuge to reinstate me in the will wasn't enough. For you, it was all—or nothing. Very well, I'm here to deliver payment. This is your moment to die, Julia—and this miserable creature as well. Then I shall put myself at the mercy of the law."

He spoke without threat, as mere statement of casual purpose, which had the effect of making his words all the more sinister. Ju

Melford's jaw trembled, but her eyes were blank, as though she had not heard clearly.

"Henry!" It was a throaty, liquid gasp of stunned terror.

Page's hand moved upward from an overcoat pocket, bringing out a heavy automatic. Maestring's breath escaped in a hiss of fear. Quinny did not move, although he caught Ju's imploring glance.

"If I find him before I lose my freedom, I shall also destroy Silburn. Ridding the world of three such scoundrels may or may not gain me some favor in a jury's eyes, but in any event will ease my humiliation."

"You don't know what you are doing!" exclaimed Ju, desperately trying to control her shaken wits. "Don't—"

"Be quiet! There'll be no argument."

The muzzle of the automatic lifted and Kyle Maestring screamed with the resounding crash that shattered the silence of the room. But it was not the gun which had made the noise. Unarmed and helpless to intervene physically, Quinny, playing against what he hoped were Page's overstrained nerves, had given the door a quick, hard shove. Swinging on its hinges, it had slammed shut with the effect of a shotgun report. And the detective dived swiftly for the hand which held the automatic. Page's startled muscles did not recover quickly enough to hold it.

"You can think up more dumb plays!" shouted Quinny wrathfully, backing away with the gun. "Just when I'm about to settle this business nice an' quiet, you come along an' louse up ever'thing."

"It would have been settled in another moment," snarled Page, his black eyes giving off sparks.

"Yeah—for good an' all. Sit down, damn it, till I tell you a couple of things." The detective motioned with the gun toward a chair across the room. "I tried to get you on the phone a while ago, but you were already on your way here."

"How did you learn I had left the house?" asked Page. He backed to the indicated chair and sat down heavily. Quinny watched him warily, convinced that the man was unpredictable and not liking the calculating expression he saw in the black eyes. "I had instructed Arthur that I was on no account to be disturbed."

"I called you on your private wire," replied Quinny. "You most likely would have answered that, if you had been there. Then I saw you standin' across th' street. I thought it was this lug here, until Ju said he had been here long enough to frisk the place for the jewelry. You heard me come in downstairs and ducked into the Silburn joint under here. Then you waited, maybe thinkin' I would go downstairs again before long. Which reminds me, Page, I located the guy which you met on the stairs last night. He knew it was eight twenty-five, on account of he was on his way to work."

"That should prove I did not stab Nailton," commented Page, his expression brightening a little. "At least, I shan't have to answer for that crime."

There wasn't any humor in Quinny's crisp smile. "No? Why not?"

Page made a gesture with his pudgy hands. "Isn't it obvious that, if I arrived at that time, the murder had already been committed—as I informed you?"

Quinny's ears cocked at the distant sound of the downstairs door to the street. He decided to stall. "Maybe you got something there," he said slowly. "Funny, I never thought of that angle. Wait a minute, I think we're goin' to have some more company."

"Phil said he was coming by," said Ju, but looking as if she didn't welcome the thought.

"I could do with some more talk with him," growled the detective.

Noise on the stairway became progressively louder. The group in the room watched the closed door in silence until the footsteps sounded on the landing outside. Quinny sidled over and turned the knob on the lock just as a heavy fist struck the panel. Tracy Madden thrust his way in. Behind him was the interested face of his favored assistant, Kelly.

"What gives here?" Madden demanded, his gaze traveling over the four in the room.

"Take him," said Quinny, motioning toward Henry Page. "There's the man who killed Nailton."

Tracy Madden howled in rage. "Y' mean to tell me, Hite, you get me all th' way up here on a goose chase? You big dope! Captain

Lendon's handed the case over to the D.A.'s office, with that Bain woman on the platter. There ain't a chance it was anybody else, an' now you come up with a screwy notion it's this guy!"

"It's absurd, Lieutenant," Page cut in. "Since I did not arrive here until nearly half past eight last night."

Quinny ignored Page. "Y' see, Trace, th' difference between me an' Bull Lendon's case is that I can prove mine an' he can't."

"Oh, yeah? Well, spill it."

Quinny turned to Page. "You had your butler give you your dinner in th' study, where he couldn't check on whether you stayed to eat it or not. You didn't. You dumped it—prob'ly out the back window—an' lammed down here right after seven. Last night, you told me about goin' into Silburn's hideout an' seein' Nailton stretched out on the floor, with the shiv in his back, didn't you?"

"Yes, of course, but—"

"You didn't tell me how you got in. That passkey you brought along wouldn't open Silburn's door—on account of he had put his own lock on it. You came in from the terrace, after crossin' the roof from the Maywood an' bustin' a pane out of a French door. That's the only way you could have got into Silburn's joint."

Page shifted uneasily before Quinny's steady, accusing stare. "Go on," he said, with an abortive effort at a sneer.

"I will. After you crashed in, you hid in the bedroom closet. Nailton comes in to phone. You see where you can make sure of not only the Page dough, but Bain's, too. You let him have it. The best I can say for you is, you maybe only meant to hurt him bad instead of kill. If that's so, you picked a bad spot to stick him. Then, after Miss Bain had run away, scared nearly to death, an' knowin' the murderer was still there, you came out in the hall and came up to this room."

"And why should I have come here?" demanded Page. "It seems that having just committed a murder, I should have concerned myself in leaving the neighborhood."

"If you had been smart, you would of," returned Quinny, unruffled. "Instead, you come here lookin' for' your jewelry. Where was it, Melford?"

"On the shelf in my closet," said Ju Melford. "I emptied Kyle's shoes on the floor in there and used the box to pack the things."

"That's what I thought." Quinny turned to Page again. "You see these shoes on the floor an' get the idea of changin' 'em for the ones you got wet crossin' the roof. I noticed these shoes we found in the box was about your size. You stuff the pretties in your pockets an' go home."

Page blew out his breath contemptuously. "You fail to account for the silver box we found in Glory's room," he said.

"That's easy. You put it there. It couldn't have been Ju here who brought the other dagger an' this silver box when she came there. She never had the Montez daggers to start with. I've got the list you gave her an' they ain't on it. An'—she wasn't in Silburn's apartment last night till after the murder, an' not in th' bedroom at all.

"When we go back uptown, we are goin' to find the rest of the stuff in the hideout you showed me under the closet floor. You figured it was a smart play to show it to me empty, so it would be passed up next time."

Page shook his head slowly. "Interesting theory, Hite, but it won't stand up. You, yourself, established that I was seen entering this building sometime after Nailton had been killed."

"Only till I got to thinkin' about it," countered the detective. "All that adds up to is that the lug who lives in 3-D saw you on the stairs. But you were on the way out—not in. When you heard this fella comin' down behind you, you turned around and started back up. You knew he'd see you before you got out, and it was a good gag to make him think you was just comin' in. Only, it didn't work."

Madden growled ominously. "How come I ain't been told about all these goin's on, Quinny?" he demanded.

"You're gettin' told now, Trace," said Quinny. "Before would of only gave you a headache, like it did me. This man had put on the damnedest act I ever run into. Four or five times I was ready to tape him for the killin' an' then he stages a song an' dance which makes me not so sure. Talk about that Doctor Jackson an' Hyde team!

"But there wasn't any chance Glory Bain pulled the job. You can see that now, yourself. She wasn't so chummy with Nailton, an' she was careful about lettin' herself get set up in any apartment alone with a guy. I heard her kick about comin' to this one, unless other people were already here. Anyhow, I can't see her packin' one of Page's daggers around on th' off chance of havin' to discourage some guy from gettin' fresh. That's nuts!

"Y' see, Trace, it had to be Page who dropped the loose ruby from the case on the closet floor, because nobody else had a dagger. It ain't goin' to be no trick to identify the shoes in the box at the Living Room as bein' Page's. I looked at the label." Quinny glanced at Maestring. "This guy don't wear twenty dollar kicks."

Page stood up. "He makes a convincing case," he said, "but it won't stand up before facts. At all events, it will not be tried here— and now. Lieutenant, I'll offer no obstacle to going with you, if you accept this fellow's accusation."

"It's all new to me," admitted Madden, uncertainly. "But, he talks a better case than we have against your sister. Guess you better come along—"

No one had been prepared for Page's willingness to go, but a lot less for his being precipitate about it. With amazingly swift agility, he rushed for the door, swerving away from Madden's belated grab and bowling over Kelly. His feet thundered in headlong flight down the stairs.

"Get him!" yelled Madden.

Kelly had already recovered his balance and started in pursuit, but Page had gained a considerable start. The detective leaped after him with reckless disregard for possible disaster. Madden and Quinny rushed out of the room, colliding heavily with each other in the narrow doorway, but even Kelly had disappeared by the time they began the descent of the stairs.

They found Kelly on the sidewalk, staring out at the street. A car had stopped, slued around with the wheels embedded in a pile of broken lumps of frozen snow. A uniformed chauffeur leaped out and crouched on his knees, trying to see under his car. Kelly looked back as Madden and Quinny burst out of the building entrance.

"He got hit, Chief!" Kelly said, excitedly. "He was runnin' for the other side of the street, slippin' an' skiddin' on the ice. You couldn't tell whether he run inta th' car, or it run inta him."

The trio climbed over the piled snow in the gutter and approached the chauffeur, still peering under his car. He looked up as their feet crunched at his side.

"Gawd, he's all—busted up," said the driver, shakily. He stood up. "It wasn't my fault. The guy run right in front of me."

It took minutes of strenuous effort to get Page out from under the car, effort that seemed hardly worthwhile. He was barely conscious, and going fast. Using a rug from the limousine, they carried him back into the building entrance. Kelly rushed toward the Maywood to phone for an ambulance.

Quinny looked down at Page's gray, wax-like face, then at Tracy Madden. He shook his head. Seeing Page's eyelids quiver, Quinny knelt at his side. The blue lips moved.

"I'll not . . . get that last meal . . ." Page murmured as Quinny strained to hear. "But . . . I'd like to tell you, that . . . you were right." He drew a quick, sharp breath at agonizing cost. "It . . . doesn't matter . . . it's all right this way . . . Tell Glory . . . I'm sorry—"

Nodding, Quinny felt for the injured man's wrist and was silent for a minute. Then he stood up.

"He beats th' chair, Trace," he said. "An' he's all yours. I been around for a long time, but I never met a fella like this one. He could of been two sep'rate guys that didn' know each other. Now, I guess I might's well scram. Landin' your client either in jail or a cemetery is no way to collect for your work. Be seein' you."

It was nearly two weeks later when Quinny got the letter. He read it several times, because it had some very unfamiliar words in it. The accompanying slip of paper was more easily comprehended. It was signed Glory Bain and had the name of a bank printed in nice, big letters across it.

Quinny leaned back in the chair behind the desk in the office Berte Dill had talked him into renting as a step toward regularity and better standing in his profession. He lit a cigarette. "Hey, Nadine!" he shouted.

A singularly uncharming female appeared in the doorway to the outer office. Nadine, his secretary, was another of Berte Dill's ideas, chosen by her on the associated theories that pulchritude had no place in a business office and that a girl would be an utter dope to provide competition for herself.

"Take a letter," ordered Quinny, like he'd seen fellows do in the movies.

Nadine sat down. She was rather tall and angular, but a collapsible model. With some contortions and twistings, she composed herself in a chair, one leg curled around the other and her knee high enough to serve as a rest for her professional looking notebook. "Shoot!" she said, rolling a wad of gum to the other cheek and applying a pencil tip to her tongue for proper moistening.

"Start off, 'Dear Miss Glory Bain,'" said Quinny, closing his eyes to avoid looking at Nadine. "An' put down th' hospital where she is at. Now: 'I have your check in hand an' am very—um—gratified—'"

"How many Cs in gratified?" interrupted Nadine, frowning.

"Make it 'glad.' 'Am very glad you are nearly okay. What I done for you—'"

"Did."

Quinny glanced at Nadine irritably. "Did what?" he demanded.

"'What I did for you.' Not 'done.'"

"Yeah? Okay. 'What I have did for you—'"

"That's worse." Nadine made an unpleasant, censorious noise with her lips.

"Oh, damn it, get th' idea an' write it down right." Quinny struggled to recall where he had left off. "'What I did—or done— for you, I did not expect to get paid for. It was for free, on account of you are a right dame, an' needed help. Of course, I can use these fish, bein' a man who don't get dough reg'lar. Any time you land in'"—Quinny wiggled his eyebrows at the secretary—"'jeopa'dy again—'"

"How do you spell that last one?" broke in Nadine.

"A-g-a-i-n."

"I mean the other one—jeppa—jeppar—"

Quinny pursed his lips thoughtfully and considered, tilting the derby back as though to cool off his cerebrum. "J-e-p-p-a-d-y," he spelled firmly.

Nadine shook her head. "No such word," she declared.

"Oh, nuts! Skip it." Quinny lunged across the desk and came back with the telephone. "I'll call her up."

THE CORPSE IN
GRAMPA'S BED

THE CORPSE IN GRAMPA'S BED

SOMEONE WAS SMACKING a fist against the door to Quinny Hite's room in the Hotel du Nord, with a violence threatening soon to admit a dash of air via a splintered panel. In the opinion of most of the hotel's tenantry, air was something properly belonging outdoors.

Quinny's eyes opened presently as the racket continued, blinking as he got them focused on his alarm clock and becoming resentful as he saw that it was only ten A.M. A hard-working homicide detective needs his sleep, but getting any in this old dump was getting tougher all the time. Only two nights before some rodeo hands living in the hotel had put on a song festival beginning at three A.M. and not piping down until four, bawling sad ditties about lugs who didn't want to be carried back to the lone prairie and such, when clearly this was where cowhands belonged. There were hardly any cows in Times Square.

Quinny sat up. "Come in!" he shouted.

The door opened, revealing a little man with a very pink face, silvery hair and black eyebrows. He stayed in the doorway a moment, regarding Quinny with shifty and suspicious eyes. Battered ears betrayed a seasoning in the prize-ring.

"Mornin'," he said tentatively.

"Don't I know it?" demanded the detective acidly. "What's the idea bustin' in on a guy which is tryin' to get some sleep? I thought you were up at Ma Holden's camp, training Bam-Bam Spilzer."

Grampa Carson shook his head sadly. "The fight's off—Bam-Bam busts his t'umb playin' a ukulele, the dope." Seeing doubt

323

rising in Quinny's sleep-heavy eyes, he rattled on. "Bam-Bam's playin' the damn thing, see, and walks right offen Ma Holden's porch. He also busts the ukulele. This was okay by everybody except Bam-Bam."

Quinny scowled, seeing no point in being aroused for bulletins on a palooka like Bam-Bam and broken ukuleles. "And so what?" he growled.

"I am on a spot," began Grampa, hesitantly. The grandfather moniker was entirely honorary, stemming from his age. Confronted with a genuine grandchild, he would have been more surprised than anybody. "I get in last night from Ma Holden's, an' I'm doggoned tired, see? Before I leave here I pay two weeks' rent, so I don't have no trouble findin' a flop when I get back. So the light bulb is stole out of my room whilst I'm gone. I say th' hell with that and pile inta bed in the dark. Right away I notice some lug is already in it, but he don't say nothin'. I figure the hotel has put over a fast play rentin' my room whilst I am away, so I lay there a while workin' out a spiel which is to cut a week offen my bill.

"The guy still don't say nothin', which I think ain't polite, considerin' it is my bed he is floppin' in. He don't move around though, so I figure he is asleep. This is okay, on account of I need sleep myself. I stick my head unner the pillow, like always, and in no time I am in the arms of orphans. This last is a gag I hear some place—"

"Yeah-yeah, I did too," Quinny cut in. "Keep on the beam."

"I kinda wake up about an hour ago. I have got my foot stuck up against this lug's—right between 'em. I think for a minute I am in the hay with Daisy, which is my ex-wife and lives in Buffalo and has feet like a hound's nose. I figure nobody but Daisy could have feet this cold and still be alive, and then I begin to notice the fella ain't breathin'. I see now where it would be a smart play to get the hell up—which I did. Sure enough—the man is dead as Heinie Himmler. So I dope it out I better come up and get a right steer offa you before I make a bum play."

Quinny thrust his feet over the side of the bed and got up, reaching for his trousers and beginning to dress. "This guy some pal of yours?" he asked.

"He is a entire stranger." Grampa rubbed the side of his nose reflectively. "Ought I go down and raise hell at the desk? Tell 'em I am sensitive about findin' corpses in my bed?"

Quinny grinned. "If you do, they'll stick a half buck on your bill for having company. We'll go have a look at this new room-mate, Grampa. Then I'll give Homicide a ring about it. Sure you didn't croak him yourself?"

"I cert'ny di'nt. Like I said, I don't even know the guy."

Grampa Carson's room was on the second floor, two flights down. En route, Quinny cadged the light bulb from a public bath-room to replace the one missing in Grampa's room. Daylight wasn't much help in the du Nord's cubicles. Hurrying after Grampa, who'd gone on, Quinny sideswiped a tall, red-eyed and snuffling jill issu-ing from the stairway in the third-floor hall. She had been too pre-occupied with her escort, a sallow-faced man, to notice a gentle-man coming from a bathroom marked "Ladies."

"Is it a fire?" asked sallow-face crossly.

"Could be," returned Quinny, flashing a glance at the woman. "Sure looks hot enough."

He went down the stairs to the second floor, finding Grampa waiting outside the door to 215, opening it as the detective joined him. There was no question of the deceased condition of the stranger in the bed, and, in Quinny's estimation, he'd been that way for two or three days. The man had not been undressed, except for shoes, and inspection showed the body had been embalmed.

"Cripes, Grampa—this fella came here from some undertaker!" exclaimed Quinny. "I'm bettin' from Lon Fischer's funeral joint next door."

"Lon's got a nerve, usin' my room for his spare corpses!" snorted Grampa. "Le's go tell him he's gotta take this one right back."

Quinny walked to the one window and looked out. The roof of a one-story taxpayer next door, housing the mortuary works of Lon Fischer, came level with this floor of the hotel. It was possible to step from the hotel window to the roof quite easily. Someone, in fact, had made use of the taxpayer roof to install a chicken-wire enclosure for pigeons.

"Okay," agreed the detective. "Even if they ganged up, carrier pigeons couldn't of unloaded the guy in your bed. We'll go downstairs and walk around to the joint."

Trailed by the still outraged Grampa, Quinny walked down the single flight to the lobby. A couple of rodeo riders were at the hotel desk, arguing with the clerk in the high-pitched, nasal tones apparently produced by outdoor life. Disputing a hotel bill wouldn't get them anywhere but out, the detective thought, as he passed toward the street entrance. If they were the ones who went in for pre-dawn cowboy ballads, eviction was just the thing for them.

Entering the sepulchral atmosphere of Fischer's Funeral Home, they found the proprietor in his small office, feet cocked up on a desk, working out a three-horse parlay and cheerfully humming one of the livelier dirges. Life was good to Lon Fischer, although death showed a better profit. He broke off his one-man musicale and nodded affably to Quinny, then cast a speculative eye on Grampa. The fight trainer didn't care for the attention.

"See here, Lon Fischer," Grampa blurted out uneasily, "don't you go lookin' at me like that, I feel okay."

"Fine, fine," returned Fischer. "Excuse it. I thought friend Hite was turning in a walking corpse."

"Nuts to you," growled the old man. "We come to tell you you gotta stop your corpses from walkin' inta my room. There's one in my bed right now."

Lon Fischer's big blue eyes—a wonderful asset in dealing with widows—drifted around to Quinny Hite, as if asking for explanation.

"Funny business going on, Lon," explained the detective. He went on to outline briefly what had brought them to the parlor.

Fischer's feet came off the desk and thudded to the floor.

"Y'mean there really is an embalmed body in Grampa's bed?" he demanded unbelievingly. "How'd he get there?"

"This is also what we want to know," interjected Grampa. "And how long it'll be before you come and get him."

Fischer got up and went to a door down a short hall, which he opened, bellowing, "Horgan!" Then he returned to his swivel chair and presently a fat, pimply man wearing an apron and with shirt sleeves rolled up came from the back room.

"Yes, boss," he said. His eyebrows were horizontal parentheses neatly duplicating the upper rim of his thick-lensed glasses.

"These boys claim to have found an embalmed body in a room of the du Nord next door," said Fischer. "Are you short one?"

Horgan shook his head, never taking his eyes from his employer.

"No, sir. The four that came in day before yesterday have been sent out—two cemetery jobs, one cremation, and one which was shipped to Columbus. Yesterday we got in two more. One of 'em went out this morning. I'm just getting through casing up the one we still got."

Quinny frowned, giving his derby a push up from his forehead as he considered the traffic problems involved in getting the departed properly headed for the pearly gates.

"You sure the ones you took in were the same you sent out?" he needled Horgan. "How do you know somebody didn't sneak in a ringer and put one of the other customers in Grampa's room?"

Horgan's eyes bulged behind his thick lenses, suggesting the stare of an emotional halibut. "What on earth would anybody do that for?" he demanded. "Ain't one corpse as good as another? Why trade 'em like that?"

Fischer got up, plainly nervous. "I can see why," he grated. "Maybe somebody had a hot corpse on hand and wanted him buried without a death certificate. Don't you ever look what you're doing, Horgan? You oughta make sure you're putting bodies in the right boxes."

"These stiffs are all strangers to me," defended the embalmer. "I don't even remember what they look like five minutes after I get 'em packaged up for delivery. I just put the job ticket on top of the lid and go on to the next one."

"I never knew that this business was run just like a cracker factory," commented Quinny wonderingly. "Well, it looks like a police job. You gotta pull in all these 'jobs' now to make sure who they are—unless you want to hire a smart detective who can straighten it all up quick-like."

"Having to recall 'em—and head off one from the crematory, if he ain't already in an urn—will put me out of business, Hite!" stormed Fischer. "Better for everybody to let things ride."

"Yeah, except it leaves you with one dead man left over. What will you do with him?"

Fischer arose and took a turn up and down his small office.

"Who's this smart dick you speak of?" he rasped.

"Me," said Quinny modestly.

Fischer looked at him doubtfully, but didn't get very far in his consideration of the suggestion. A short, stocky and belligerently disposed man named O'Hara came in from the street, stern purpose shining from under beetling brows.

"Ye're a scut, Lon Fischer!" he roared. "A low-life an' a bum!"

"I am?" replied the mortician, with the air of having made a discovery.

"Y' sure are. Lat night fri'nds and relatives of the late Jug Dooley gather in his flat to throw a wake. After drinkin' up all the booze an' gittin' to the p'nt where we are not so sensitive, Slim Dooley, a cousin Jug had no use for, unscrews the lid offa the coffin for a last look. After all this mournin', we discover Jug does not show up for his own wake. He is not in the casket."

"What?" exclaimed the harassed undertaker. "You mean the box was empty?"

"I do not," denied Mr. O'Hara firmly. "What I mean is, old Mrs. Ginsberg, who dies last Tuesday, was in it. Mrs. Ginsberg was a fine old woman, but not Irish, and she would not go for a wake. What are yez going to do about it?"

Lon Fischer's expression indicated that he had no idea. "But we buried Mrs. Ginsberg yesterday afternoon," he objected weakly.

"That must have been Jug." A look of sudden dismay spread over the stocky Irishman's face. "Holy St. Pathrick, Lon, if ye've gone and buried Jug in a Jewish cemetery— What are yez goin' to do about it, man?"

"Why—why—" Mr. Fischer gulped, then went on with forced heartiness, "I'll send Mr. Dooley around, as soon as I can get him back, and pick up Mrs. Ginsberg. Accidents will happen, you know."

"Sure, but that ain't all. We drunk up ever'thin' before finding out we were having a wake for the wrong desisted. Ye'll have to stand fer the likker, if we have to start all over ag'in."

"I'll send a case of good stuff and a half-keg of beer," agreed Fischer promptly, "if you promise not to let this mix-up get around."

Grampa eyed Mr. O'Hara with fresh interest. "Tip me off when you get this wake goin' again," he said "I'll drop in."

The Irishman received Grampa's proposal coldly. "Were yez a friend of Jug's?" he demanded.

"Not good," admitted Grampa. "But, after what I been through, I could get as drunk and holler as loud as anybody. Prob'bly more."

Mr. O'Hara went out and Fischer's interest swung to his embalmer. "Horgan," he said tensely, "I ought to bust you one right on your fat jaw. You see how your bungling costs me dough?"

"Yes, sir," replied Horgan politely.

Fischer turned to Quinny. "Okay, Hite. You're hired. Twenty-five fish, if you get this fixed up before the whole neighborhood hears about it."

"Fifty—and anyhow everybody's going to know about it. Thing to do is show 'em you're a man who does the right thing."

The mortician nodded despondently and Quinny walked through the hall into the workroom at the rear. He wanted to see how Grampa's find had made the passage to the hotel, if possible. It was simple enough. Horgan, to reach the crude cote on the roof for his pigeons, had placed a ladder to the skylight over the workroom. Quinny climbed up, followed by both Horgan and Grampa.

From the roof it had been easy to take the body through Grampa's window, although getting it up the ladder was no simple task for one man. Near the parapet the detective picked up a buckskin bag about four or five inches long, closed at the top with a purse clasp. It contained two dollars and sixty cents—all in silver. He dropped it into his coat pocket and climbed through Grampa's window, the two men following.

"He didn't scram whilst we was out," observed Grampa morosely, viewing the intruder in his bed. "Wunner who he is?"

"Looks kinda familiar," hazarded the embalmer uncertainly. "Anyhow, I can tell he's a Fischer body."

"With a conked motor," growled Quinny. "Well, you take him back before Grampa gets stuck for two-in-a-room rates."

It took the combined efforts of the detective and Horgan, with Grampa getting in the way, to accomplish it. They rolled him in a sheet before carrying him across the roof to the skylight. Mrs. Urdlebinder, retired from a career as costume woman at a Forty-second Street burlesque, wasn't taken in by the camouflaging sheet. Sitting at her window on the fifth floor of the du Nord, she promptly fainted at the macabre procession across the roof, a sheer waste of emotion, as there was no one else in her room to appreciate it.

But it wasn't to the customary solemn silence of Lou Fischer's elite mortuary that the corpse was returned. At least, not for long. With the proprietor watching grimly, they had no more than got the stranger comfortably disposed on a slab when a tall young man in morning clothes came in briskly through the side door. Joe Herk, whose naturally melancholy expression had built him up to become Fischer's star director, was trembling with outraged and betrayed dignity.

"Damn it, Lon, what's getting to be the matter with this outfit?" he demanded. "Here I am, working a smooth job with the funeral of the Greek's wife, and what happens? I ask you, what happens?"

"I know," responded the shaken Fischer. "Somebody else is in her coffin. It's getting to be the regular thing around here."

"Well, it's no way to run an undertaking establishment," snapped Mr. Herk. "A grocery, okay—but you can't deliver substitute goods in this business."

"What turned up?" asked Quinny curiously. "Dame or guy?"

"Dame." Mr. Herk scowled at the detective who had prompted him into coarse language. "I mean, it was a woman. Quite good looking, too. Nick said if his late wife had looked anything like her, he would have hired better doctors."

"You're getting closer, Horgan," commented Quinny. "At least, now you ain't sending out women where they're expecting men.

What've you got in that case?" He nodded toward a plain casket on horses across the room.

Horgan colored and dropped his gaze. "Pigeon feed," he said. "If you mean what other stiffs are in the works, there's only one. I—I guess this must be Mrs. Pappapadolous. I *did* get the tickets mixed up on that job, so I sent Nick the best-looking one. Greeks always go for good-looking women."

Lon Fischer let out a bawl like a lonesome moolycow and waved his arms in an eloquent gesture of bitter despair.

"Pappapadolous and his family were good for two de luxe funerals a year—and now I lose that business," he moaned. "Get going, Hite."

"Okay. I am going," assented Quinny. "Now, look, according to Horgan, you had four jobs day before yesterday. How's for giving 'em names, so we can sort out what happened to 'em?"

Fischer walked over to a hook on the wall and pulled off a handful of manila envelopes—Horgan's "job tickets"—and riffled through them.

"Dooley and Witzbaum were funeral jobs, Schlosselmeyer went to the oven—catching the idea from the bakery he ran over on Ninth, I suppose—and a woman named Smithley was shipped to Columbus. Yesterday we had Mrs. Pappapadolous and—"

"Mrs. Ginsberg," finished Quinny. "Like you said a while ago, some lug has run in an added starter, but we don't know from which stable. All we do know is that Jug Dooley is knocking around some place where he don't belong—and prob'ly some other customers. You better get the crematory on the phone and hold up that job, if it ain't already too late. Flip a wire to Columbus, too. It looks like the Greek got the Smithley dame out of your grab-bag, and could be Jug is on the way to Columbus.

"What we got to find out is who and where is this extra corpse. I got this to go on: whoever brought him in and left the other guy in Grampa's bed was somebody who knew Grampa was out of town. He knew that du Nord maids don't look for work and would skip any room not bein' used. While you're sorting this out, I'm going back to the hotel and see what I can find out there."

Grampa, unpleasantly conscious of the somber surroundings and aseptic aroma, went along. The two men reentered the hotel through the street entrance, where Quinny collared Hugh Brenning, the hotel manager, on his way to lunch. A lengthy conversation ensued, during which Grampa almost worked up eye-strain darting glances from one to the other as they talked. In the end, Mr. Brenning forgot about lunch and decided to explore the second floor with Quinny.

Besides Grampa's, there were four other rooms on this floor with windows giving access to the roof of the funeral parlor. One was cancelled from the investigation because of occupancy by a newspaper pressman who worked all night and couldn't have been home during the significant hours. Another was occupied by a pair of midgets lacking the physical ability to have accomplished the feat.

Brenning rapped on 219 professionally. There was the sound of scurrying within and a cigarette-soprano voice called excitedly to know who was at the door.

"The manager—Brenning."

This must also have sounded professional to the woman inside.

"I paid my bill yesterday afternoon," she shouted.

"This is another matter. Open up."

She didn't seem to be in any hurry about complying, but after a wait the door opened a mere crack and Quinny saw part of the face of the tall woman he had bumped into earlier in the third-floor hall. She seemed to get around.

"What the hell kind of a dump is this?" she rasped.

"You ought to know—you been living in it long enough," growled Quinny. He leaned heavily against the door and, despite the woman's effort, pushed it open for a view of the room. A skinny, anemic-looking man suffering acute jitters, the one Quinny had seen before with the woman, sat on the bed. His coat had been hung over a chair.

Mr. Brenning, seeing the fellow, glanced sharply at the woman.

"Mrs. Lutterbury, it is against the hotel rules for ladies to entertain men in their rooms. If this occurs again, I must ask—"

"Skip the act, Hugh," interrupted Quinny. "This lug don't look much like he's being entertained, like you say. If he has already paid, I'd say he's stuck. Is there a Mr. Lufflebury?"

"*Lutter*bury," corrected the woman acidly. "There sure is. The louse walked out on me. This man is his cousin."

People certainly stick to the old gags, Quinny reflected, looking around the room. There wasn't much to mark it different from other rooms in the hotel—a wash stand in a corner, windows covered with sleazy and torn lace curtains, and one closet. The latter was well filled with dresses and gay shoes, plus a man's suit and a single pair of male oxfords bearing the sheepish air of having blundered into a ladies' toilet. The coat of the man's suit seemed to sag from a weight in a side pocket. Quinny stuck his hand in and brought out a small revolver. He turned, glowering at the woman.

"Mr. Lutterbury forgot his hardware," he said succinctly, and pocketed the weapon. "I better keep this, Hugh. People get hurt with them things. Come on, let's look into the other room." He strode out into the hall, with the wondering manager at his heels, stopping at 217—the room next to Grampa's. He glanced at Brenning.

"Who's in here?"

"Three men—rodeo riders from the Garden. The show left last week, but they're still here—two of 'em. They're not in, though. I saw 'em going out a while ago. Look, Hite, do you suppose Mrs. Lutterbury and that unhealthy-looking character with her are mixed up in this? Good gracious, I hope we aren't having another murder in the hotel—people will begin to think we cater to an undesirable element."

He unlocked the door and Quinny pushed in. This room was somewhat larger than the others, with one double and a single bed. Scattered around were the trappings of men who ride horses for a living—making dough the hard way in Quinny's estimation—and these interpreters of life on the range had found lace curtains practically ideal for hanging up spurs. Apparently this gear was carried around in canvas sacks similar to duffle bags, as there were only three cheap suitcases for clothes. Quinny read the names stenciled on the sides of these—Tucson Bill, Cameroon Cal and Tex Bonham—with moderate interest but considerable help to his conclusions.

"You said there was only two guys still here," he said to Brenning. "How come there are three suitcases?"

"One of 'em sneaked out on me," complained the hotel man. "The two that are still here assured me this morning that they would take care of his bill, as soon as they got a remittance. All three of 'em staged a drinking party the night the show left—last Monday— and got left behind."

Grampa, who had tagged faithfully along, was losing interest. "I'm gonna see if I can find a maid to fix up my room," he said, leaving.

"These buckaroos didn't care what they drank," said Quinny, with a glance at the exiting Grampa. There were a couple of empty fifths on the bureau which had contained the cheapest brand of whiskey obtainable. There was also an empty pint bottle on the floor. Quinny picked it up to sniff gingerly at its uncorked neck. He almost choked at the remaining fumes. "I get it—kinda," he said recovering. He straightened up as he heard a noise in the hallway that definitely had not been made by Grampa.

The door was shoved in violently, banging back, against the wall, revealing the tall figures of two men in cowhand outfits. One of them gripped a big Colt revolver, with lowered muzzle, mean-while crouching and glaring from slitted eyes like William S. Hart at his best.

"Stick 'em up, yo' thievin' coyotes!" he snarled. "Befo' I gun yo' down."

"Now, just 'a minute," barked Hugh Brenning, used to almost anything in the Hotel du Nord. "We are not thieves, my friend. I am the hotel manager—"

"That's a bad beginning, Hugh," intruded Quinny.

Brenning didn't hear him, but eyed the newcomers sternly. "Where is the money you promised my clerk for your room?"

This demand had stopped tougher men than these children of nature, but this time it didn't work.

"Plug 'em, Cal," encouraged the man looming over the one with the gun. "Shoot 'em down like coyotes. Robbin' a man's room. Prob'bly hoss thieves."

"Skip it!" Quinny cut in firmly. "Horses are about the only thing I know of which ain't allowed in du Nord rooms. Where's the other guy—your buddy?"

"You—mean Tucson Bill?" Cal's grim fierceness faded a little. "He left town with the rody-oshow."

"He did not," contradicted Quinny. "He croaked himself on wood alcohol outa that pint flask. You two guys lugged him over and left him in Fischer's undertaking shop next door. You brought another body back, so Fischer wouldn't notice he had one too many corpses on hand, and left it in the next room to this. A fine couple of ghouls you are!"

"Oh, yeah? I'm Cameroon Cal, an' I'm a rootin,' tootin', shootin' son of a—"

"Tut-tut!" interrupted Mr. Brenning sharply.

Snarling Cameroon Cal jerked his chin up, then his gun hand. Perhaps Wild Bill Hickok would have managed it more efficiently, but Cal underestimated the weight of the Colt. Unexpectedly, it flew out of his hand and over his shoulder into the hall. It struck something that gave forth a pop similar to a batted ping-pong ball.

This was Grampa's head. He had come back from his room to look into the noisy situation he had overheard, but beaned by the shooting iron, he lost interest forthwith and sank to the hall carpet.

"Whadda we do now, Tex?" croaked the suddenly disarmed Cal.

"We scram."

Tex put his idea into action. Backing and turning to flee down the hall, he fell over Grampa, joining him on the floor in a tangled mass. Cal, also in retreat, stumbled over them and thudded to the floor with a deflating grunt. Quinny walked out into the hall, exhibiting the little gun he'd taken from Mrs. Lutterbury's closet. With this persuasion, it wasn't difficult to herd his captives back into their room.

"You fellas forget about the rootin', tootin' stuff," he advised. "You're in a serious jam. Why didn't you report your buddy's dying, instead of pulling all this monkey business?"

The rodeo hands, sitting side by side on the bed, exchanged worried glances, then both spoke at once. "We—" They stopped, each waiting for the other to go on. Quinny, deciding that the one called Tex was the most scared, indicated him with the little revolver. Tex seemed not honored.

"You tell it," the detective ordered. "For a couple of wild westerners, you mugs are a hundred percent pantywaist."

"We ain't never been west," confessed Tex. "We ain't even sure-enough cowboys. The only horse I ever was on was at Steeplechase at Coney Island, an' I fell offa that one. I'm from Canarsie and Cal's from Boston. We didn't mean to do wrong, officer. Tucson Bill and us two were celebratin' a couple of nights ago and run out of liquor. Bill didn't have enough left to buy another bottle, but he found a flask hid behind the john in the bathroom down the ball which said alcohol on it. We didn't want to drink it, on account of maybe it wasn't drinking alcohol, but Bill said the hell what other kind is there. The next thing we know Bill is down on the floor kickin'. Before we could do anything he was dead."

"I figured something like that," nodded Quinny. "But didn't you dopes know that even if a man is dead, you still got to send for a doctor?"

Cal nodded somberly.

"Yeah—we knew, but Bill only had two bucks sixty. Tex an' me didn't have nothin'." He shrugged helplessly. "We couldn't pay no doctor."

Tex took over. "Besides, after we talked it over, we knew they'd bury poor Bill in potter's field. Bill was a sure-enough cowboy from Arizona, and he always said he wanted to be put away in a desert grave when he died. There ain't any deserts around New York, but we thought we owed it to him as a pal to get him laid away in a reg'lar cemetery. What we done was all we could think of. It wasn't goin' to hurt anybody."

"You'd be surprised how this noble idea turned out," commented Quinny. "You upset everybody from Times Square to Columbus."

"We was mightily upset, too, pardner," said Cal, reverting to the dialect he'd stayed up nights to acquire. "Bill was a fine hombre an' we jes' couldn't let him git planted in no potter's field. After we took him down an' put him in a coffin, we sat on the edge of the skylight singin' the cowboy songs he liked—for mighty near an hour, I reckon—"

"I heard you, which is what gave me the first tip-off," interrupted Quinny. "Sounded like them coyotes you were talking about a while back."

"Bill always liked cowboy songs," insisted Cal, hurt.

"He liked liquor, too, and see what it got him." Quinny turned to Brenning. "Take these two sawhorse jockeys down to your office, Hugh, and we'll let the cops figure out what to do with 'em. Come on—I got fifty bucks to collect from Lon Fischer."

"Bet he'll want to keep it for a down-payment on your funeral," offered Grampa from the hall. He felt his head gingerly. "What'll they do to these guys? I hope they burn for just maybe killing this other mug. I got a lump on my head you could hang one of Ma Holden's towels on."

Quinny shook his head. "They ain't in for much," he said. "All I can think of is holding out on a death and moving a body without a permit. Let's get going."

On the way to the stairs and about to pass 219, the door flew open and Mr. Lutterbury's alleged cousin flew out. Inside there was an excited babble of voices, a stormy male and a tear-choked soprano.

"So, the minute I turn my back." the male voice boomed, "you take in this skinny lizard from Perth Amboy—"

"I guess," said Quinny, admiring the way the fleeing lizard took the stairs, "Mr. Lutterbury is back home. Sounds like."

Coachwhip Publications

CoachwhipBooks.com

MURDER
À LA RICHELIEU
THE ADELAIDE ADAMS MYSTERIES
ANITA BLACKMON

ISBN 978-1-61646-222-2

VULTURES
IN THE SKY
A HUGH RENNERT MYSTERY

TODD DOWNING

ISBN 978-1-61646-149-2

COACHWHIP PUBLICATIONS

COACHWHIPBOOKS.COM

MURDER
IN BERMUDA

WILLOUGHBY SHARP

ISBN 978-1-61646-198-0

COACHWHIP PUBLICATIONS

NOW AVAILABLE

THE STRAWSTACK
MURDER CASE
KIRKE
MECHEM

ISBN 978-1-61646-179-9

COACHWHIP PUBLICATIONS

COACHWHIPBOOKS.COM

ISBN 978-1-61646-232-1

ISBN 978-1-61646-233-8

www.ingramcontent.com/pod-product-compliance
Lightning Source LLC
Chambersburg PA
CBHW020531020726
47494CB00006B/1725